Unicorn for a Day

Another Phoebe and Her Unicorn Adventure

Complete Your Phoebe and Her Unicorn Collection

Phoebe and Her Unicorn
Dana Simpson

Unicorn on a Roll
Another Phoebe and Her Unicorn Adventure
Dana Simpson

Unicorn vs. Goblins
Another Phoebe and Her Unicorn Adventure
Dana Simpson

Razzle Dazzle Unicorn
Another Phoebe and Her Unicorn Adventure
Dana Simpson

Unicorn Crossing
Another Phoebe and Her Unicorn Adventure
Dana Simpson

Phoebe and Her Unicorn in
The Magic Storm
Dana Simpson

Unicorn of Many Hats
Another Phoebe and Her Unicorn Adventure
Dana Simpson

Phoebe and Her Unicorn in
Unicorn Theater
Dana Simpson

Unicorn Bowling
Another Phoebe and Her Unicorn Adventure
Dana Simpson

The Unicorn Whisperer
Another Phoebe and Her Unicorn Adventure
Dana Simpson

Camping with Unicorns
Another Phoebe and Her Unicorn Adventure
Dana Simpson

Virtual Unicorn Experience
Another Phoebe and Her Unicorn Adventure
Dana Simpson

Unicorn Famous
Another Phoebe and Her Unicorn Adventure
Dana Simpson

Unicorn Playlist
Another Phoebe and Her Unicorn Adventure
Dana Simpson

Unicorn Selfies
Another Phoebe and Her Unicorn Adventure
Dana Simpson

Unicornado
Another Phoebe and Her Unicorn Adventure
Dana Simpson

Punk Rock Unicorn
Another Phoebe and Her Unicorn Adventure
Dana Simpson

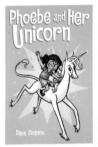

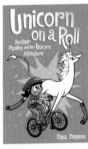

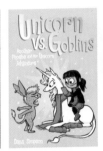

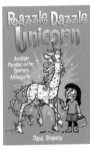

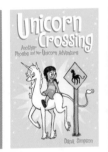

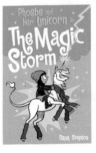

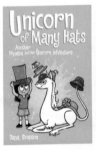

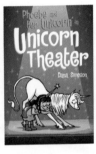

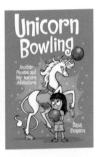

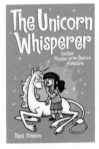

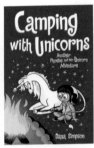

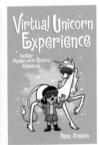

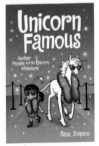

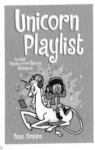

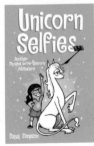

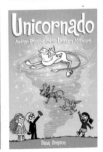

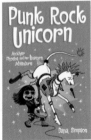

Unicorn for a Day

Another Phoebe and Her Unicorn Adventure

Dana Simpson

Andrews McMeel
PUBLISHING®

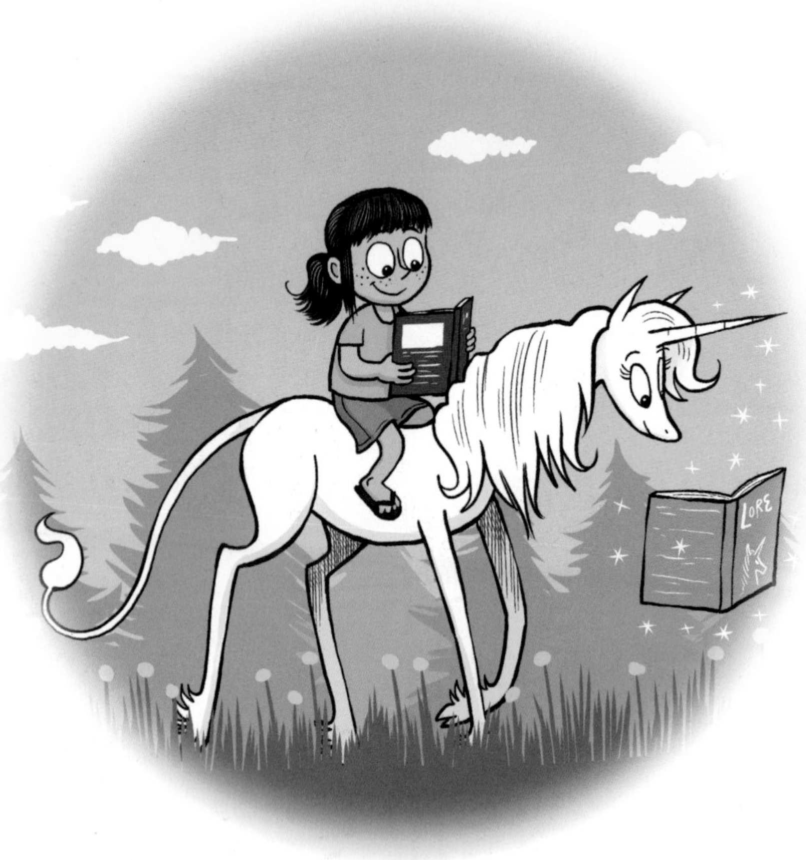
LORE

Hey, kids!

Check out the glossary on page 172
if you come across words you don't know.

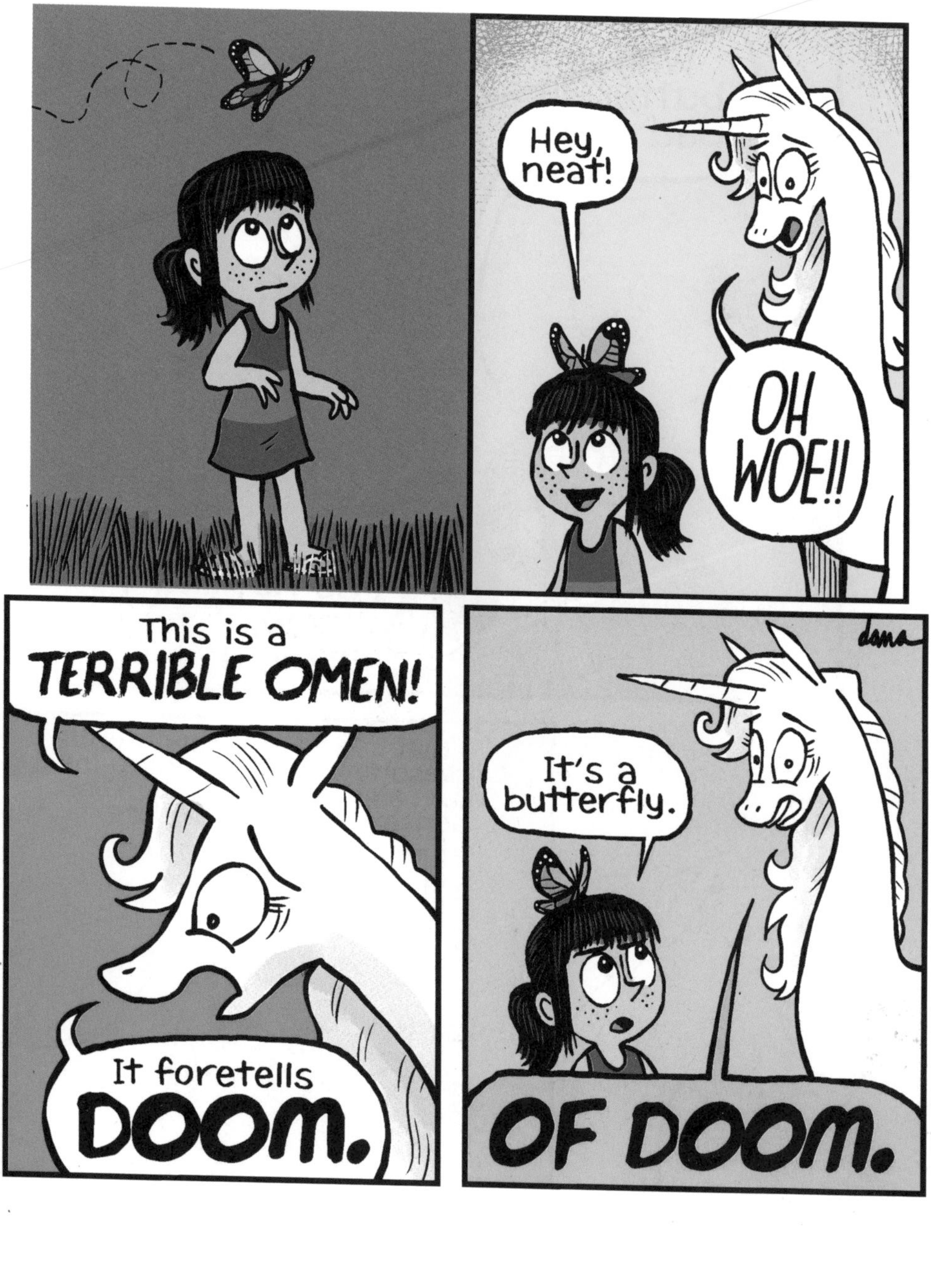
Hey, neat!
OH WOE!!
This is a TERRIBLE OMEN!
It foretells DOOM.
It's a butterfly.
OF DOOM.
dana

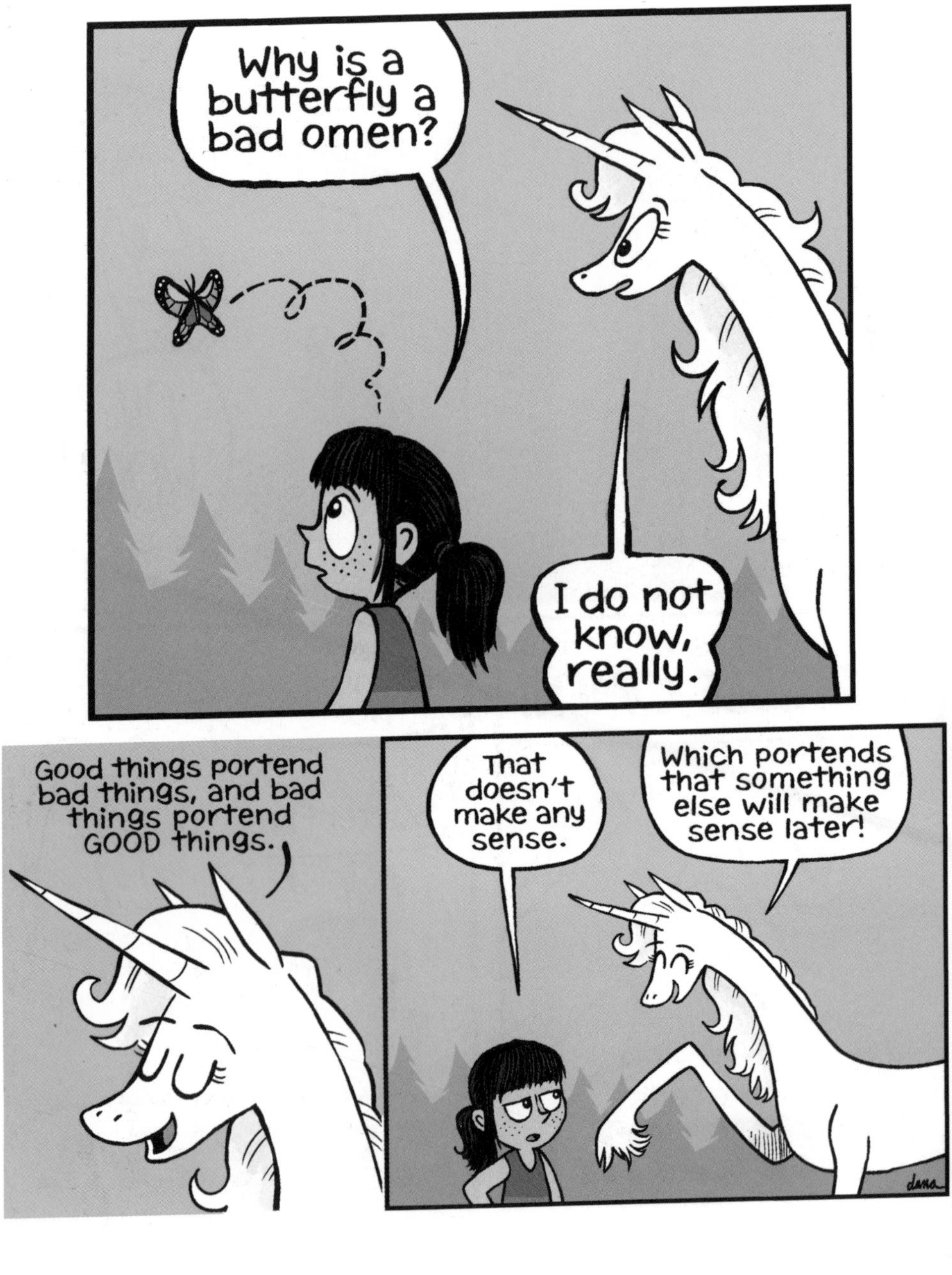
Why is a butterfly a bad omen?
I do not know, really.
Good things portend bad things, and bad things portend GOOD things.
That doesn't make any sense.
Which portends that something else will make sense later!
dana

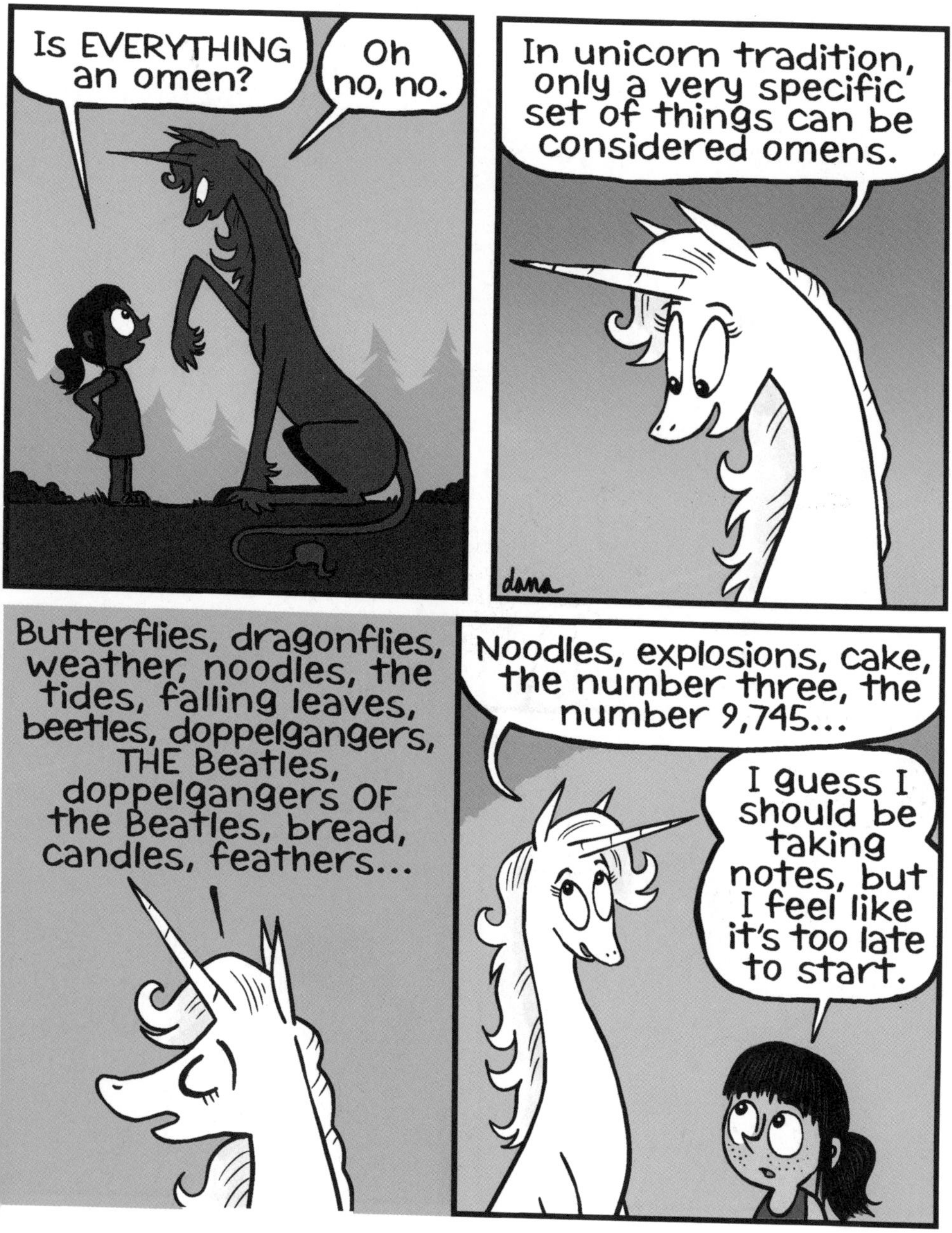
Is EVERYTHING an omen?
Oh no, no.
In unicorn tradition, only a very specific set of things can be considered omens.
dana
Butterflies, dragonflies, weather, noodles, the tides, falling leaves, beetles, doppelgangers, THE Beatles, doppelgangers OF the Beatles, bread, candles, feathers...
Noodles, explosions, cake, the number three, the number 9,745...
I guess I should be taking notes, but I feel like it's too late to start.

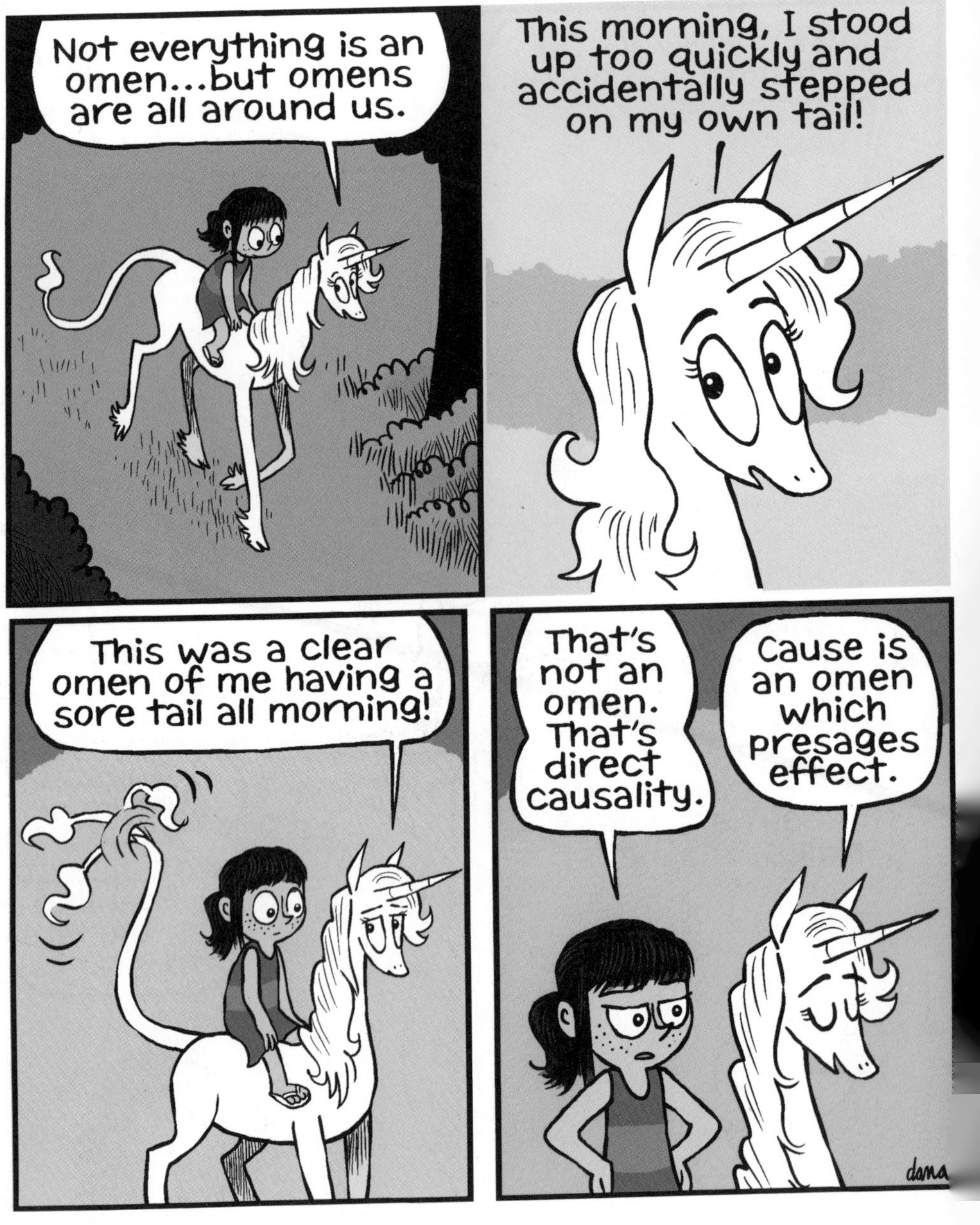
Not everything is an omen...but omens are all around us.
This morning, I stood up too quickly and accidentally stepped on my own tail!
This was a clear omen of me having a sore tail all morning!
That's not an omen. That's direct causality.
Cause is an omen which presages effect.
dana

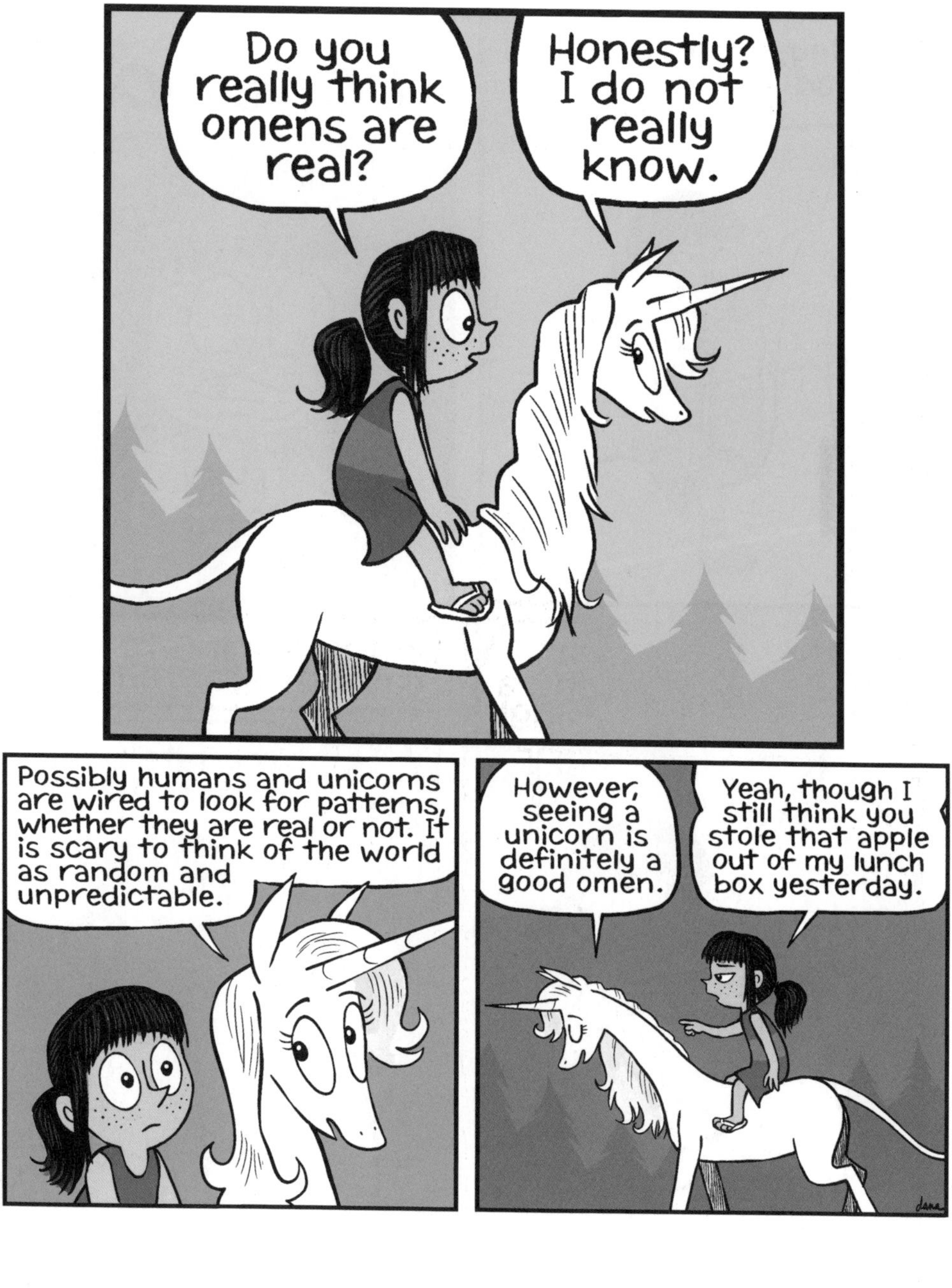
Do you really think omens are real?
Honestly? I do not really know.
Possibly humans and unicorns are wired to look for patterns, whether they are real or not. It is scary to think of the world as random and unpredictable.
However, seeing a unicorn is definitely a good omen.
Yeah, though I still think you stole that apple out of my lunch box yesterday.
dana

Hey, I forgot I had this pencil.
This pencil...of
DOOOOOM.
I am beginning to wish I had not started this.
Too late now.
dana

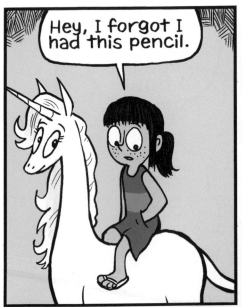

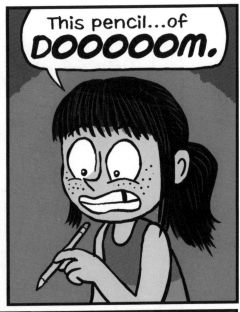

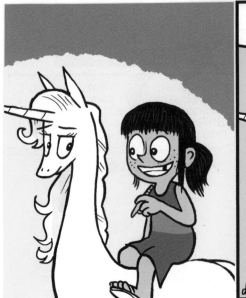

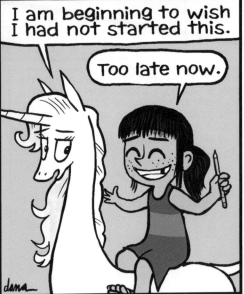

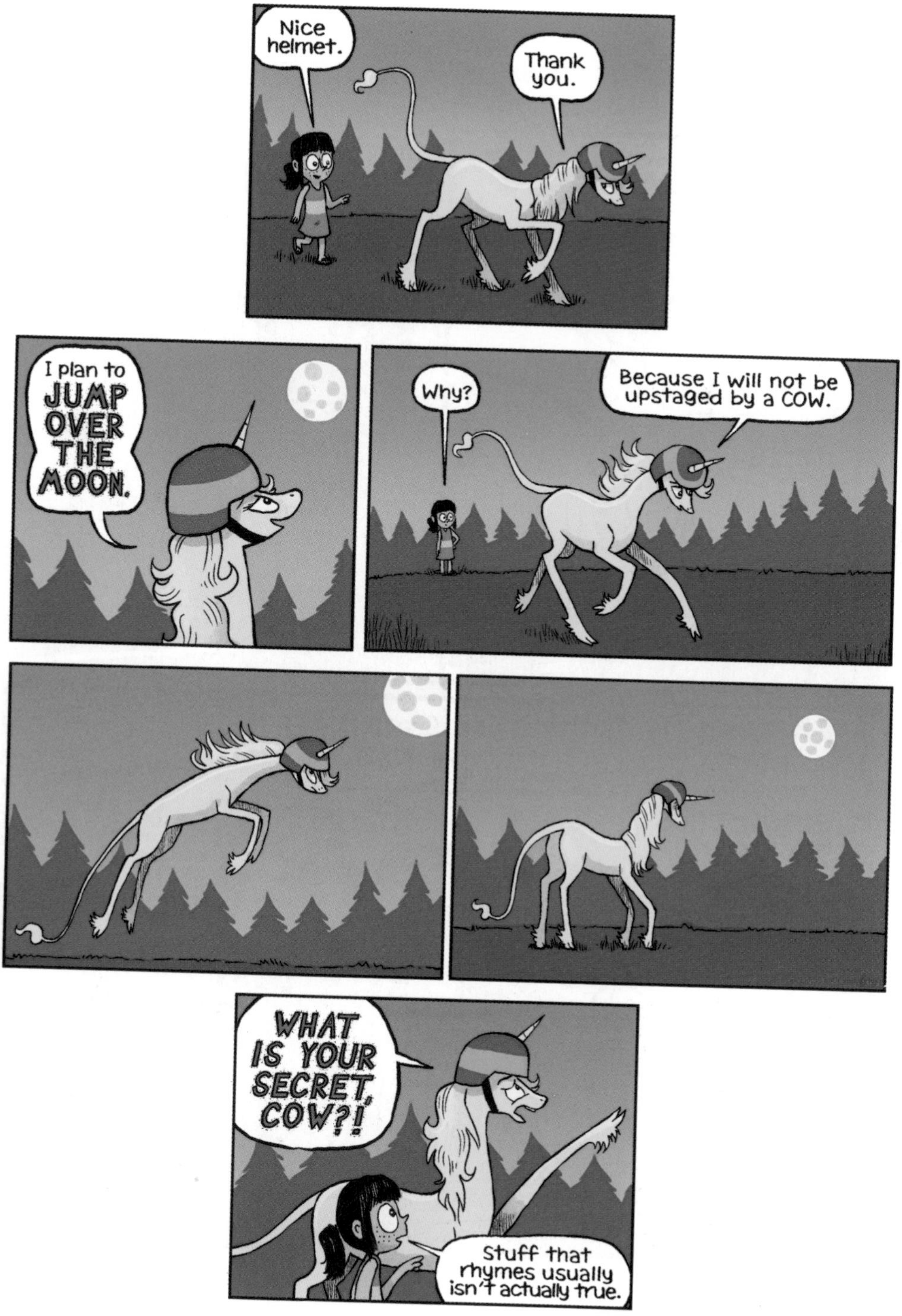
Nice helmet.
Thank you.
I plan to JUMP OVER THE MOON.
Why?
Because I will not be upstaged by a COW.
WHAT IS YOUR SECRET, COW?!
Stuff that rhymes usually isn't actually true.

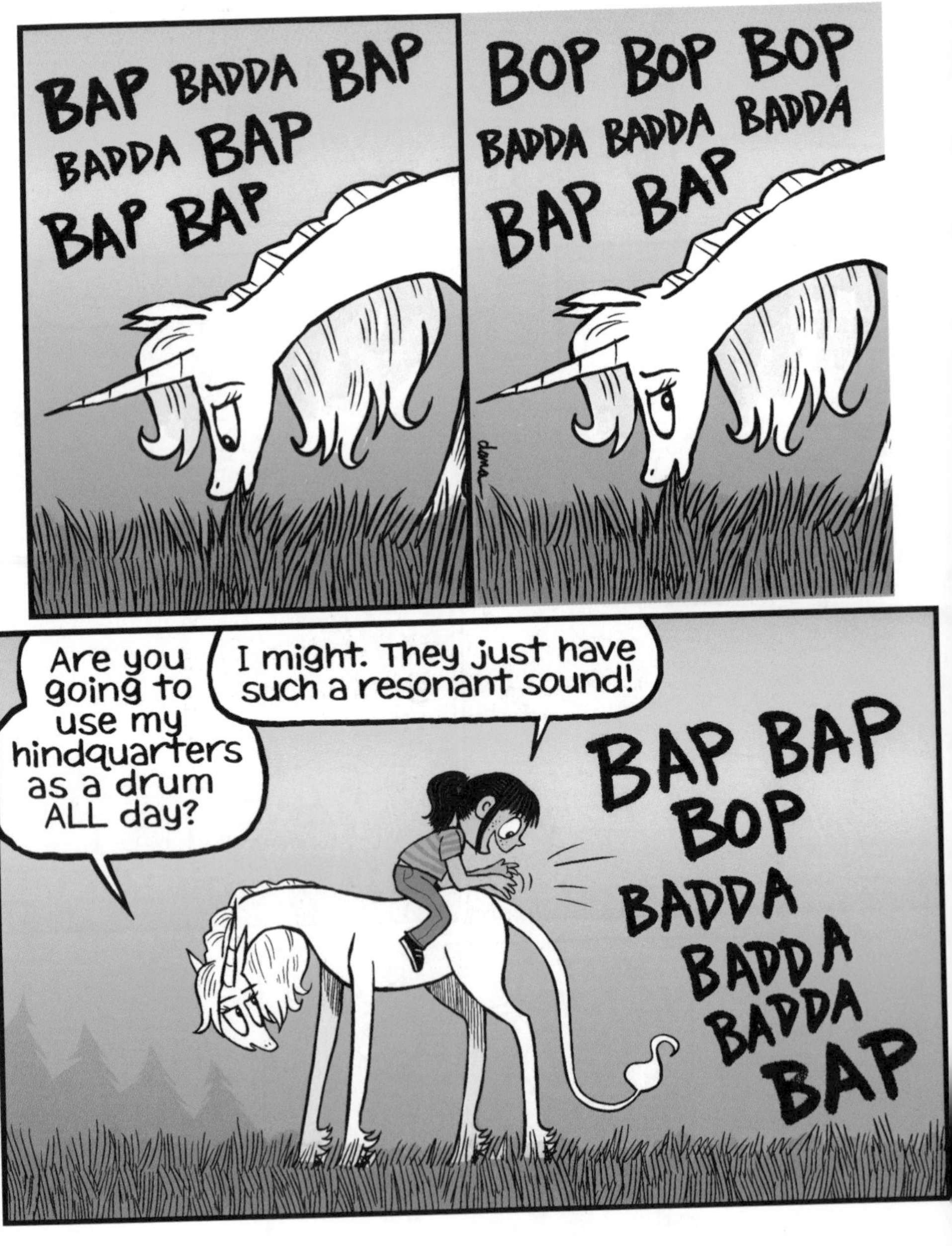
BAP BADDA BAP
BADDA BAP
BAP BAP
BOP BOP BOP
BADDA BADDA BADDA
BAP BAP
Are you going to use my hindquarters as a drum ALL day?
I might. They just have such a resonant sound!
BAP BAP
BOP
BADDA
BADDA
BADDA
BAP

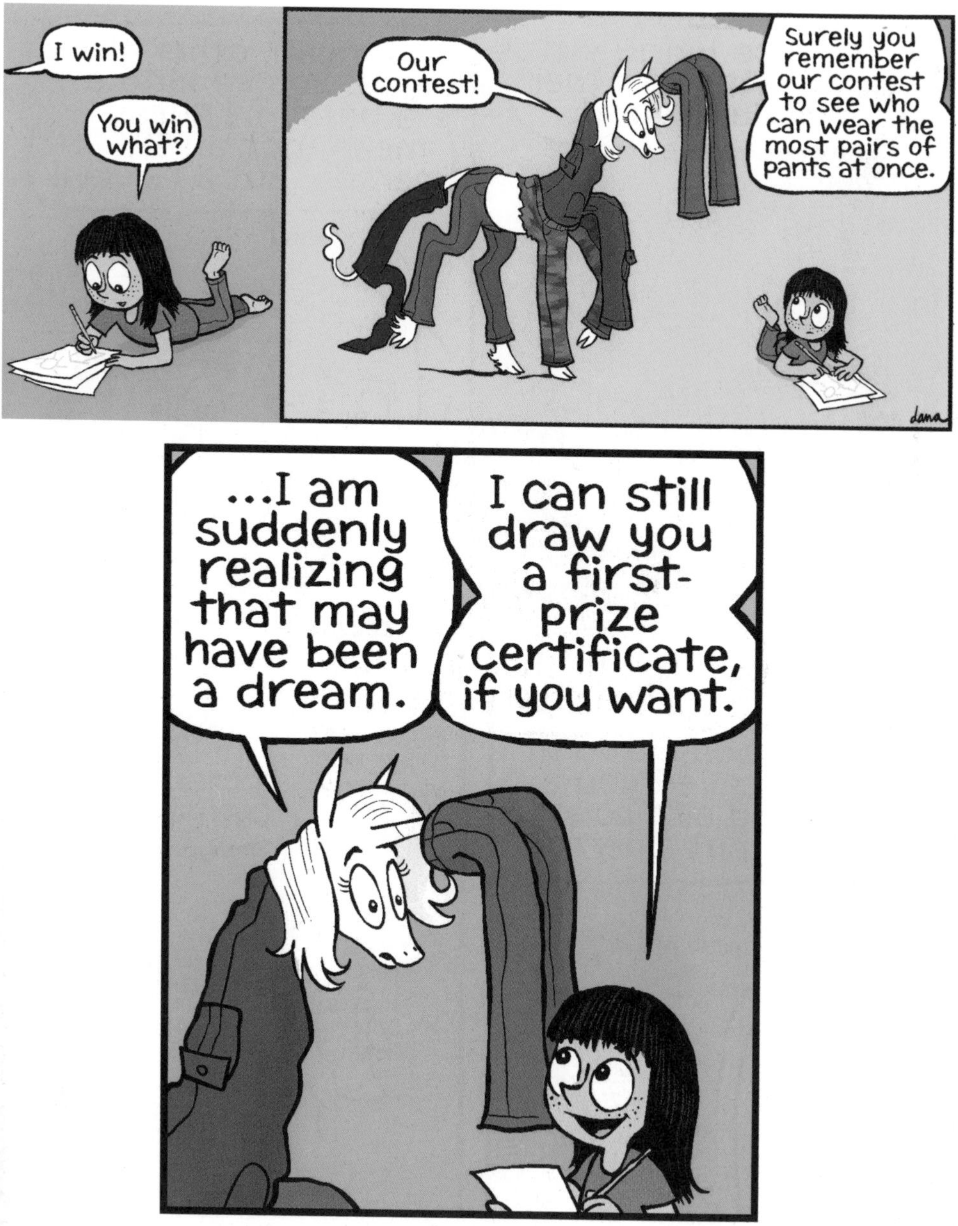

I win!
You win what?
Our contest!
Surely you remember our contest to see who can wear the most pairs of pants at once.
dana
...I am suddenly realizing that may have been a dream.
I can still draw you a first-prize certificate, if you want.

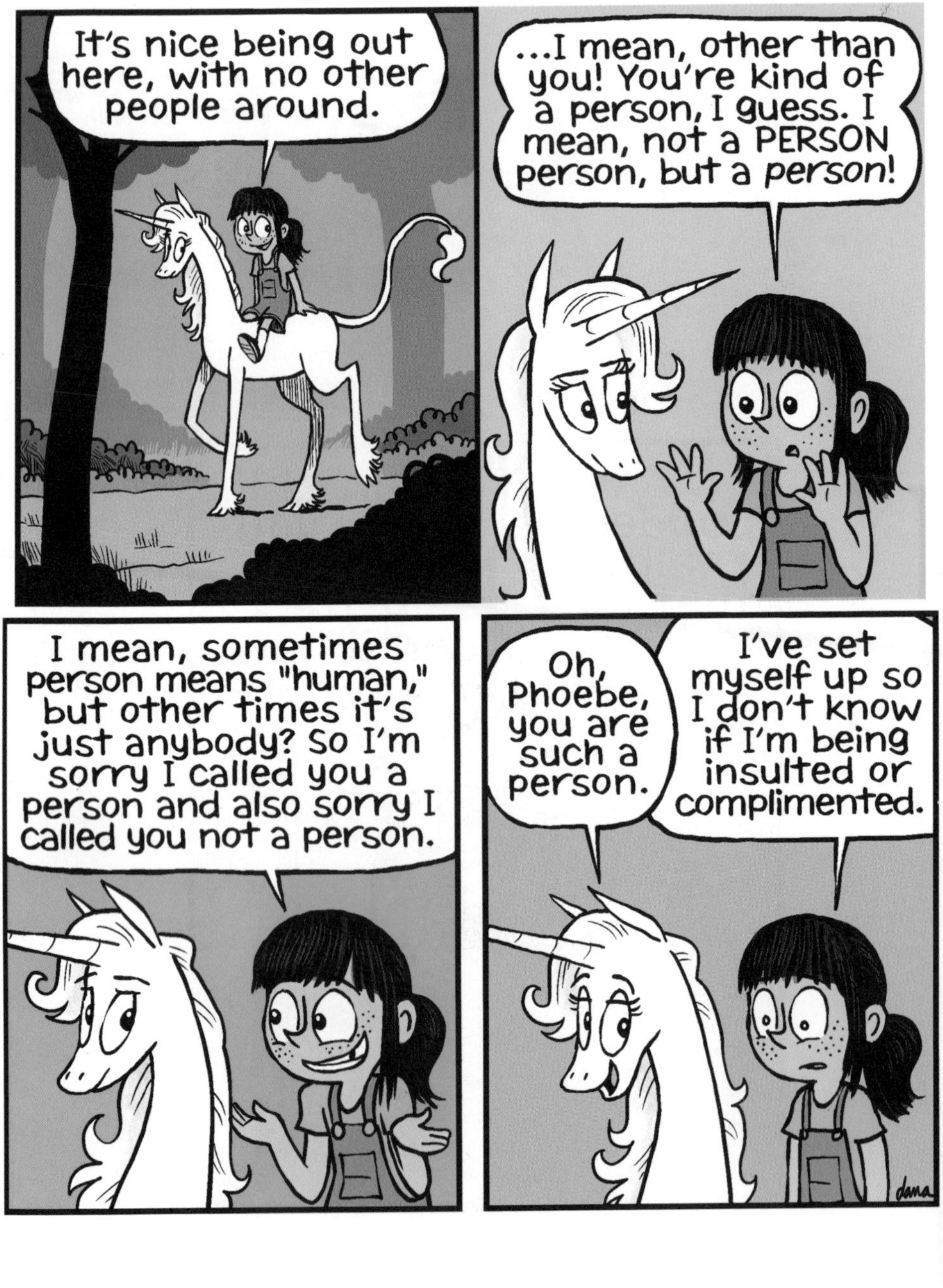
It's nice being out here, with no other people around.
...I mean, other than you! You're kind of a person, I guess. I mean, not a PERSON person, but a *person*!
I mean, sometimes person means "human," but other times it's just anybody? So I'm sorry I called you a person and also sorry I called you not a person.
Oh, Phoebe, you are such a person.
I've set myself up so I don't know if I'm being insulted or complimented.
dana

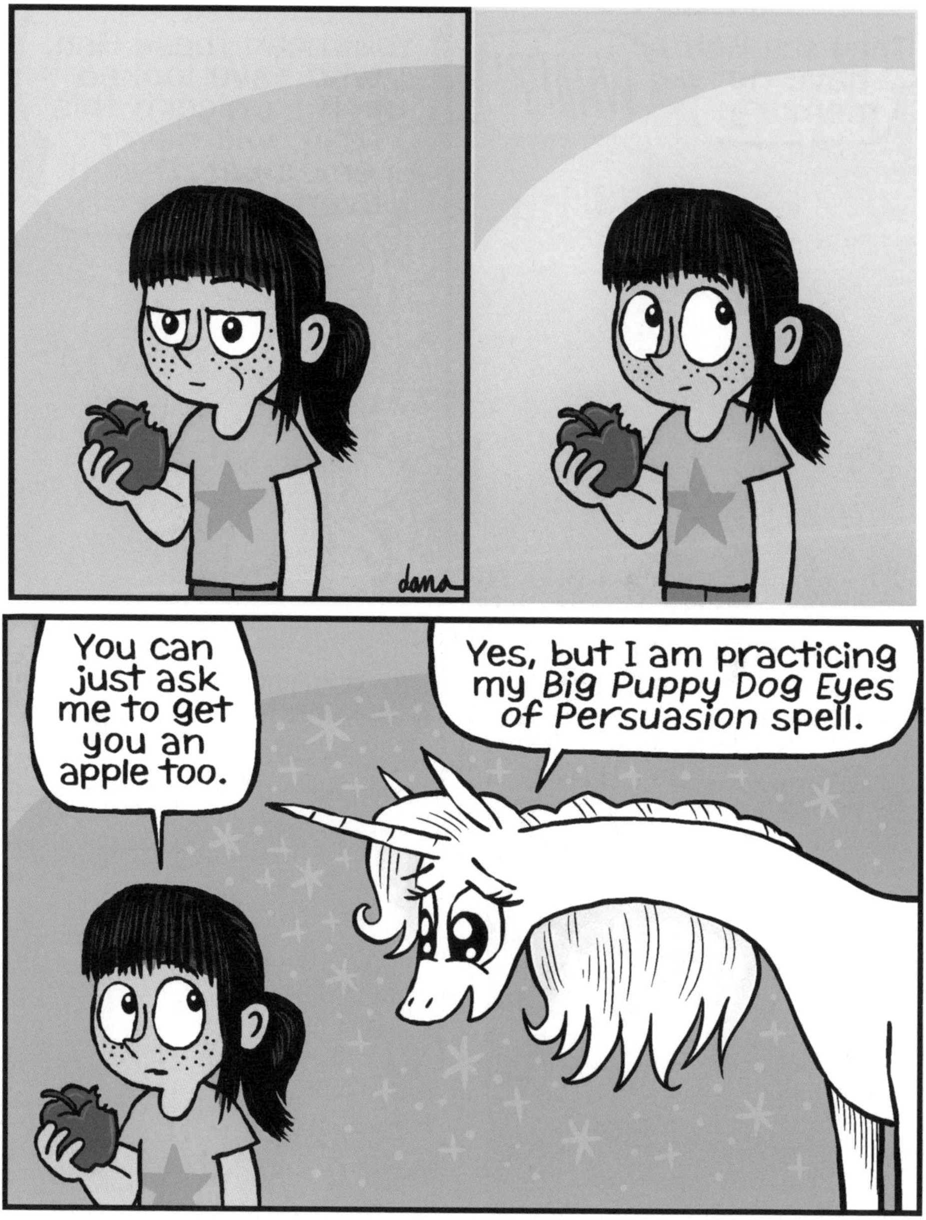
dana
You can just ask me to get you an apple too.
Yes, but I am practicing my *Big Puppy Dog Eyes of Persuasion* spell.

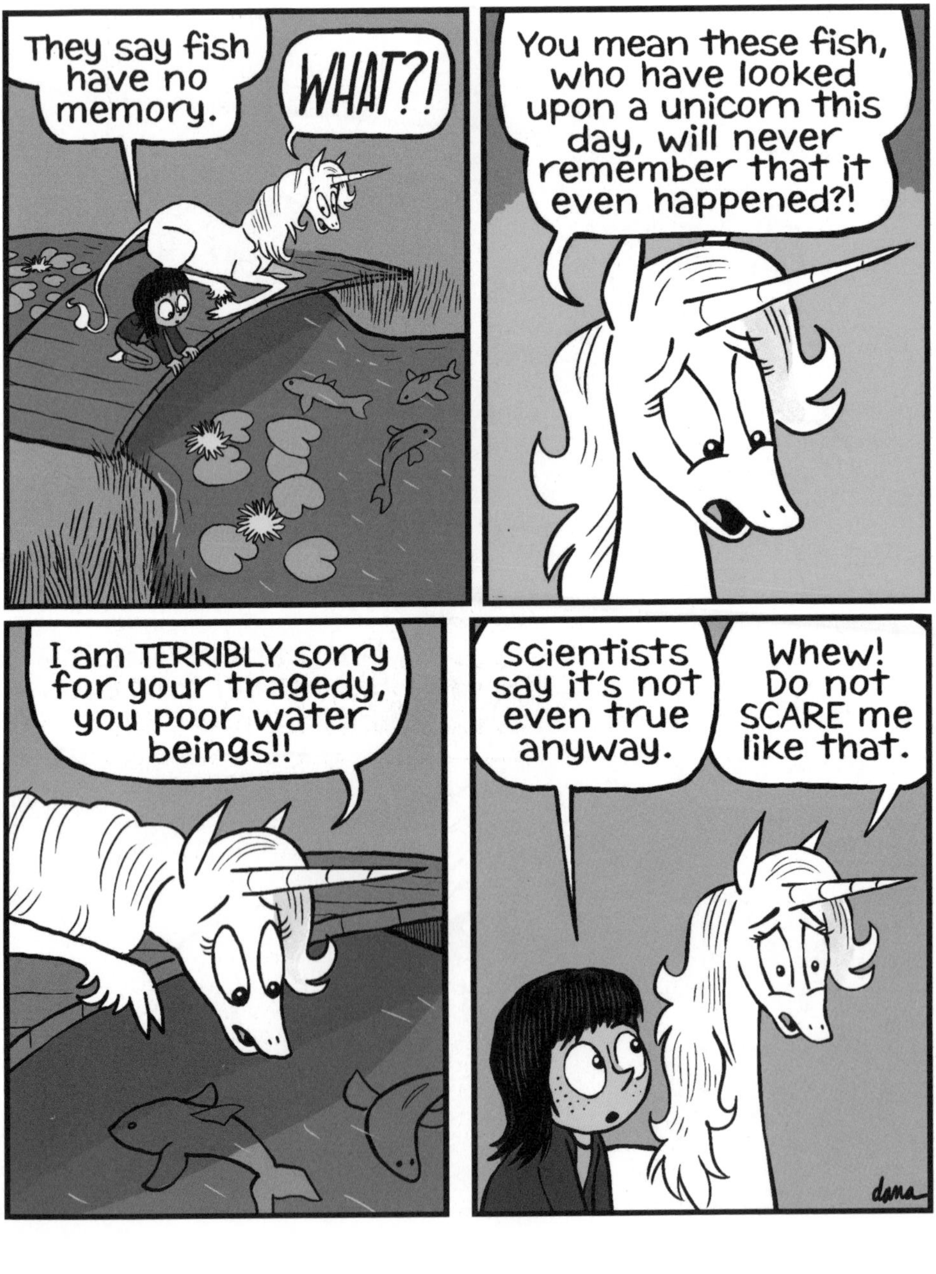
They say fish have no memory.
WHAT?!
You mean these fish, who have looked upon a unicorn this day, will never remember that it even happened?!
I am TERRIBLY sorry for your tragedy, you poor water beings!!
Scientists say it's not even true anyway.
Whew! Do not SCARE me like that.
dana

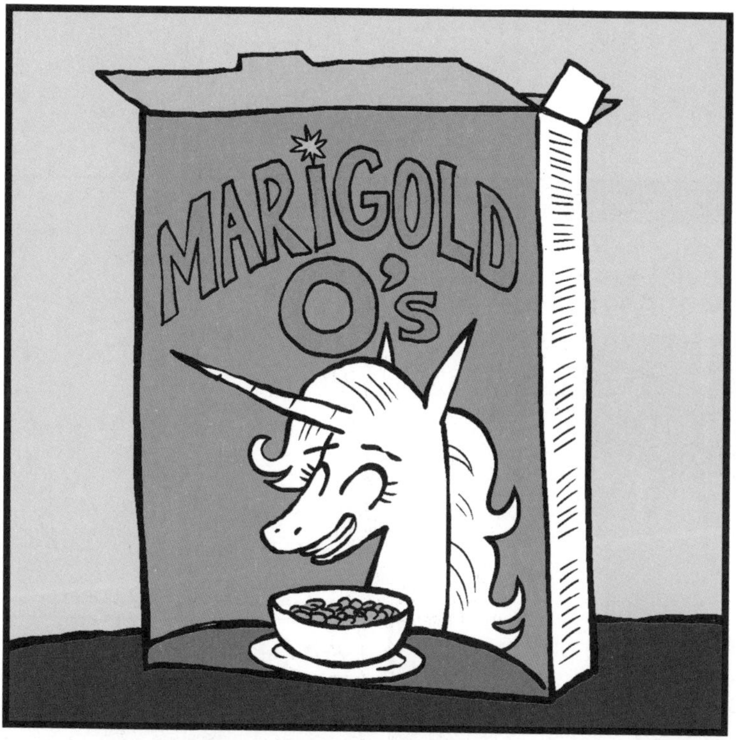
MARIGOLD O's

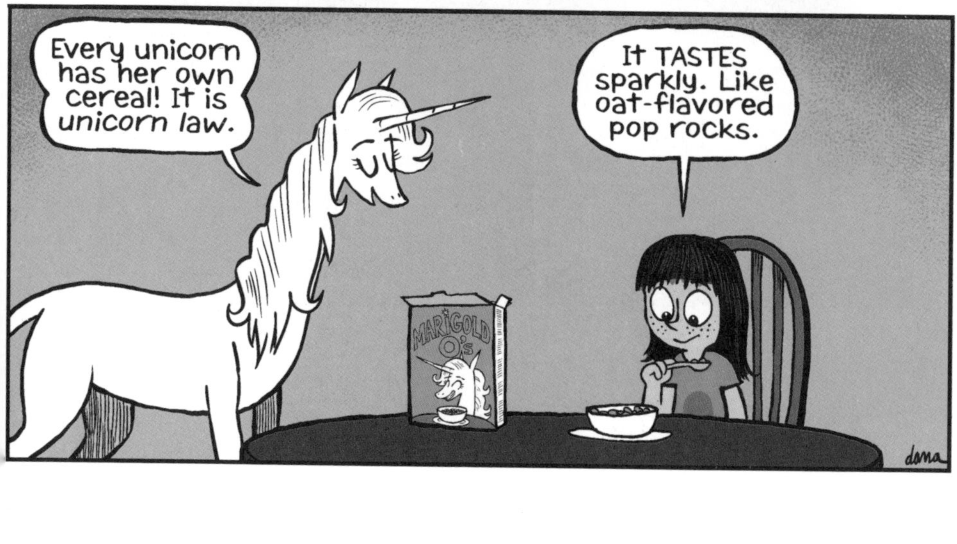
Every unicorn has her own cereal! It is unicorn law.
It TASTES sparkly. Like oat-flavored pop rocks.
MARIGOLD O's
dana

I saw this in a movie! Ready to be hypnotized?
I am ready.
You are getting very sleeeeeeeepy.
I am getting very sleepy.

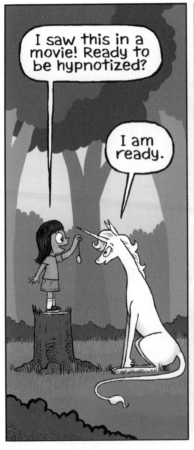

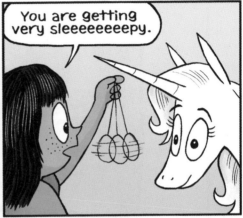

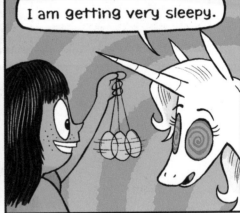

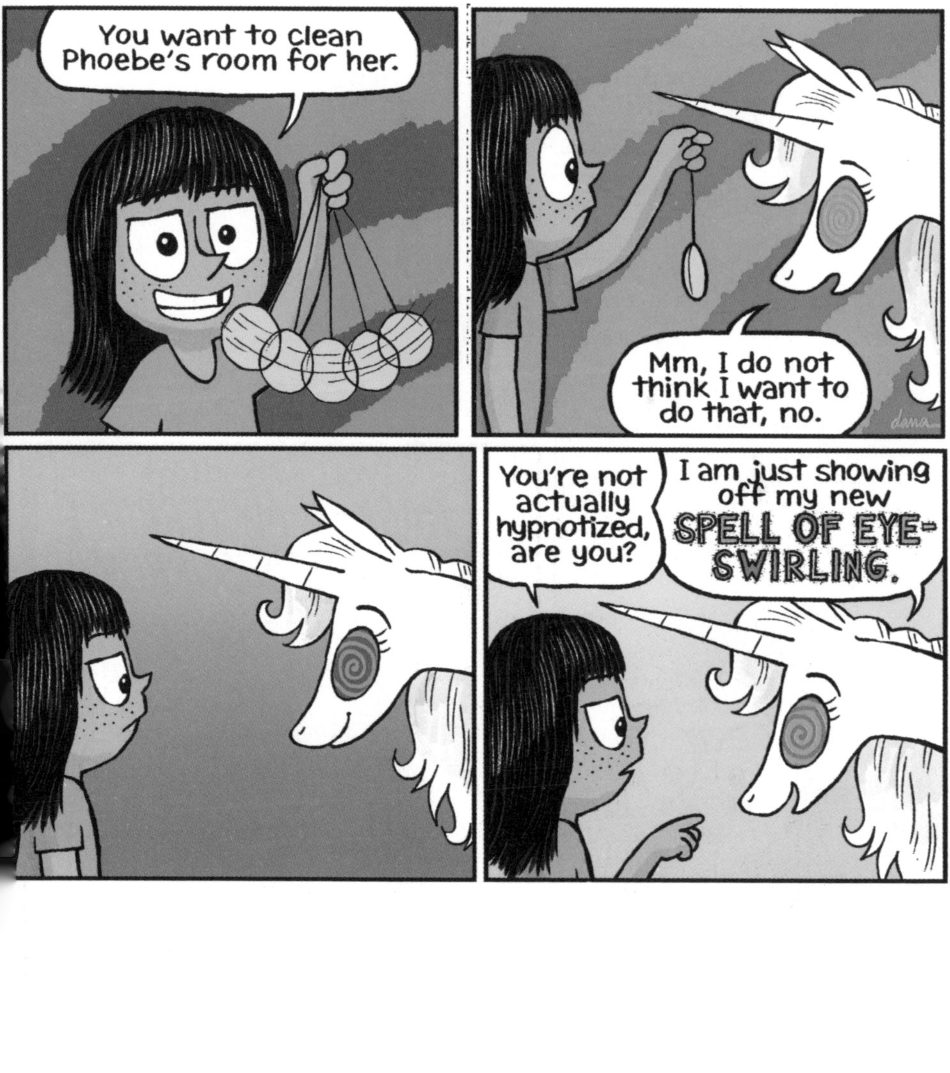
You want to clean Phoebe's room for her.
Mm, I do not think I want to do that, no.
You're not actually hypnotized, are you?
I am just showing off my new SPELL OF EYE-SWIRLING.

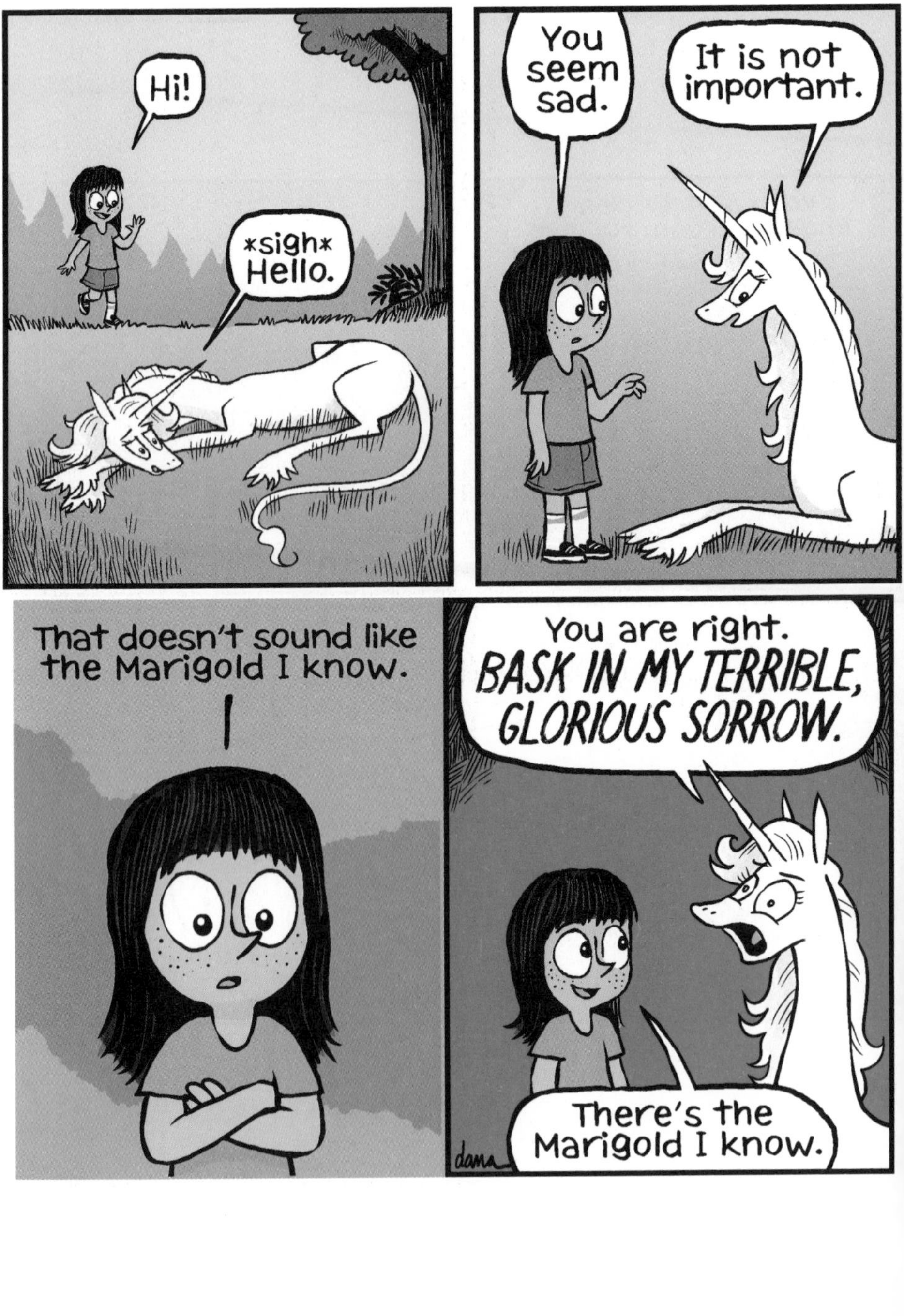
Hi!
sigh Hello.
You seem sad.
It is not important.
That doesn't sound like the Marigold I know.
You are right. BASK IN MY TERRIBLE, GLORIOUS SORROW.
There's the Marigold I know.
dana

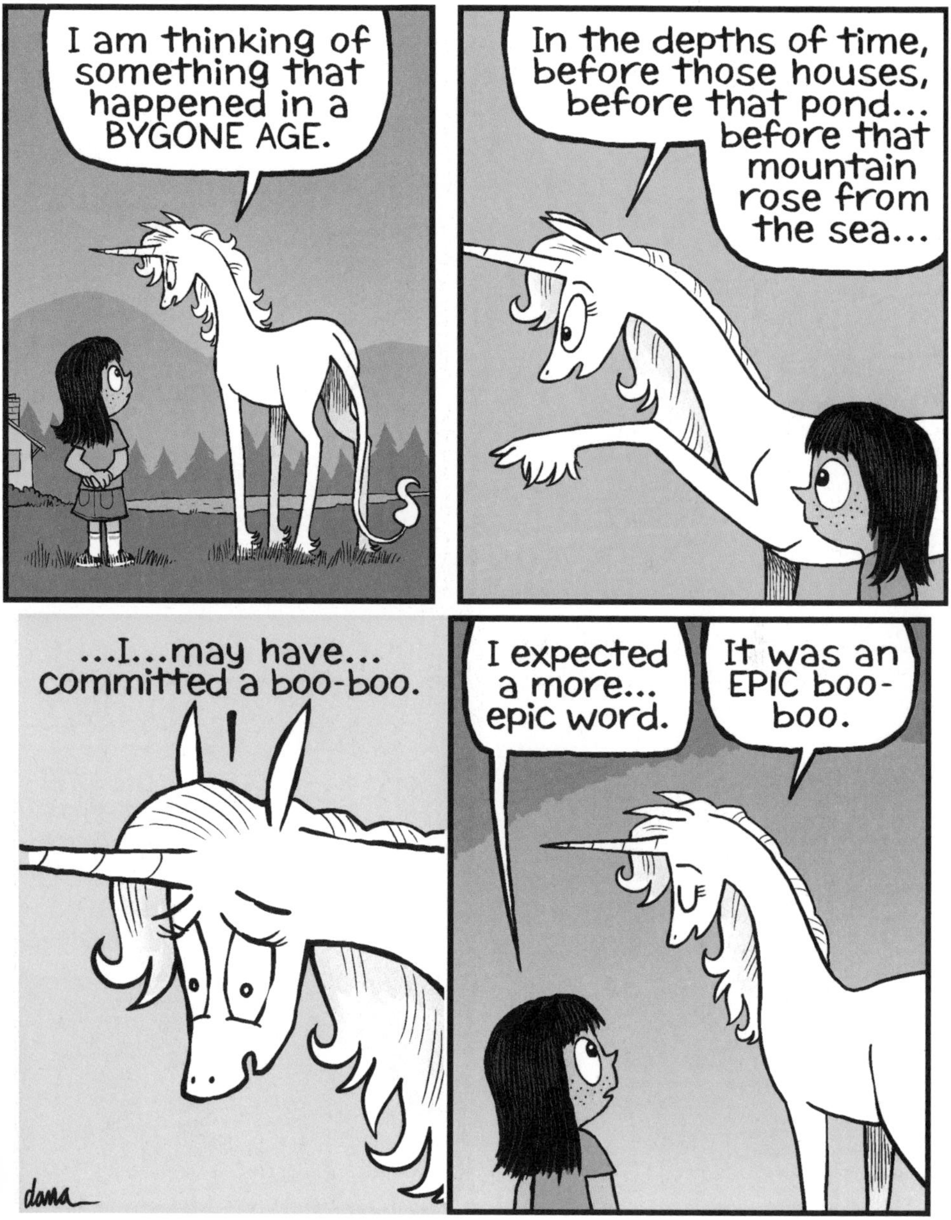
I am thinking of something that happened in a BYGONE AGE.
In the depths of time, before those houses, before that pond... before that mountain rose from the sea...
...I...may have... committed a boo-boo.
dana
I expected a more... epic word.
It was an EPIC boo-boo.

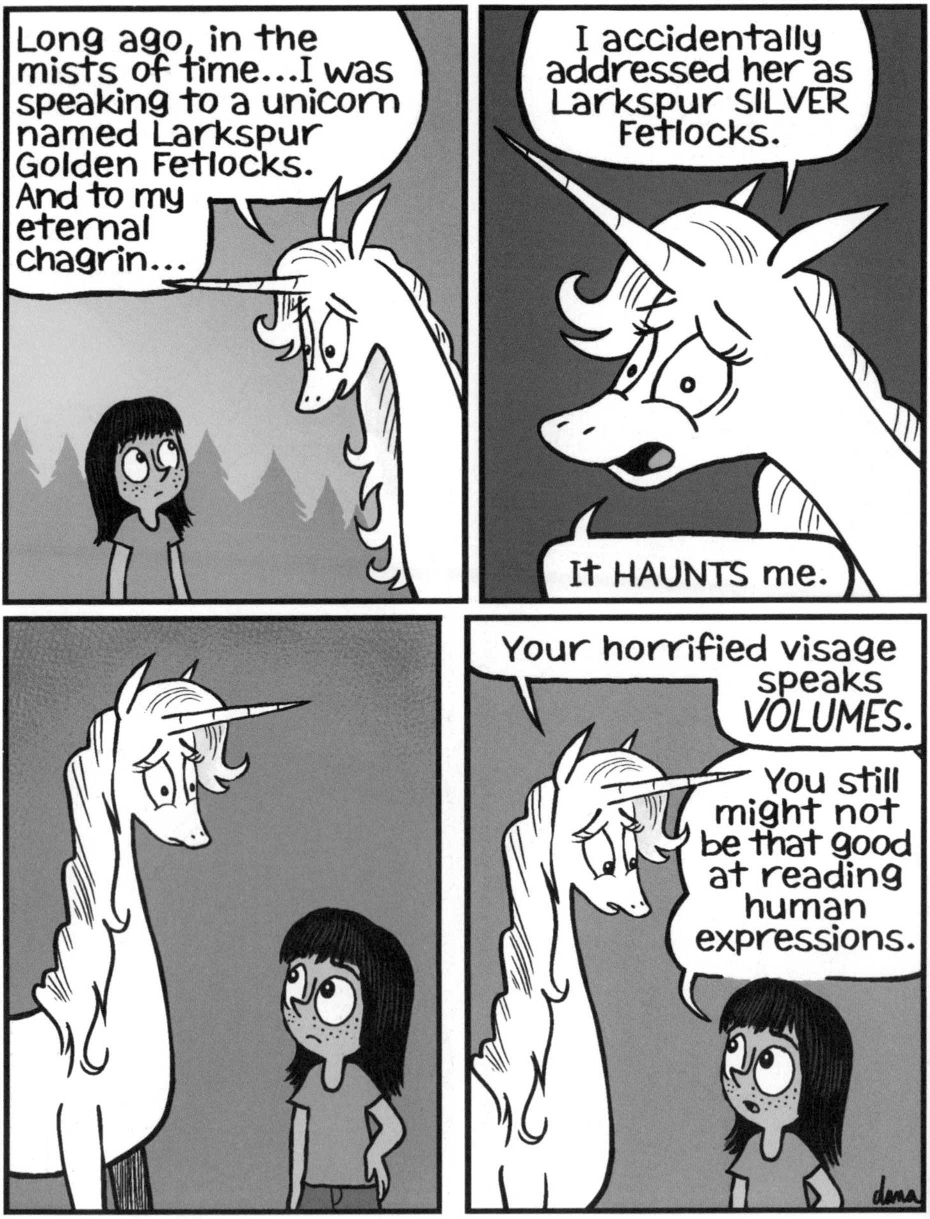
Long ago, in the mists of time...I was speaking to a unicorn named Larkspur Golden Fetlocks. And to my eternal chagrin...
I accidentally addressed her as Larkspur SILVER Fetlocks.
It HAUNTS me.
Your horrified visage speaks *VOLUMES*.
You still might not be that good at reading human expressions.
dana

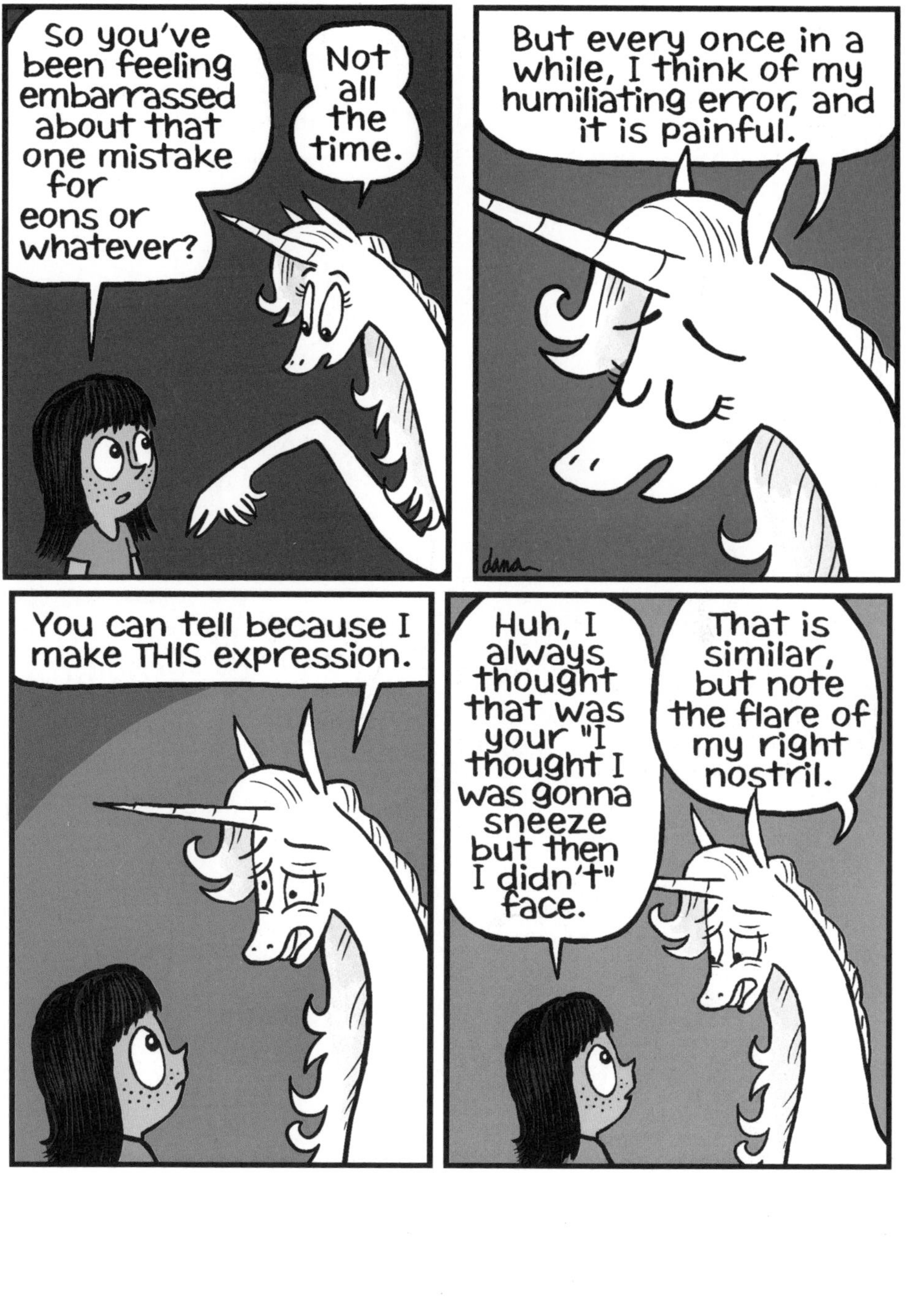
So you've been feeling embarrassed about that one mistake for eons or whatever?
Not all the time.
But every once in a while, I think of my humiliating error, and it is painful.
dana
You can tell because I make THIS expression.
Huh, I always thought that was your "I thought I was gonna sneeze but then I didn't" face.
That is similar, but note the flare of my right nostril.

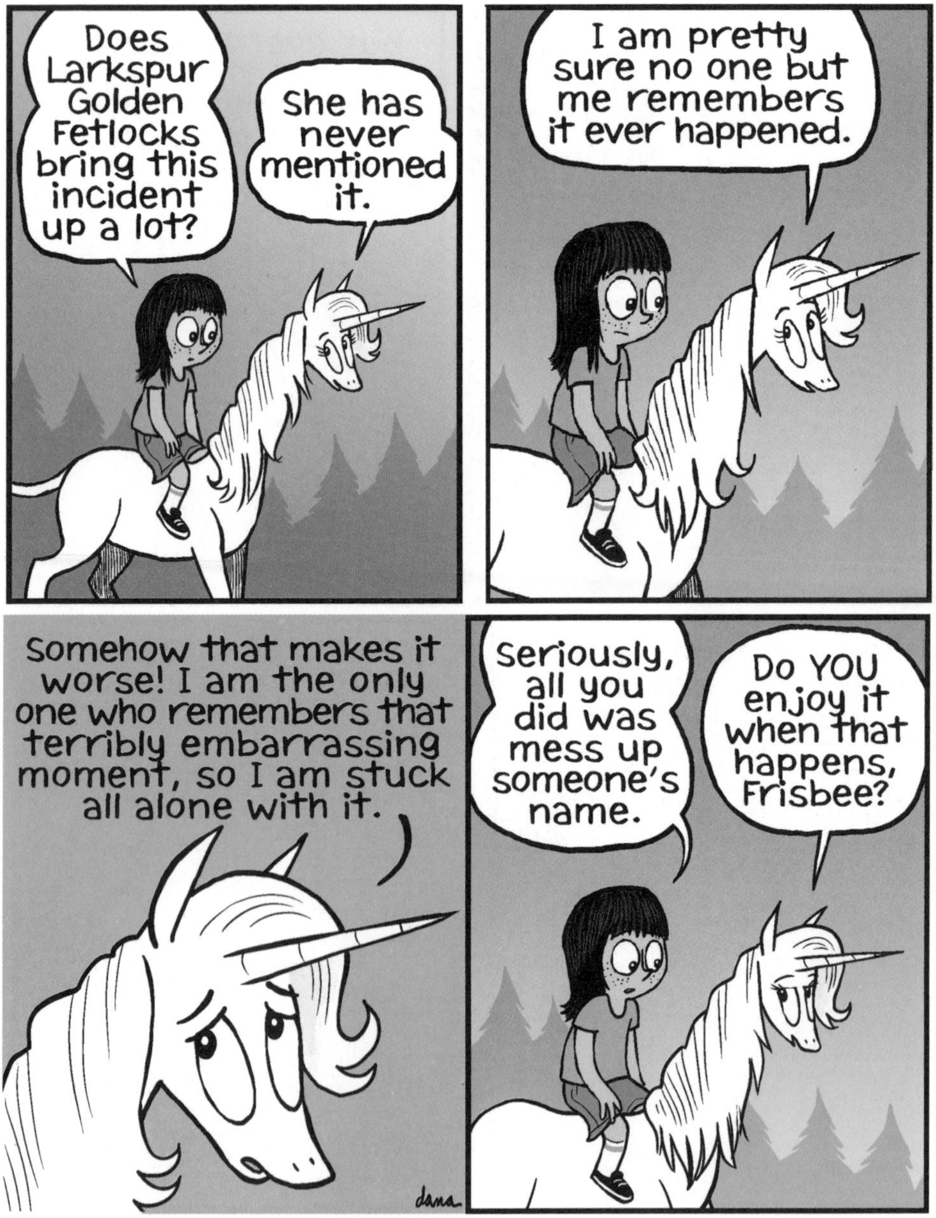
Does Larkspur Golden Fetlocks bring this incident up a lot?
She has never mentioned it.
I am pretty sure no one but me remembers it ever happened.
Somehow that makes it worse! I am the only one who remembers that terribly embarrassing moment, so I am stuck all alone with it.
Seriously, all you did was mess up someone's name.
Do YOU enjoy it when that happens, Frisbee?
dana

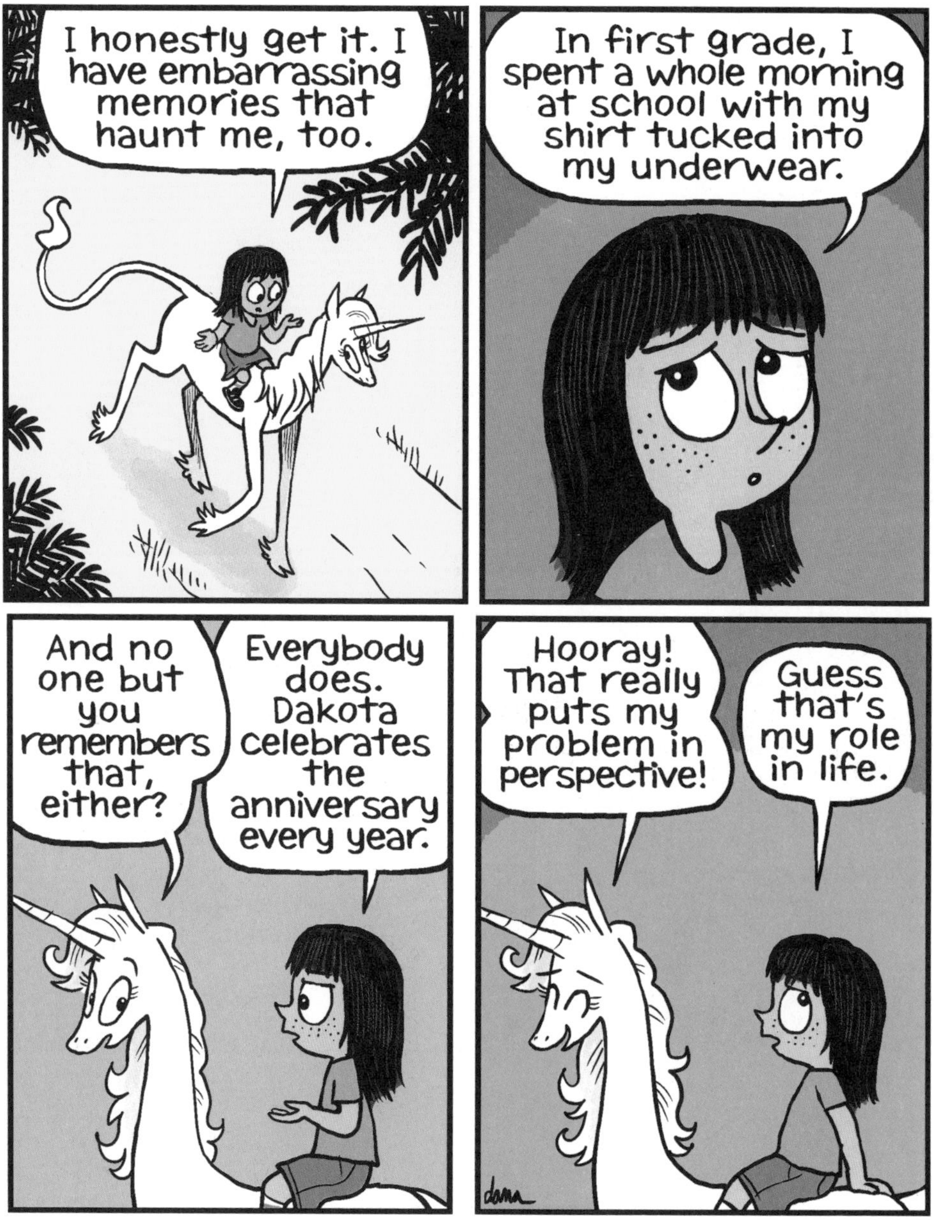
I honestly get it. I have embarrassing memories that haunt me, too.
In first grade, I spent a whole morning at school with my shirt tucked into my underwear.
And no one but you remembers that, either?
Everybody does. Dakota celebrates the anniversary every year.
Hooray! That really puts my problem in perspective!
Guess that's my role in life.
dana

Boop!
You have booped me!
Yup.
You have disrespected me, and my entire family, and all of unicornkind!
What?
To be booped is a GRAVE dishonor.

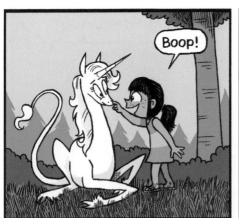

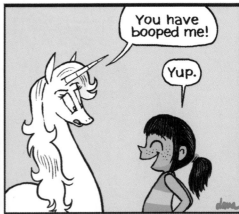

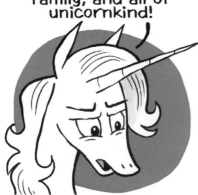

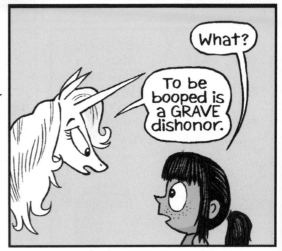

Since ancient times, booping has been a matter of utmost seriousness. The Booping Wars were a terrible era for unicornkind!
BOOP BOOP BOOP BOOP BOOP
BOOP
BOOP
Wow. Is that true?
No. I made it up to mess with you.
BOOP BOOP BOOP
BOOP BOOP

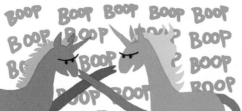

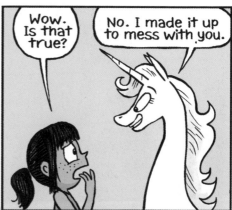

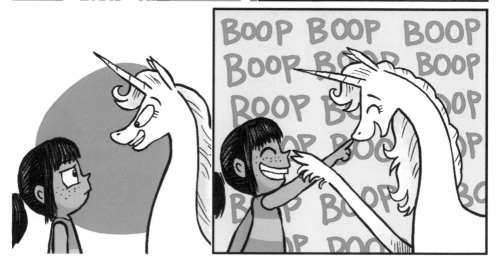

Marigold? Is that you?
PHOEBE!
Thank goodness! I am hopelessly lost!
But my house is just over there! How are you lost?
I...cannot remember. How strange.
Wait...it is all coming back to me now!

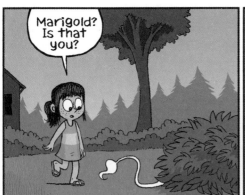

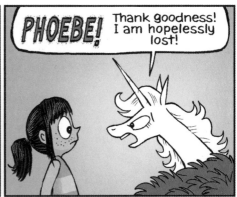

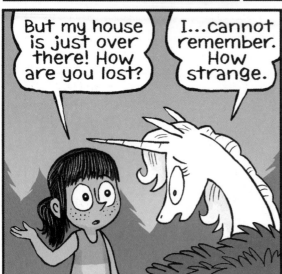

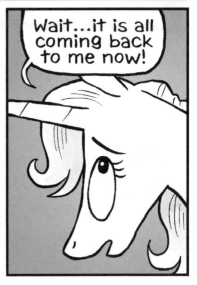

I wanted to play hide-and-seek, but you were not here.
So I cast a
Spell of forgetting
so I could forget where I was!
And then, because I did not know where I was, I panicked and hid in this bush, and remained there until you came along.
A true friend will always help you find yourse- WHAT IS THAT STRANGE SWISHY THING I SEE BEHIND ME?
You should stop with the forgetting spells. You might be bad at them.
dana

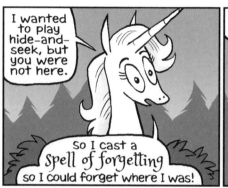

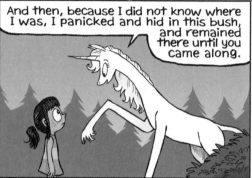

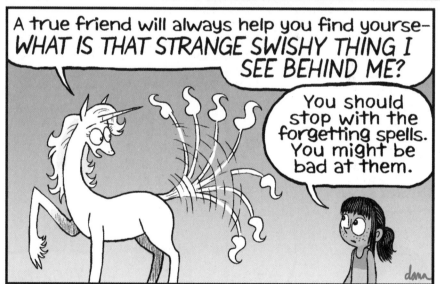

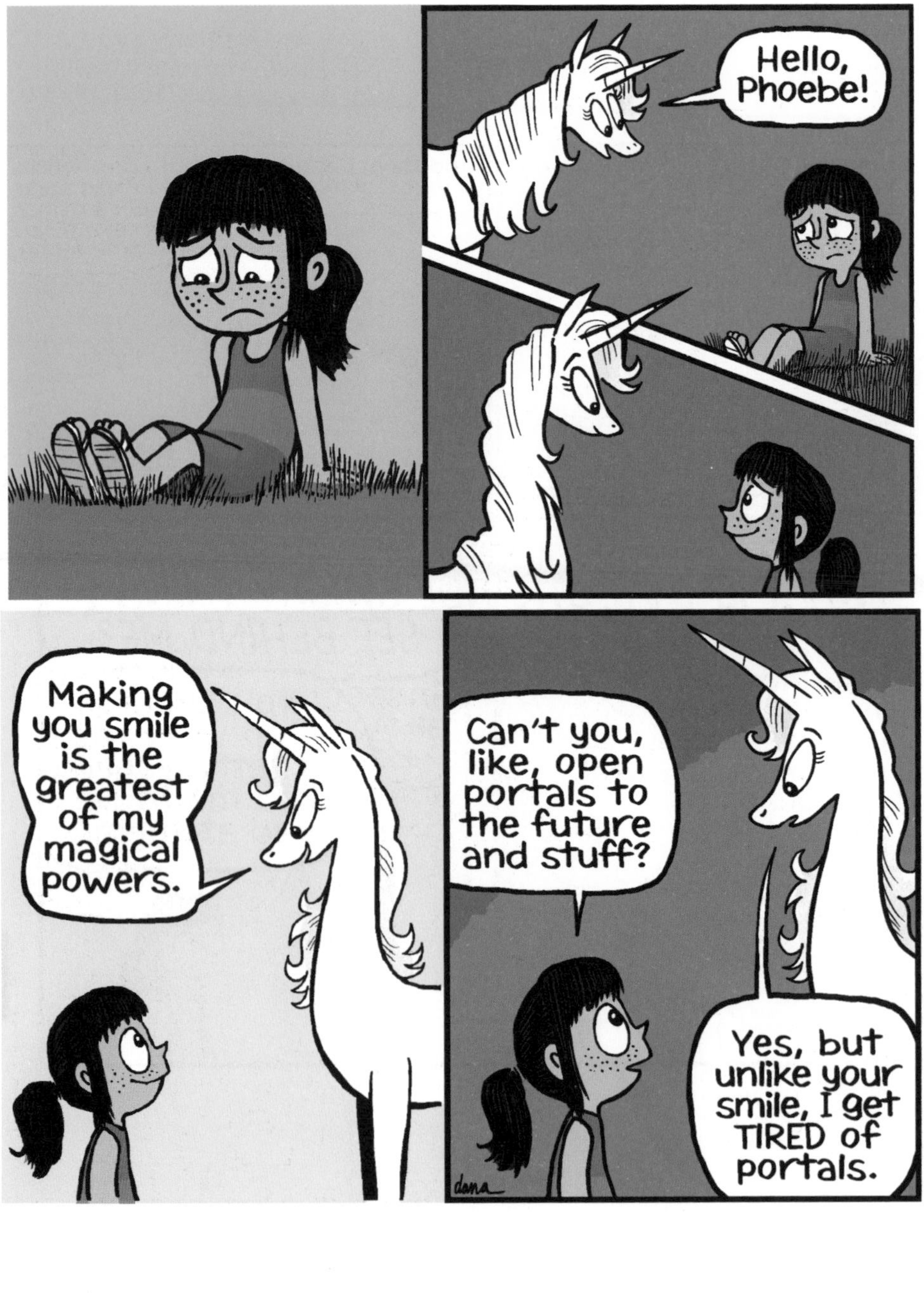
Hello, Phoebe!
Making you smile is the greatest of my magical powers.
Can't you, like, open portals to the future and stuff?
Yes, but unlike your smile, I get TIRED of portals.
dana

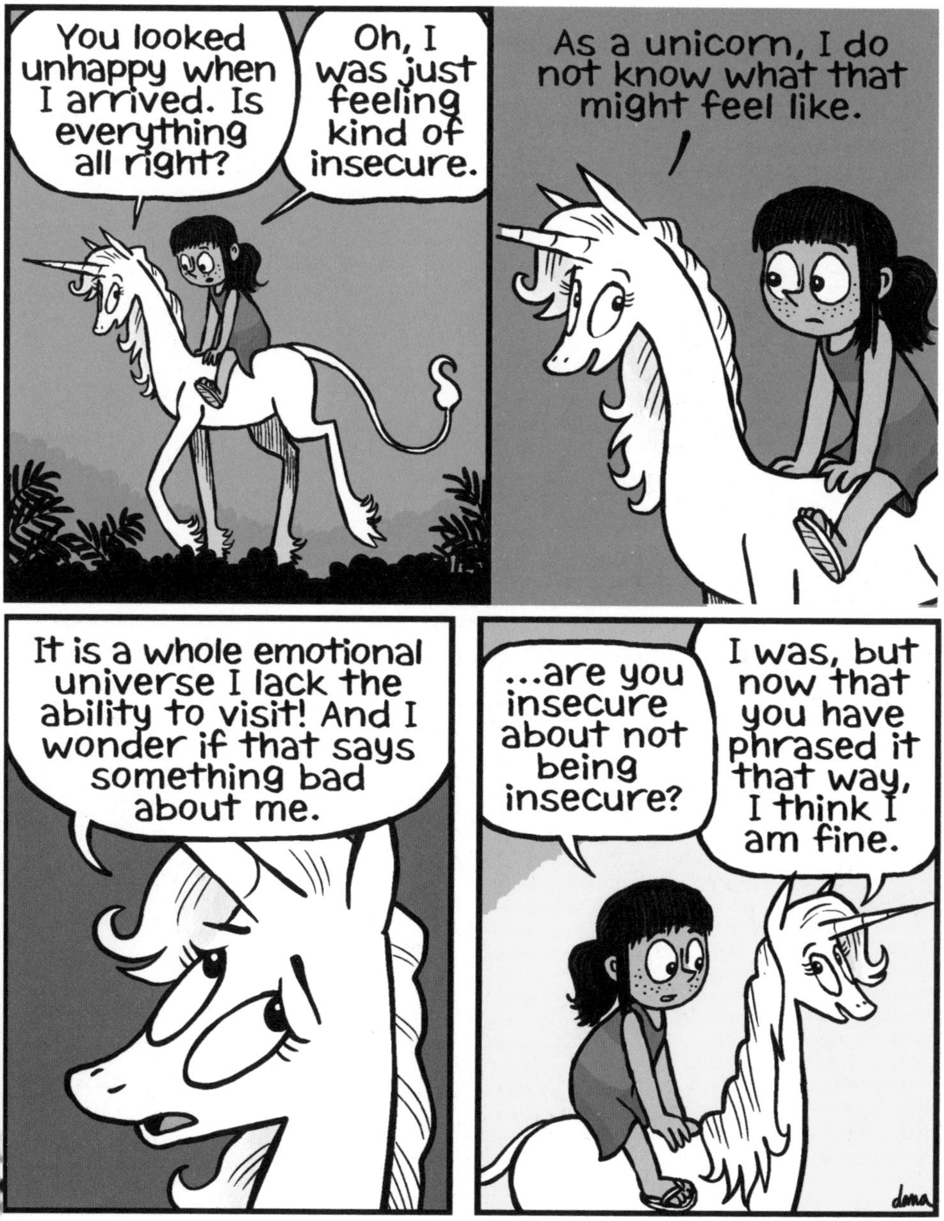
You looked unhappy when I arrived. Is everything all right?
Oh, I was just feeling kind of insecure.
As a unicorn, I do not know what that might feel like.
It is a whole emotional universe I lack the ability to visit! And I wonder if that says something bad about me.
...are you insecure about not being insecure?
I was, but now that you have phrased it that way, I think I am fine.
dana

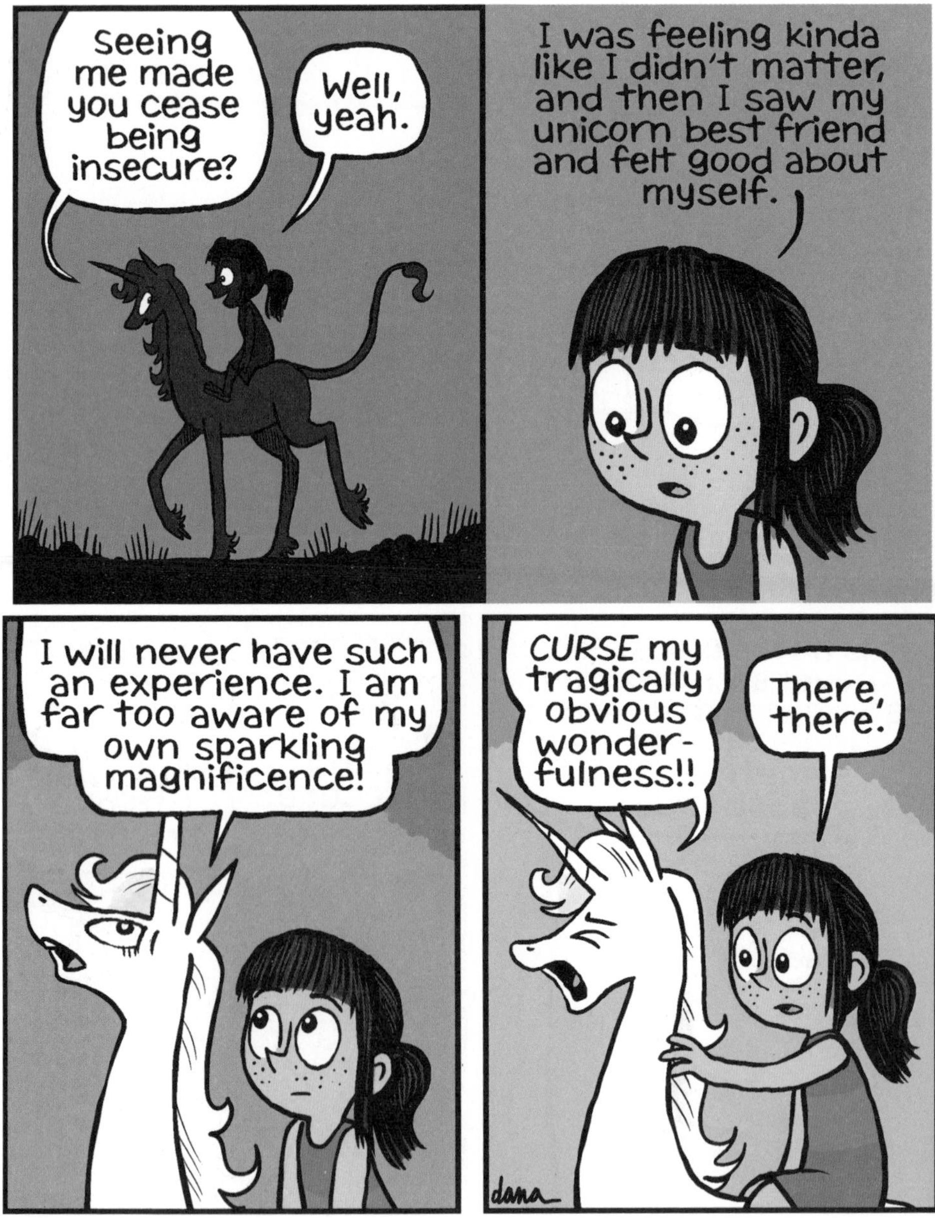
Seeing me made you cease being insecure?
Well, yeah.
I was feeling kinda like I didn't matter, and then I saw my unicorn best friend and felt good about myself.
I will never have such an experience. I am far too aware of my own sparkling magnificence!
CURSE my tragically obvious wonder-fulness!!
There, there.
dana

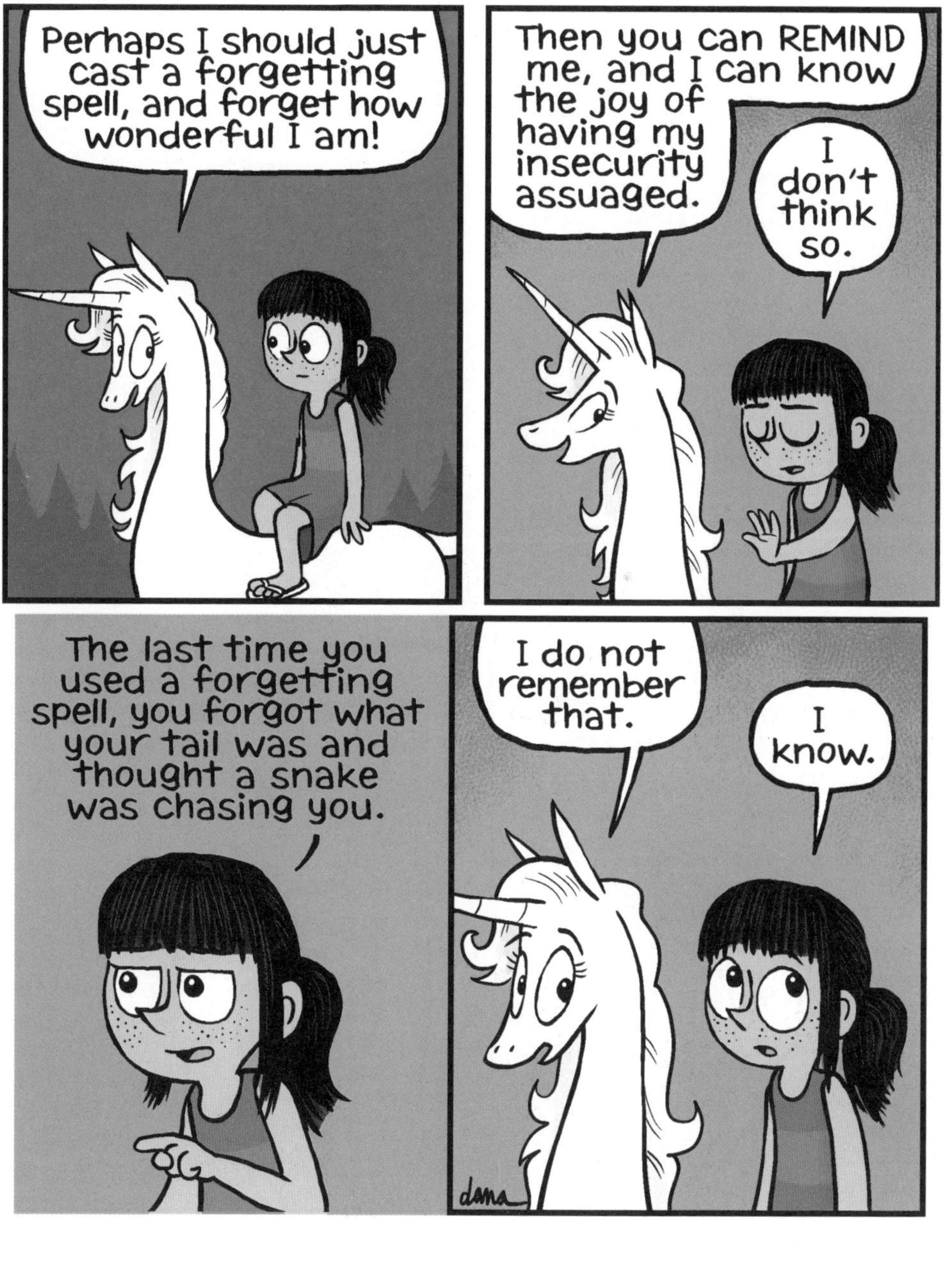
Perhaps I should just cast a forgetting spell, and forget how wonderful I am!
Then you can REMIND me, and I can know the joy of having my insecurity assuaged.
I don't think so.
The last time you used a forgetting spell, you forgot what your tail was and thought a snake was chasing you.
I do not remember that.
I know.
dana

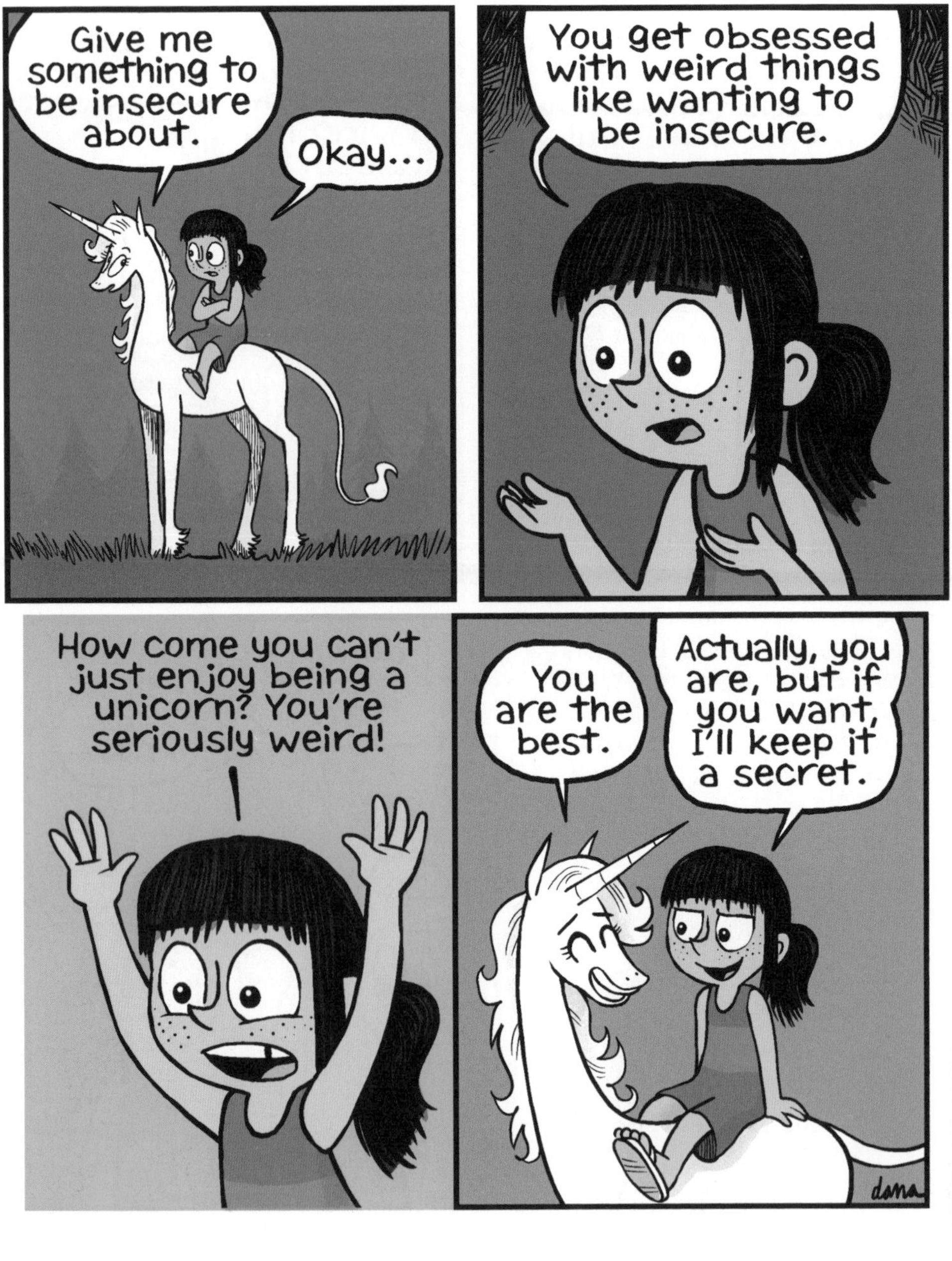
Give me something to be insecure about.
Okay...
You get obsessed with weird things like wanting to be insecure.
How come you can't just enjoy being a unicorn? You're seriously weird!
You are the best.
Actually, you are, but if you want, I'll keep it a secret.
dana

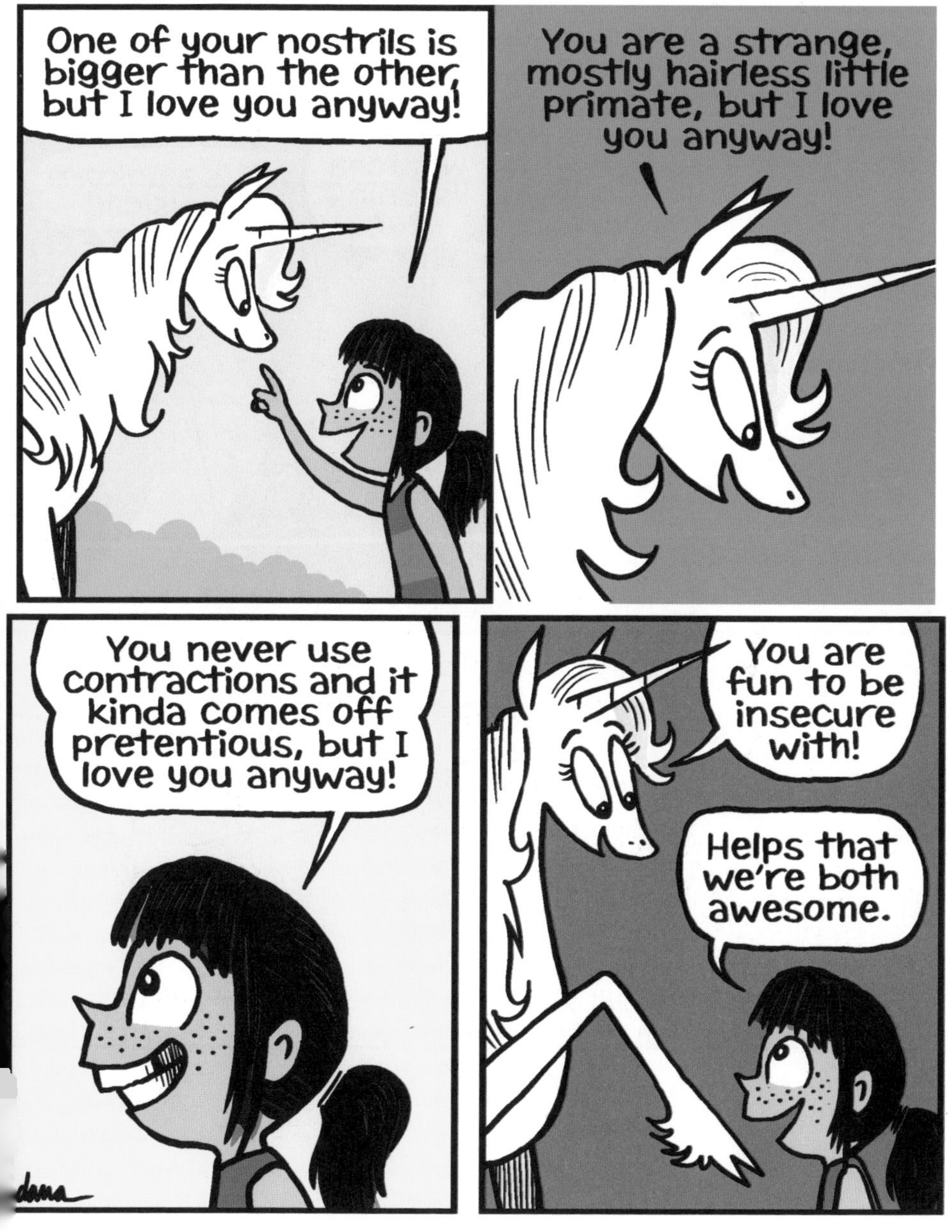
One of your nostrils is bigger than the other, but I love you anyway!
You are a strange, mostly hairless little primate, but I love you anyway!
You never use contractions and it kinda comes off pretentious, but I love you anyway!
You are fun to be insecure with!
Helps that we're both awesome.
dana

Whatcha listening to?
It is a unicorn musical!
GRASS IS DELICIOOOUS
Oh, like "Grass: The Musical."
No! Not at all.
"Grass: The Musical" is a JOYOUS CELEBRATION.

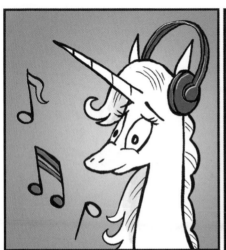

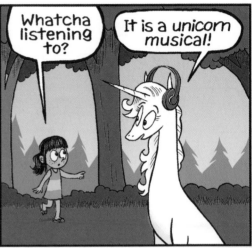

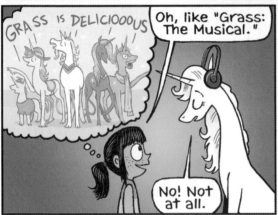

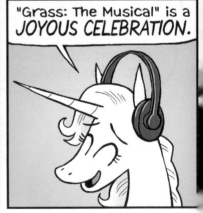

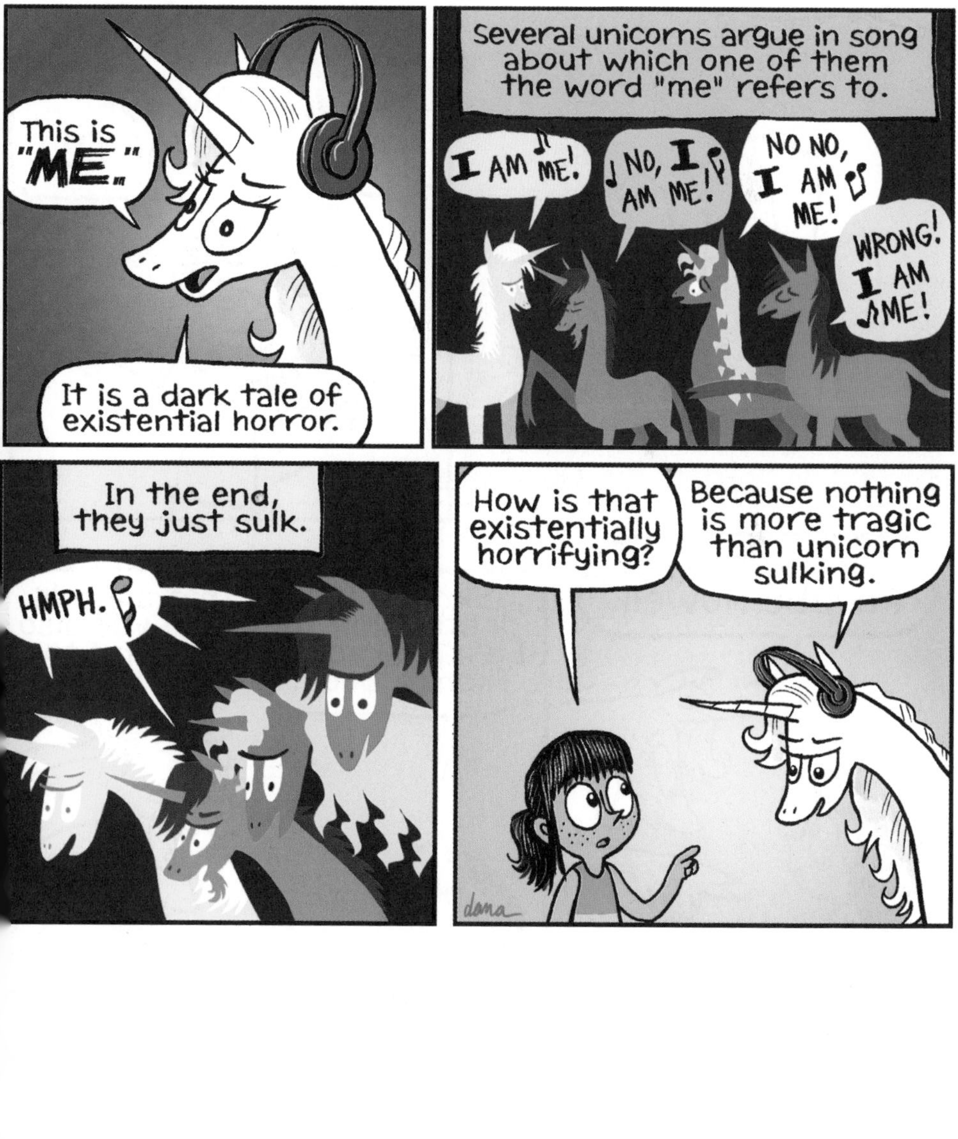
This is "ME."
It is a dark tale of existential horror.
Several unicorns argue in song about which one of them the word "me" refers to.
I AM ME!
NO, I AM ME!
NO NO, I AM ME!
WRONG! I AM ME!
In the end, they just sulk.
HMPH.
How is that existentially horrifying?
Because nothing is more tragic than unicorn sulking.

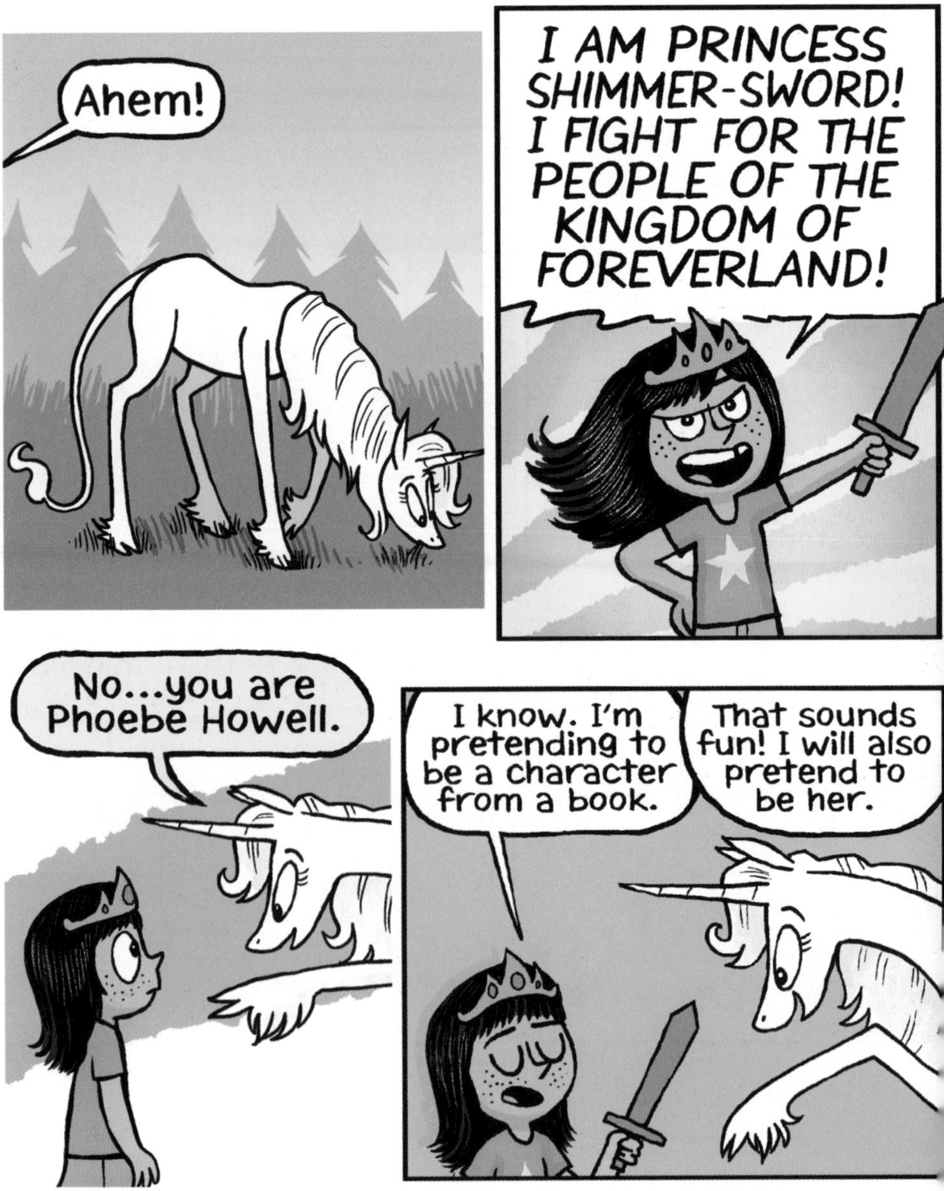
Ahem!
I AM PRINCESS SHIMMER-SWORD! I FIGHT FOR THE PEOPLE OF THE KINGDOM OF FOREVERLAND!
No...you are Phoebe Howell.
I know. I'm pretending to be a character from a book.
That sounds fun! I will also pretend to be her.

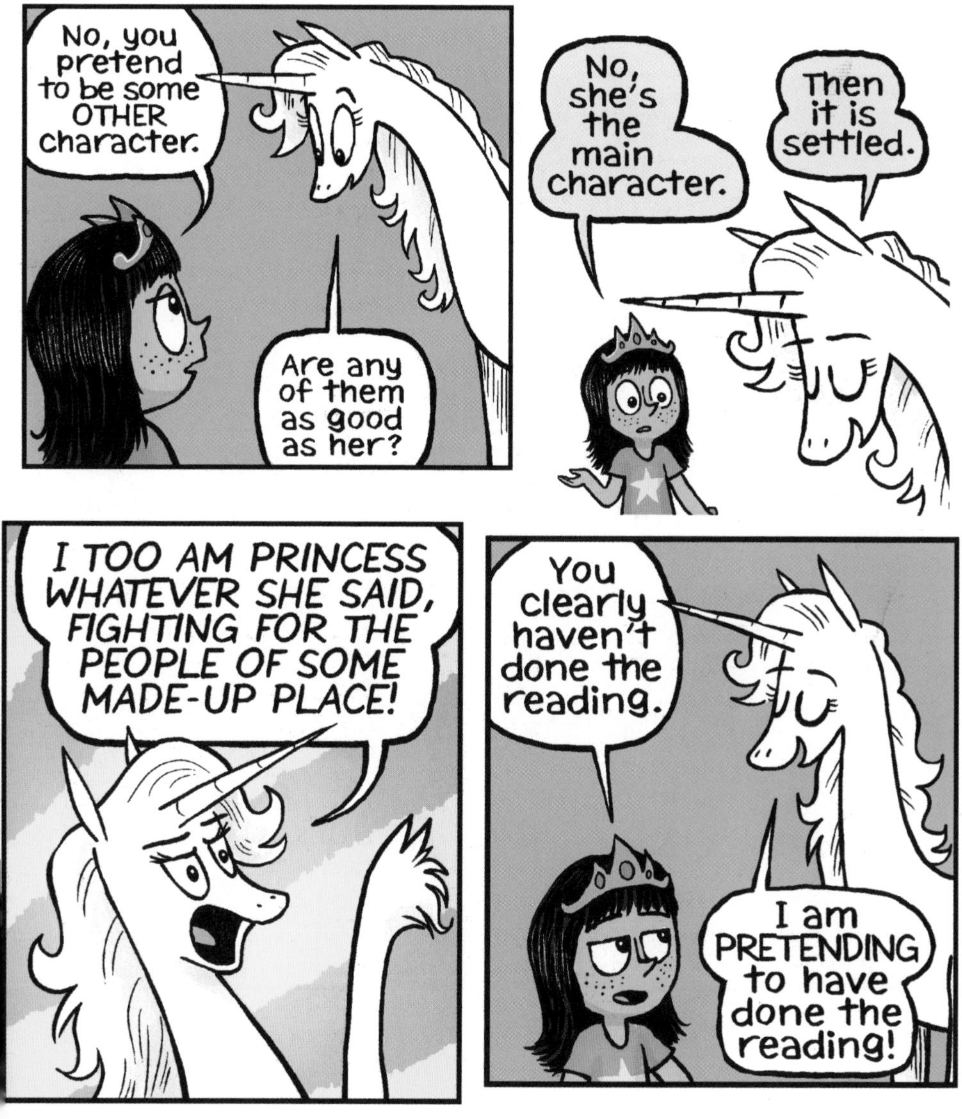
No, you pretend to be some OTHER character.
Are any of them as good as her?
No, she's the main character.
Then it is settled.
I TOO AM PRINCESS WHATEVER SHE SAID, FIGHTING FOR THE PEOPLE OF SOME MADE-UP PLACE!
You clearly haven't done the reading.
I am PRETENDING to have done the reading!

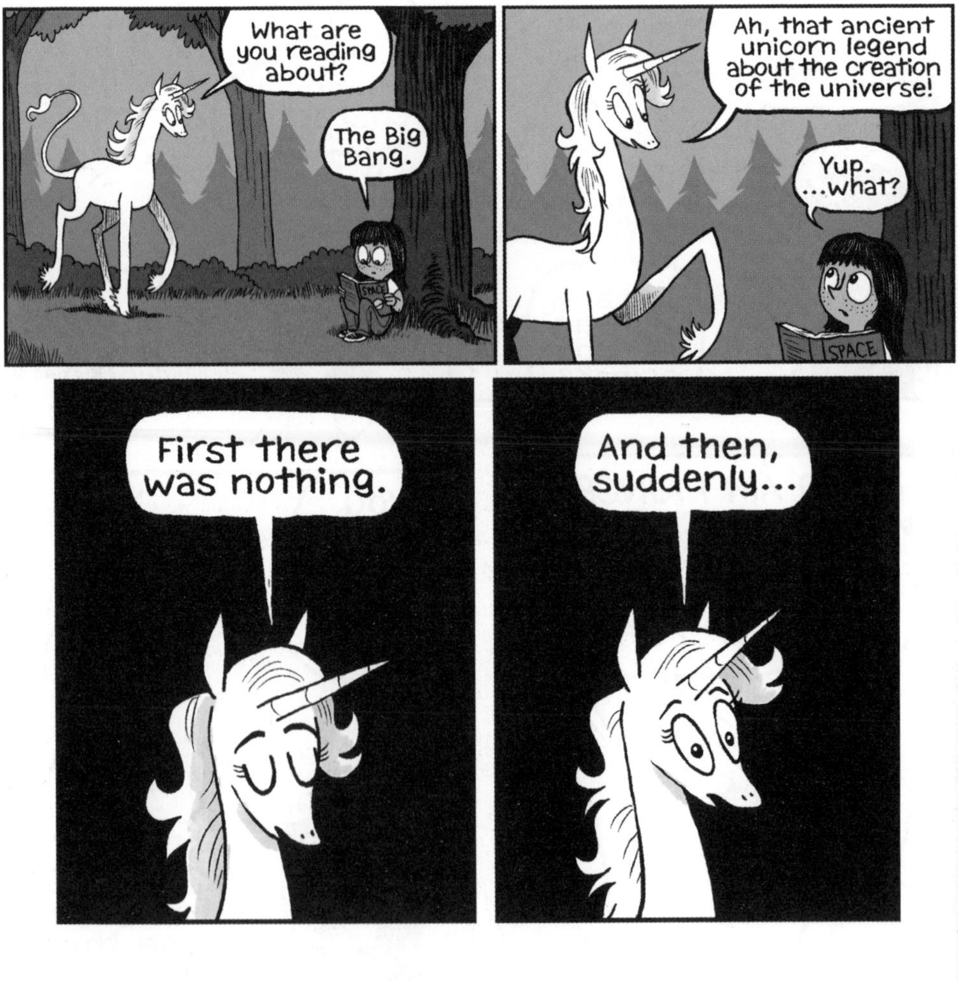
What are you reading about?
The Big Bang.
Ah, that ancient unicorn legend about the creation of the universe!
Yup. ...what?
SPACE
First there was nothing.
And then, suddenly...

The nothingness exploded in unicorns!

Oh dear!

We exist now!

How vexing!

This went on for eons, because getting over things had not yet been invented.

Mine is different.

I will get over it, since that HAS been invented now.

Oh, hey. What've you been up to?
Oh, not too much. Only...
ALCHEMY.
The ancient art of turning non-gold stuff into gold?
You humans and your silly obsession with gold! Who really needs gold?
Unicorn Alchemy is the art of making non-unicorn materials into unicorns!

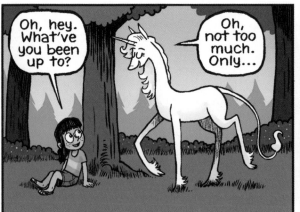

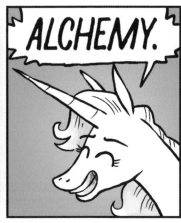

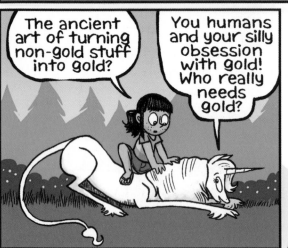

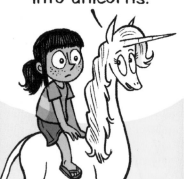

What, like living, breathing unicorns?
No, no. We just... arrange inanimate materials to look more like unicorns! Three-dimensional pictures of unicorns, if you will.
So... sculpture.
No! It is ALCHEMY.
For instance, this is the unicorn I alchemized this morning!
You made it OUT of gold?
Oh, unicorns always have some lying around.
Marigold is Excellent

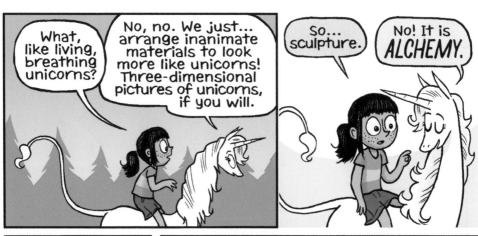

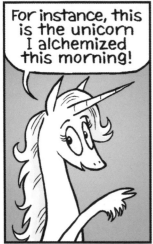

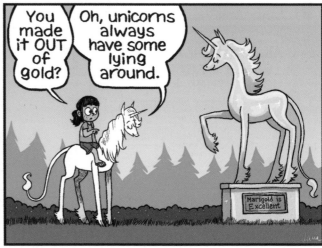

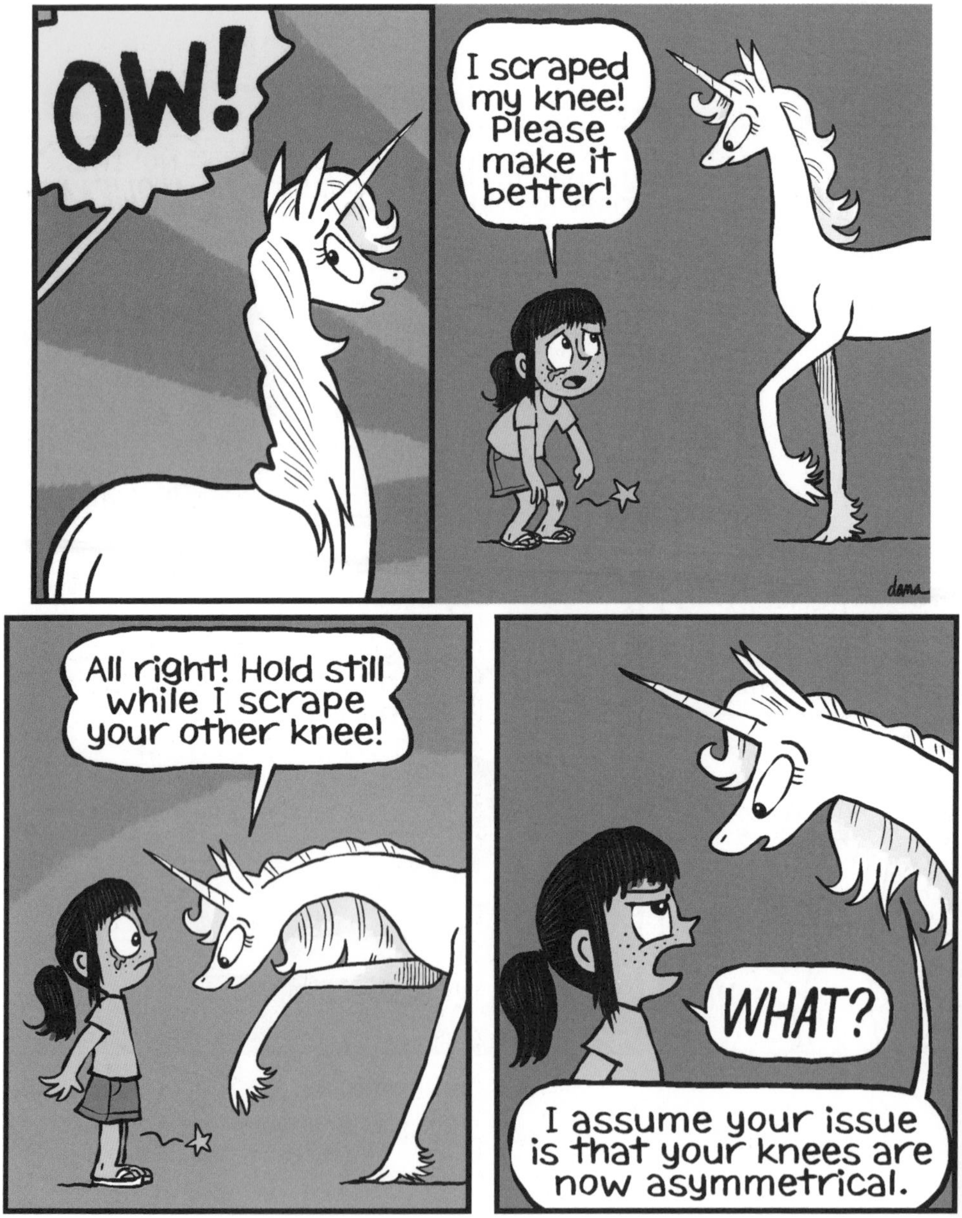
OW!
I scraped my knee! Please make it better!
dana
All right! Hold still while I scrape your other knee!
WHAT?
I assume your issue is that your knees are now asymmetrical.

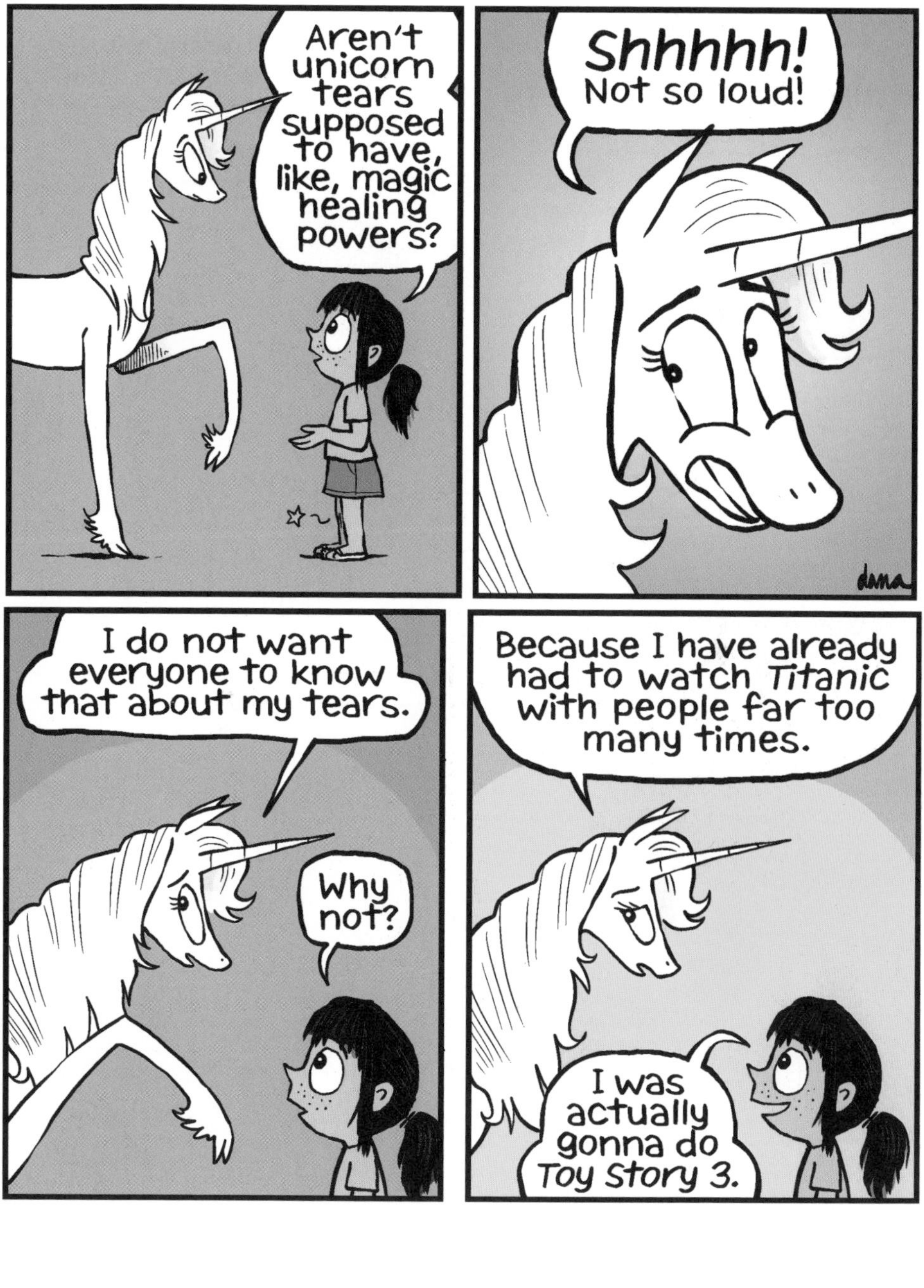
Aren't unicorn tears supposed to have, like, magic healing powers?
Shhhhh! Not so loud!
I do not want everyone to know that about my tears.
Why not?
Because I have already had to watch *Titanic* with people far too many times.
I was actually gonna do *Toy Story 3*.

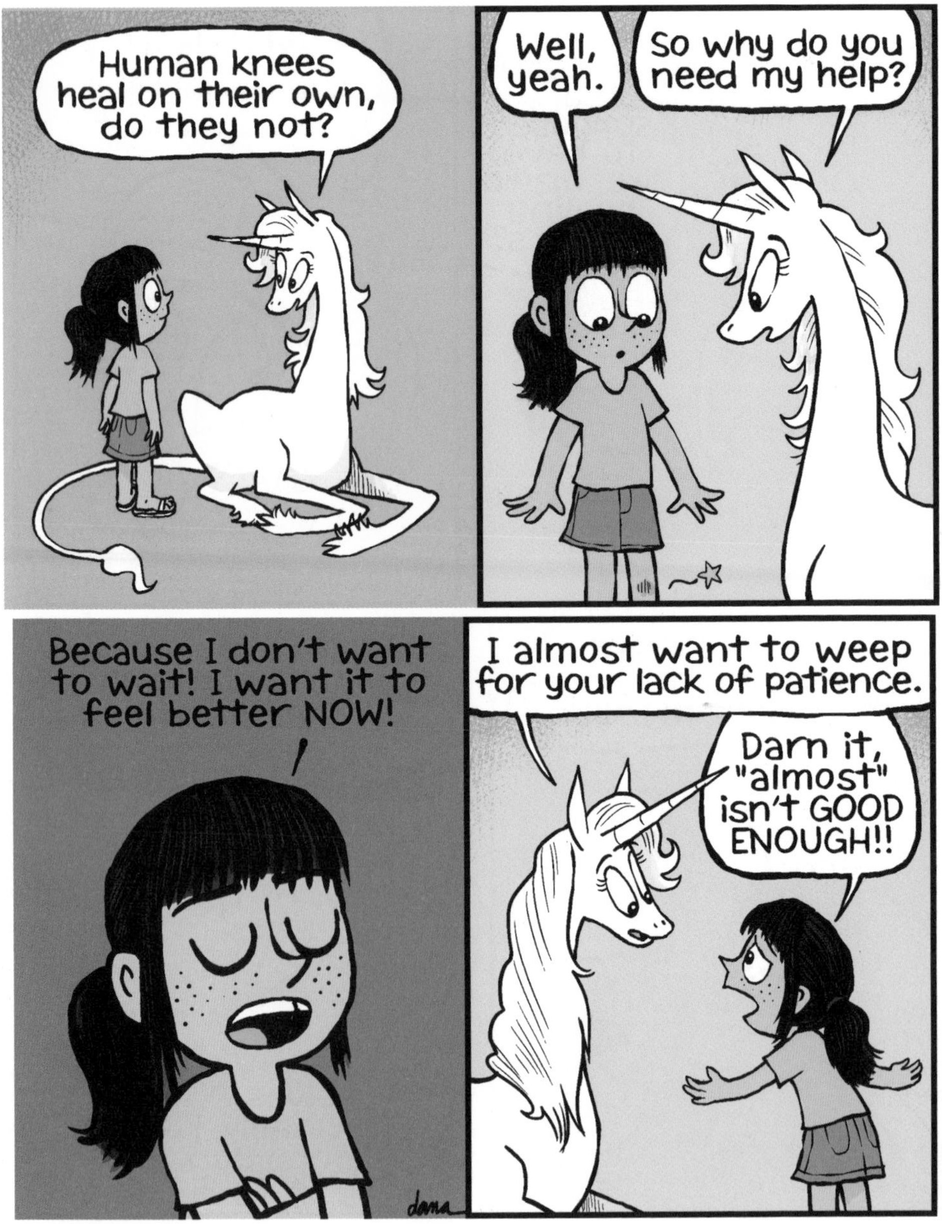

Human knees heal on their own, do they not?
Well, yeah.
So why do you need my help?
Because I don't want to wait! I want it to feel better NOW!
I almost want to weep for your lack of patience.
Darn it, "almost" isn't GOOD ENOUGH!!
dana

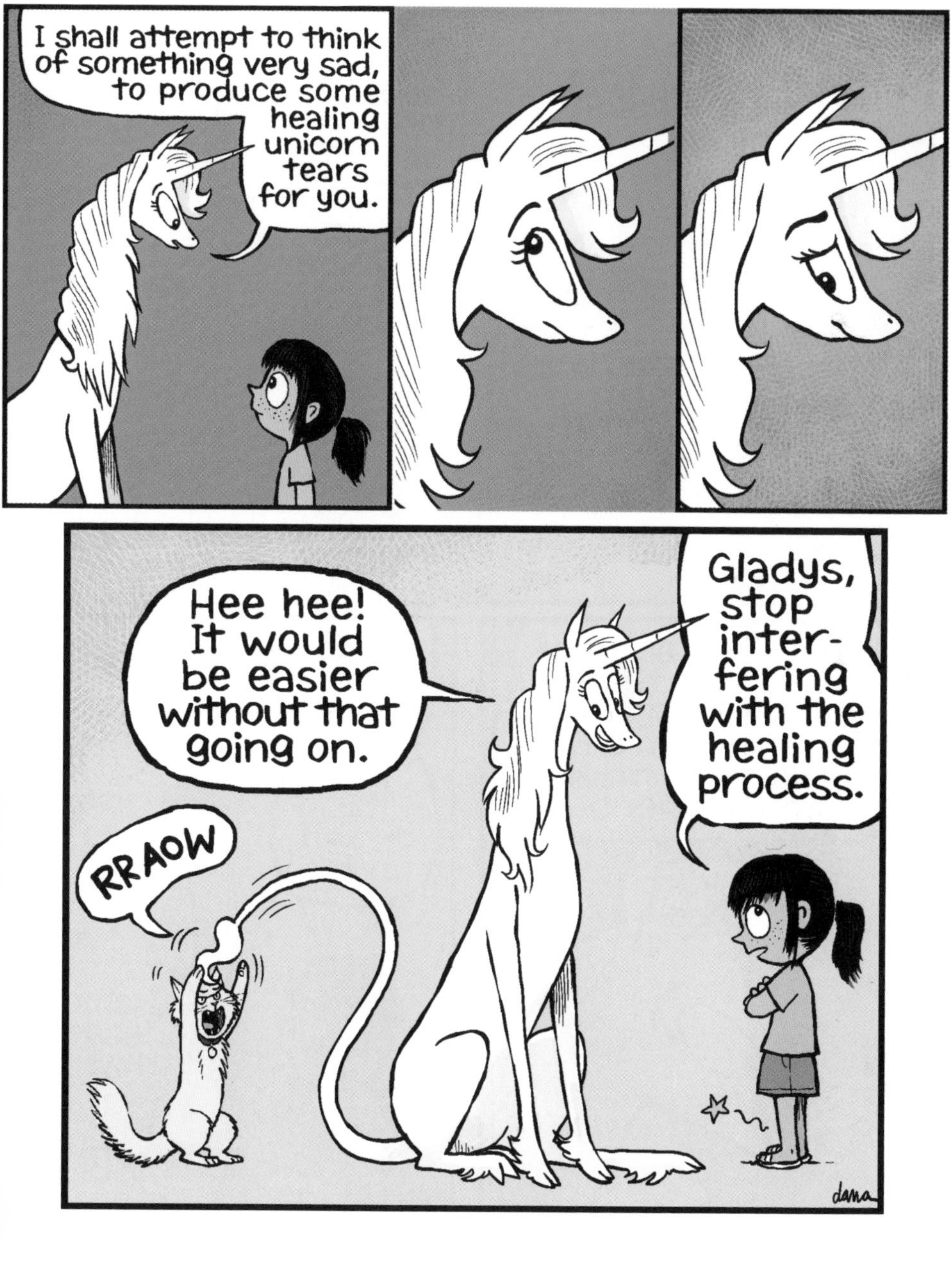
I shall attempt to think of something very sad, to produce some healing unicorn tears for you.
Hee hee! It would be easier without that going on.
Gladys, stop inter-fering with the healing process.
RRAOW
dana

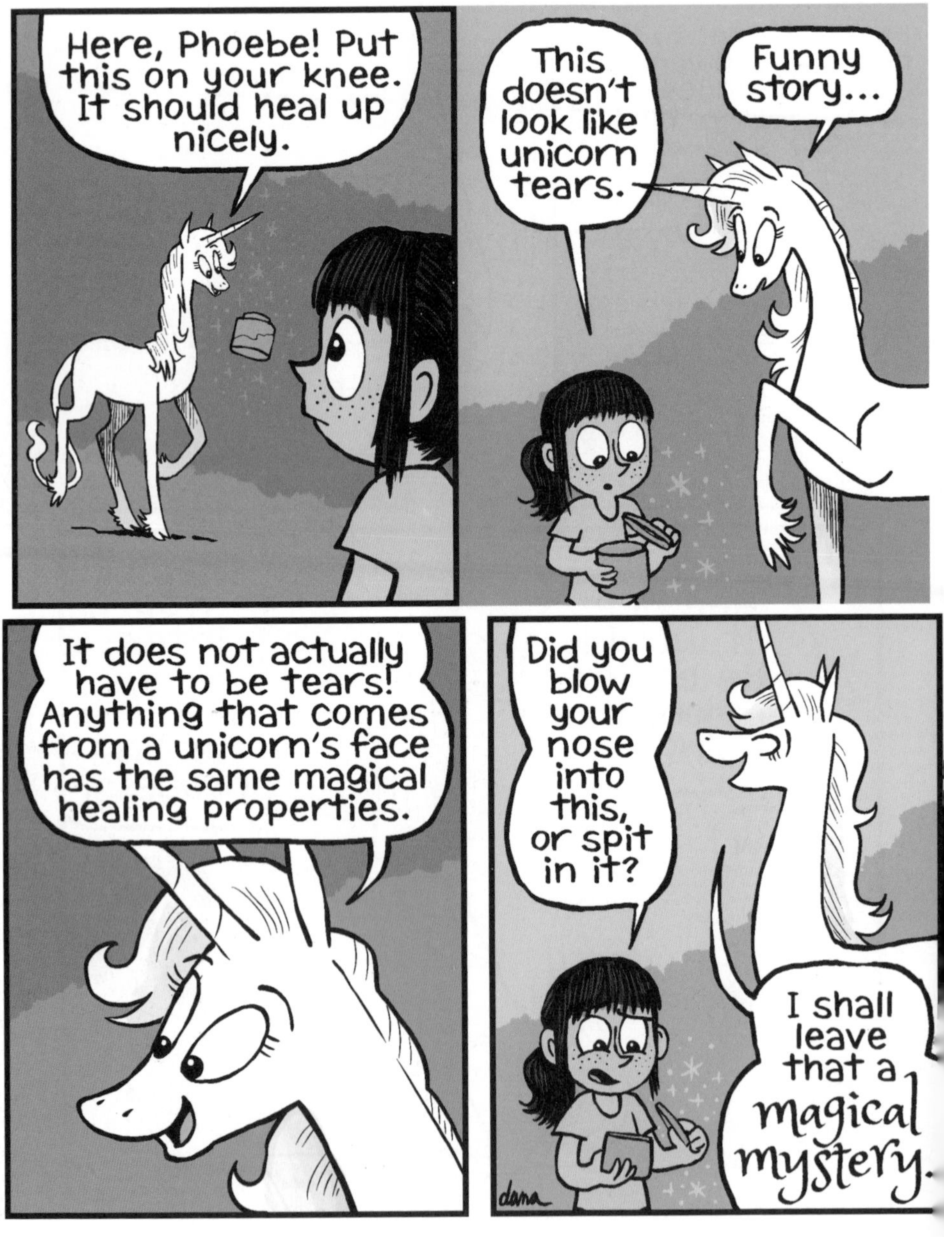
Here, Phoebe! Put this on your knee. It should heal up nicely.
This doesn't look like unicorn tears.
Funny story...
It does not actually have to be tears! Anything that comes from a unicorn's face has the same magical healing properties.
Did you blow your nose into this, or spit in it?
I shall leave that a magical mystery.
dana

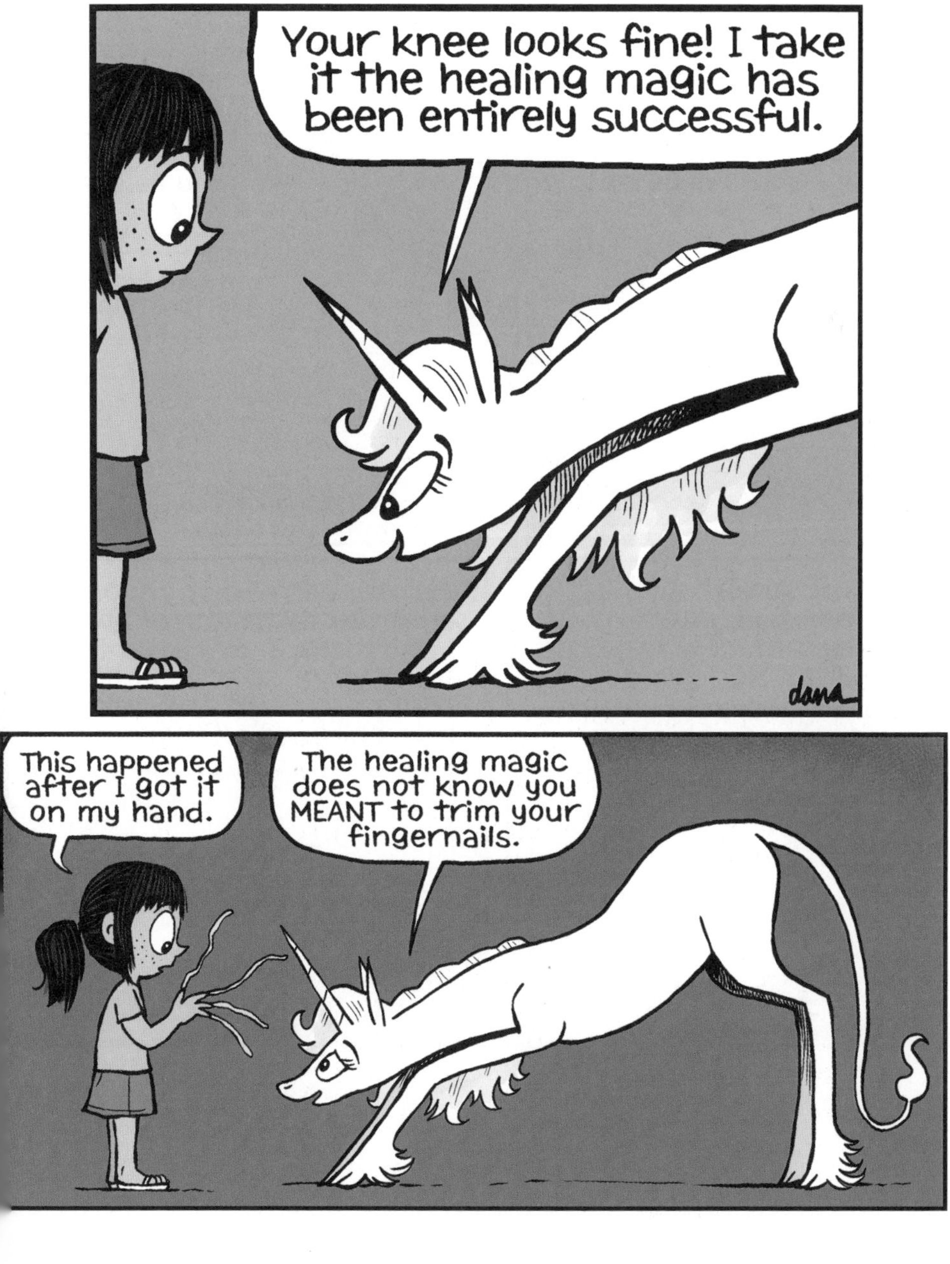
Your knee looks fine! I take it the healing magic has been entirely successful.
dana
This happened after I got it on my hand.
The healing magic does not know you MEANT to trim your fingernails.

Hey!
Hello. I am being an artist.
No you're not. You're just sitting around.
To the untrained eye, perhaps.
But great art is mainly subtraction. It is the art of knowing what NOT to do.
Sculpture is about choosing what parts to chisel away. Painting is defined by negative space. Music truly soars in the notes one chooses NOT to play.
dana

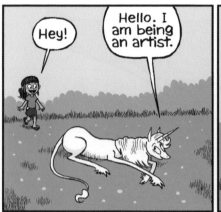

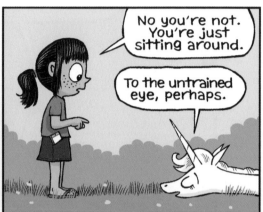

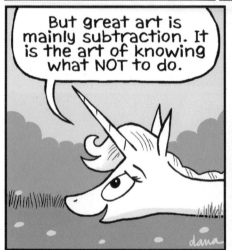

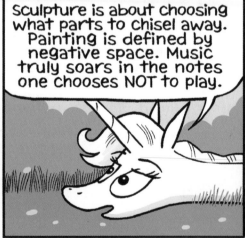

By doing *nothing*, I am the world's greatest artist!
Can I join you?
The nothing we do together shall echo throughout the ages.
It's really hard to resist poking at my phone.
We all must suffer for our art.

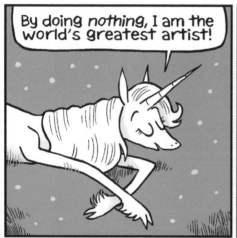

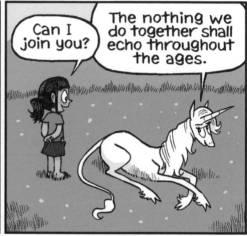

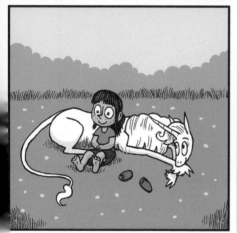

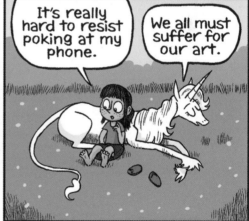

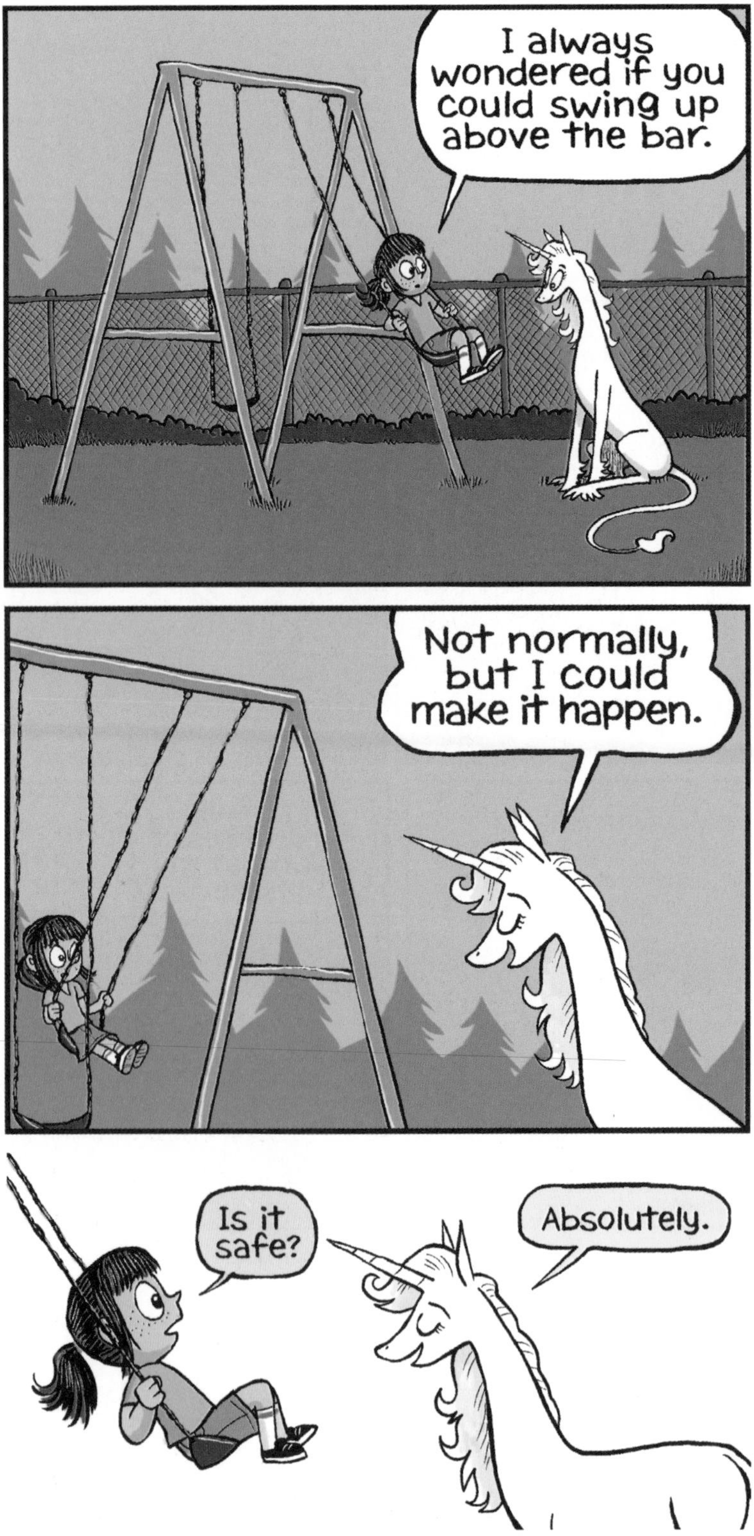
I always wondered if you could swing up above the bar.
Not normally, but I could make it happen.
Is it safe?
Absolutely.

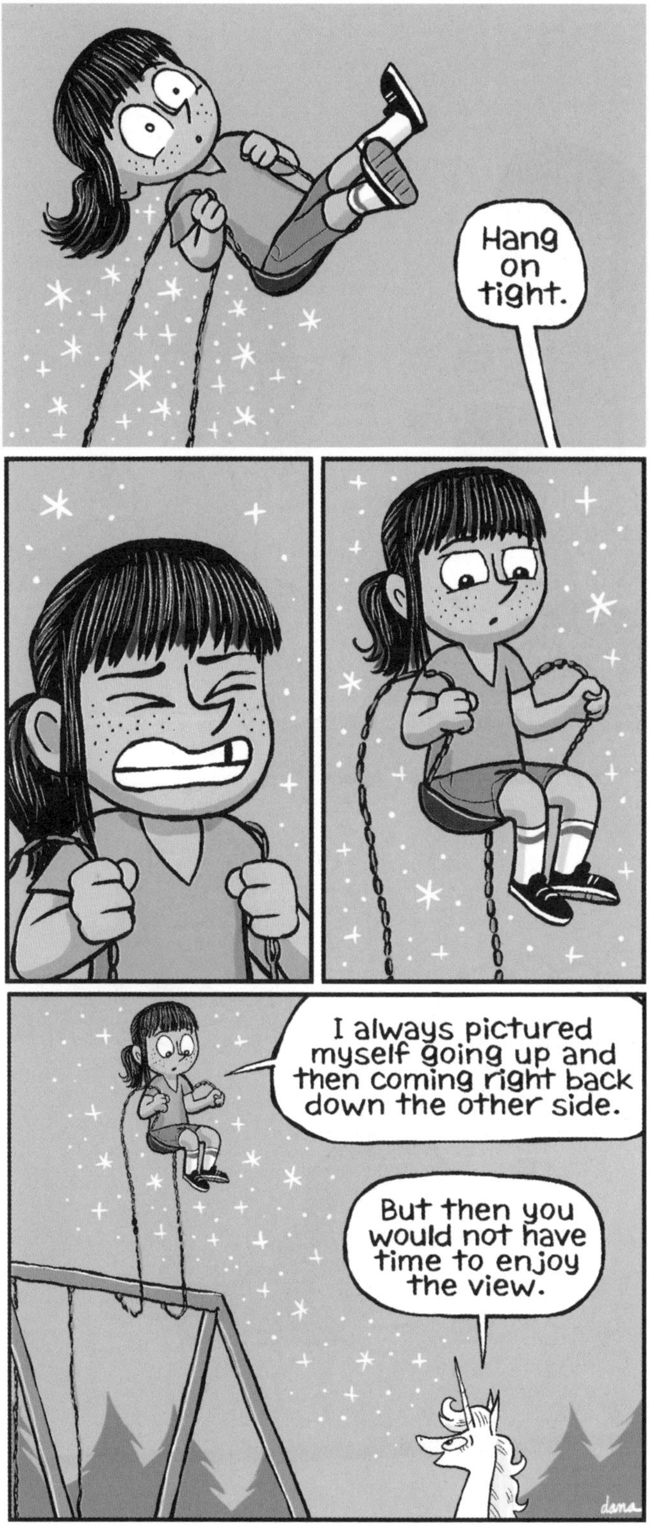
Hang on tight.
I always pictured myself going up and then coming right back down the other side.
But then you would not have time to enjoy the view.
dana

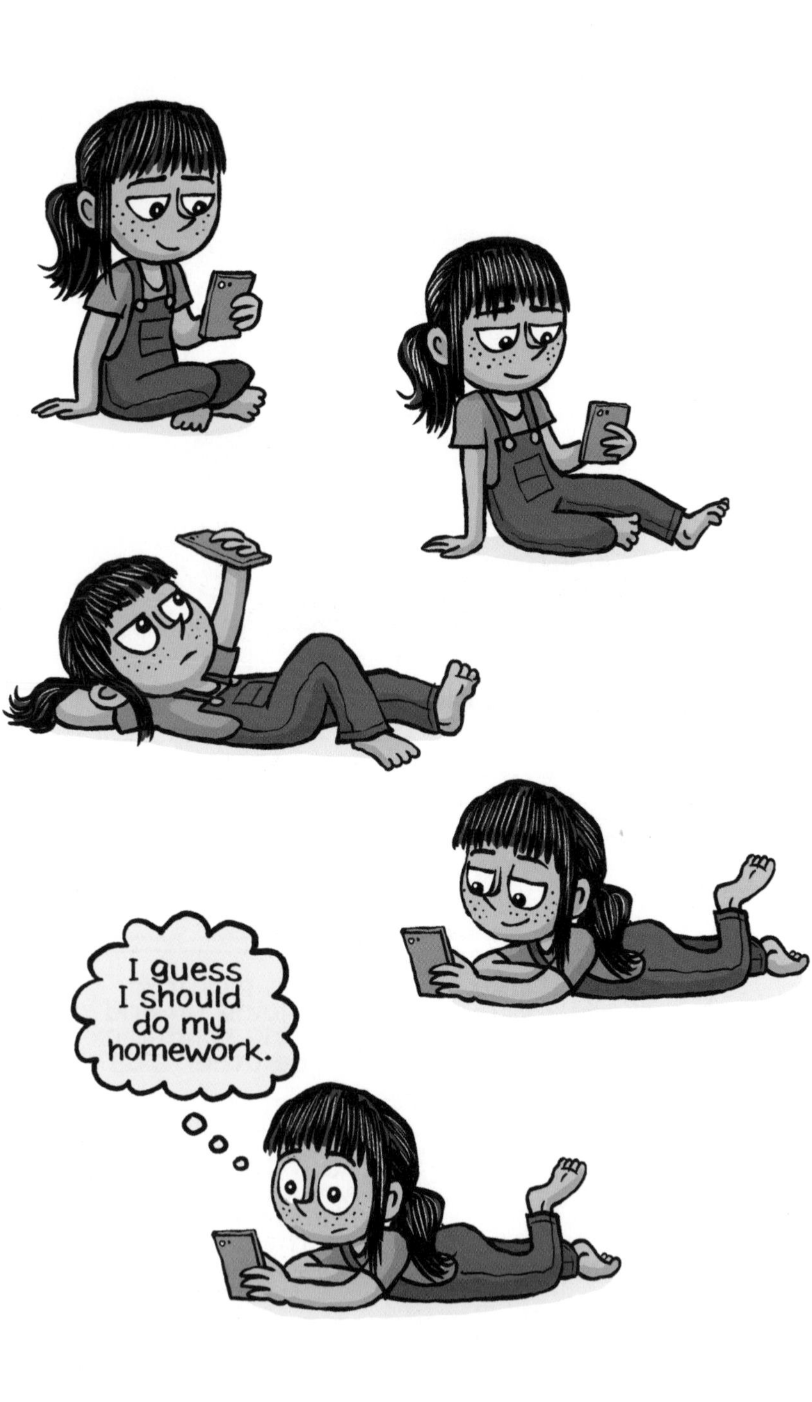
I guess I should do my homework.

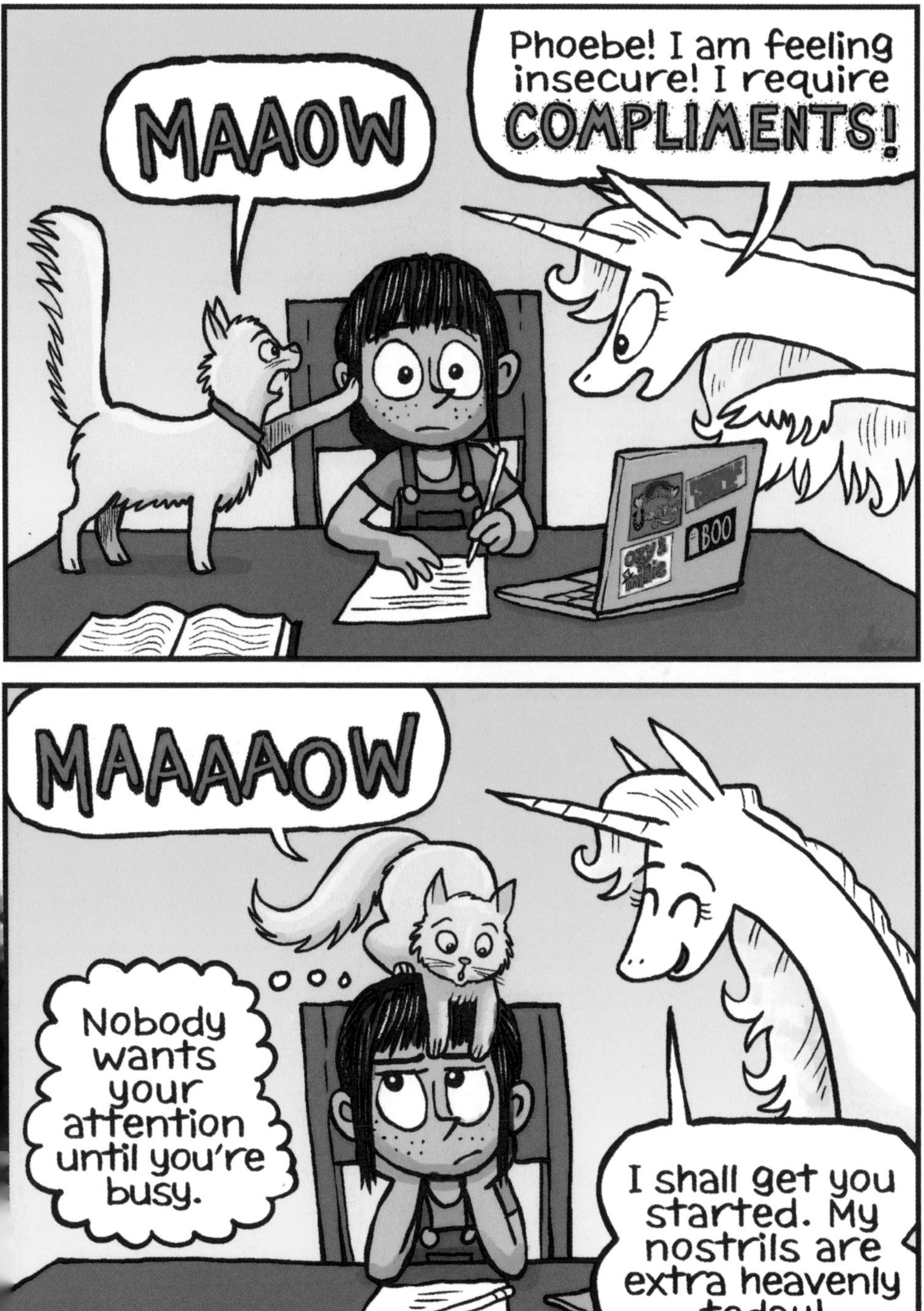
MAAOW
Phoebe! I am feeling insecure! I require COMPLIMENTS!
BOO
MAAAAOW
Nobody wants your attention until you're busy.
I shall get you started. My nostrils are extra heavenly today!

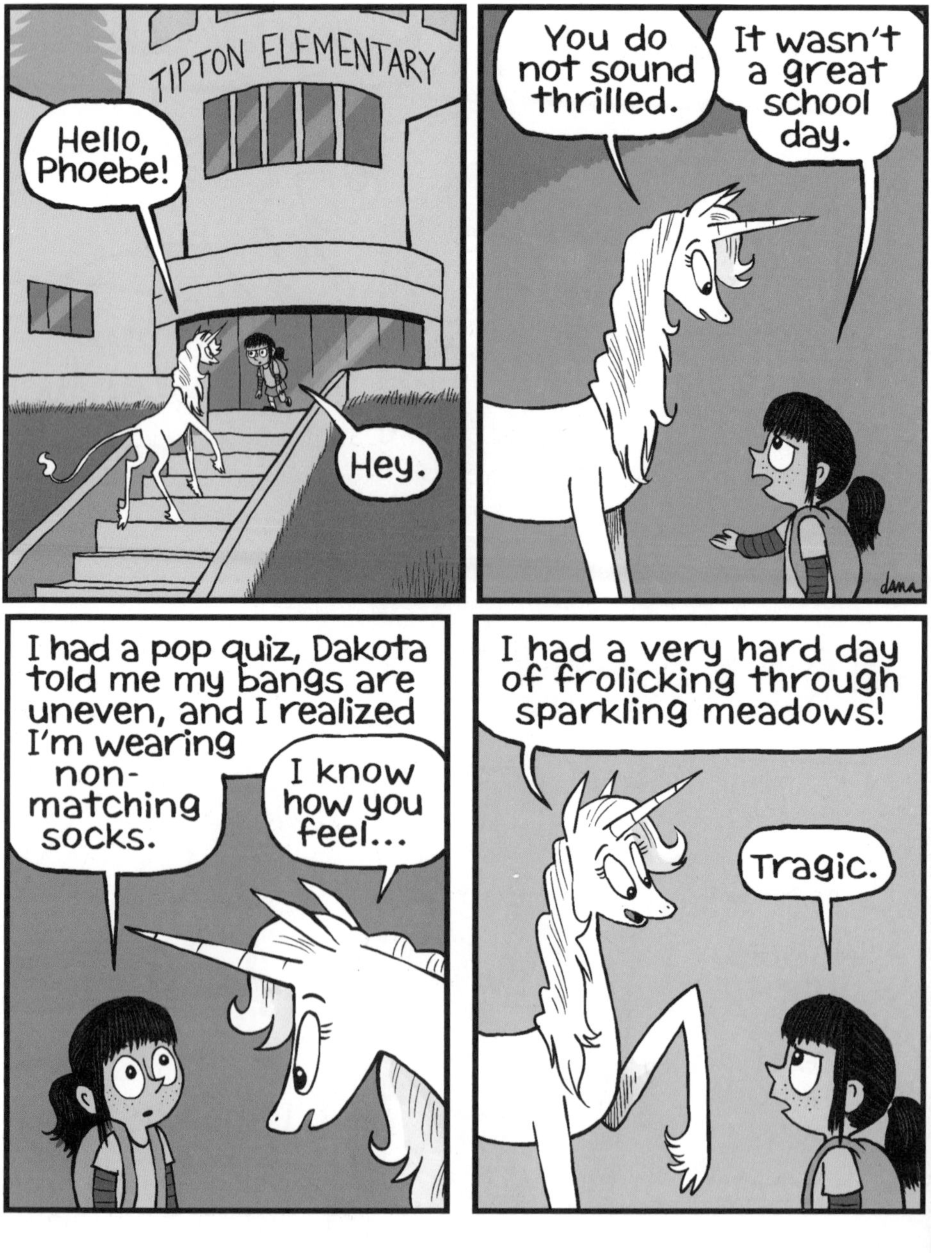
TIPTON ELEMENTARY
Hello, Phoebe!
Hey.
You do not sound thrilled.
It wasn't a great school day.
I had a pop quiz, Dakota told me my bangs are uneven, and I realized I'm wearing non-matching socks.
I know how you feel...
I had a very hard day of frolicking through sparkling meadows!
Tragic.

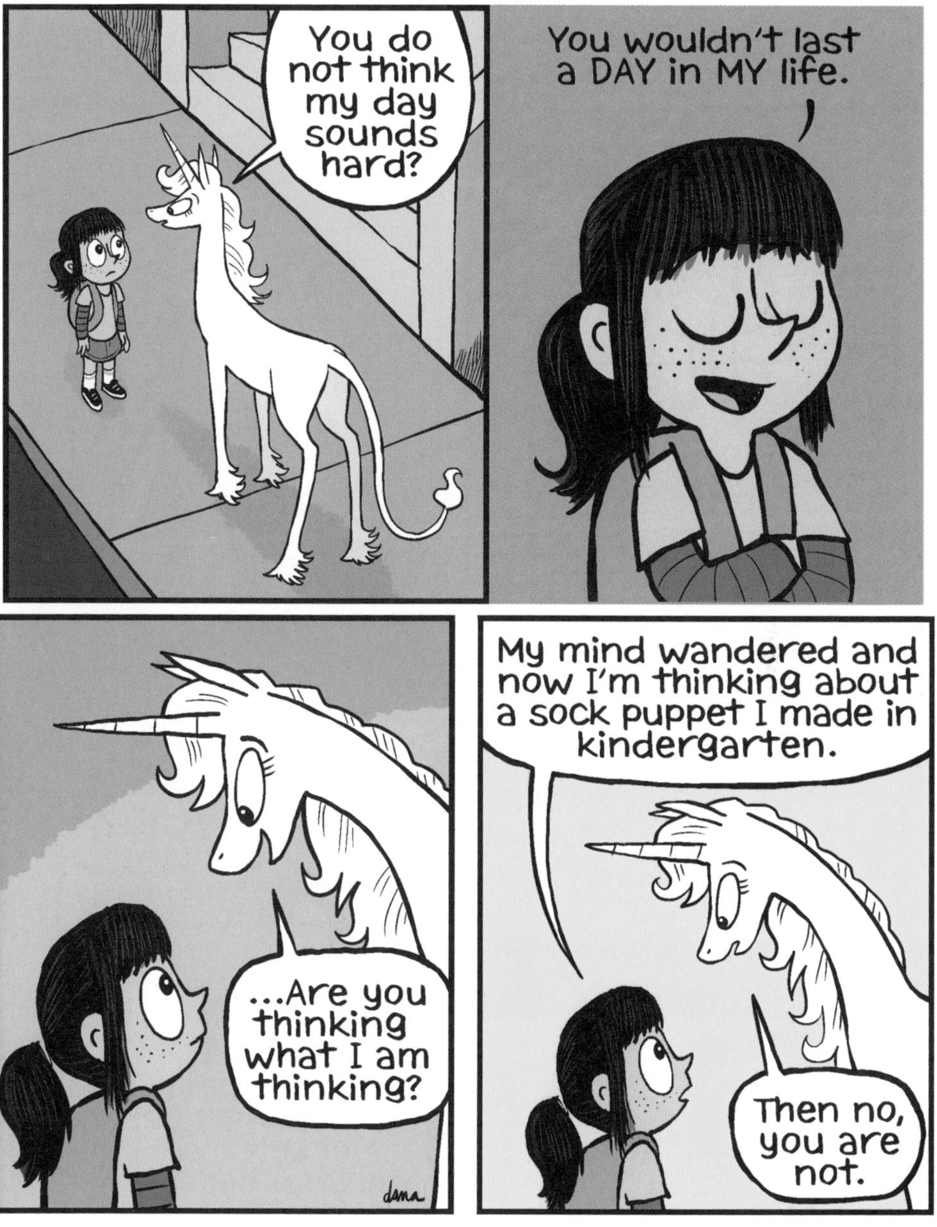
You do not think my day sounds hard?
You wouldn't last a DAY in MY life.
...Are you thinking what I am thinking?
My mind wandered and now I'm thinking about a sock puppet I made in kindergarten.
Then no, you are not.

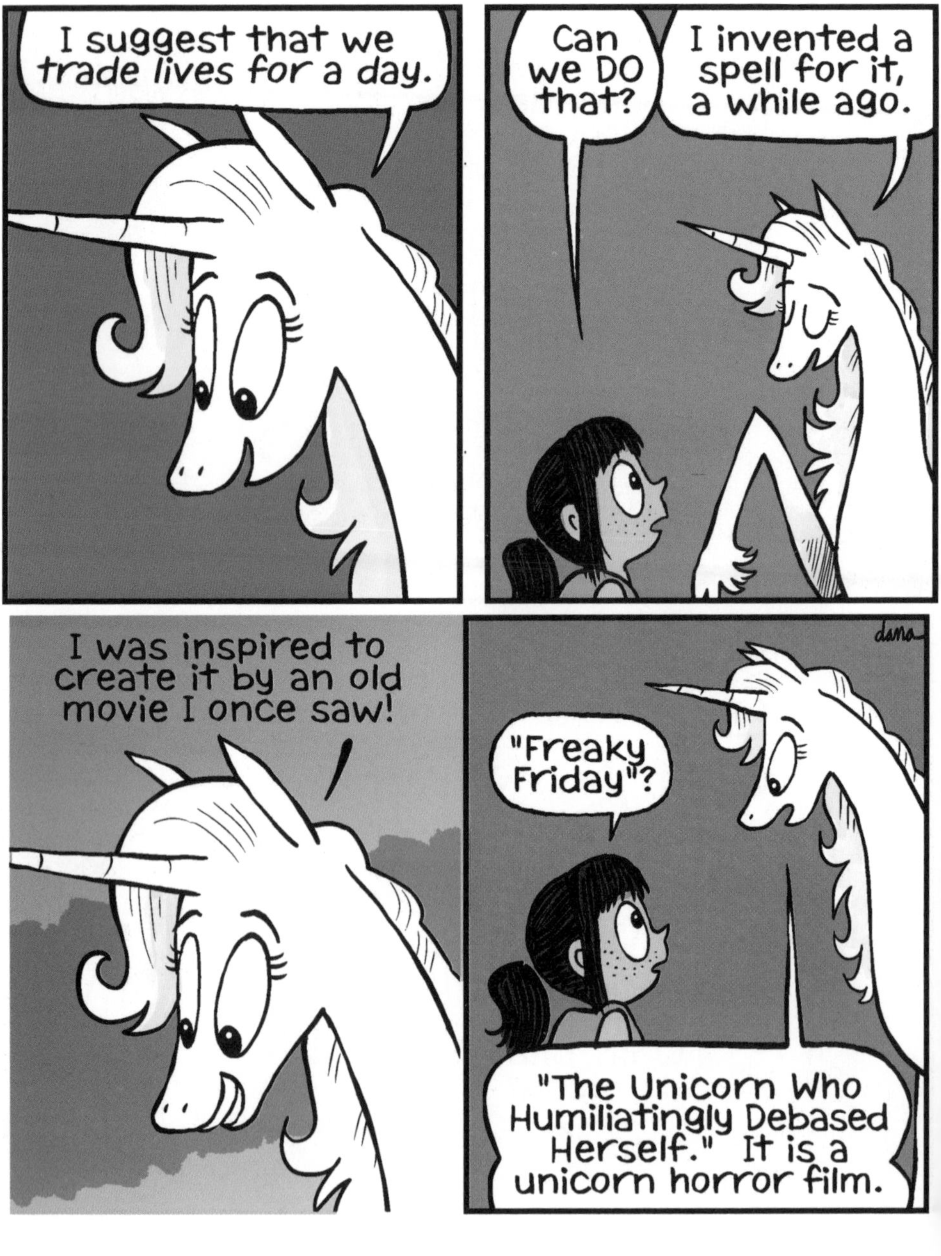
I suggest that we trade lives for a day.
Can we DO that?
I invented a spell for it, a while ago.
I was inspired to create it by an old movie I once saw!
"Freaky Friday"?
"The Unicorn Who Humiliatingly Debased Herself." It is a unicorn horror film.
dana

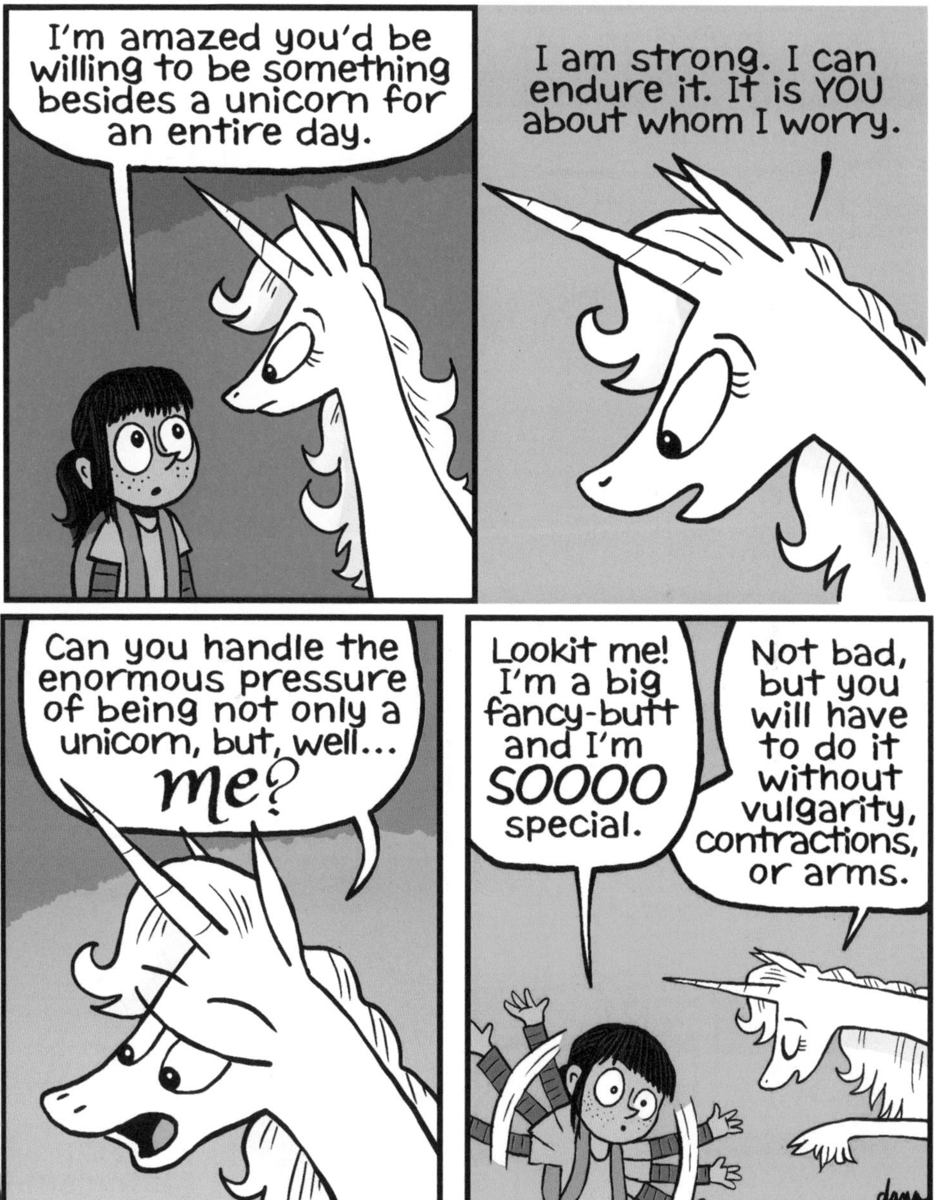
I'm amazed you'd be willing to be something besides a unicorn for an entire day.
I am strong. I can endure it. It is YOU about whom I worry.
Can you handle the enormous pressure of being not only a unicorn, but, well... *me?*
Lookit me! I'm a big fancy-butt and I'm SOOOO special.
Not bad, but you will have to do it without vulgarity, contractions, or arms.
dana

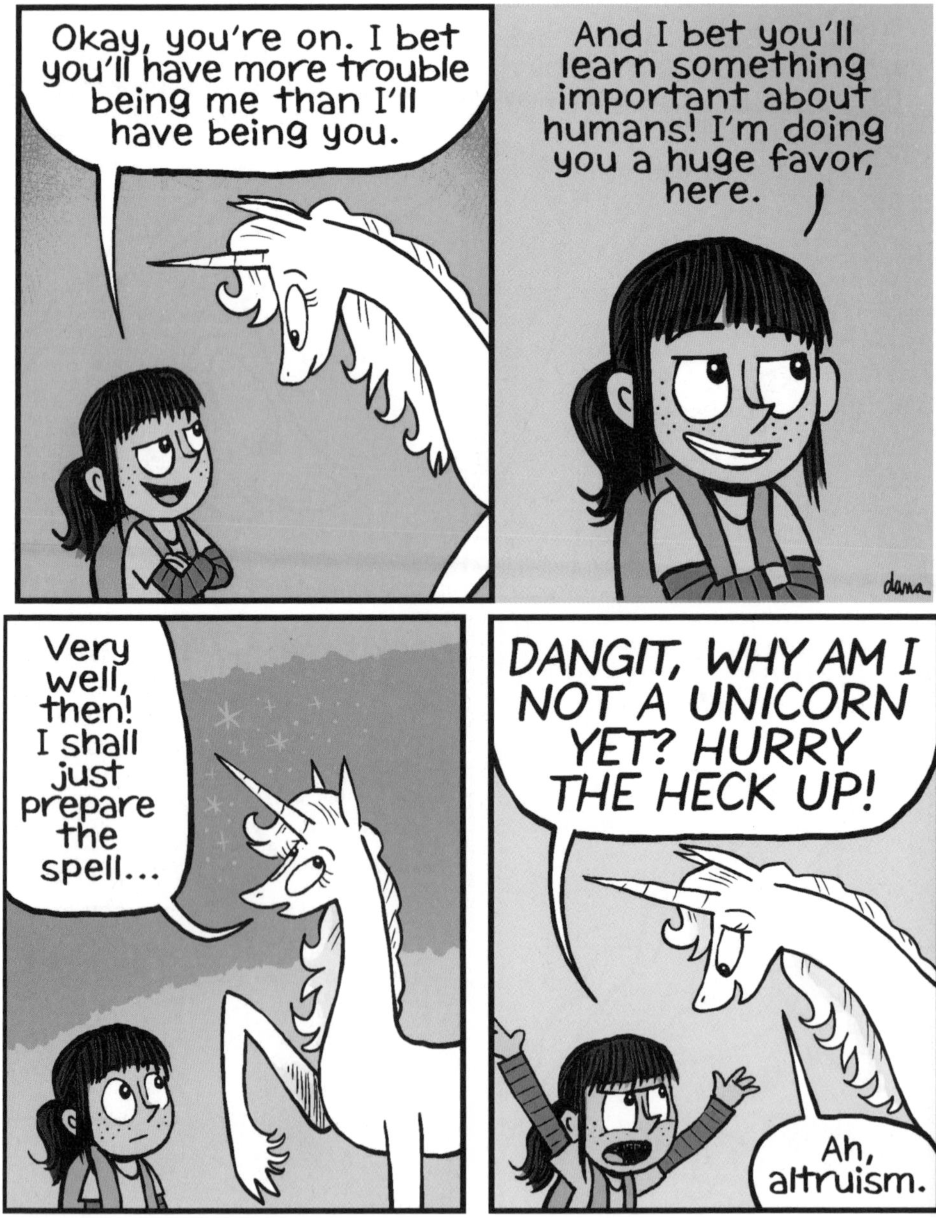
Okay, you're on. I bet you'll have more trouble being me than I'll have being you.
And I bet you'll learn something important about humans! I'm doing you a huge favor, here.
dana
Very well, then! I shall just prepare the spell...
DANGIT, WHY AM I NOT A UNICORN YET? HURRY THE HECK UP!
Ah, altruism.

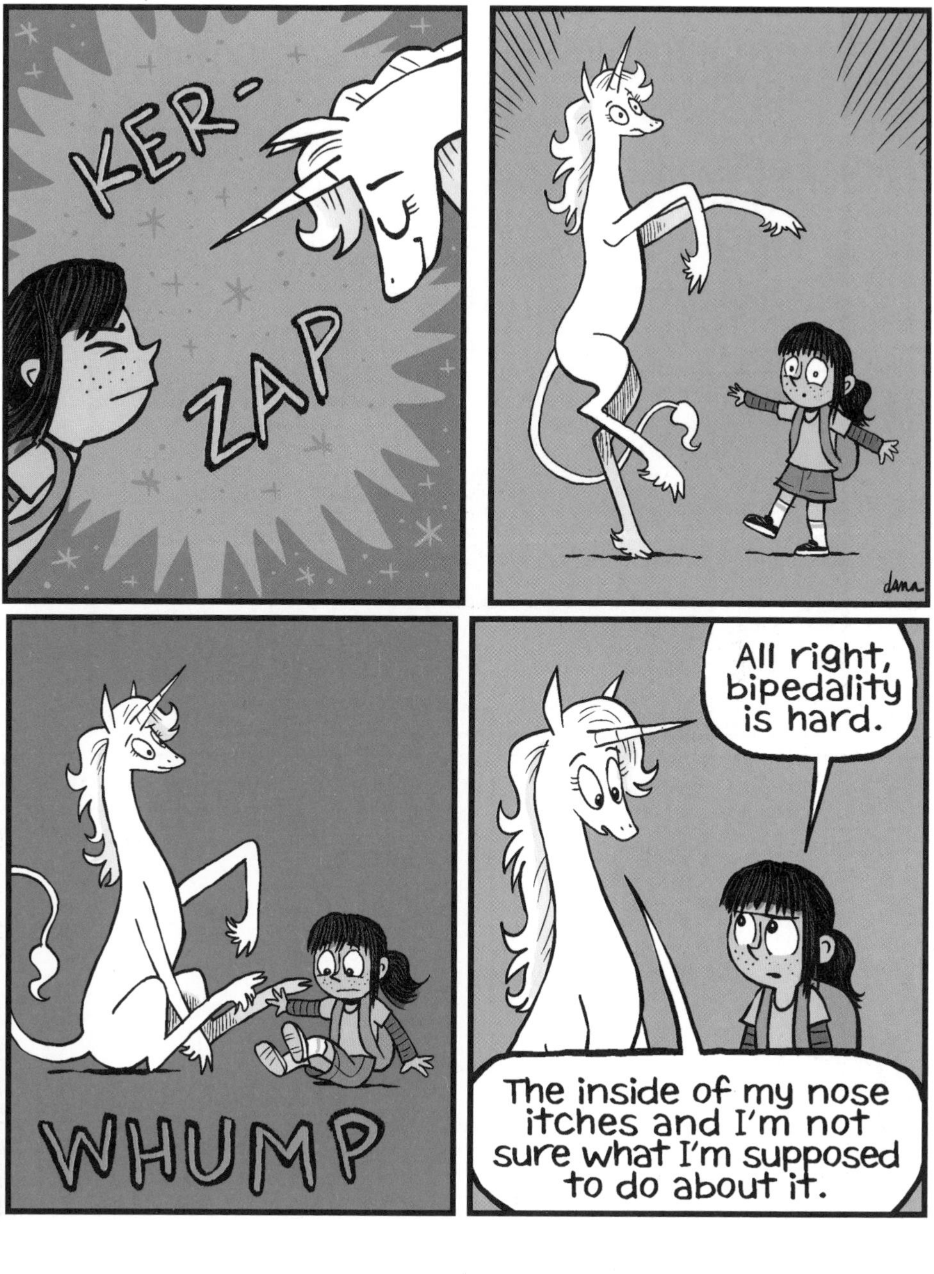
KER-
ZAP
WHUMP
All right, bipedality is hard.
The inside of my nose itches and I'm not sure what I'm supposed to do about it.

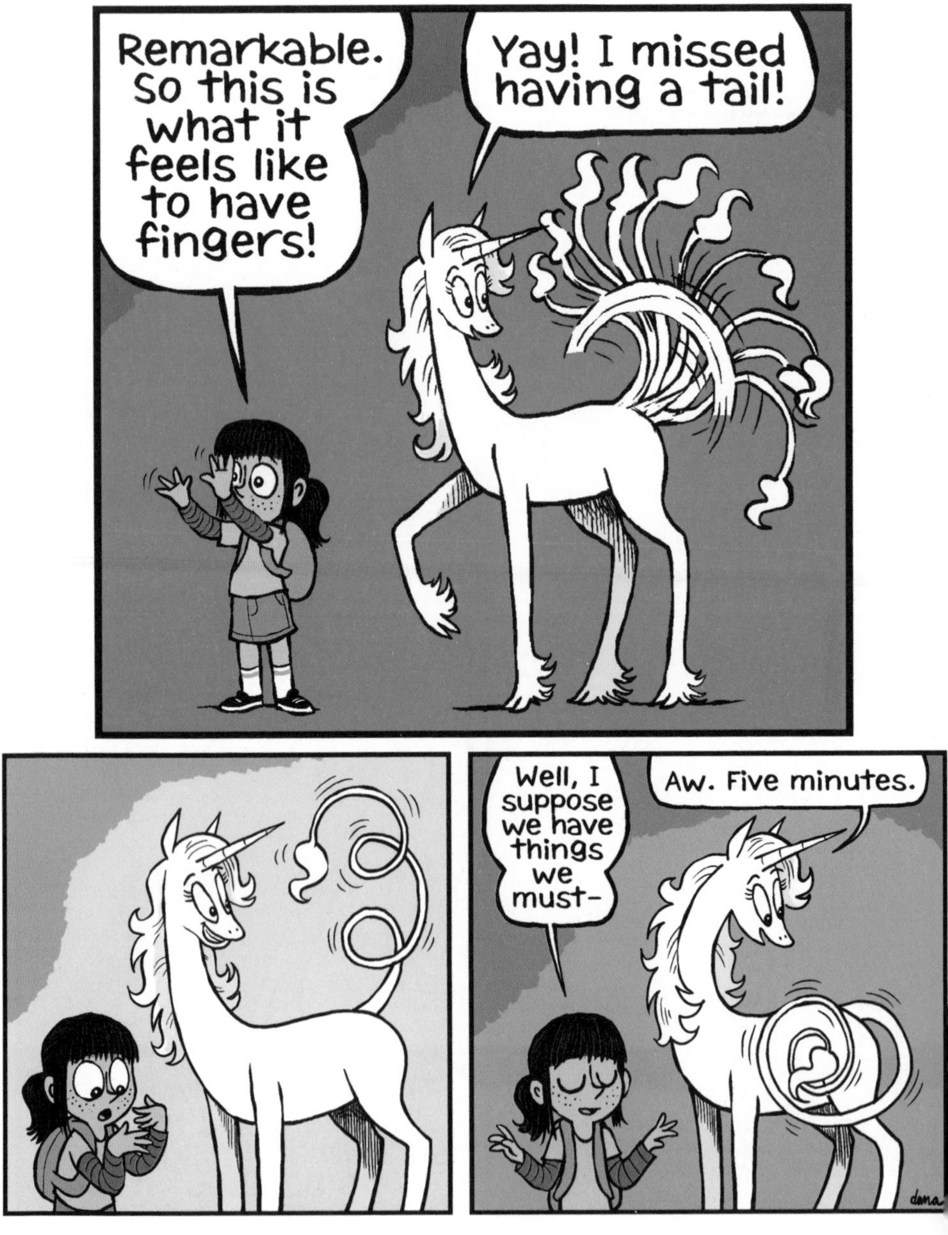
Remarkable. So this is what it feels like to have fingers!
Yay! I missed having a tail!
Well, I suppose we have things we must-
Aw. Five minutes.
dana

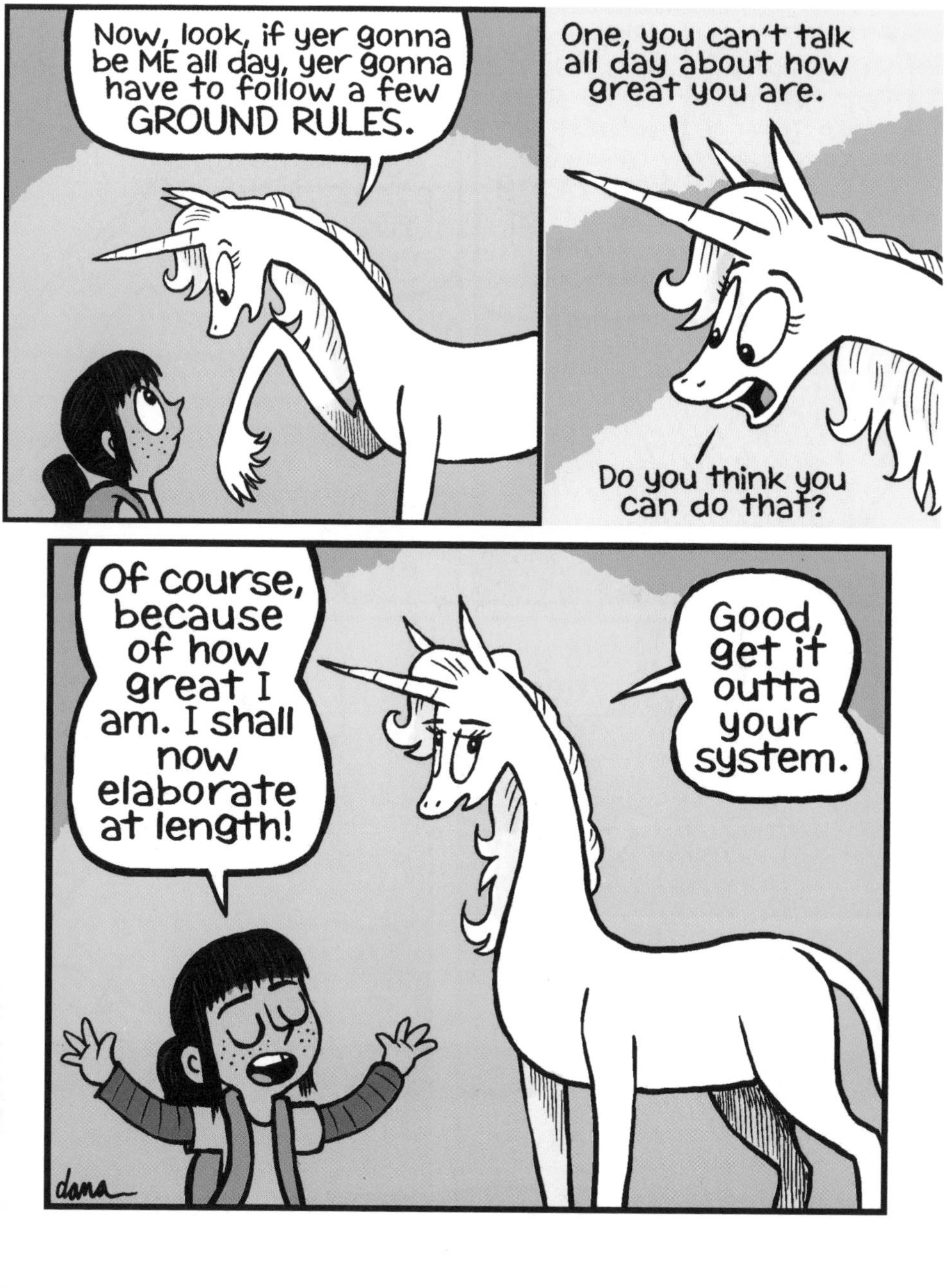

Now, look, if yer gonna be ME all day, yer gonna have to follow a few GROUND RULES.
One, you can't talk all day about how great you are.
Do you think you can do that?
Of course, because of how great I am. I shall now elaborate at length!
Good, get it outta your system.
dana

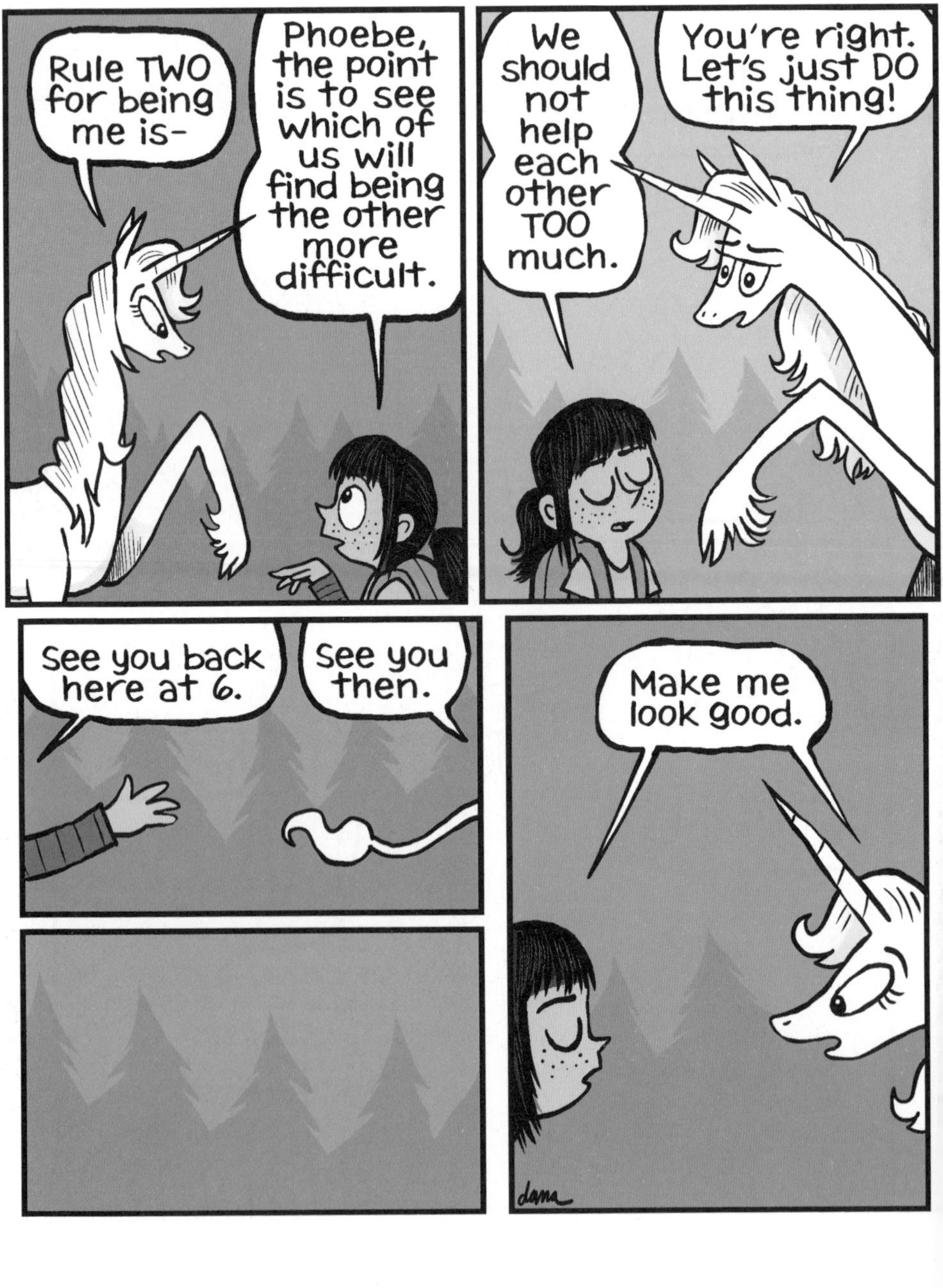
Rule TWO for being me is-
Phoebe, the point is to see which of us will find being the other more difficult.
We should not help each other TOO much.
You're right. Let's just DO this thing!
See you back here at 6.
See you then.
Make me look good.
dana

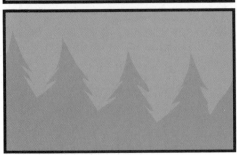

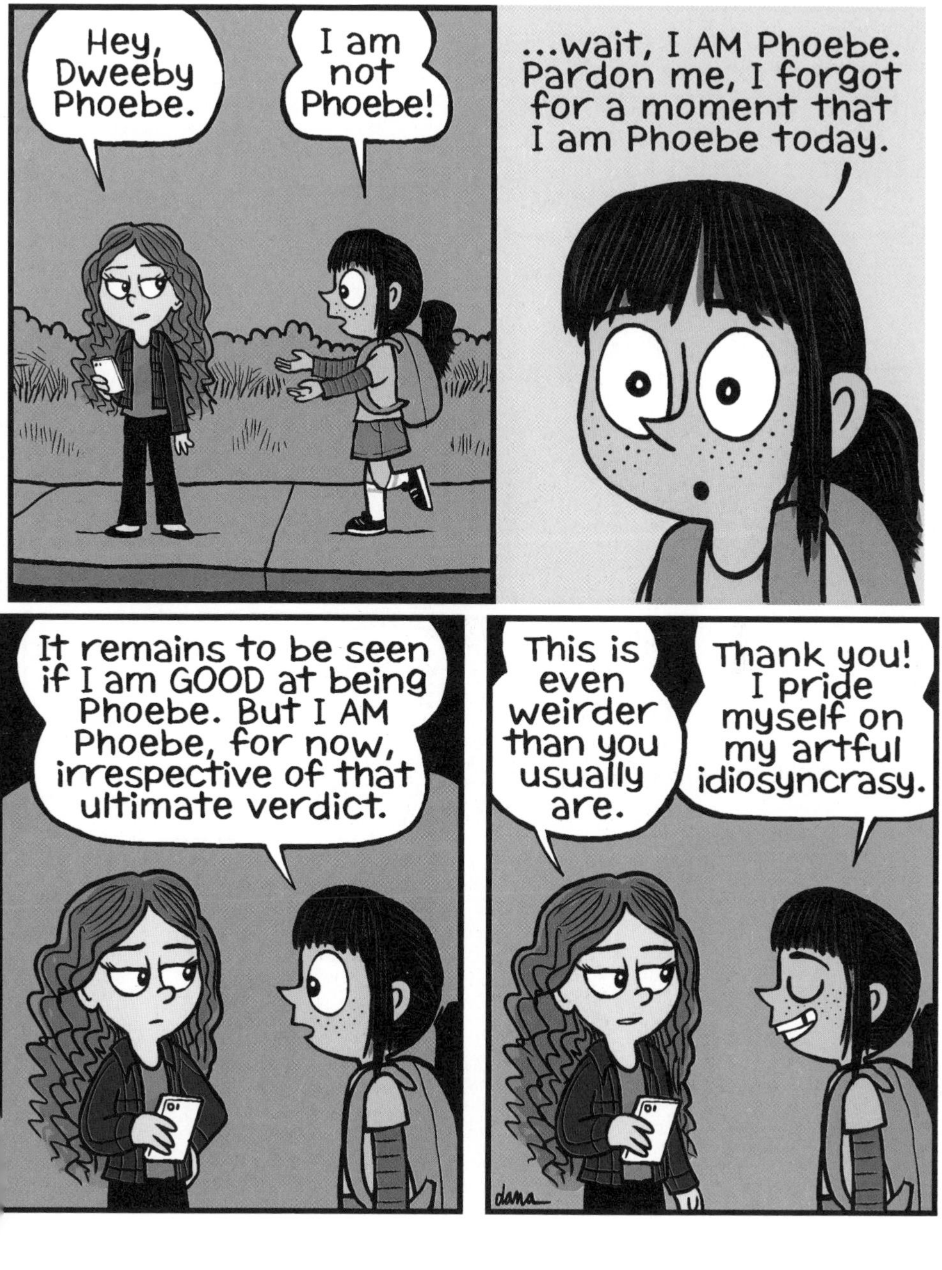
Hey, Dweeby Phoebe.
I am not Phoebe!
...wait, I AM Phoebe. Pardon me, I forgot for a moment that I am Phoebe today.
It remains to be seen if I am GOOD at being Phoebe. But I AM Phoebe, for now, irrespective of that ultimate verdict.
This is even weirder than you usually are.
Thank you! I pride myself on my artful idiosyncrasy.
dana

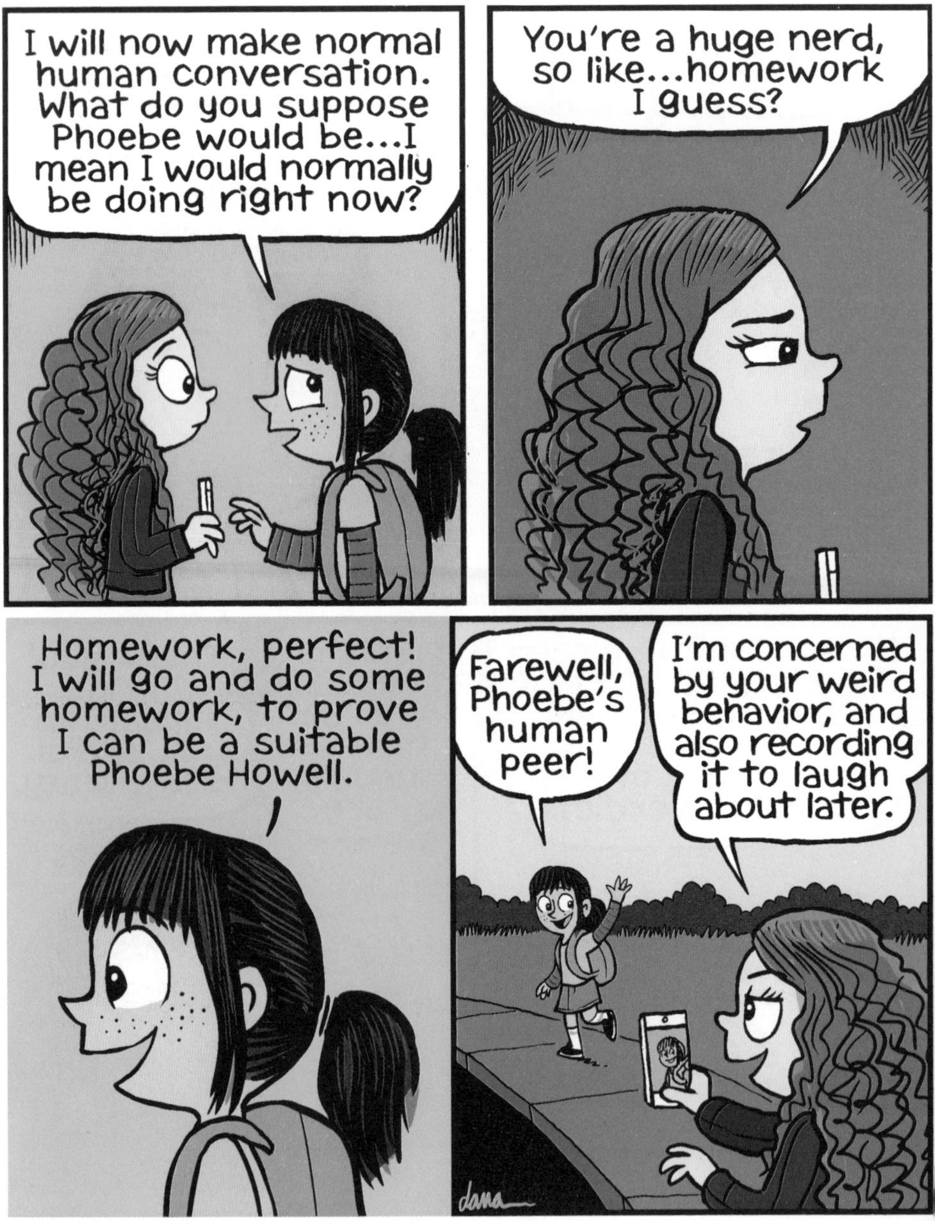
I will now make normal human conversation. What do you suppose Phoebe would be...I mean I would normally be doing right now?
You're a huge nerd, so like...homework I guess?
Homework, perfect! I will go and do some homework, to prove I can be a suitable Phoebe Howell.
Farewell, Phoebe's human peer!
I'm concerned by your weird behavior, and also recording it to laugh about later.
dana

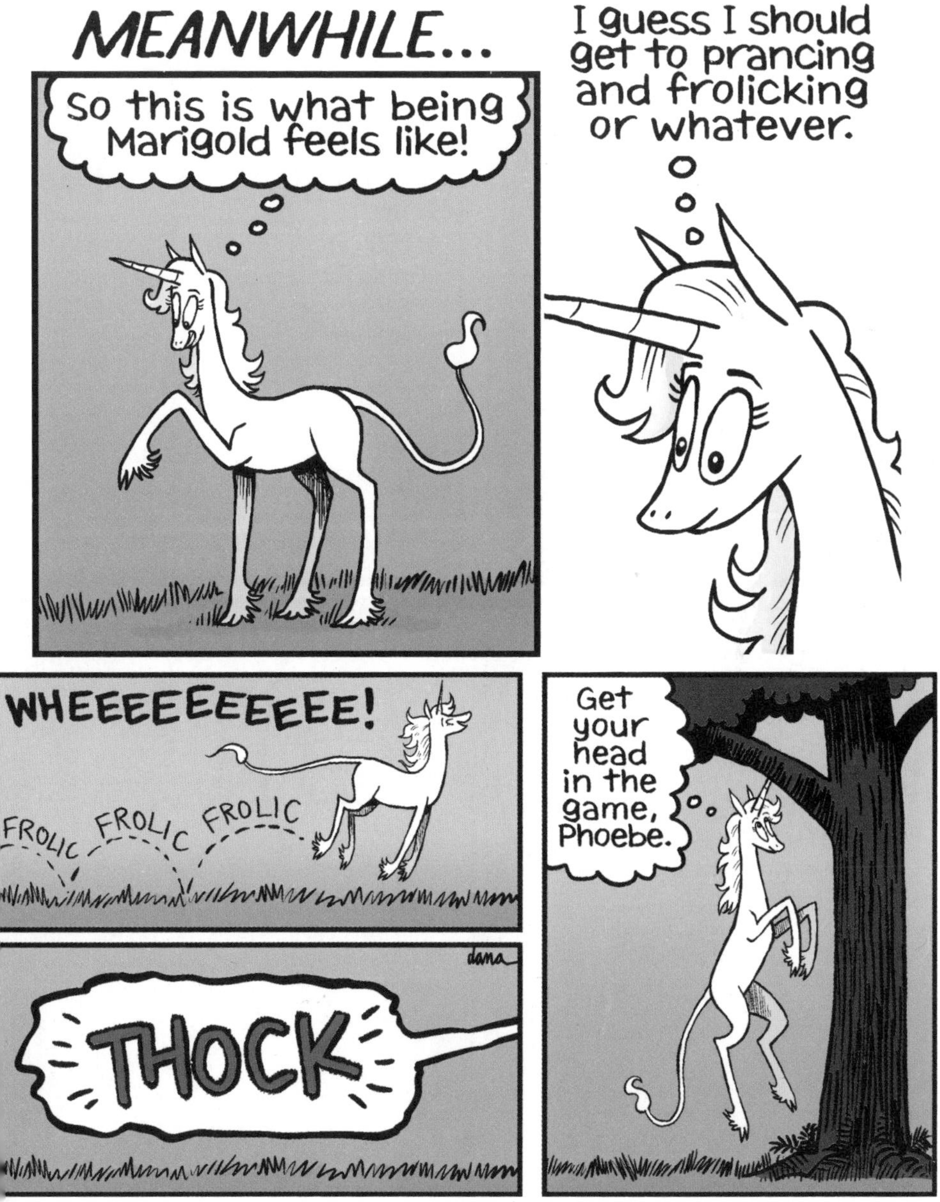
MEANWHILE...
So this is what being Marigold feels like!
I guess I should get to prancing and frolicking or whatever.
WHEEEEEEEEEEE!
FROLIC
FROLIC
FROLIC
THOCK
dana
Get your head in the game, Phoebe.

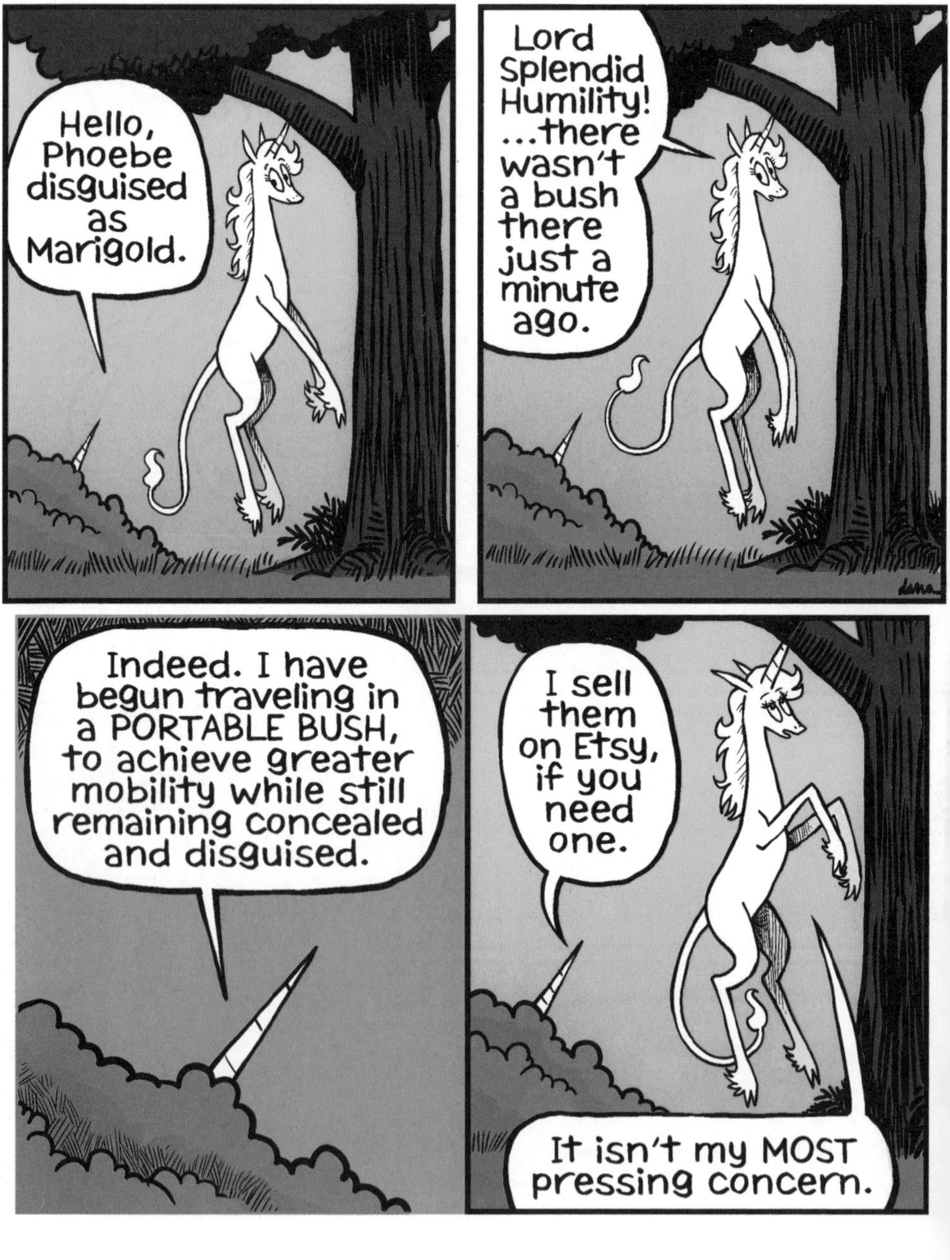
Hello, Phoebe disguised as Marigold.
Lord Splendid Humility! ...there wasn't a bush there just a minute ago.
Indeed. I have begun traveling in a PORTABLE BUSH, to achieve greater mobility while still remaining concealed and disguised.
I sell them on Etsy, if you need one.
It isn't my MOST pressing concern.

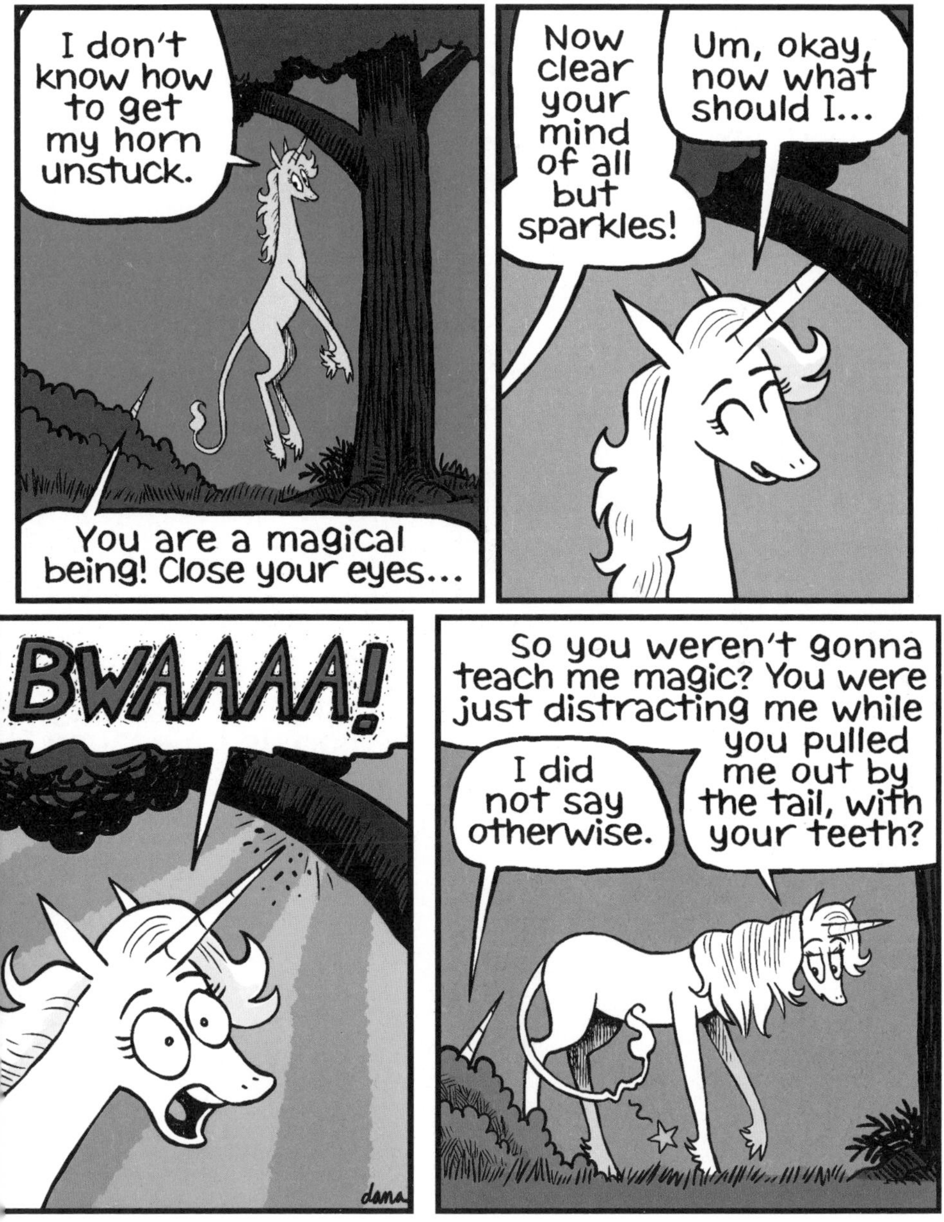
I don't know how to get my horn unstuck.
You are a magical being! Close your eyes...
Now clear your mind of all but sparkles!
Um, okay, now what should I...
BWAAAA!
So you weren't gonna teach me magic? You were just distracting me while you pulled me out by the tail, with your teeth?
I did not say otherwise.
dana

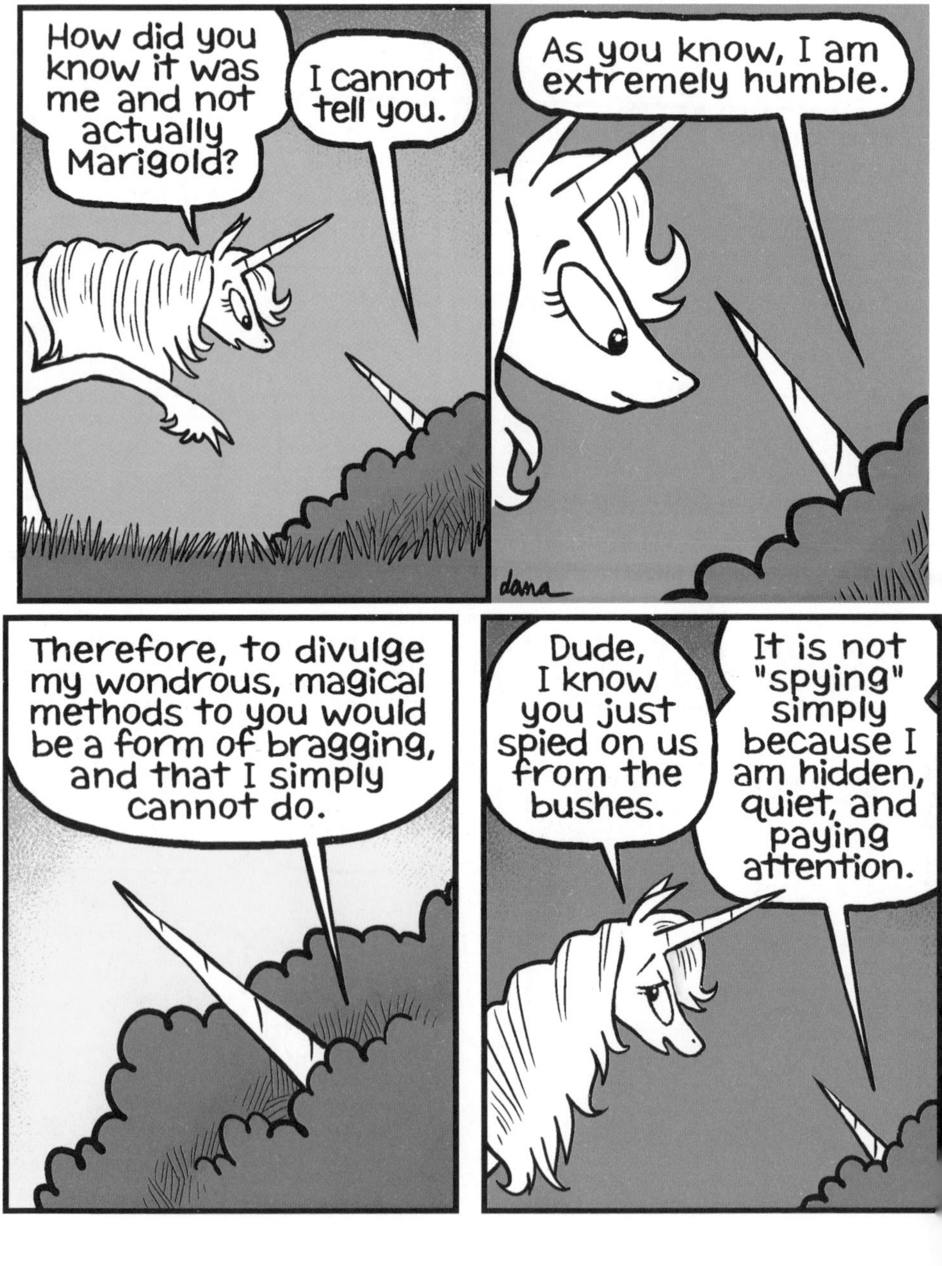
How did you know it was me and not actually Marigold?
I cannot tell you.
As you know, I am extremely humble.
dana
Therefore, to divulge my wondrous, magical methods to you would be a form of bragging, and that I simply cannot do.
Dude, I know you just spied on us from the bushes.
It is not "spying" simply because I am hidden, quiet, and paying attention.

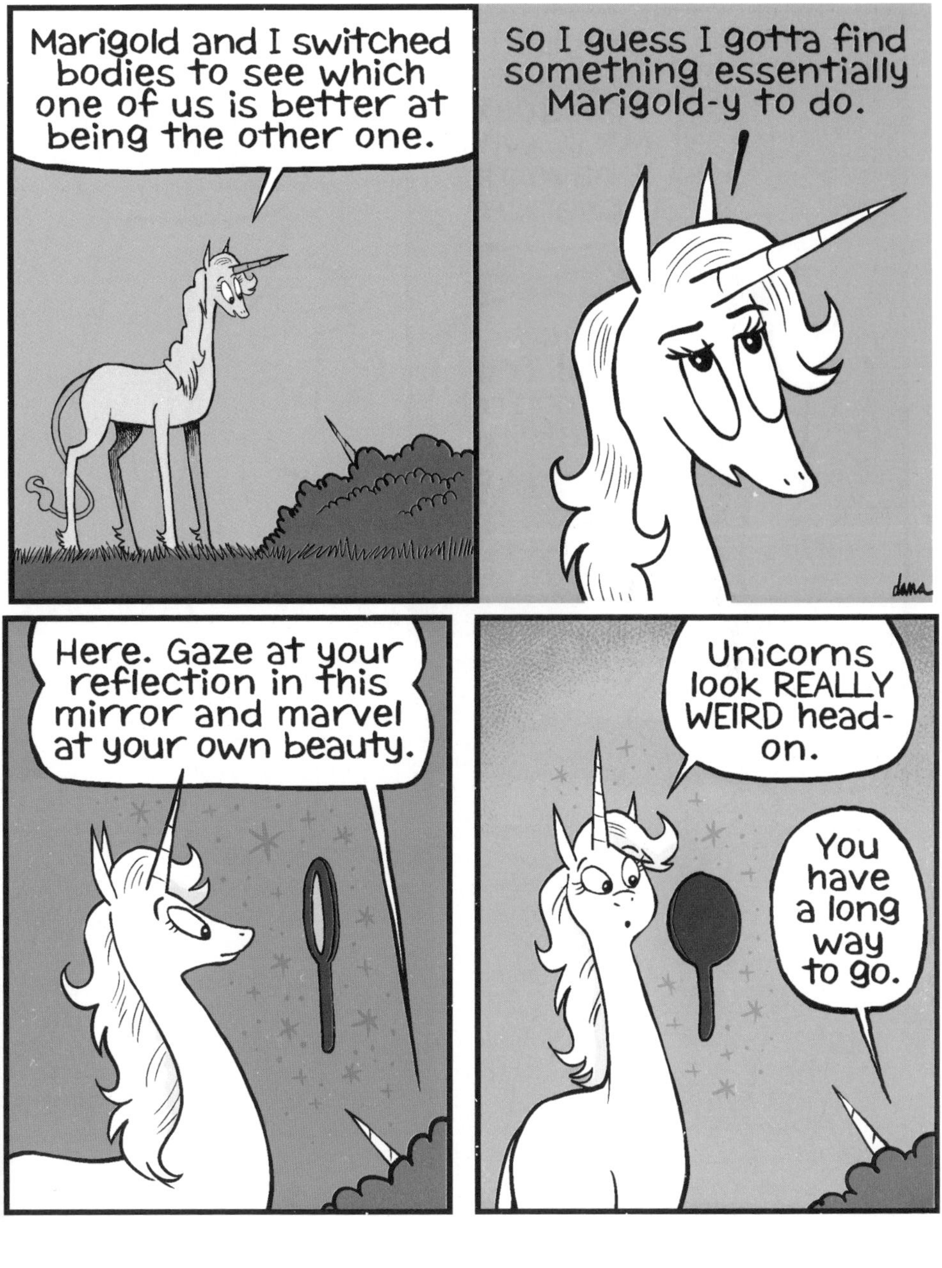
Marigold and I switched bodies to see which one of us is better at being the other one.
So I guess I gotta find something essentially Marigold-y to do.
dana
Here. Gaze at your reflection in this mirror and marvel at your own beauty.
Unicorns look REALLY WEIRD head-on.
You have a long way to go.

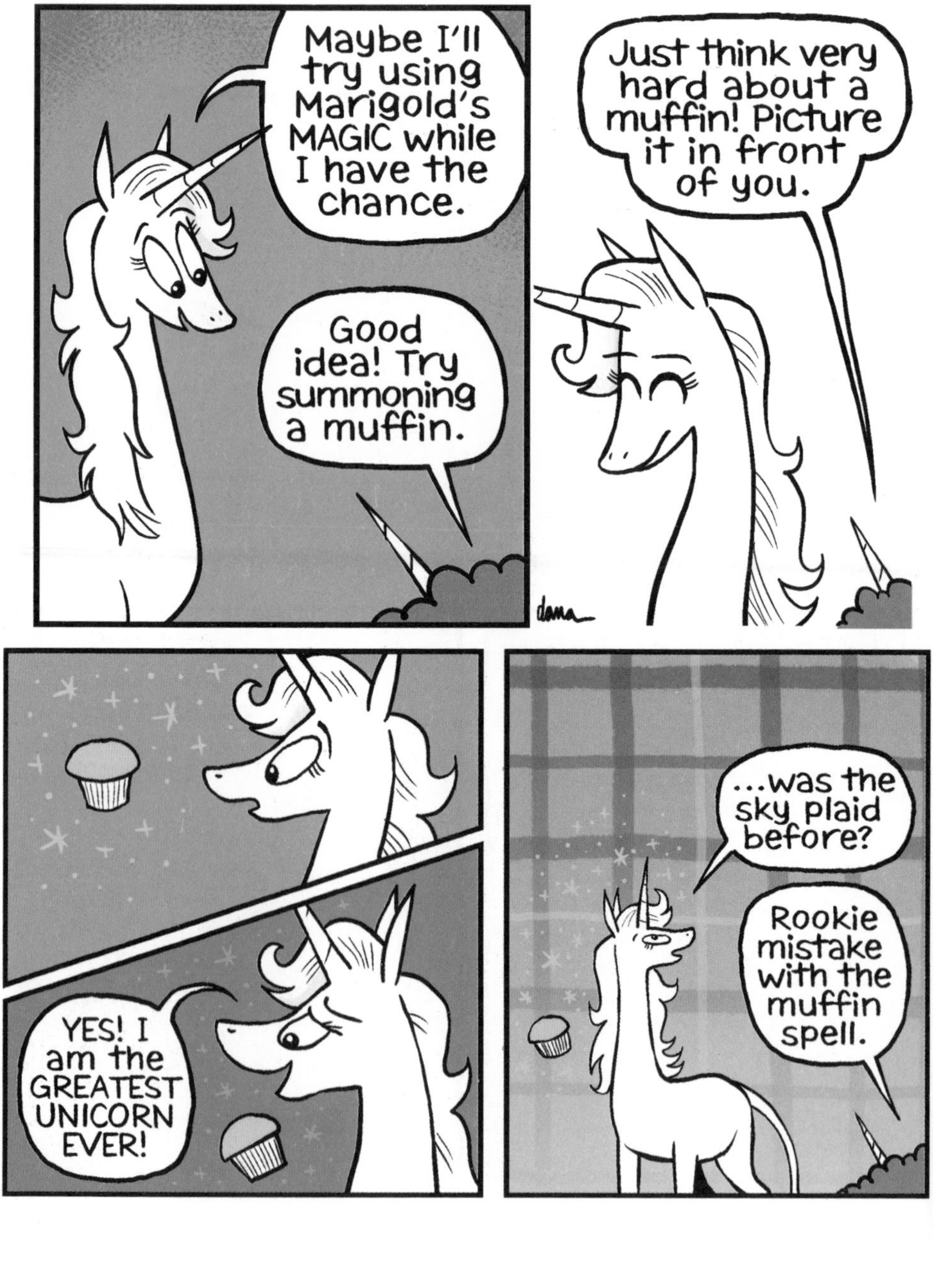

Maybe I'll try using Marigold's MAGIC while I have the chance.
Good idea! Try summoning a muffin.
Just think very hard about a muffin! Picture it in front of you.
YES! I am the GREATEST UNICORN EVER!
...was the sky plaid before?
Rookie mistake with the muffin spell.

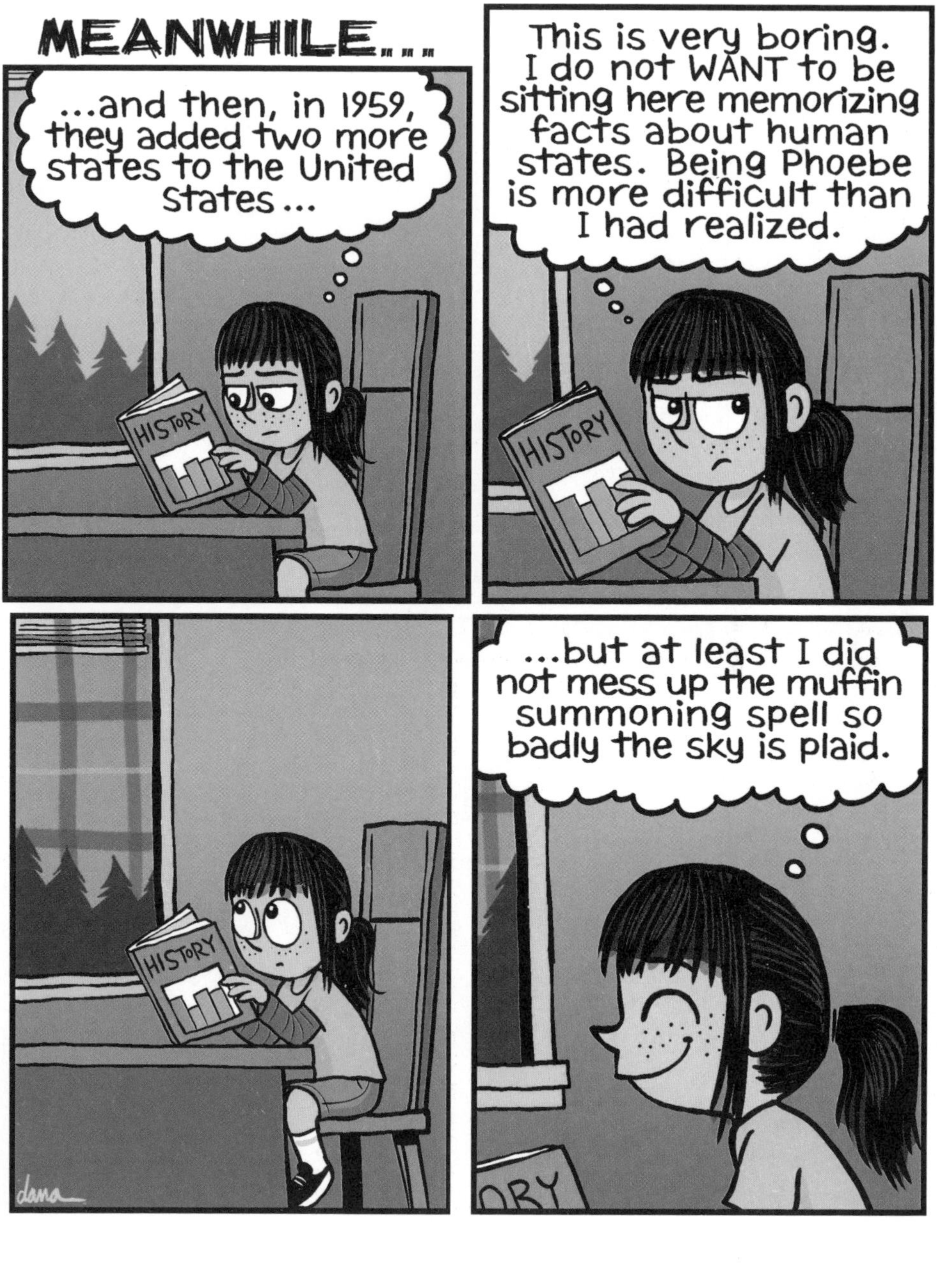
MEANWHILE....
...and then, in 1959, they added two more states to the United States...
HISTORY
This is very boring. I do not WANT to be sitting here memorizing facts about human states. Being Phoebe is more difficult than I had realized.
HISTORY
HISTORY
dana
...but at least I did not mess up the muffin summoning spell so badly the sky is plaid.
ORY

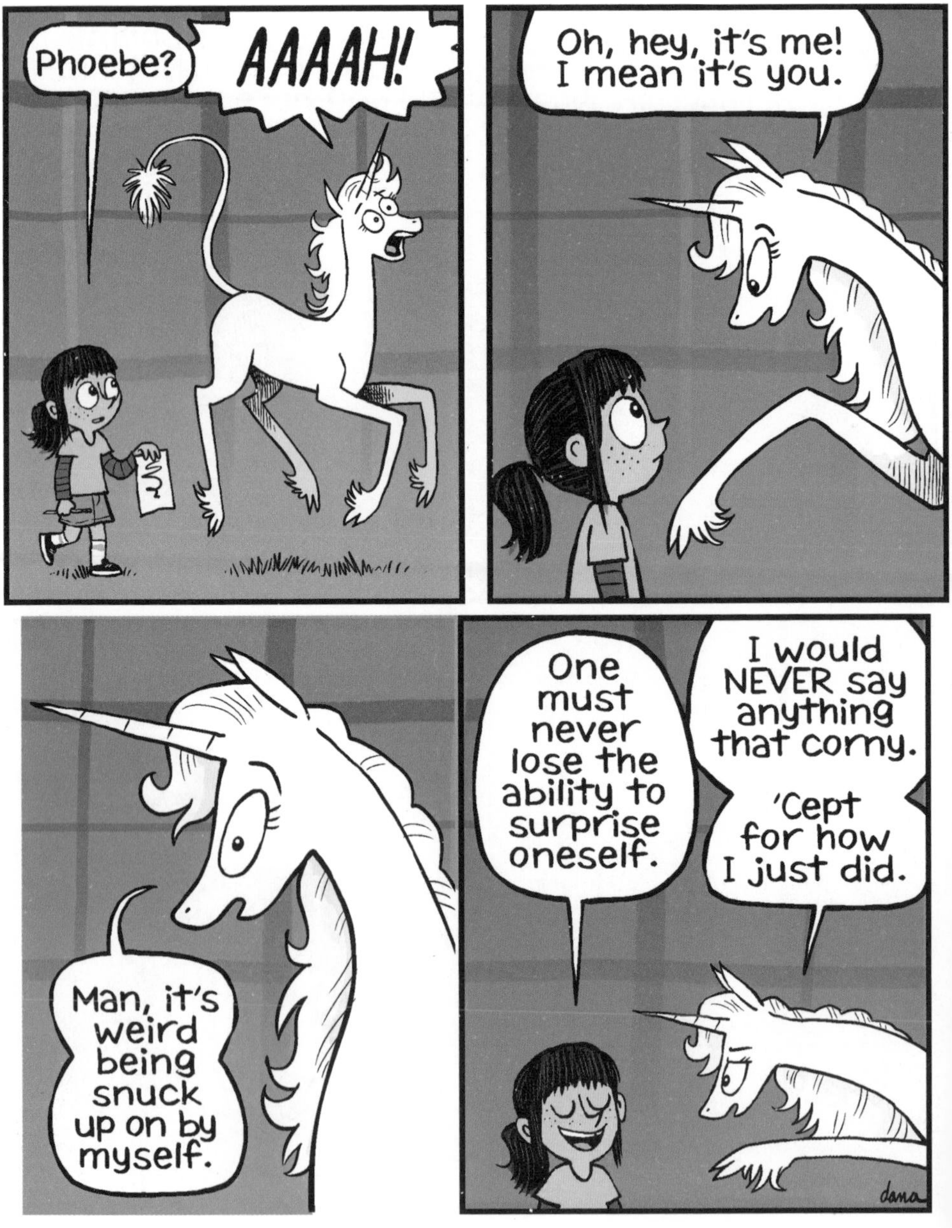
Phoebe?
AAAAH!
Oh, hey, it's me! I mean it's you.
Man, it's weird being snuck up on by myself.
One must never lose the ability to surprise oneself.
I would NEVER say anything that corny.
'Cept for how I just did.
dana

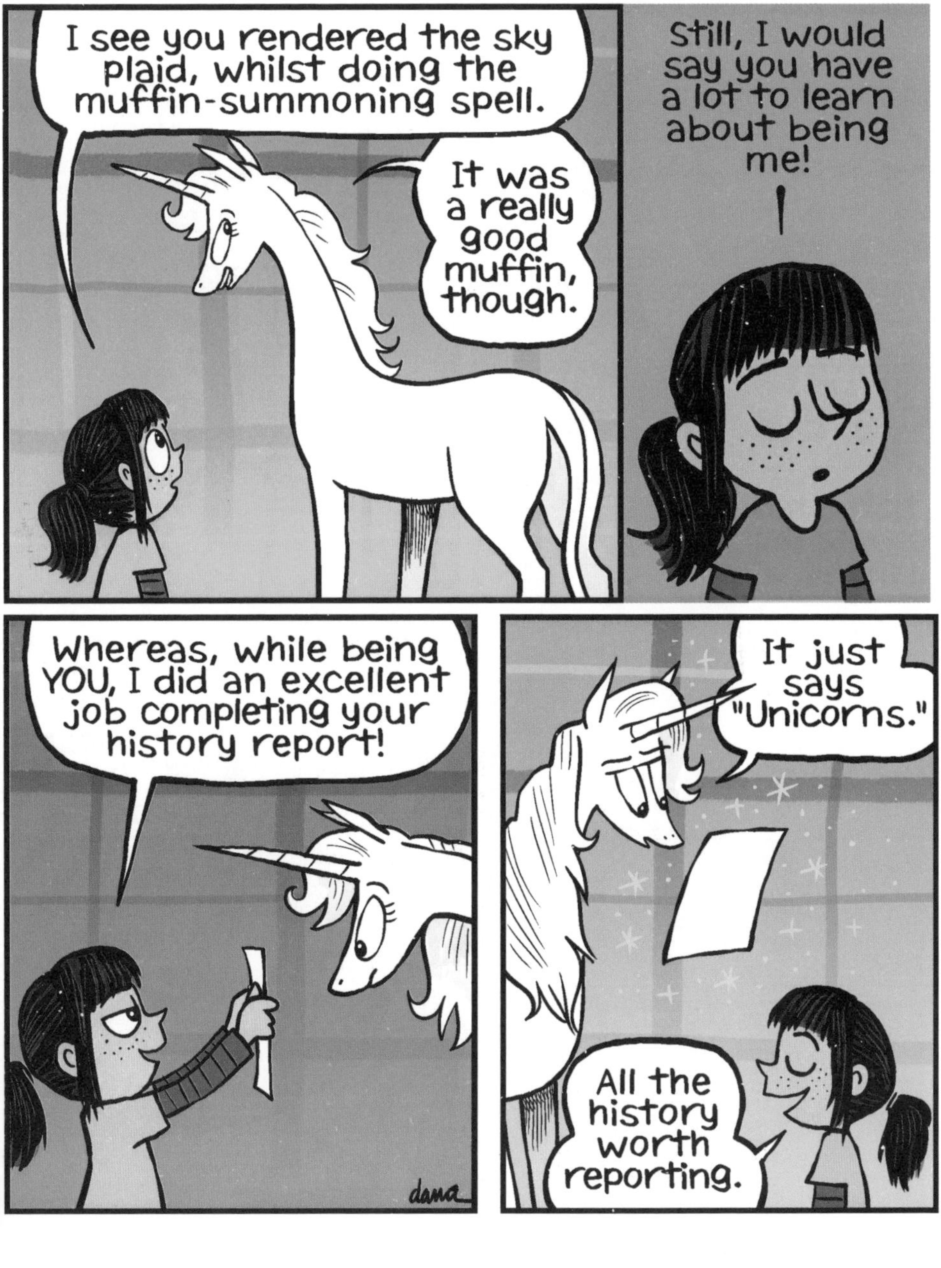
I see you rendered the sky plaid, whilst doing the muffin-summoning spell.
It was a really good muffin, though.
Still, I would say you have a lot to learn about being me!
Whereas, while being YOU, I did an excellent job completing your history report!
dana
It just says "Unicorns."
All the history worth reporting.

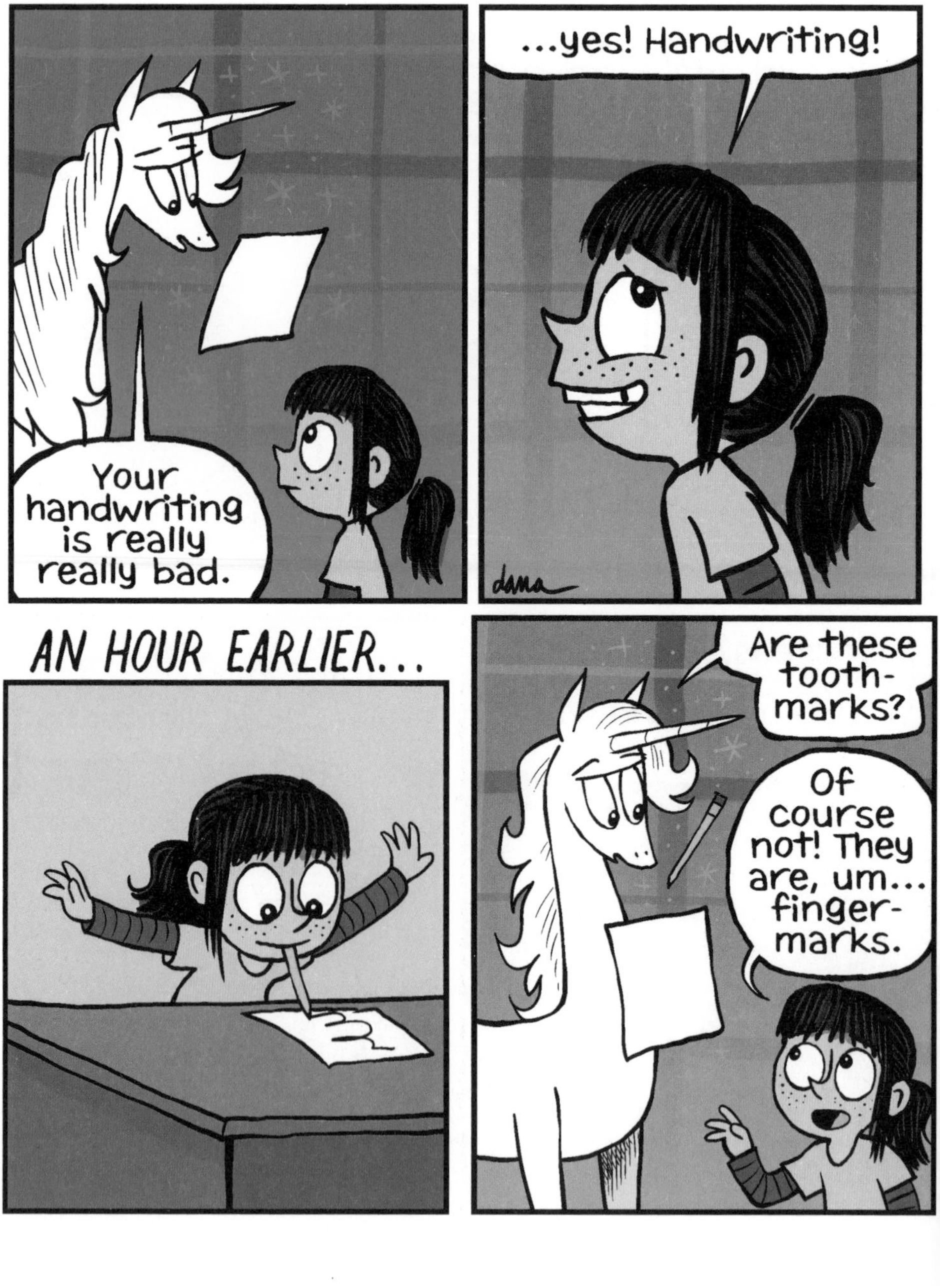
Your handwriting is really really bad.
...yes! Handwriting!
AN HOUR EARLIER...
Are these tooth-marks?
Of course not! They are, um... finger-marks.

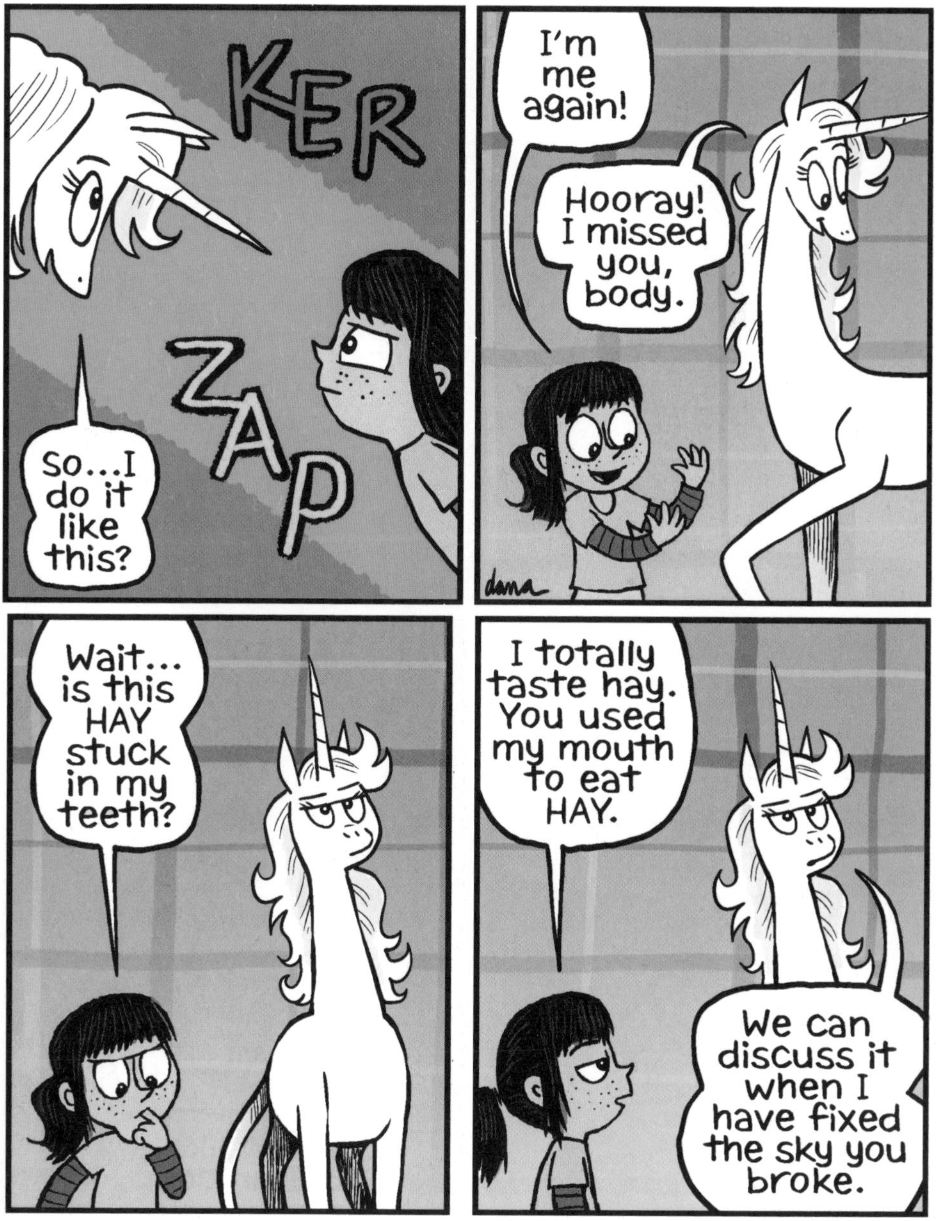
KER
ZAP
So...I do it like this?
I'm me again!
Hooray! I missed you, body.
dana
Wait... is this HAY stuck in my teeth?
I totally taste hay. You used my mouth to eat HAY.
We can discuss it when I have fixed the sky you broke.

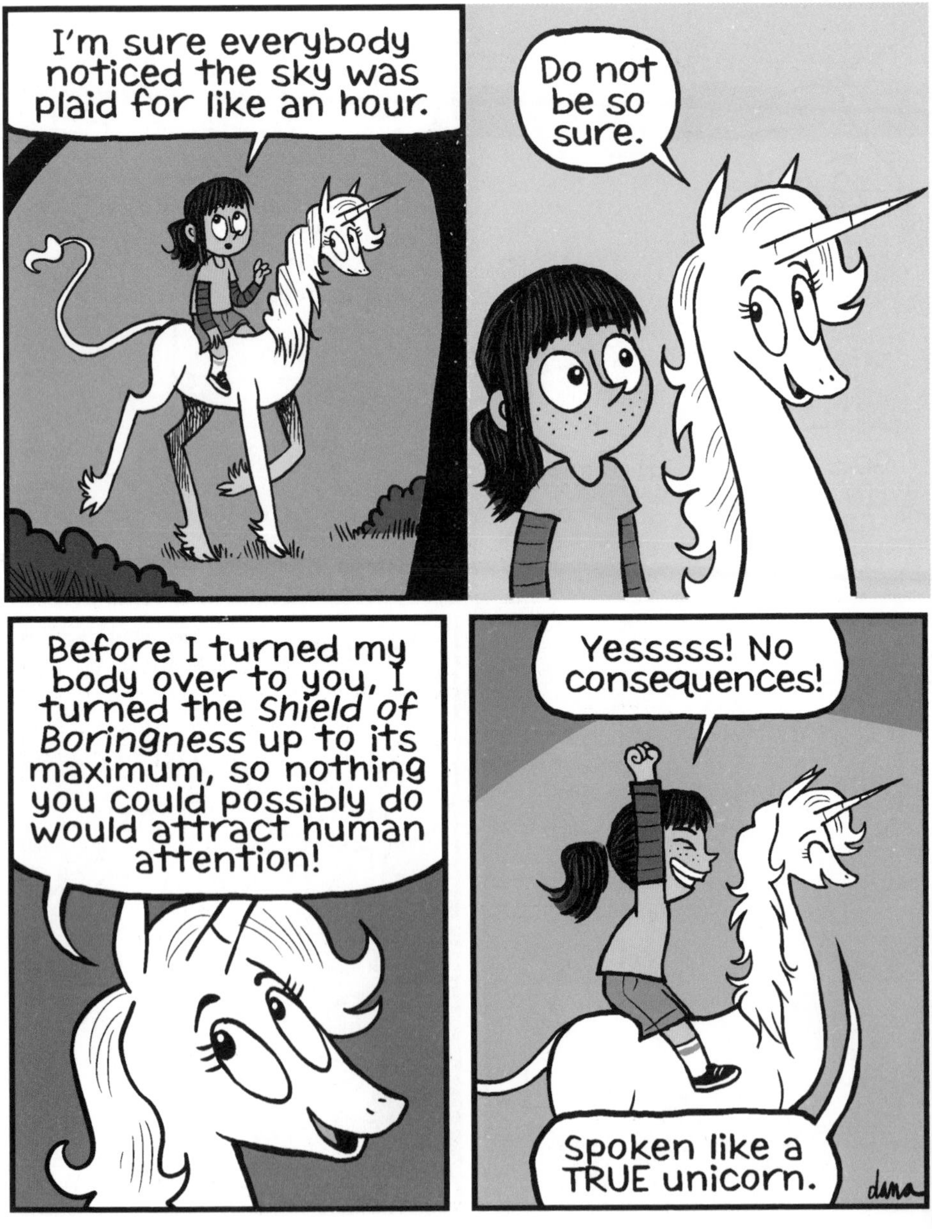
I'm sure everybody noticed the sky was plaid for like an hour.
Do not be so sure.
Before I turned my body over to you, I turned the *Shield of Boringness* up to its maximum, so nothing you could possibly do would attract human attention!
Yesssss! No consequences!
Spoken like a TRUE unicorn.
dana

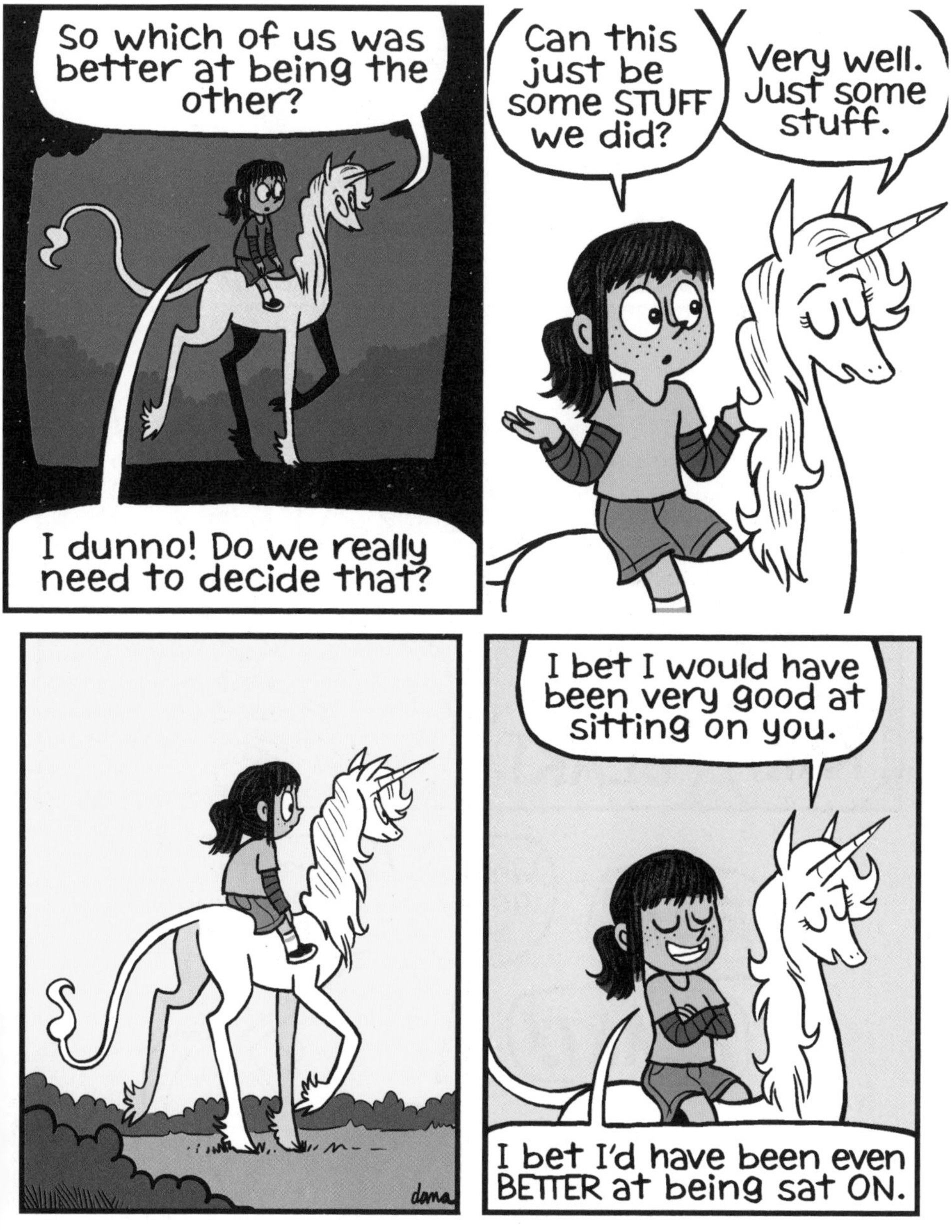
So which of us was better at being the other?
I dunno! Do we really need to decide that?
Can this just be some STUFF we did?
Very well. Just some stuff.
I bet I would have been very good at sitting on you.
I bet I'd have been even BETTER at being sat ON.

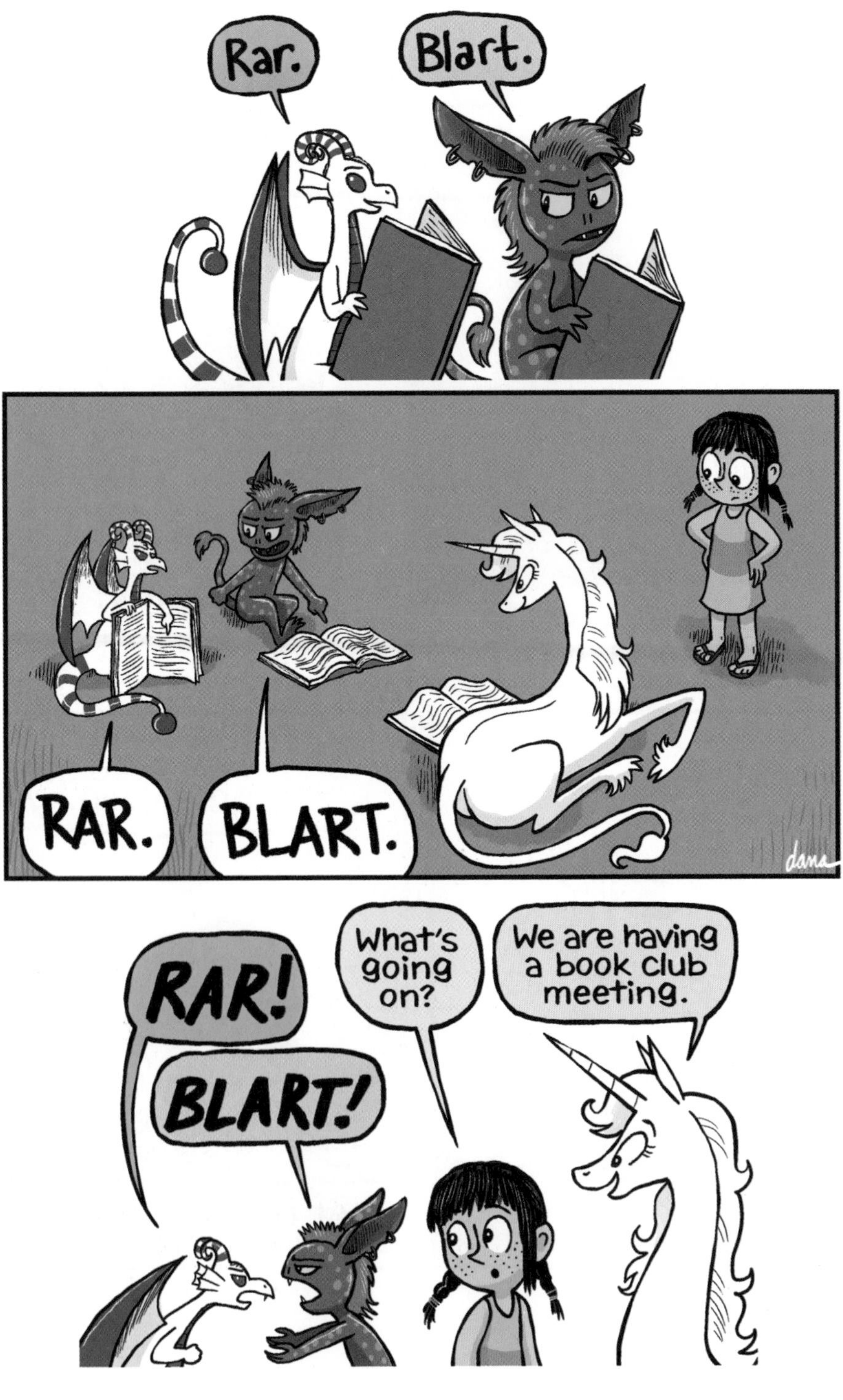
Rar.
Blart.
RAR.
BLART.
RAR!
BLART!
What's going on?
We are having a book club meeting.
dana

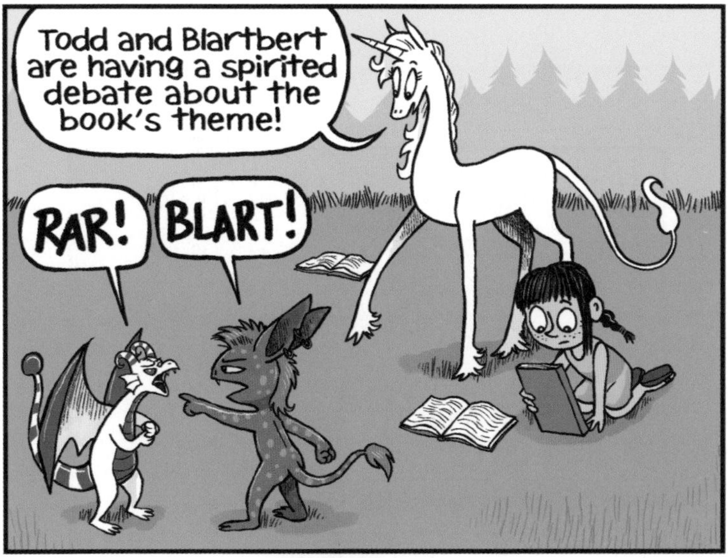
Todd and Blartbert are having a spirited debate about the book's theme!
RAR!
BLART!

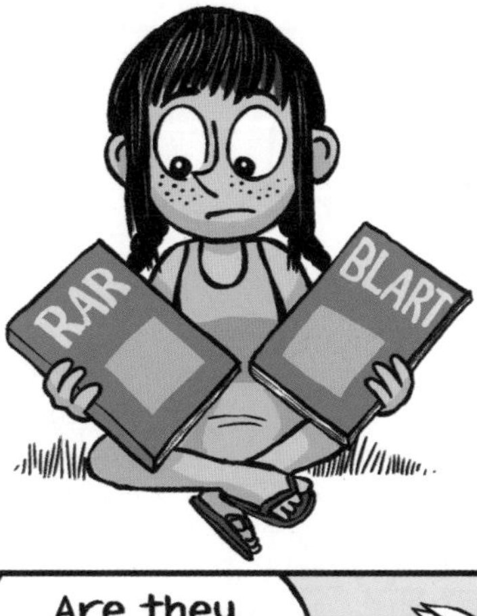
RAR
BLART

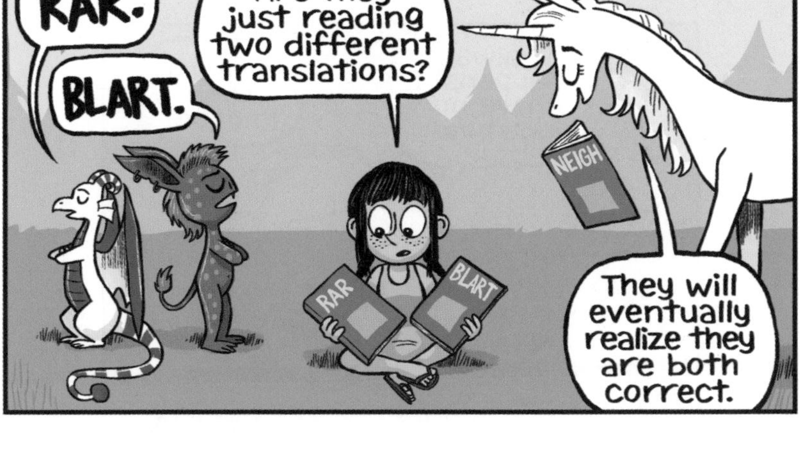
RAR.
BLART.
Are they just reading two different translations?
NEIGH
RAR
BLART
They will eventually realize they are both correct.

Why does this always happen?
This sock had a mate when I put it in the wash. Now it definitely isn't here.
It always happens! I have no idea how-
Have you seen Phoebe?

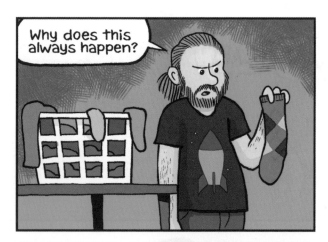

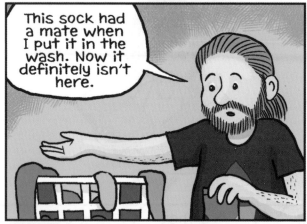

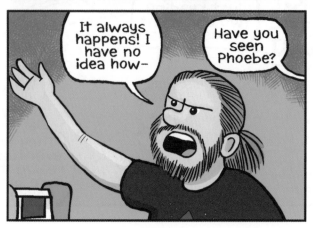

She's in her room.
Thank you!
I almost preferred the mystery.
Remind me to return the 73 other horn-cozies I have borrowed since I met you.

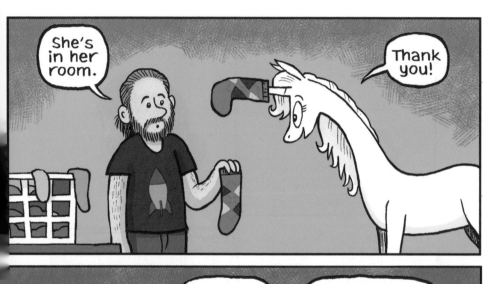

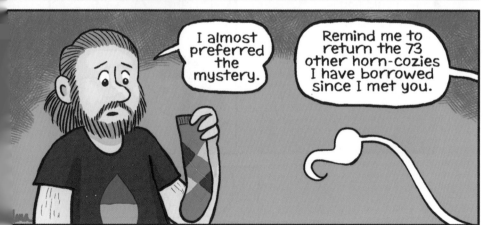

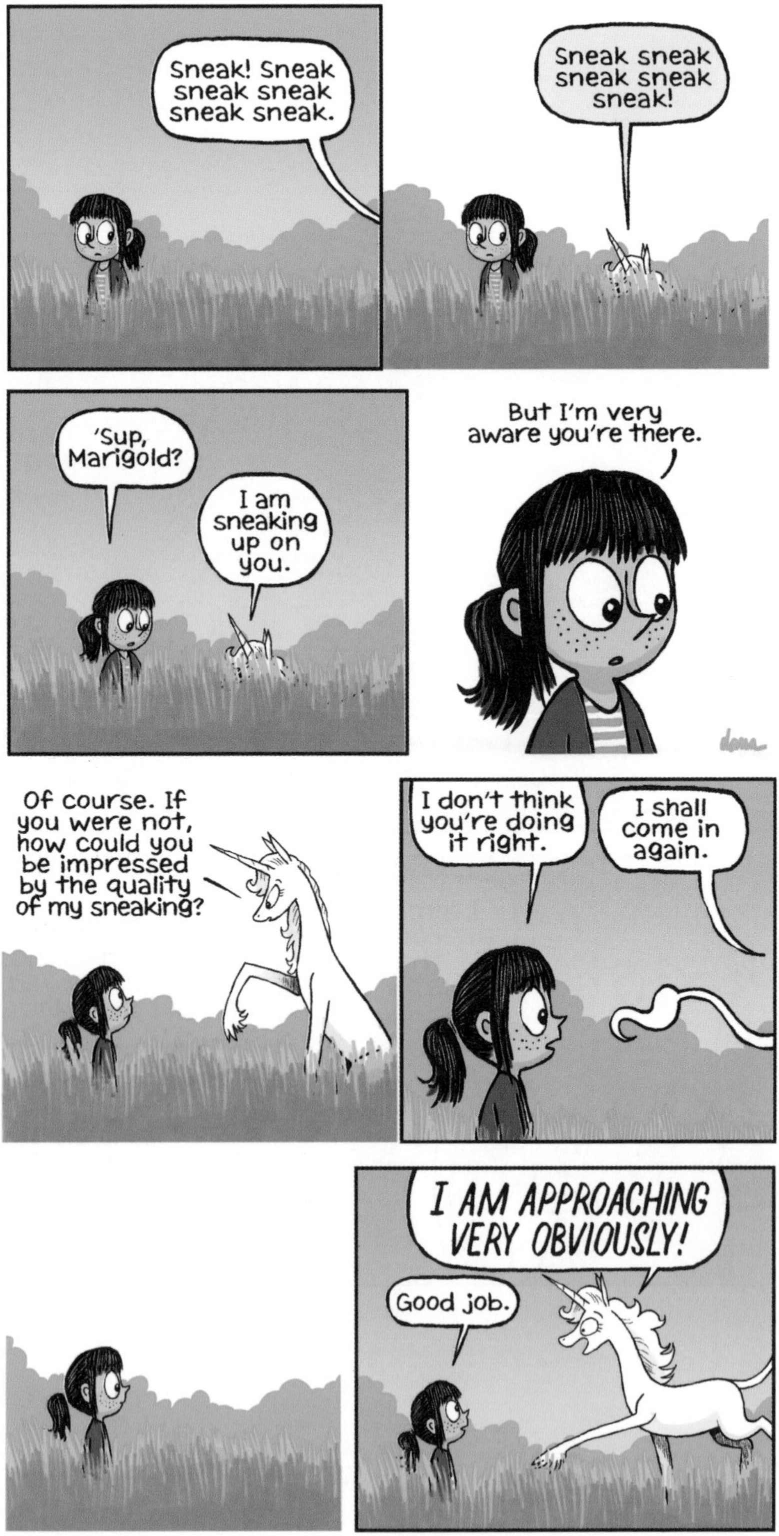
Sneak! Sneak sneak sneak sneak sneak.
Sneak sneak sneak sneak sneak!
'Sup, Marigold?
I am sneaking up on you.
But I'm very aware you're there.
Of course. If you were not, how could you be impressed by the quality of my sneaking?
I don't think you're doing it right.
I shall come in again.
I AM APPROACHING VERY OBVIOUSLY!
Good job.

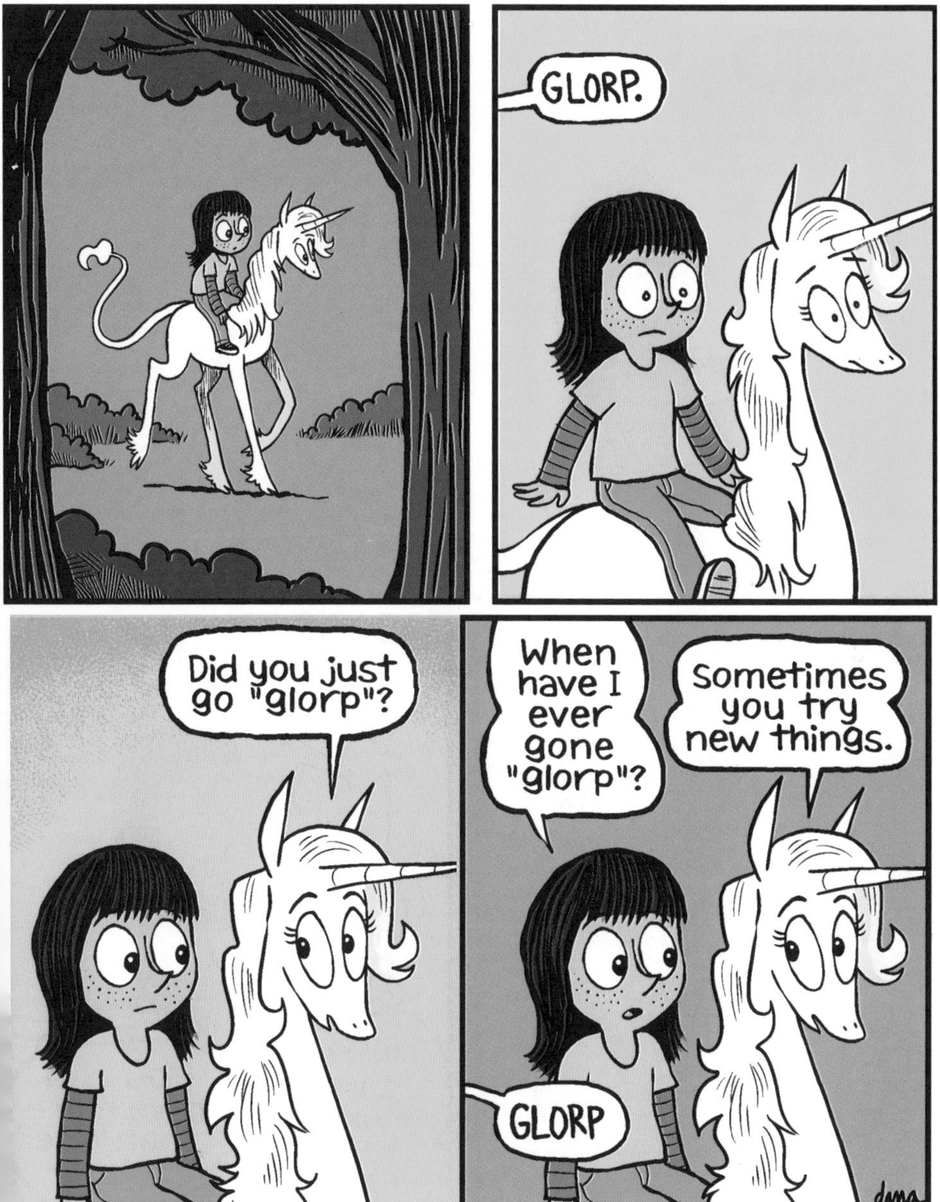
GLORP.
Did you just go "glorp"?
When have I ever gone "glorp"?
Sometimes you try new things.
GLORP
dana

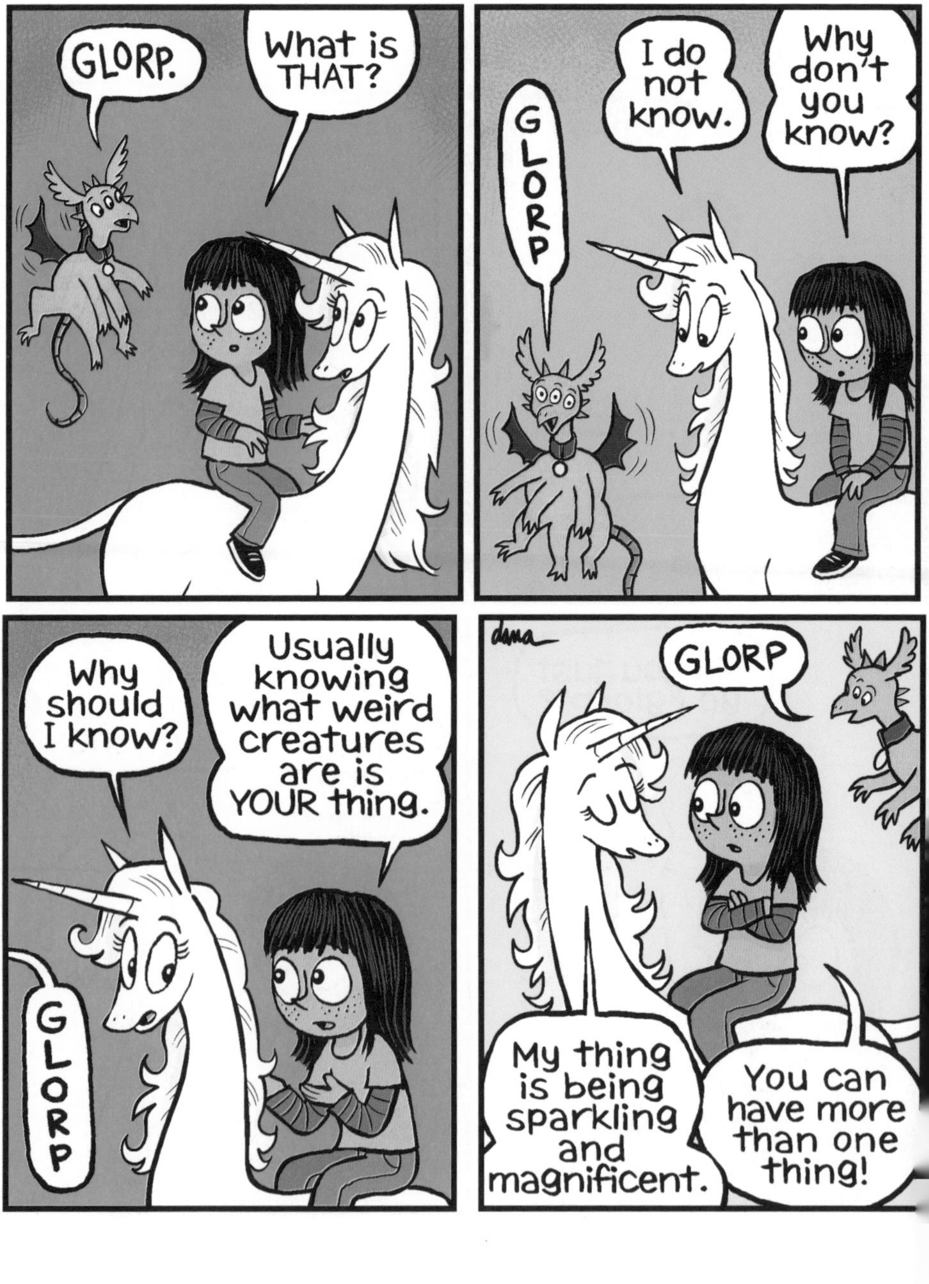
GLORP.
What is THAT?
GLORP
I do not know.
Why don't you know?
Why should I know?
Usually knowing what weird creatures are is YOUR thing.
GLORP
dana
GLORP
My thing is being sparkling and magnificent.
You can have more than one thing!

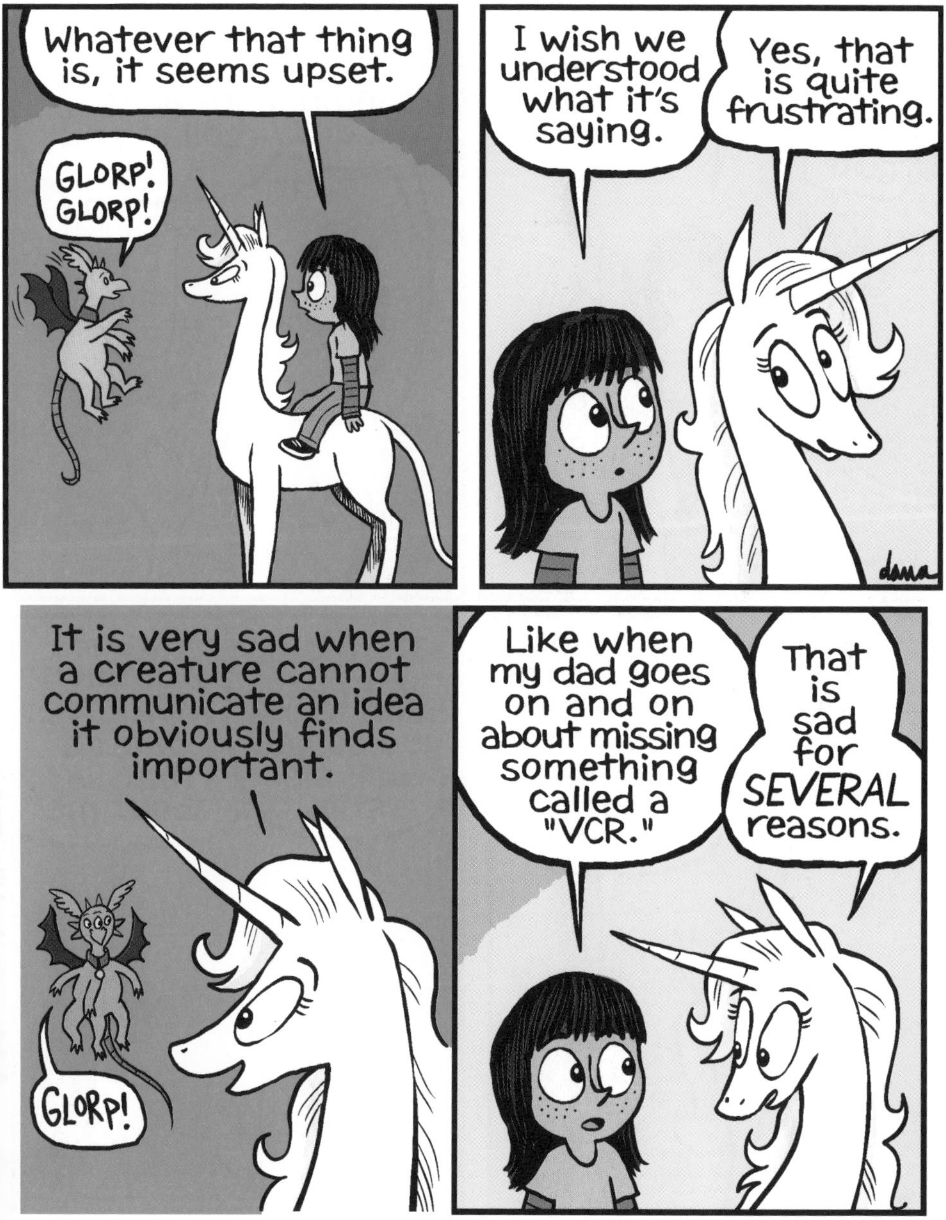
Whatever that thing is, it seems upset.
GLORP! GLORP!
I wish we understood what it's saying.
Yes, that is quite frustrating.
It is very sad when a creature cannot communicate an idea it obviously finds important.
GLORP!
Like when my dad goes on and on about missing something called a "VCR."
That is sad for SEVERAL reasons.

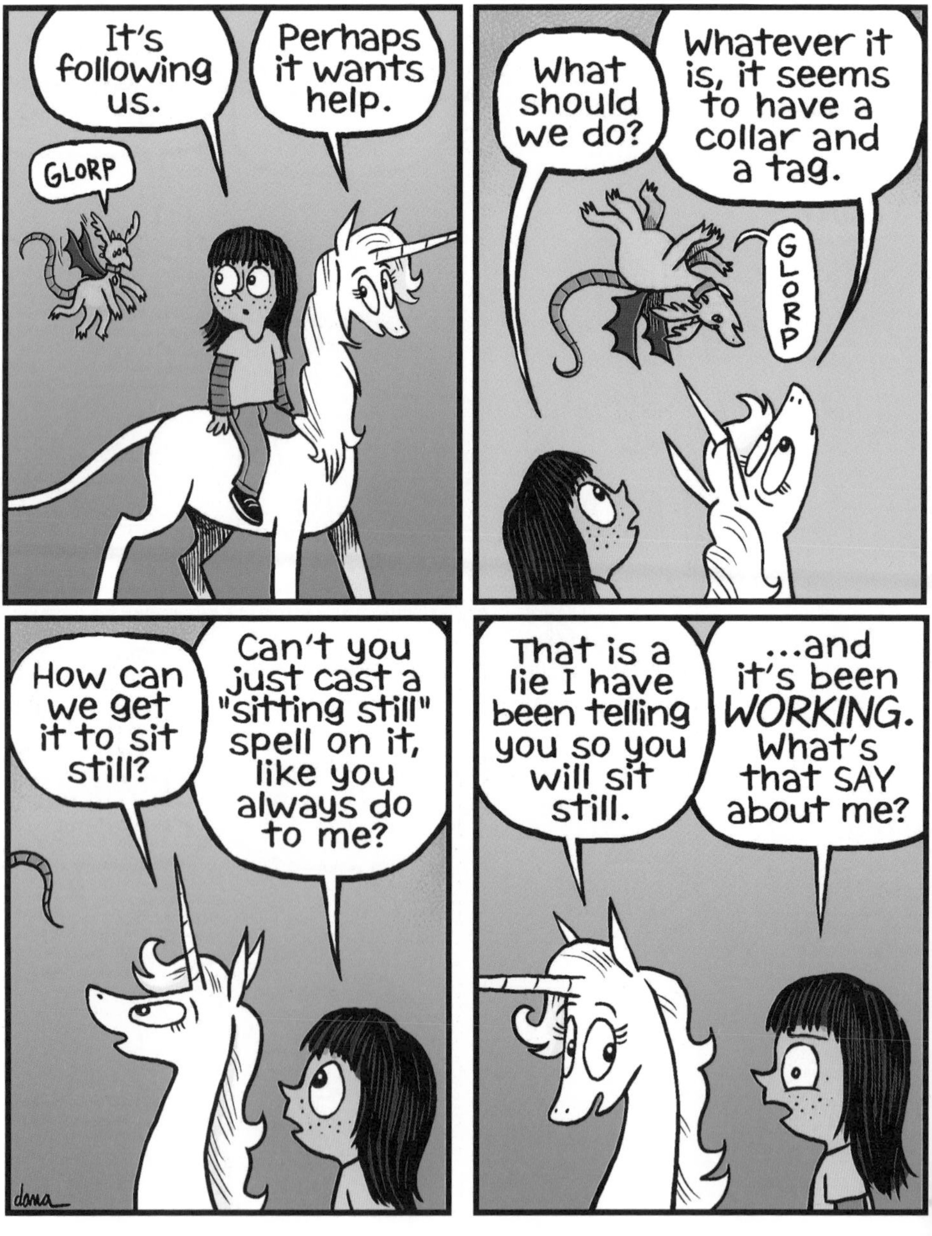
It's following us.
Perhaps it wants help.
GLORP
What should we do?
Whatever it is, it seems to have a collar and a tag.
GLORP
How can we get it to sit still?
Can't you just cast a "sitting still" spell on it, like you always do to me?
That is a lie I have been telling you so you will sit still.
...and it's been *WORKING*. What's that SAY about me?

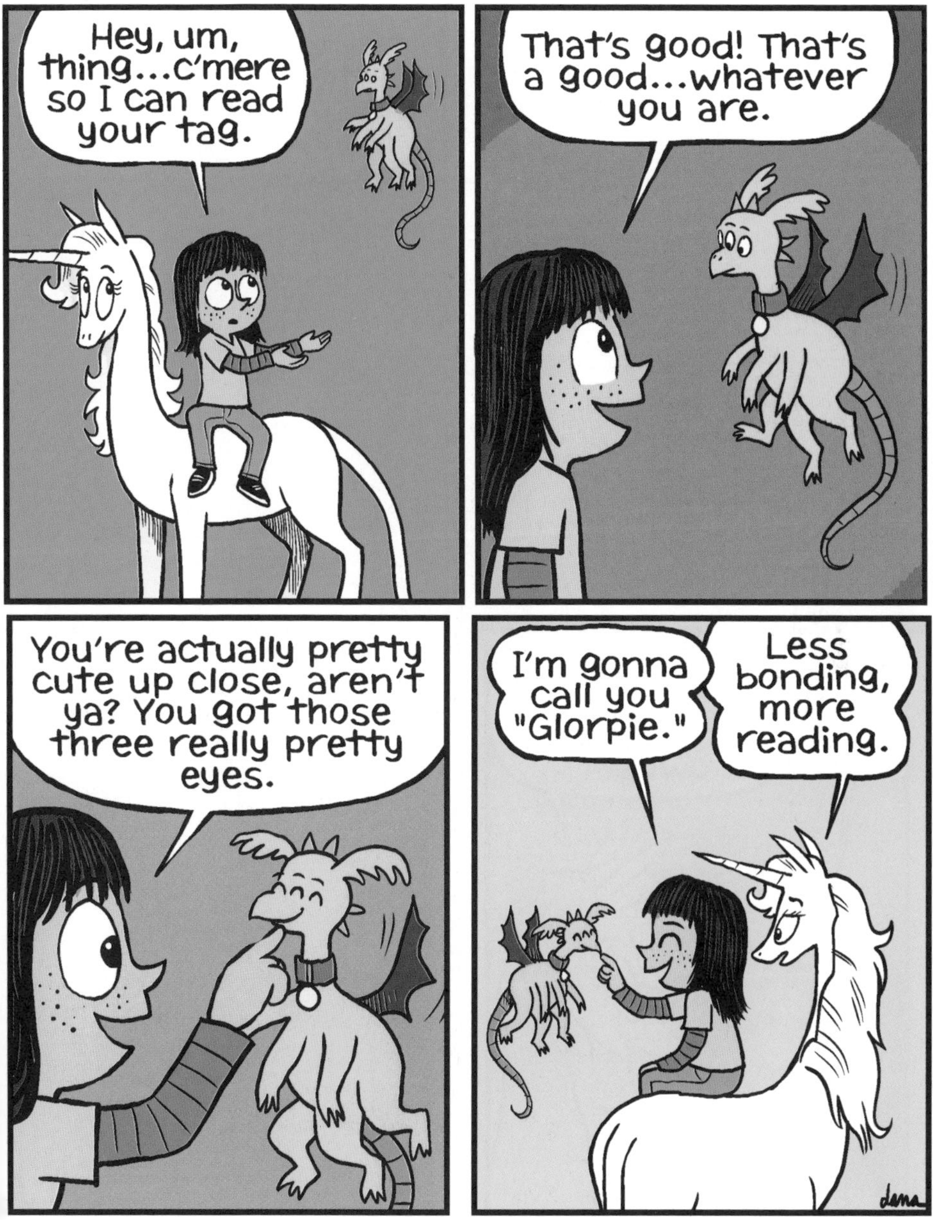

Hey, um, thing...c'mere so I can read your tag.
That's good! That's a good...whatever you are.
You're actually pretty cute up close, aren't ya? You got those three really pretty eyes.
I'm gonna call you "Glorpie."
Less bonding, more reading.
dana

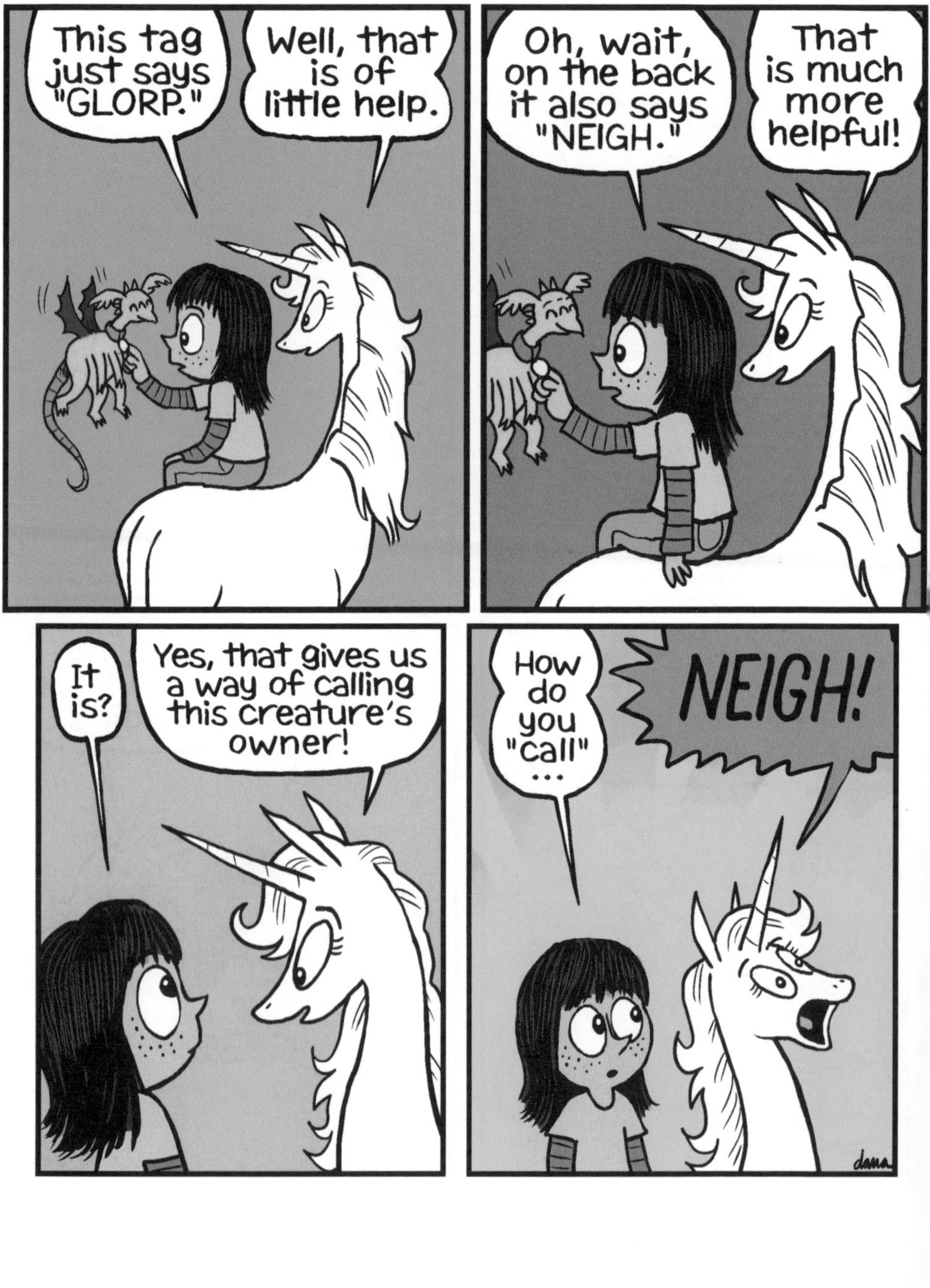
This tag just says "GLORP."
Well, that is of little help.
Oh, wait, on the back it also says "NEIGH."
That is much more helpful!
It is?
Yes, that gives us a way of calling this creature's owner!
How do you "call" ...
NEIGH!
dana

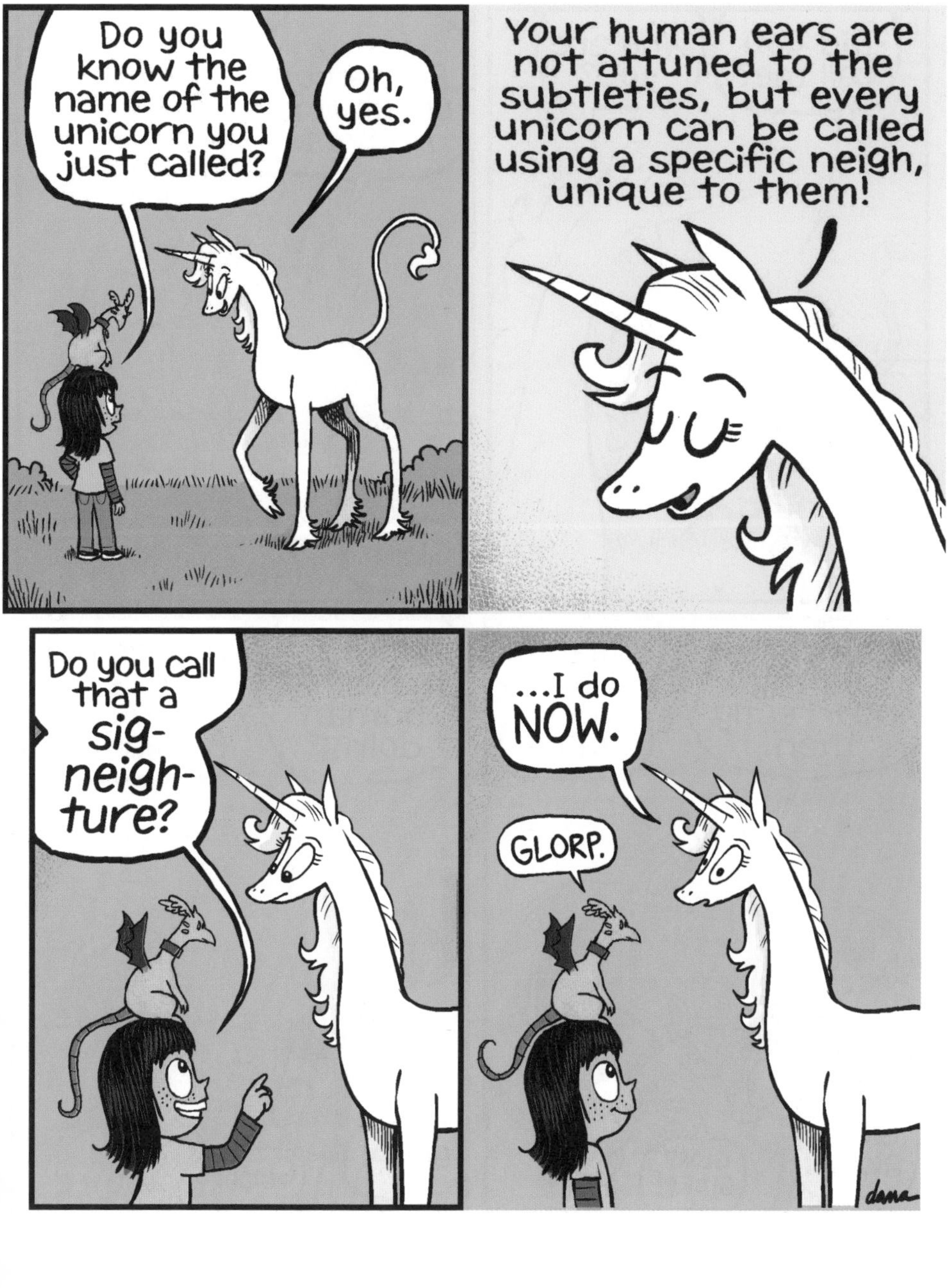
Do you know the name of the unicorn you just called?
Oh, yes.
Your human ears are not attuned to the subtleties, but every unicorn can be called using a specific neigh, unique to them!
Do you call that a sig-neigh-ture?
...I do NOW.
GLORP.
dana

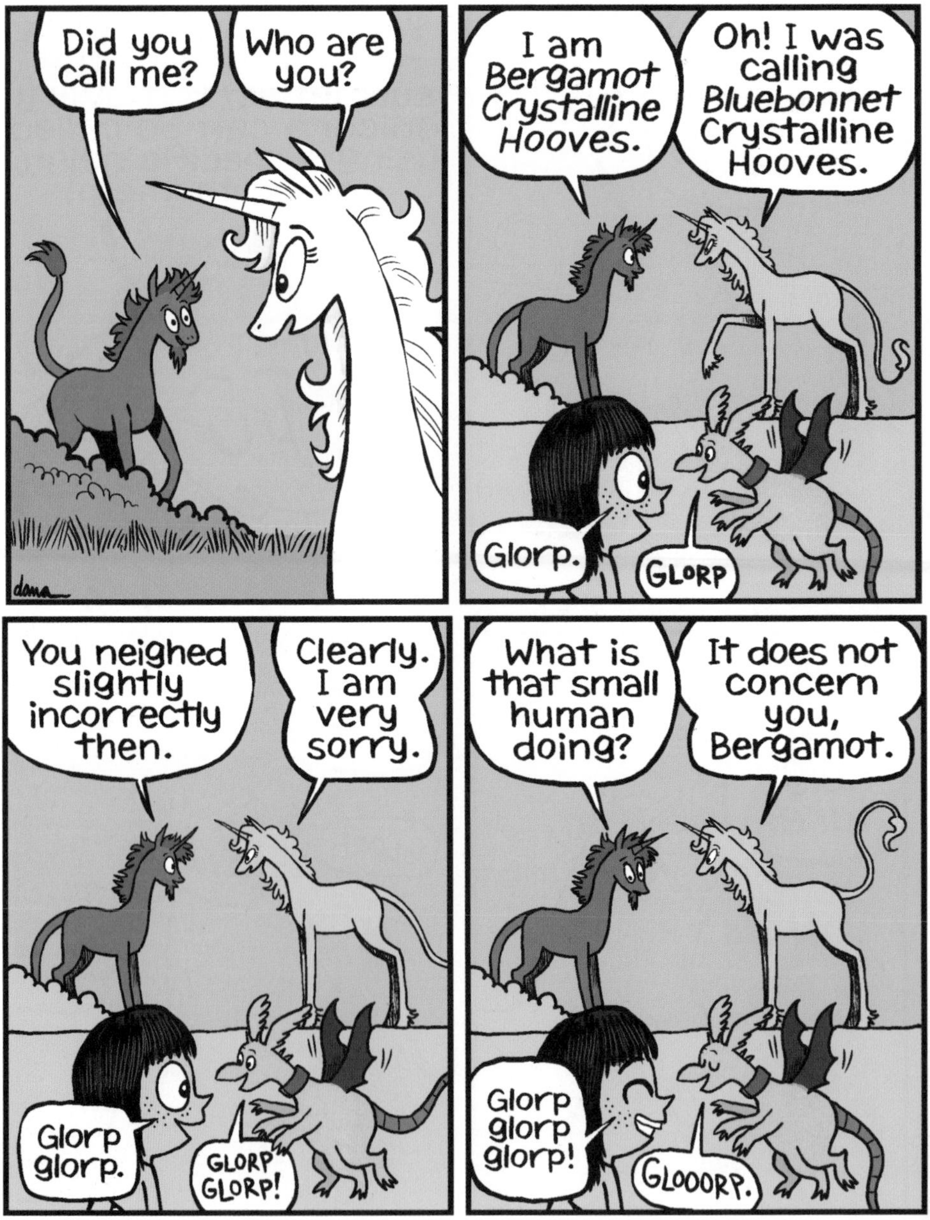
Did you call me?
Who are you?
I am Bergamot Crystalline Hooves.
Oh! I was calling Bluebonnet Crystalline Hooves.
Glorp.
GLORP
You neighed slightly incorrectly then.
Clearly. I am very sorry.
Glorp glorp.
GLORP GLORP!
What is that small human doing?
It does not concern you, Bergamot.
Glorp glorp glorp!
GLOOORP.

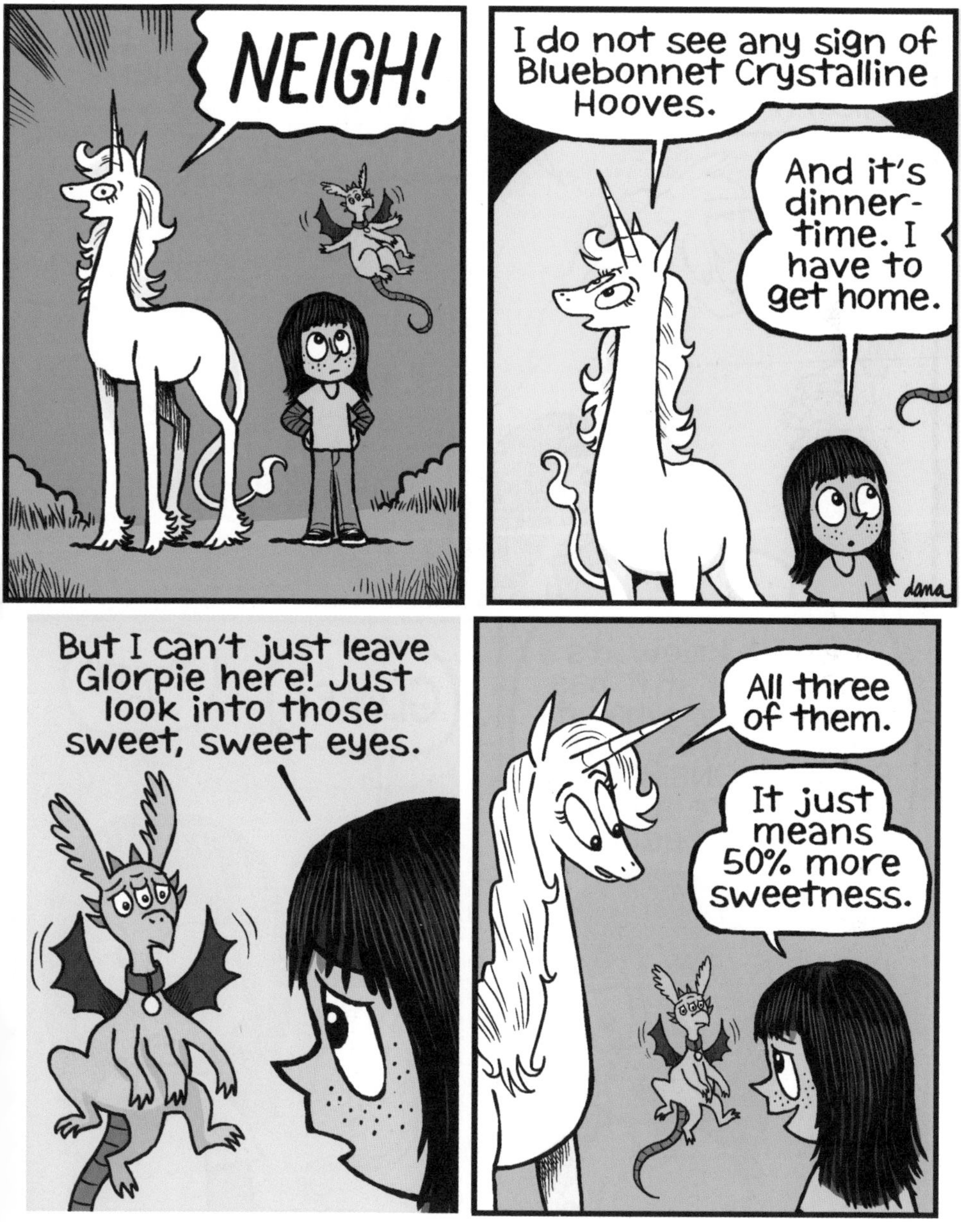
NEIGH!
I do not see any sign of Bluebonnet Crystalline Hooves.
And it's dinner-time. I have to get home.
dana
But I can't just leave Glorpie here! Just look into those sweet, sweet eyes.
All three of them.
It just means 50% more sweetness.

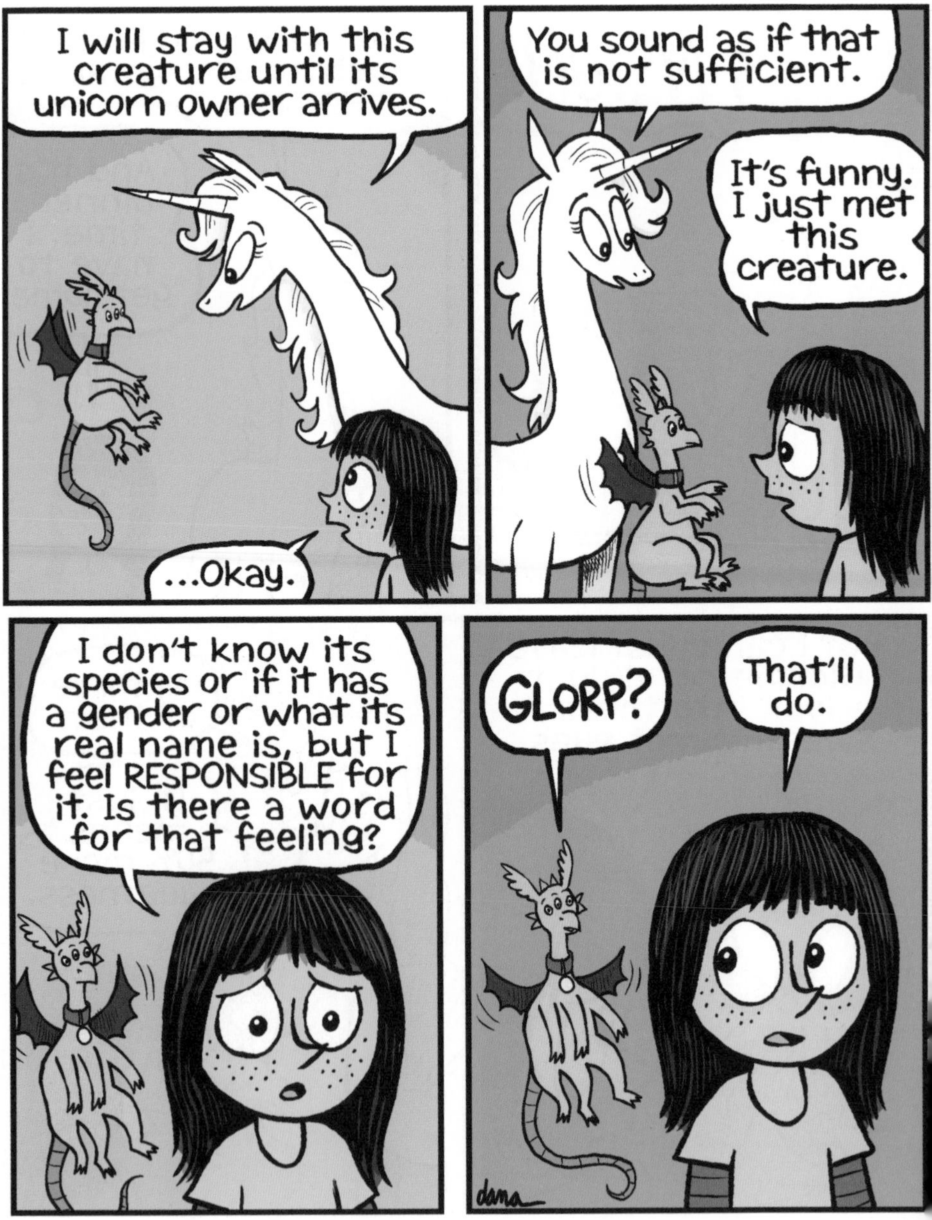
I will stay with this creature until its unicorn owner arrives.
...Okay.
You sound as if that is not sufficient.
It's funny. I just met this creature.
I don't know its species or if it has a gender or what its real name is, but I feel RESPONSIBLE for it. Is there a word for that feeling?
GLORP?
That'll do.
dana

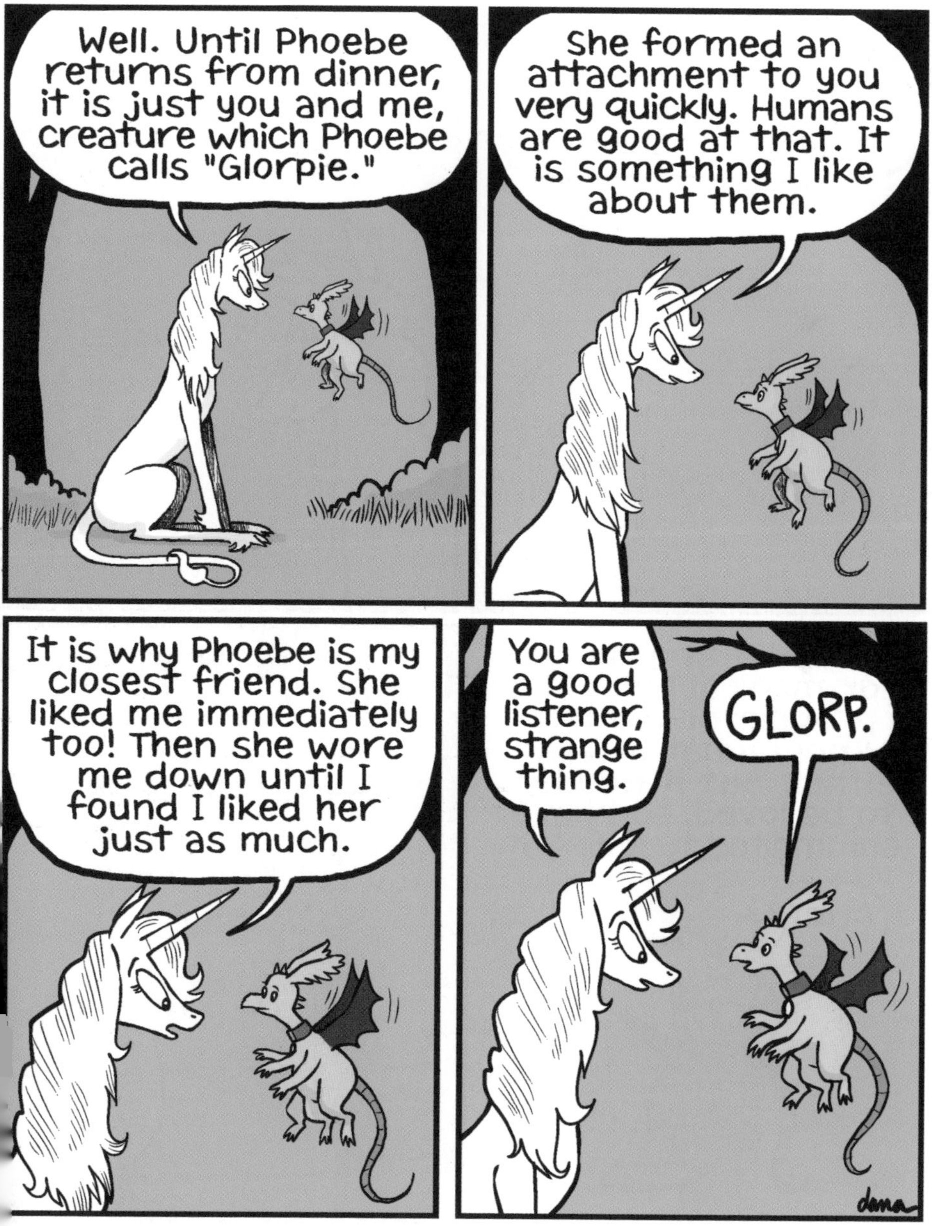
Well. Until Phoebe returns from dinner, it is just you and me, creature which Phoebe calls "Glorpie."
She formed an attachment to you very quickly. Humans are good at that. It is something I like about them.
It is why Phoebe is my closest friend. She liked me immediately too! Then she wore me down until I found I liked her just as much.
You are a good listener, strange thing.
GLORP.
dana

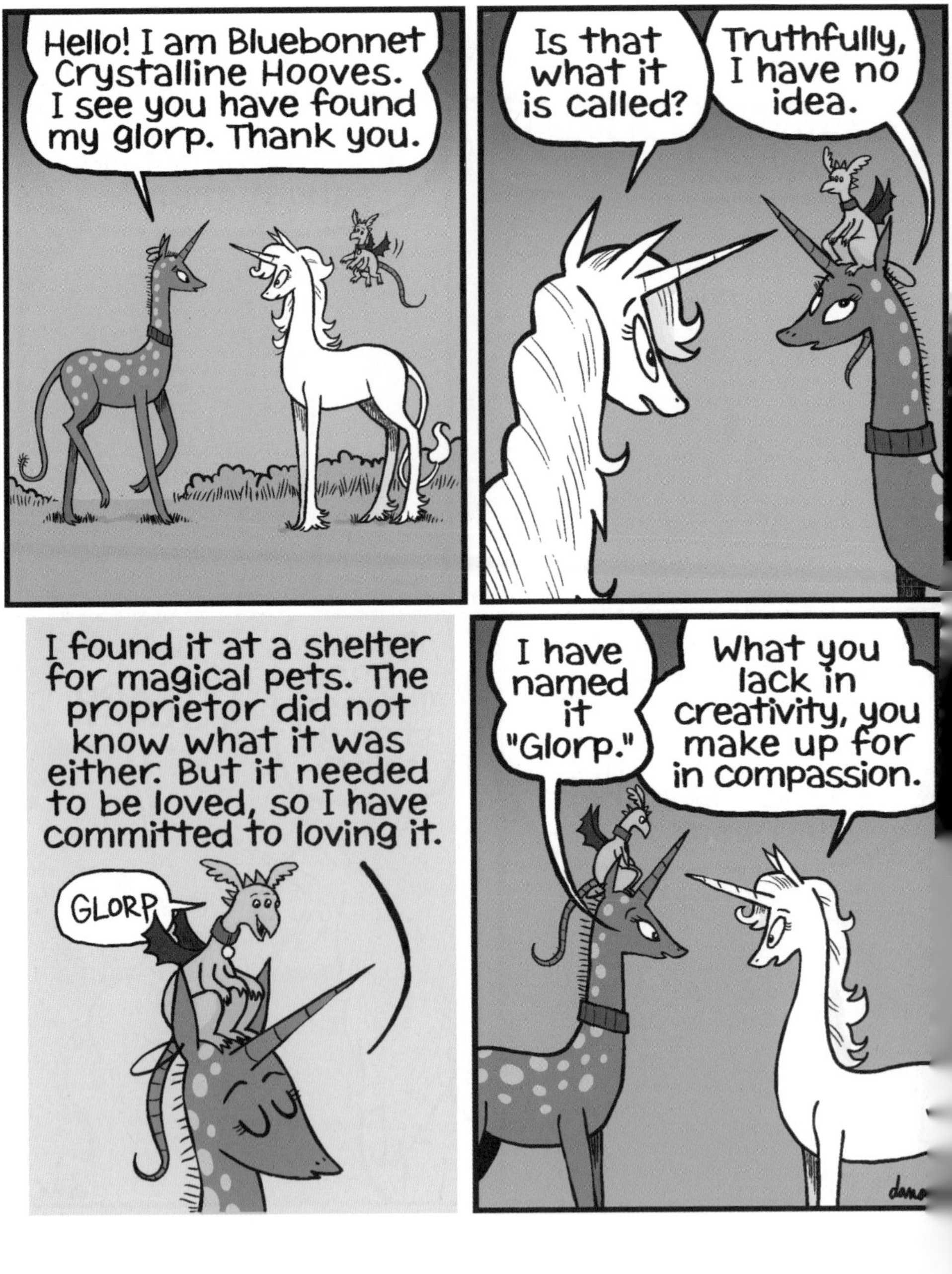
Hello! I am Bluebonnet Crystalline Hooves. I see you have found my glorp. Thank you.
Is that what it is called?
Truthfully, I have no idea.
I found it at a shelter for magical pets. The proprietor did not know what it was either. But it needed to be loved, so I have committed to loving it.
GLORP
I have named it "Glorp."
What you lack in creativity, you make up for in compassion.

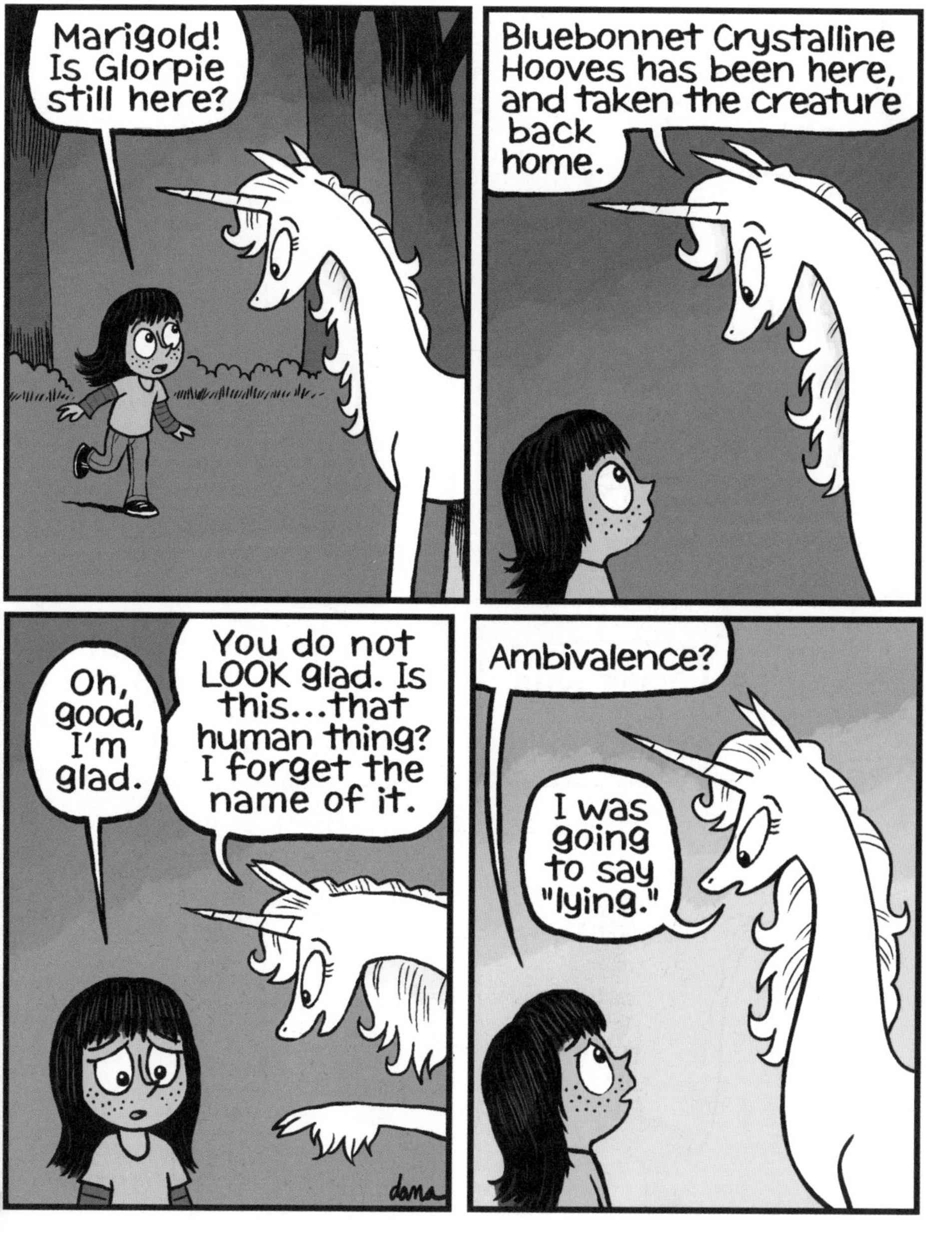
Marigold! Is Glorpie still here?
Bluebonnet Crystalline Hooves has been here, and taken the creature back home.
Oh, good, I'm glad.
You do not LOOK glad. Is this...that human thing? I forget the name of it.
dana
Ambivalence?
I was going to say "lying."

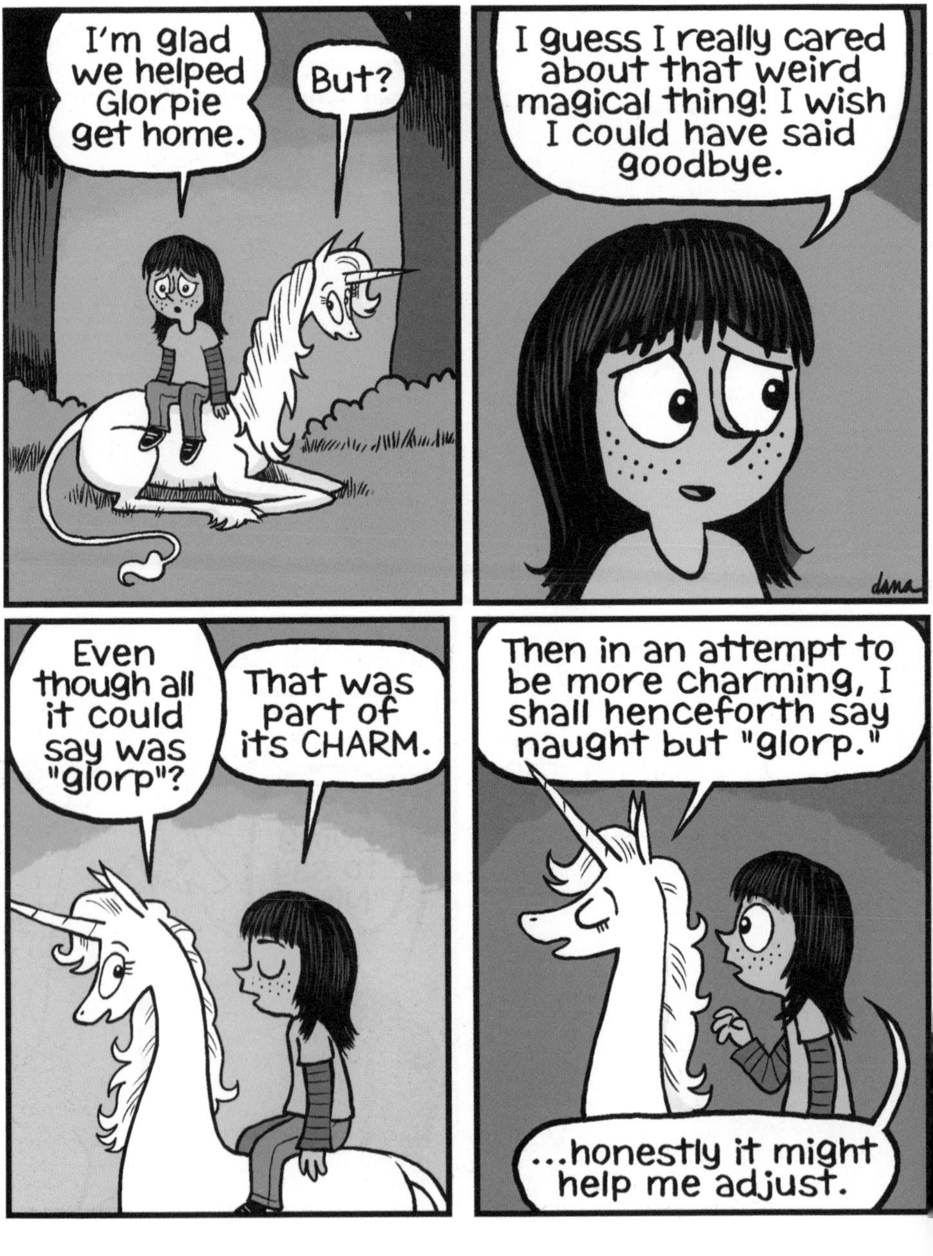

I'm glad we helped Glorpie get home.
But?
I guess I really cared about that weird magical thing! I wish I could have said goodbye.
dana
Even though all it could say was "glorp"?
That was part of its CHARM.
Then in an attempt to be more charming, I shall henceforth say naught but "glorp."
...honestly it might help me adjust.

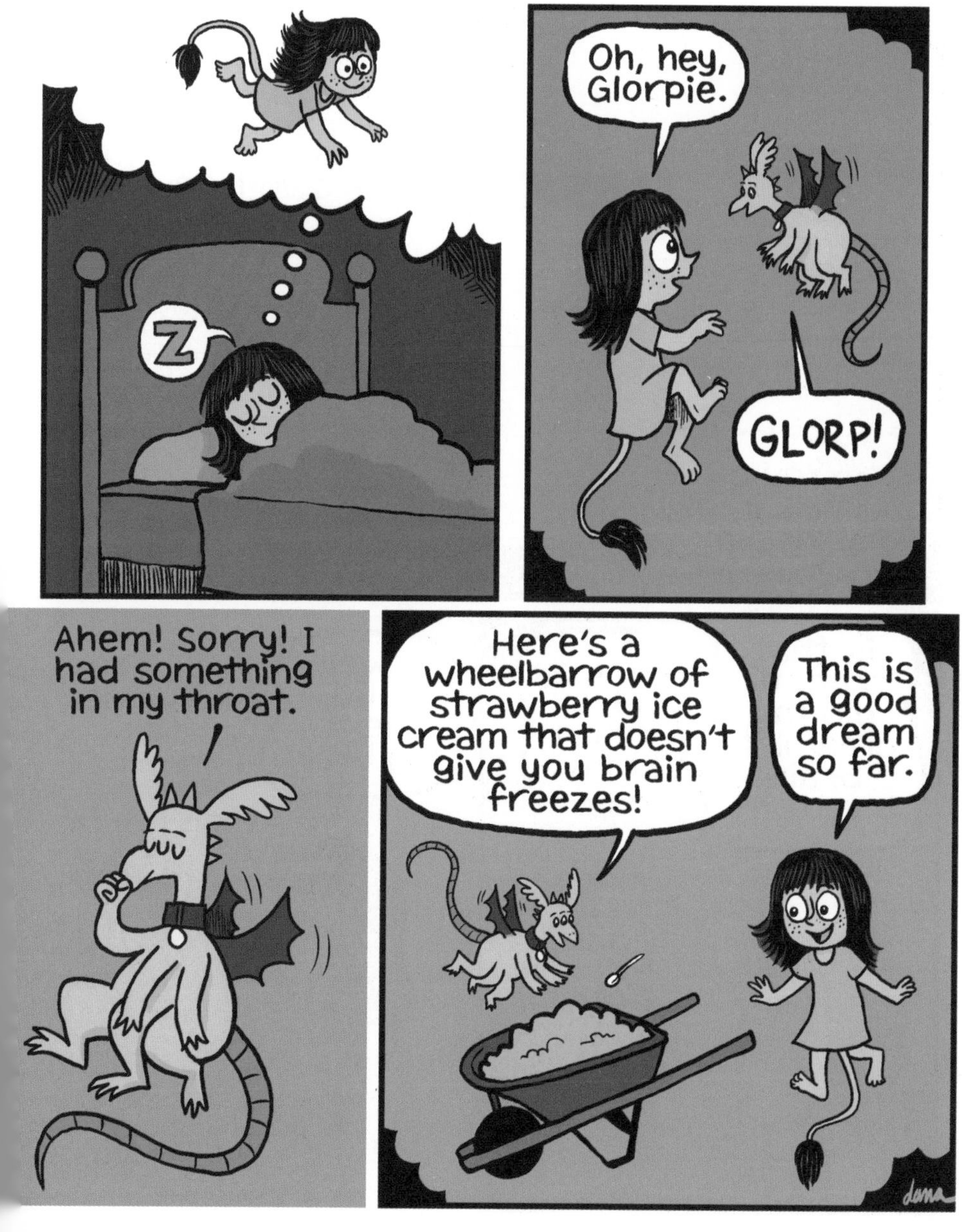

Z
Oh, hey, Glorpie.
GLORP!
Ahem! Sorry! I had something in my throat.
Here's a wheelbarrow of strawberry ice cream that doesn't give you brain freezes!
This is a good dream so far.
dana

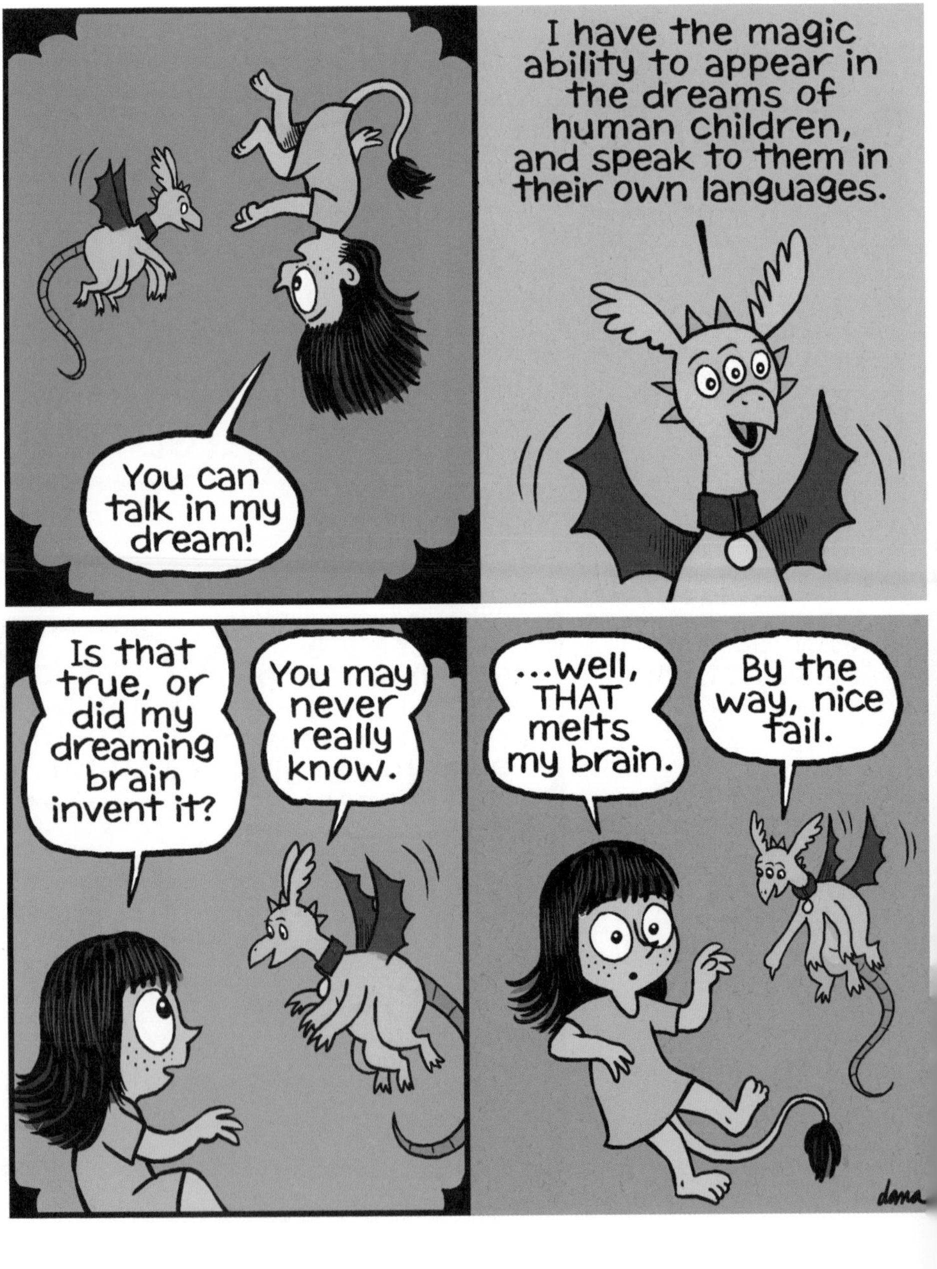
You can talk in my dream!
I have the magic ability to appear in the dreams of human children, and speak to them in their own languages.
Is that true, or did my dreaming brain invent it?
You may never really know.
...well, THAT melts my brain.
By the way, nice tail.
dana

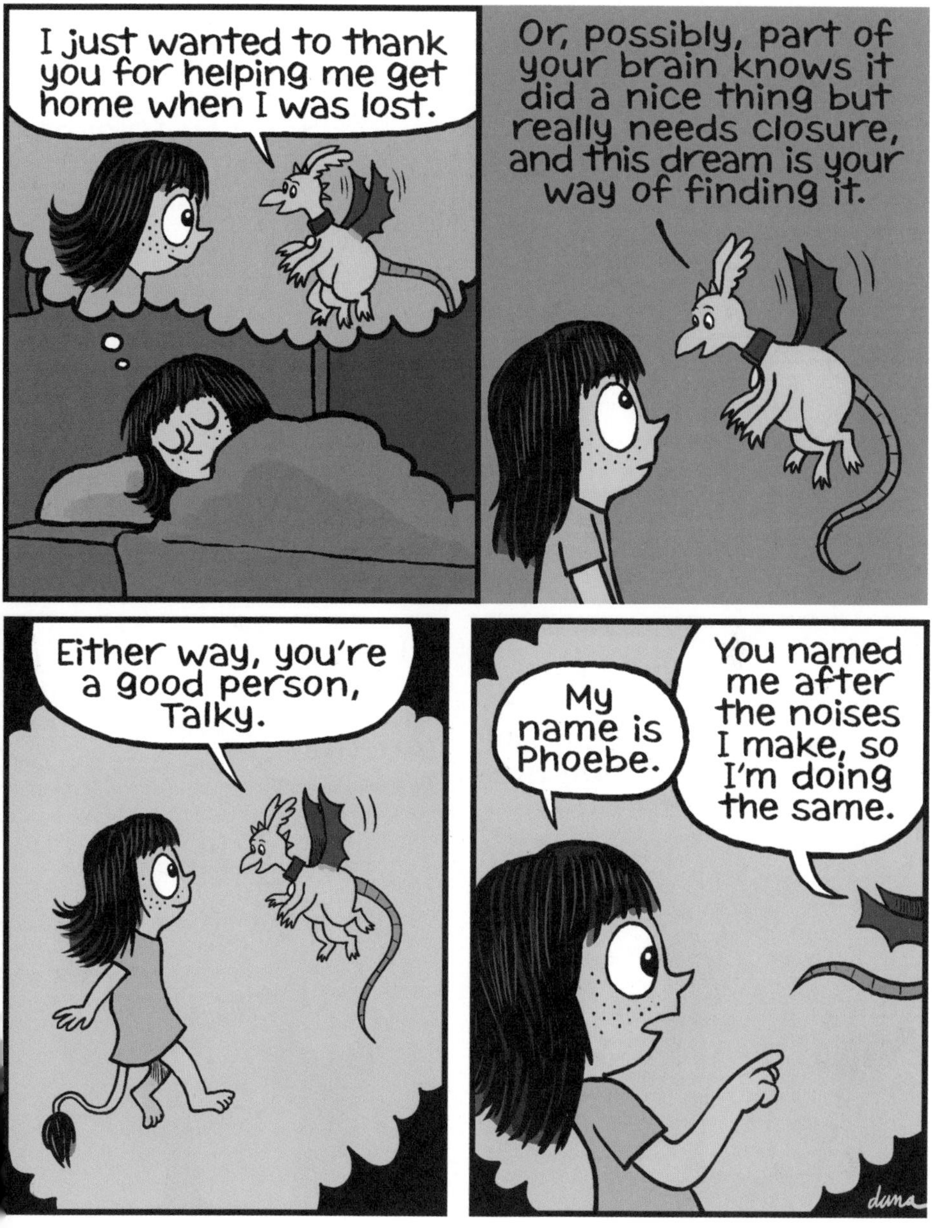
I just wanted to thank you for helping me get home when I was lost.
Or, possibly, part of your brain knows it did a nice thing but really needs closure, and this dream is your way of finding it.
Either way, you're a good person, Talky.
My name is Phoebe.
You named me after the noises I make, so I'm doing the same.
dana

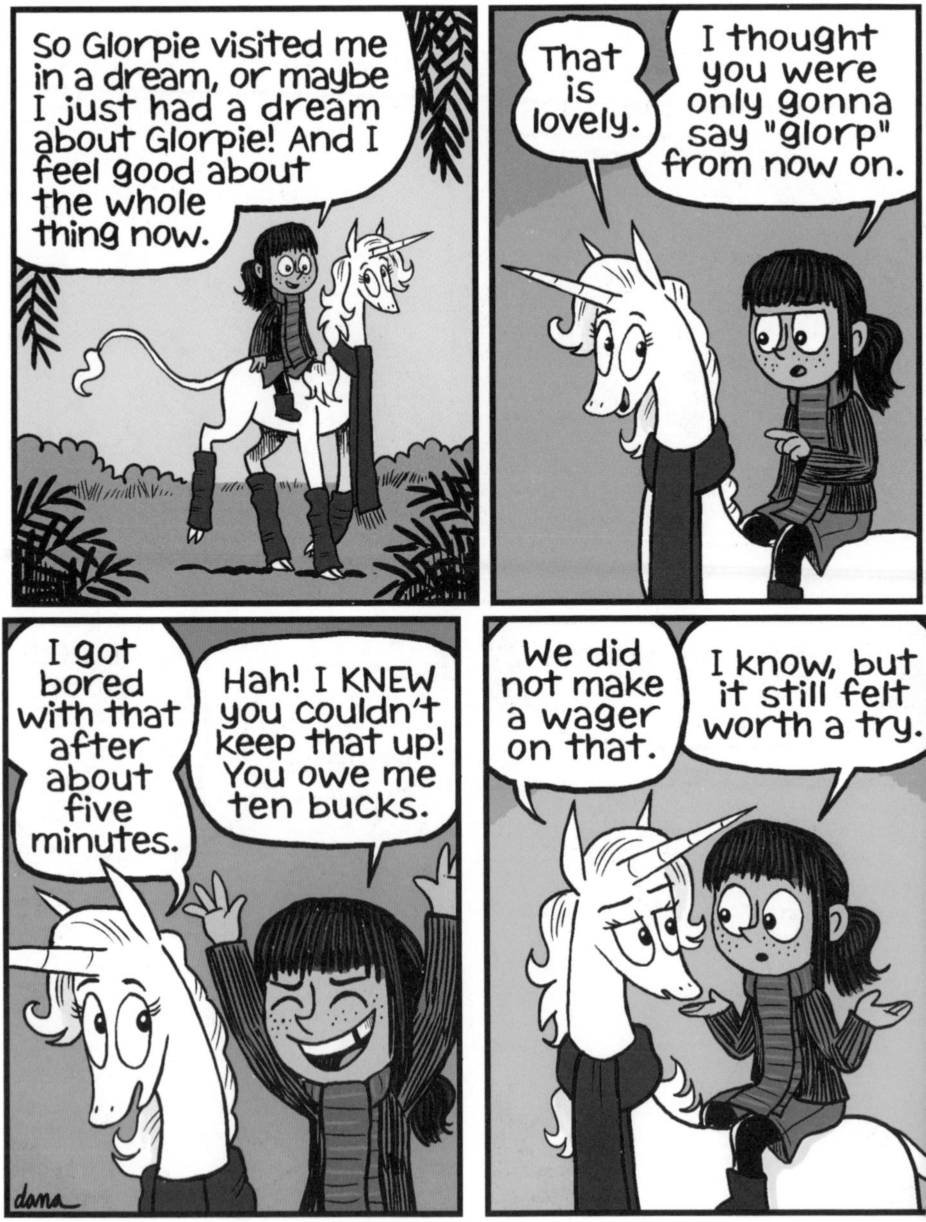
So Glorpie visited me in a dream, or maybe I just had a dream about Glorpie! And I feel good about the whole thing now.
That is lovely.
I thought you were only gonna say "glorp" from now on.
I got bored with that after about five minutes.
Hah! I KNEW you couldn't keep that up! You owe me ten bucks.
We did not make a wager on that.
I know, but it still felt worth a try.
dana

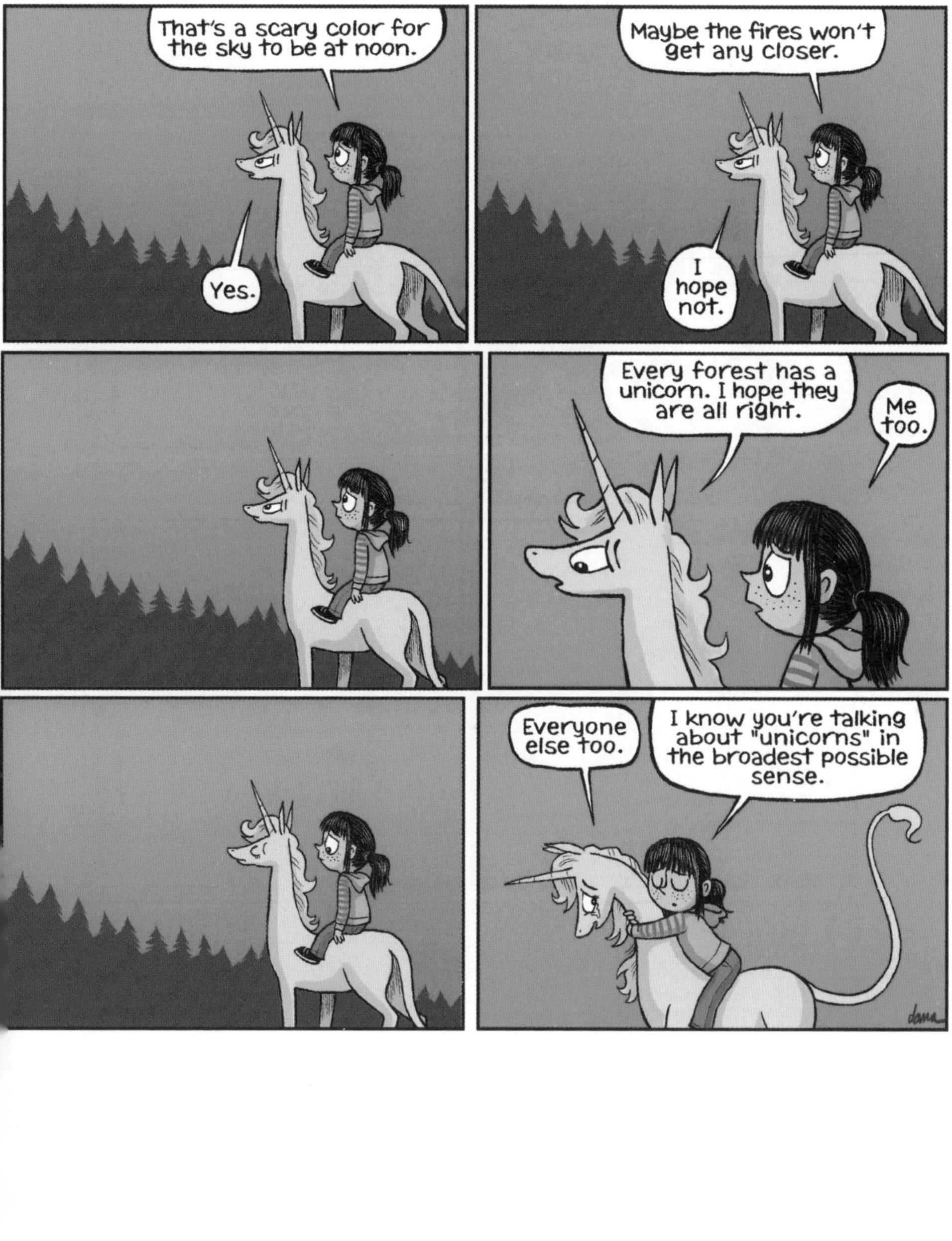
That's a scary color for the sky to be at noon.
Yes.
Maybe the fires won't get any closer.
I hope not.
Every forest has a unicorn. I hope they are all right.
Me too.
Everyone else too.
I know you're talking about "unicorns" in the broadest possible sense.

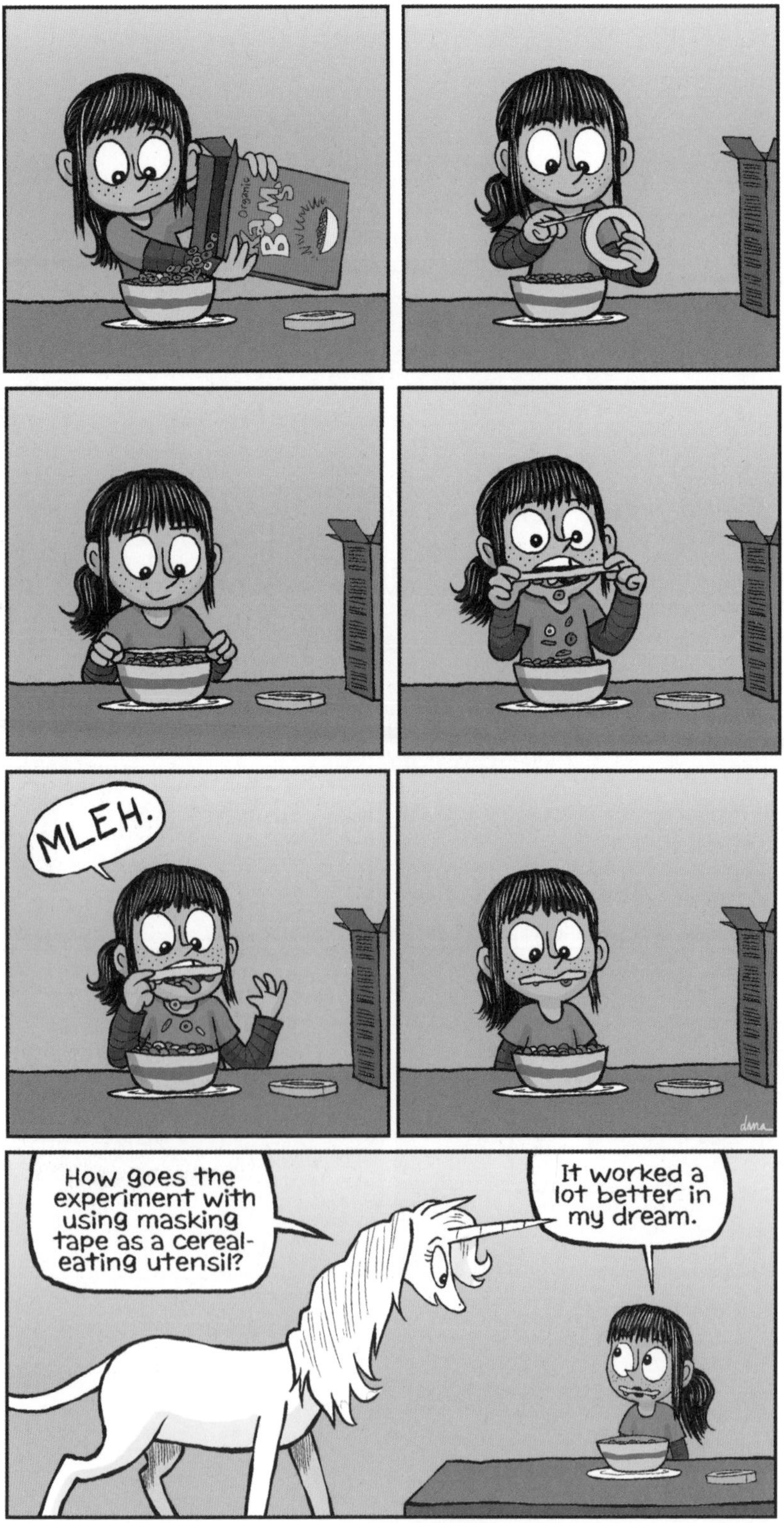
MLEH.
How goes the experiment with using masking tape as a cereal-eating utensil?
It worked a lot better in my dream.

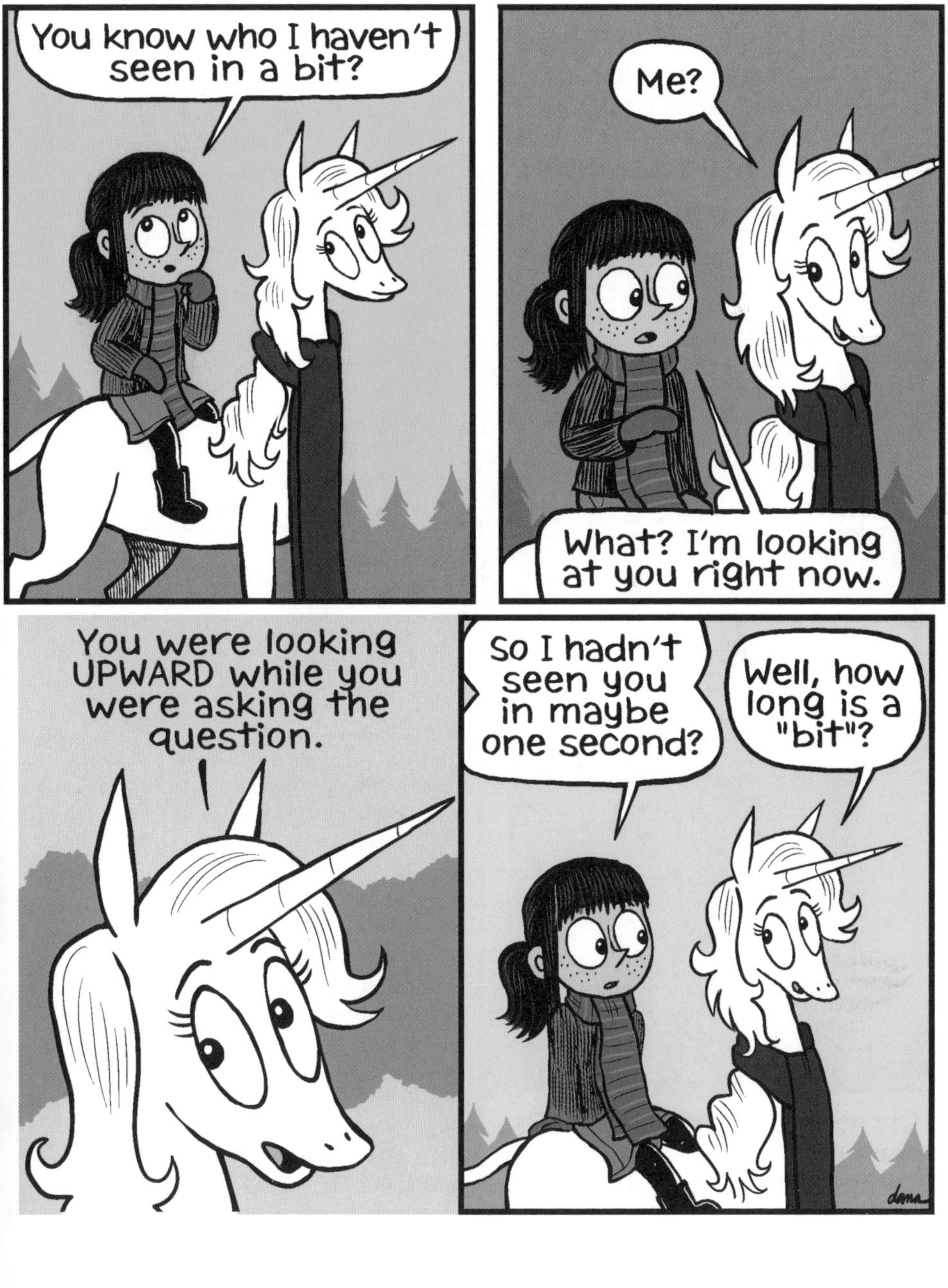
You know who I haven't seen in a bit?
Me?
What? I'm looking at you right now.
You were looking UPWARD while you were asking the question.
So I hadn't seen you in maybe one second?
Well, how long is a "bit"?
dana

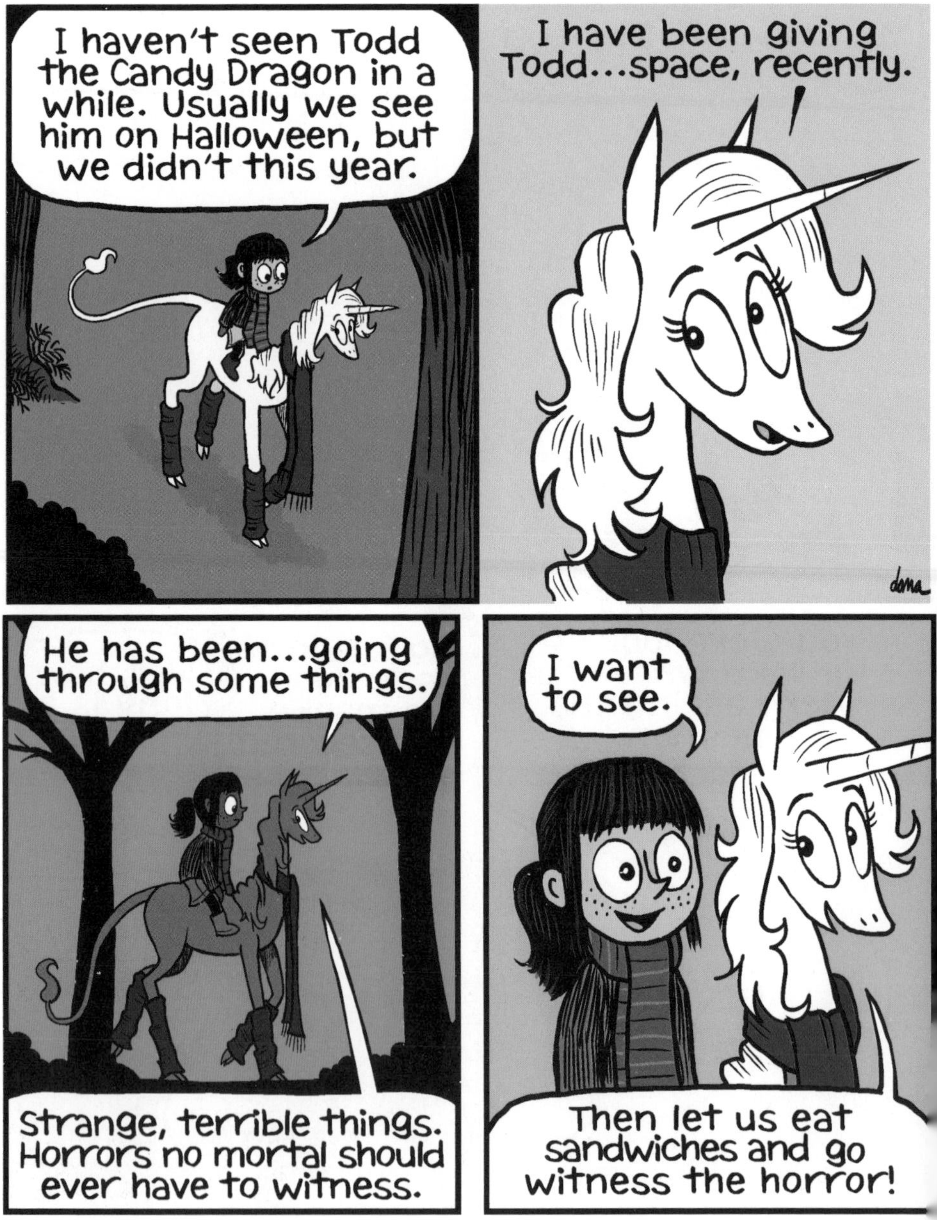
I haven't seen Todd the Candy Dragon in a while. Usually we see him on Halloween, but we didn't this year.
I have been giving Todd...space, recently.
He has been...going through some things.
Strange, terrible things. Horrors no mortal should ever have to witness.
I want to see.
Then let us eat sandwiches and go witness the horror!

You must promise not to be TOO afraid when we see Todd.
Um... okay.
RAAAR!
RAR
Aaaaaaaaa.
Good, that is a proper amount of being afraid.

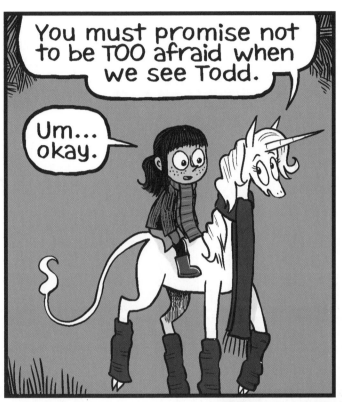

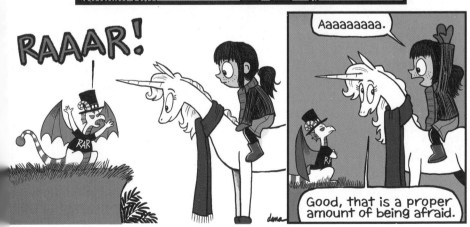

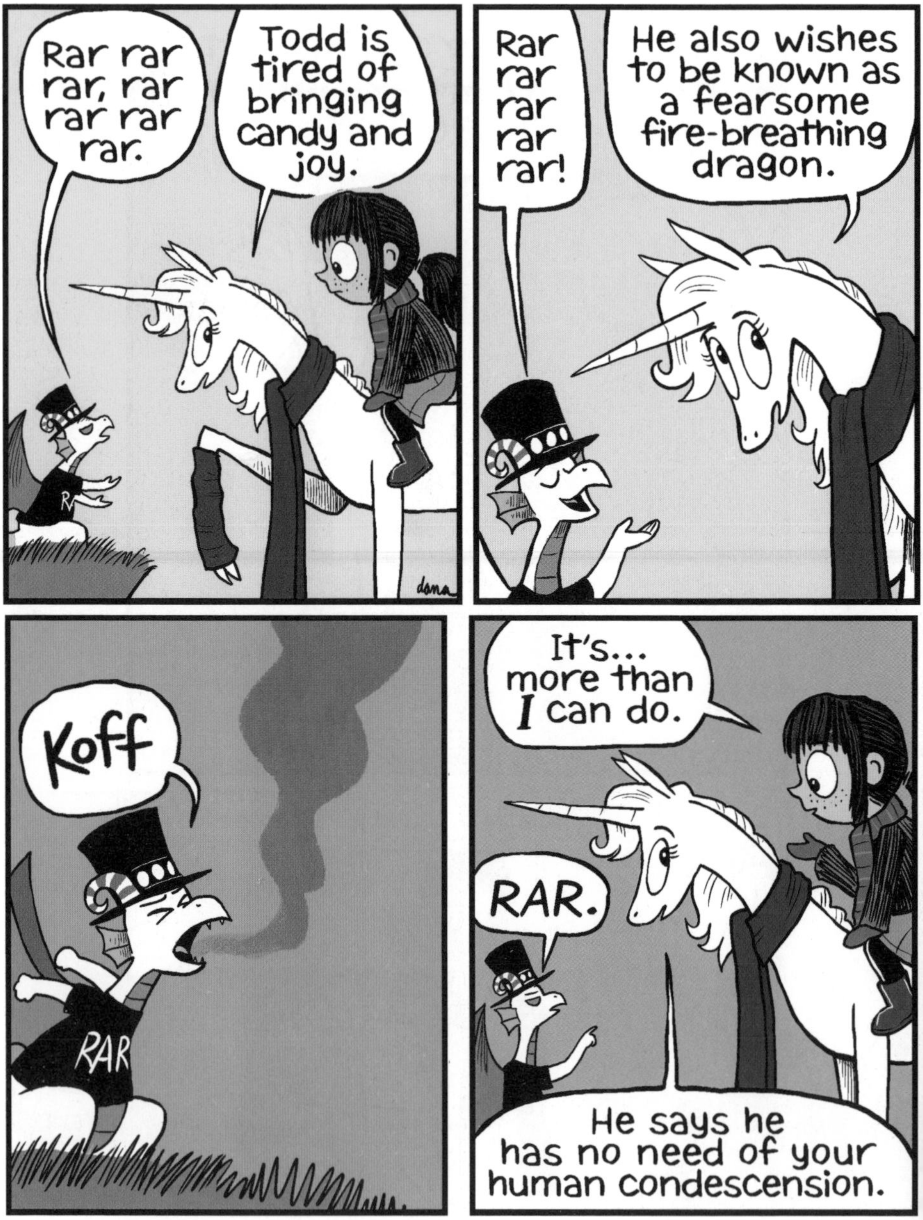
Rar rar rar, rar rar rar rar.
Todd is tired of bringing candy and joy.
Rar rar rar rar rar!
He also wishes to be known as a fearsome fire-breathing dragon.
Koff
RAR
It's... more than I can do.
RAR.
He says he has no need of your human condescension.

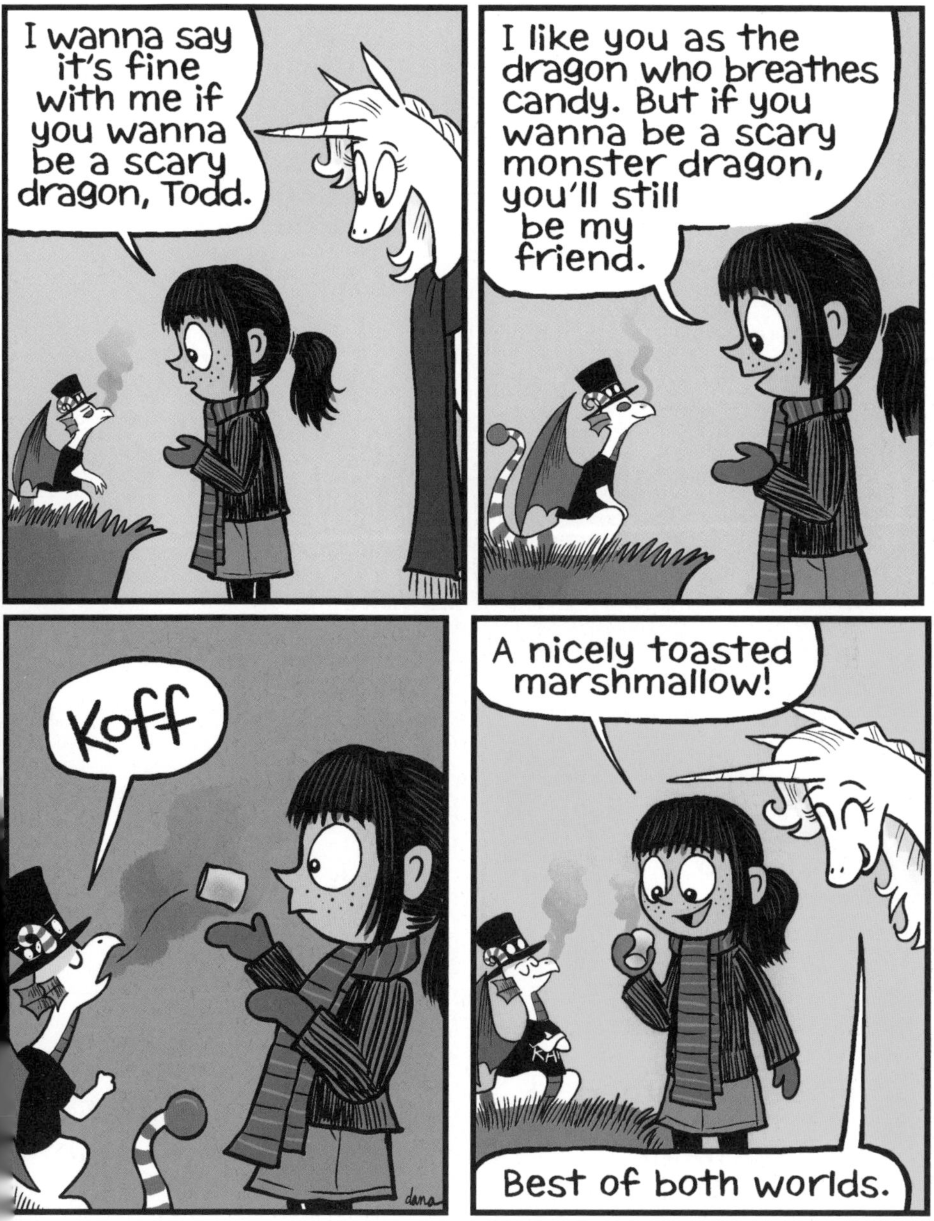
I wanna say it's fine with me if you wanna be a scary dragon, Todd.
I like you as the dragon who breathes candy. But if you wanna be a scary monster dragon, you'll still be my friend.
Koff
A nicely toasted marshmallow!
Best of both worlds.

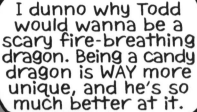

I dunno why Todd would wanna be a scary fire-breathing dragon. Being a candy dragon is WAY more unique, and he's so much better at it.

I think many of us sometimes rebel against the roles life has assigned us, however good they may seem from the outside.

Do you ever get tired of being a unicorn?

Honestly, I have daydreamed of being the only thing twice as magical and sparkling as a unicorn.

Two unicorns?

TWO UNI-
...yes.

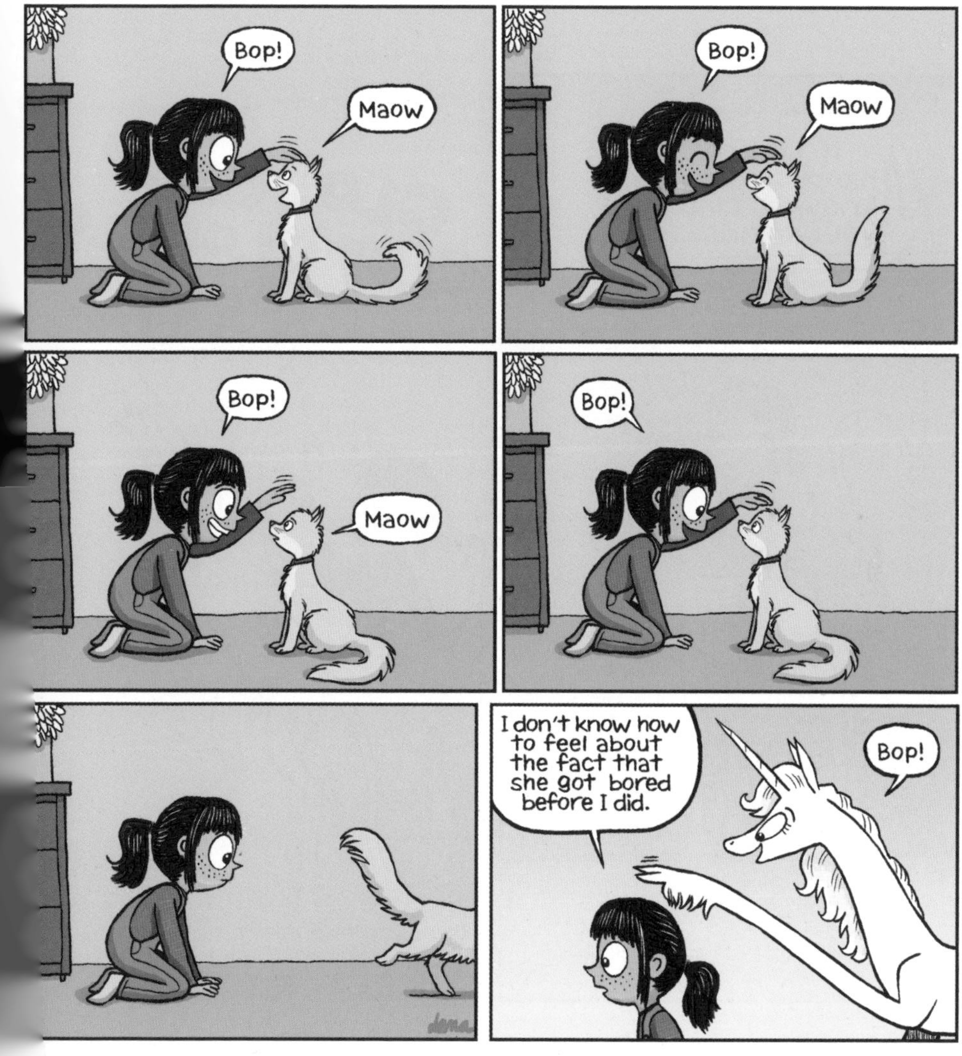
Bop!
Maow
Bop!
Maow
Bop!
Maow
Bop!
I don't know how to feel about the fact that she got bored before I did.
Bop!

If you're happy and you know it, clap your hands...
CLOP CLOP
CLOP CLOP CLOP CLOP

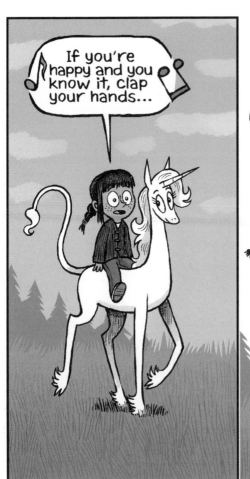

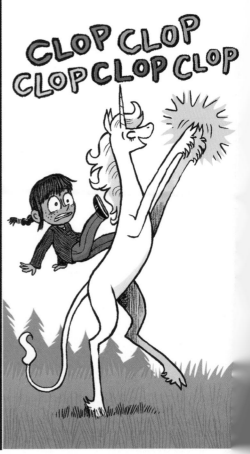

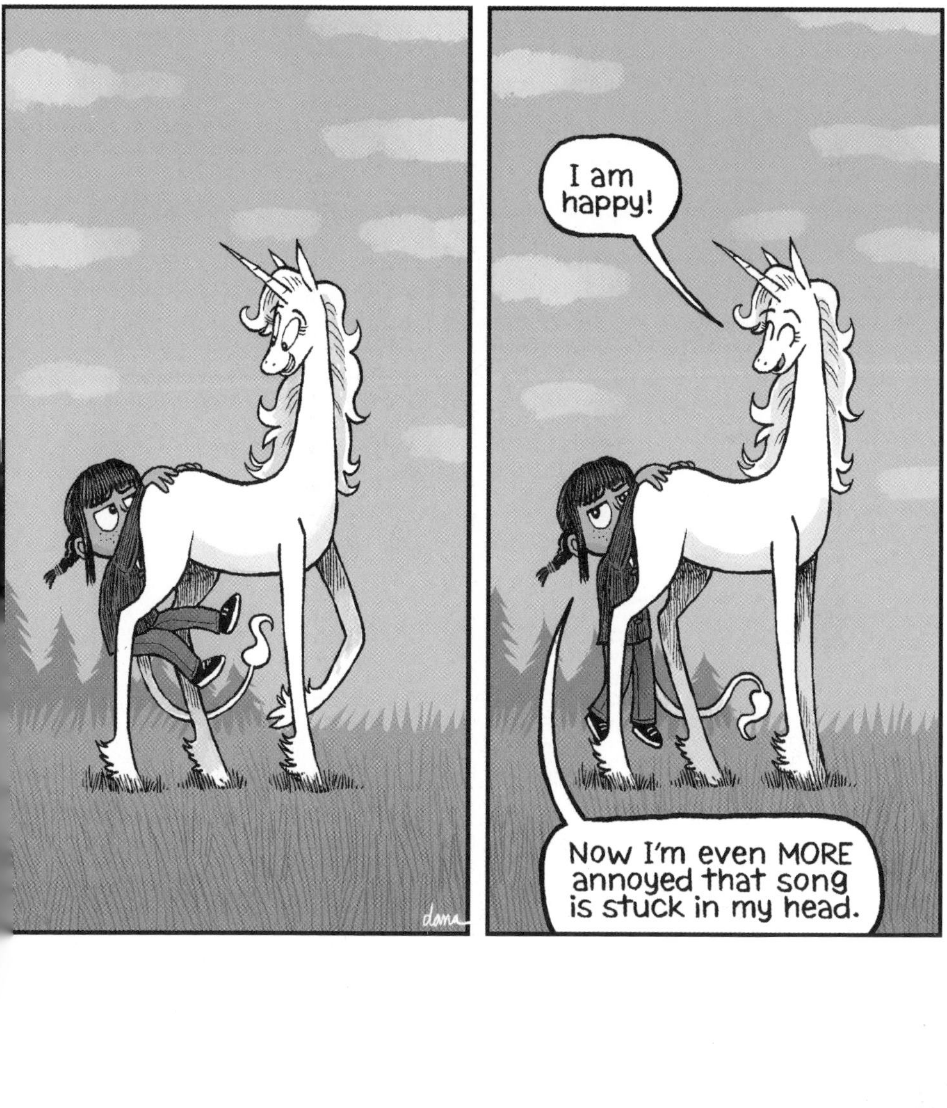
I am happy!
Now I'm even MORE annoyed that song is stuck in my head.
dana

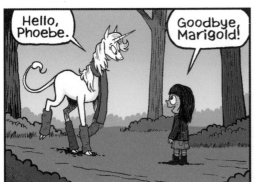

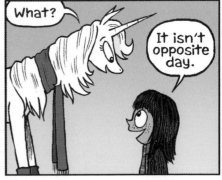

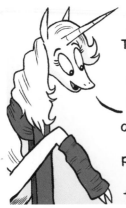

Hello, Phoebe.
Goodbye, Marigold!
What?
It isn't opposite day.
Ah, I know of this day. This human ritual wherein one says the OPPOSITE of what one means.
I shall participate in this human tradition.
I am horrid! I am NOT the loveliest creature in this forest!

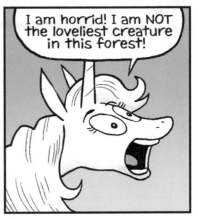

My nose is bulbous and not at all delicate! My hooves are big and clumsy! My legs are stumpy and awkward! My mane is stringy and ill-groomed! And I smell like unwashed human feet!

Delete the video of me saying those things.

Yes.

I dislike opposite day.

It totally isn't my favorite day.

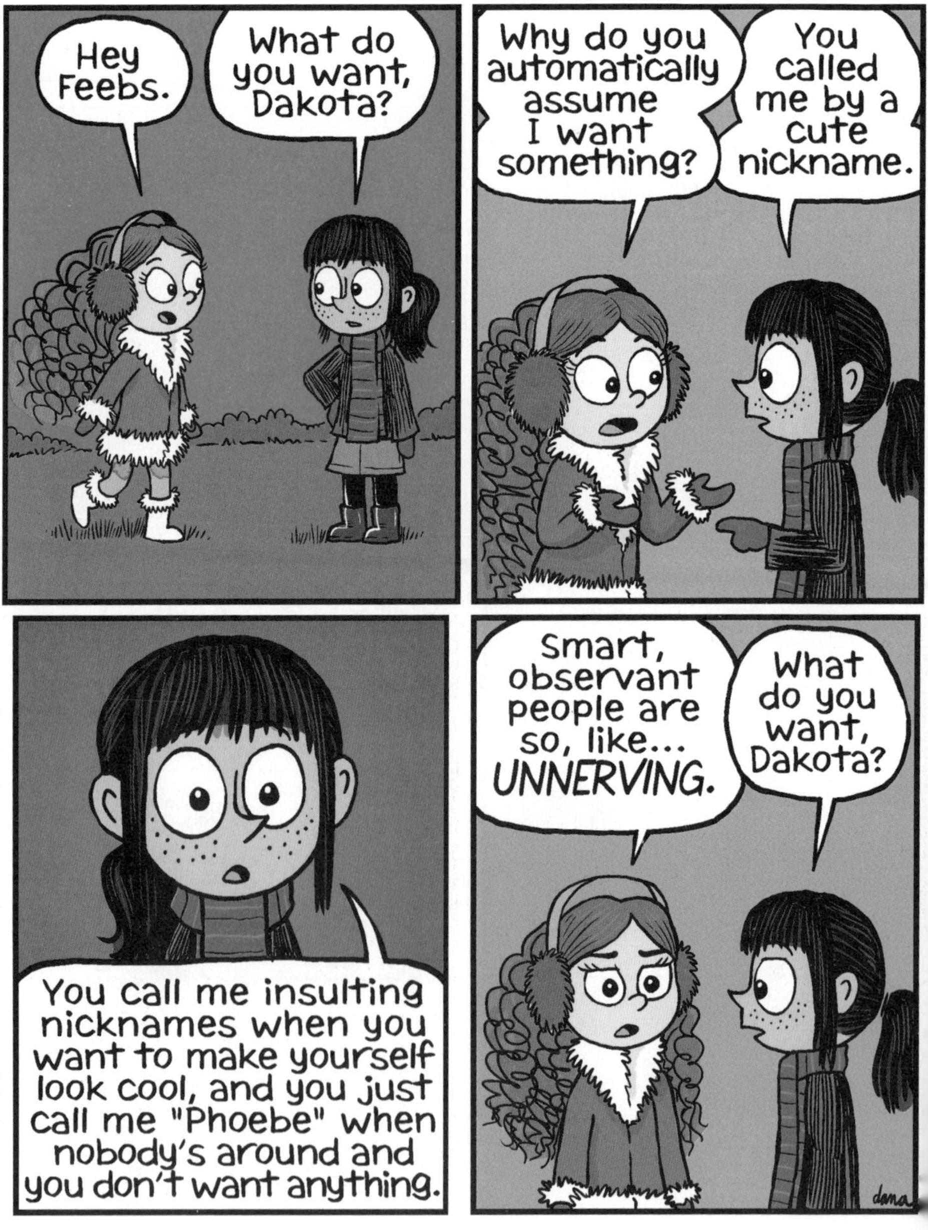
Hey Feebs.
What do you want, Dakota?
Why do you automatically assume I want something?
You called me by a cute nickname.
You call me insulting nicknames when you want to make yourself look cool, and you just call me "Phoebe" when nobody's around and you don't want anything.
Smart, observant people are so, like... UNNERVING.
What do you want, Dakota?
dana

I need to tell you something, and you gotta promise you won't laugh at me.
My cooler friends would, but you I think I can trust.
...I promise.
Okay. Here it is...
I think I'm being haunted.
HA!
dana

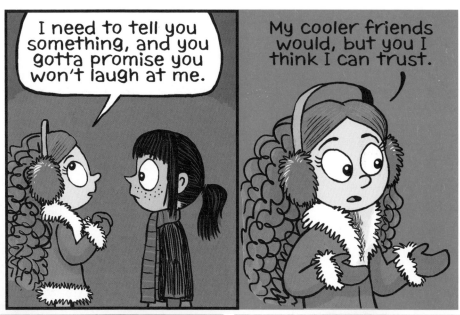

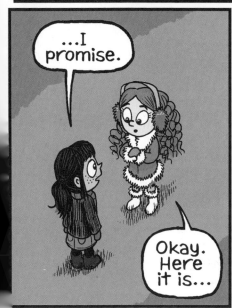

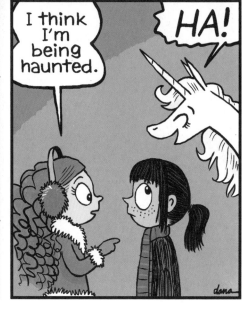

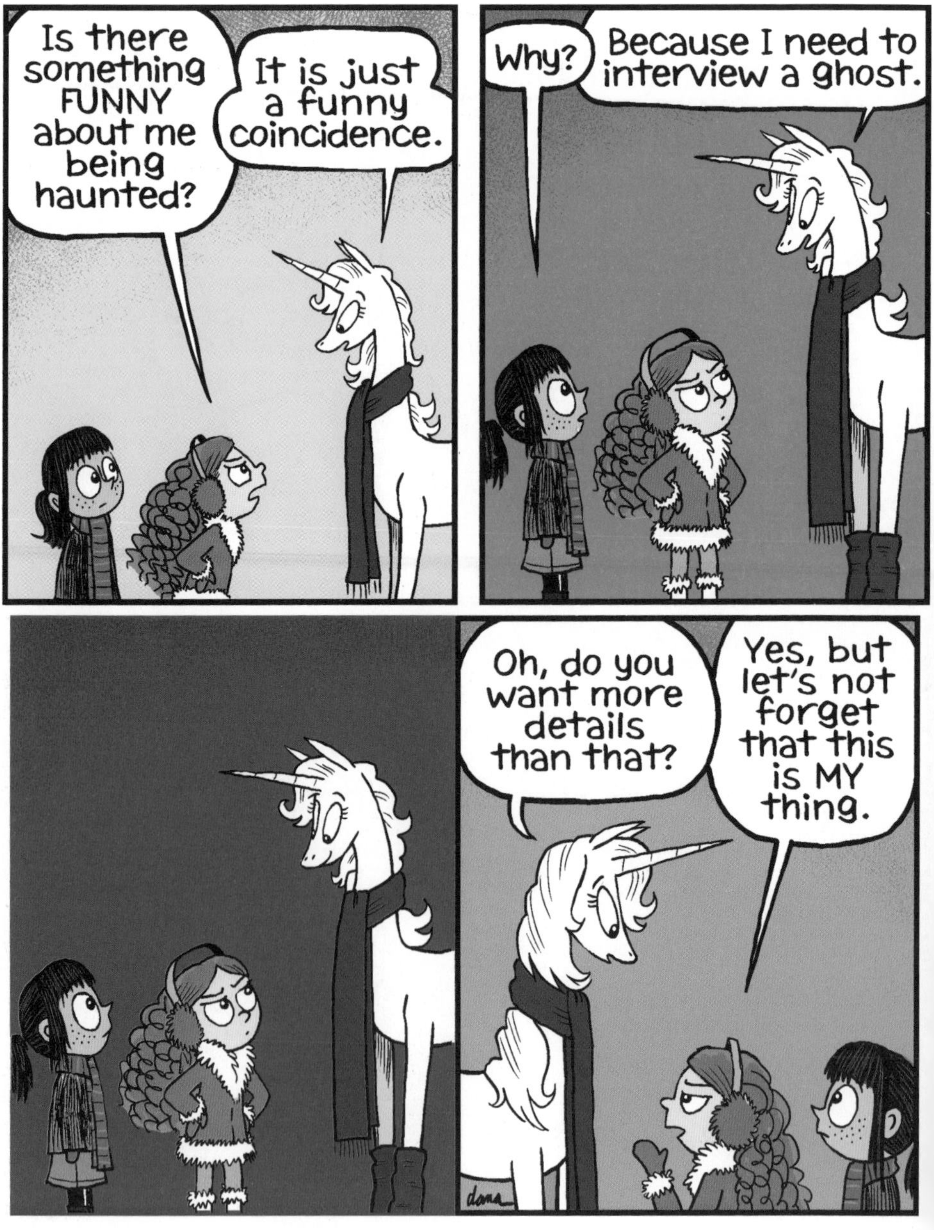

Is there something FUNNY about me being haunted?
It is just a funny coincidence.
Why?
Because I need to interview a ghost.
Oh, do you want more details than that?
Yes, but let's not forget that this is MY thing.
dana

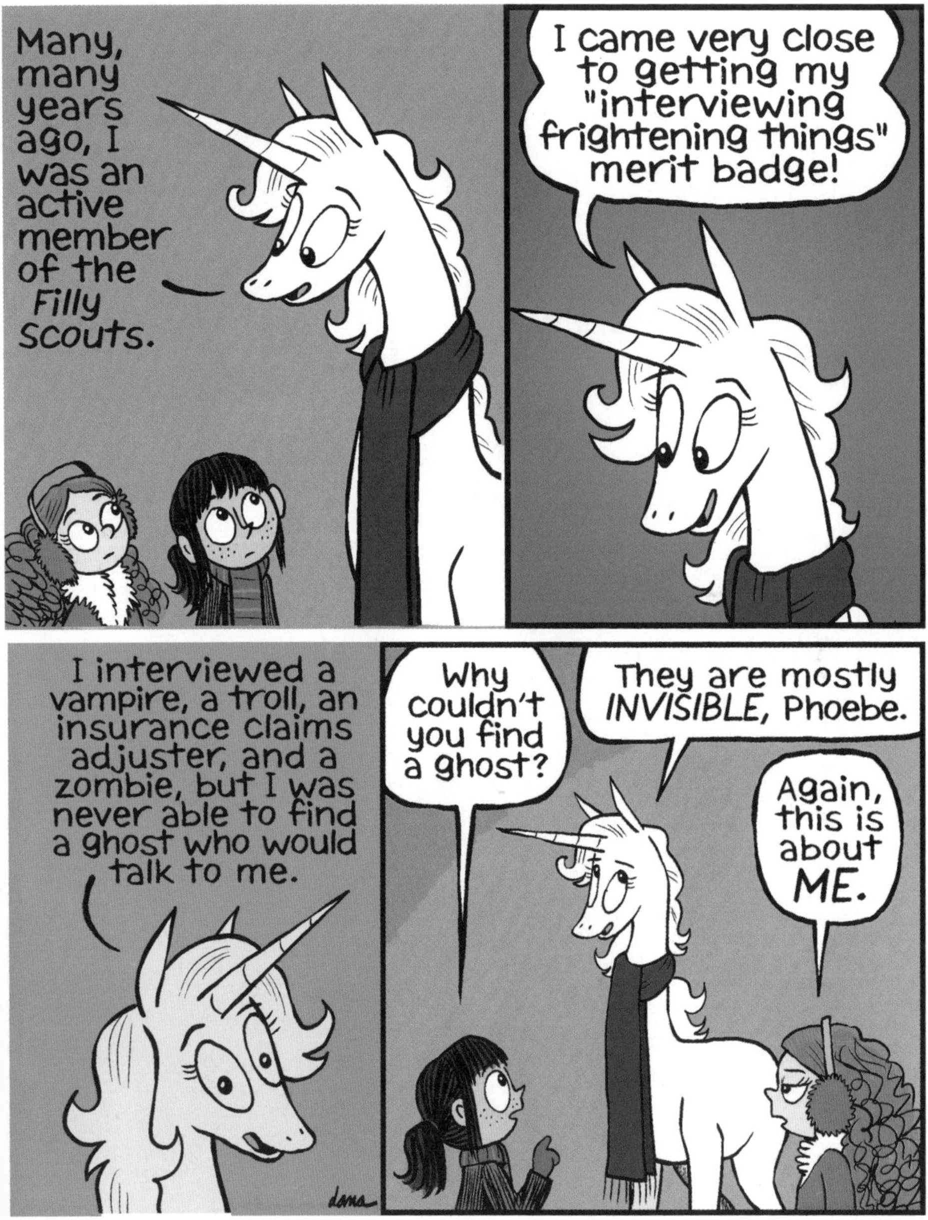

Many, many years ago, I was an active member of the *Filly scouts.*
I came very close to getting my "interviewing frightening things" merit badge!
I interviewed a vampire, a troll, an insurance claims adjuster, and a zombie, but I was never able to find a ghost who would talk to me.
Why couldn't you find a ghost?
They are mostly *INVISIBLE*, Phoebe.
Again, this is about **ME.**
dana

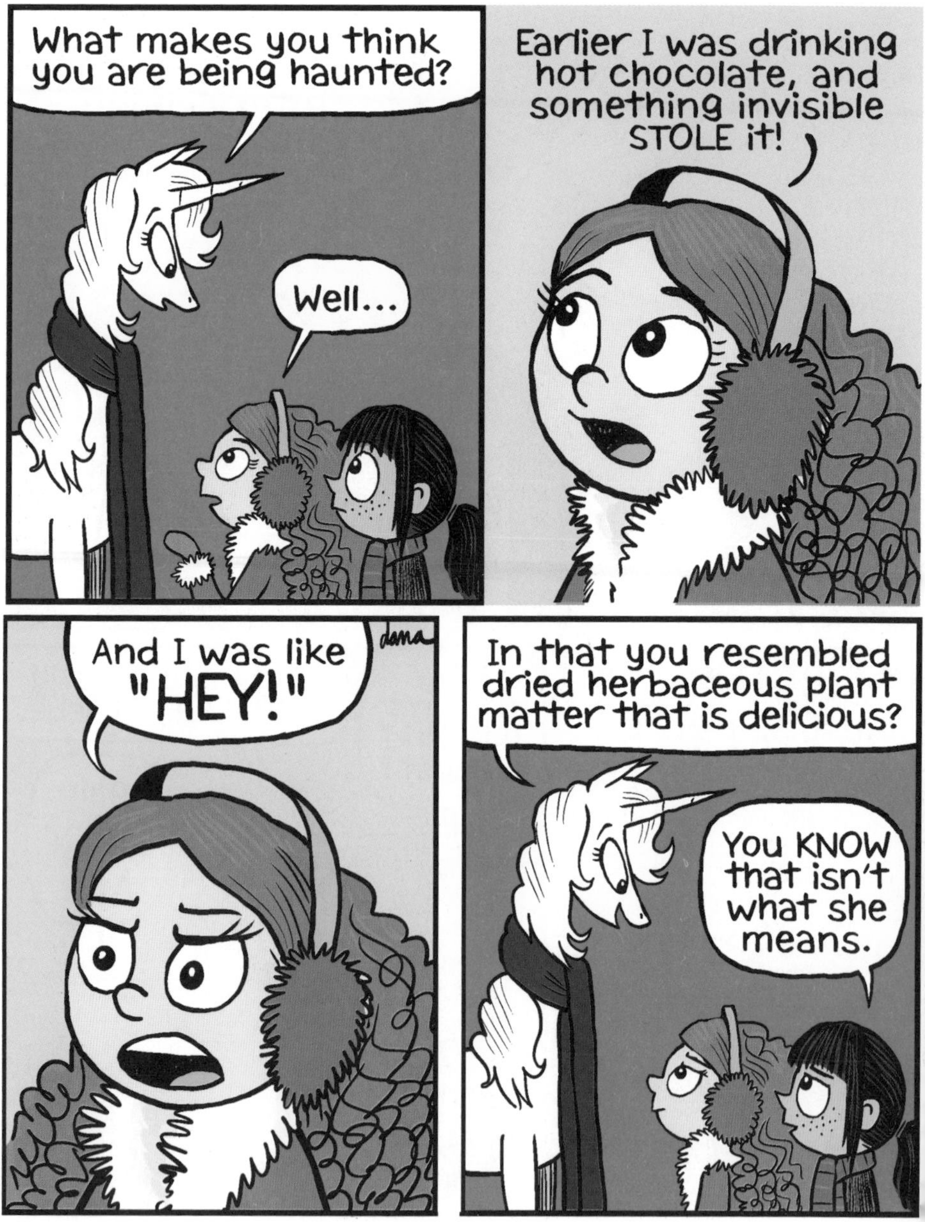
What makes you think you are being haunted?
Well...
Earlier I was drinking hot chocolate, and something invisible STOLE it!
And I was like "HEY!"
dana
In that you resembled dried herbaceous plant matter that is delicious?
You KNOW that isn't what she means.

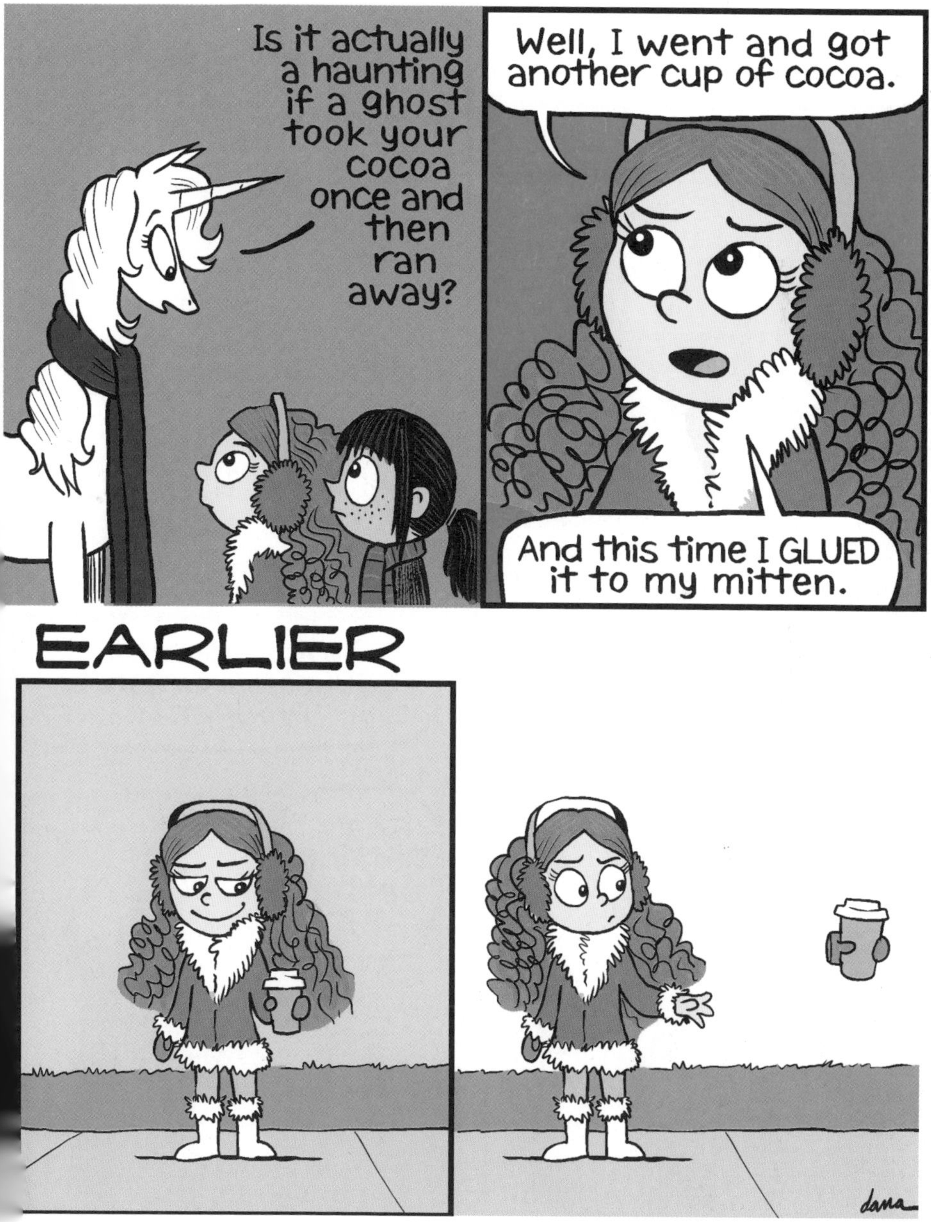

Is it actually a haunting if a ghost took your cocoa once and then ran away?
Well, I went and got another cup of cocoa.
And this time I GLUED it to my mitten.
EARLIER
dana

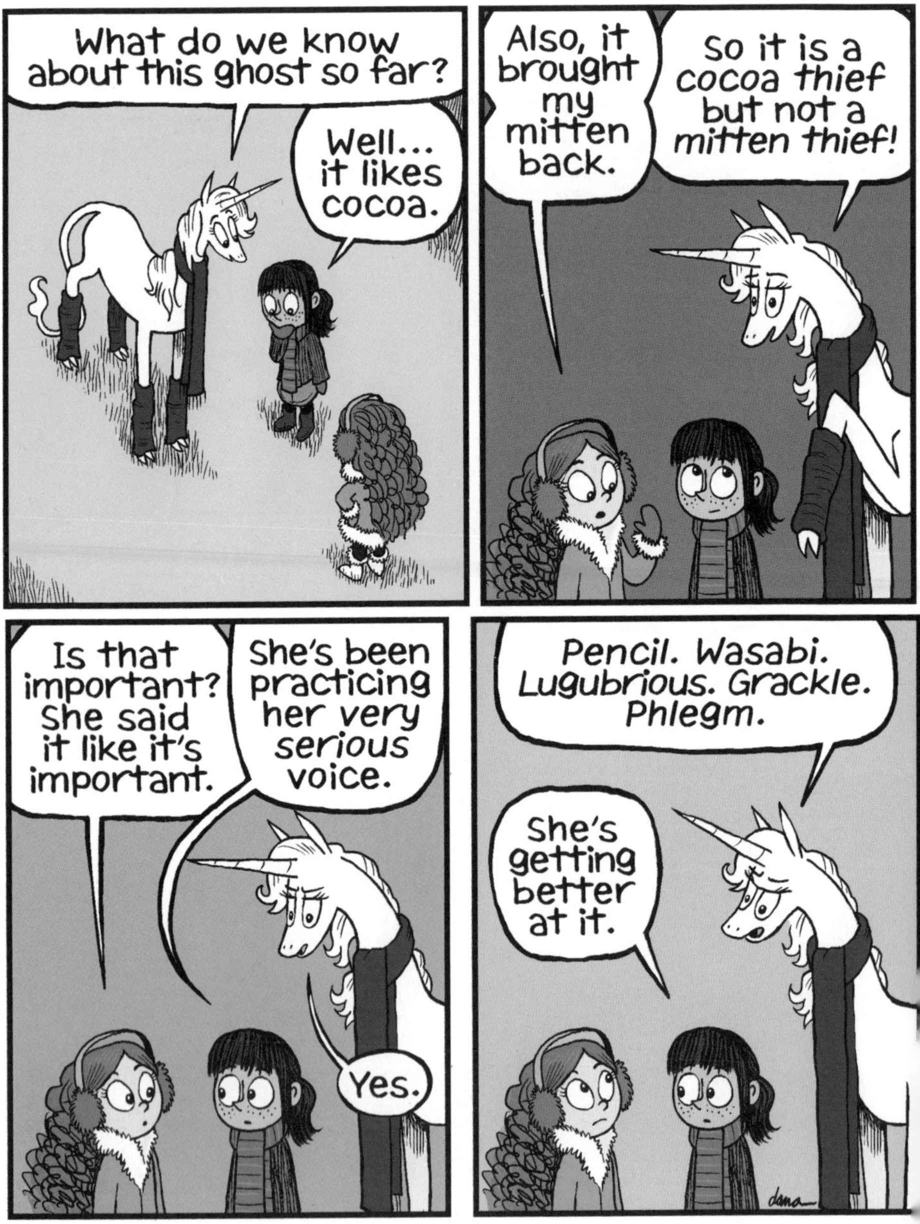
What do we know about this ghost so far?
Well... it likes cocoa.
Also, it brought my mitten back.
So it is a cocoa thief but not a mitten thief!
Is that important? She said it like it's important.
She's been practicing her very serious voice.
Yes.
Pencil. Wasabi. Lugubrious. Grackle. Phlegm.
She's getting better at it.
dana

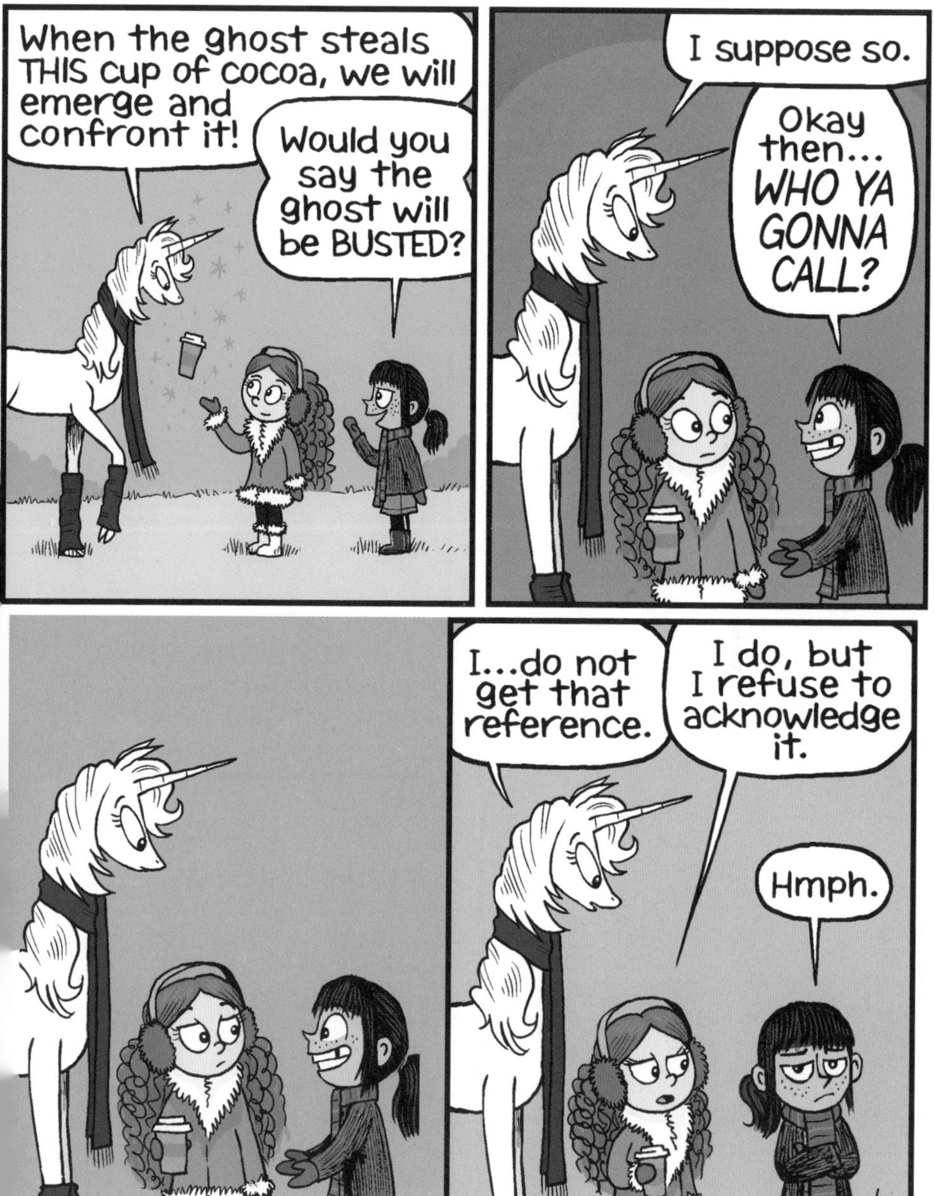

When the ghost steals THIS cup of cocoa, we will emerge and confront it!
Would you say the ghost will be BUSTED?
I suppose so.
Okay then... WHO YA GONNA CALL?
I...do not get that reference.
I do, but I refuse to acknowledge it.
Hmph.

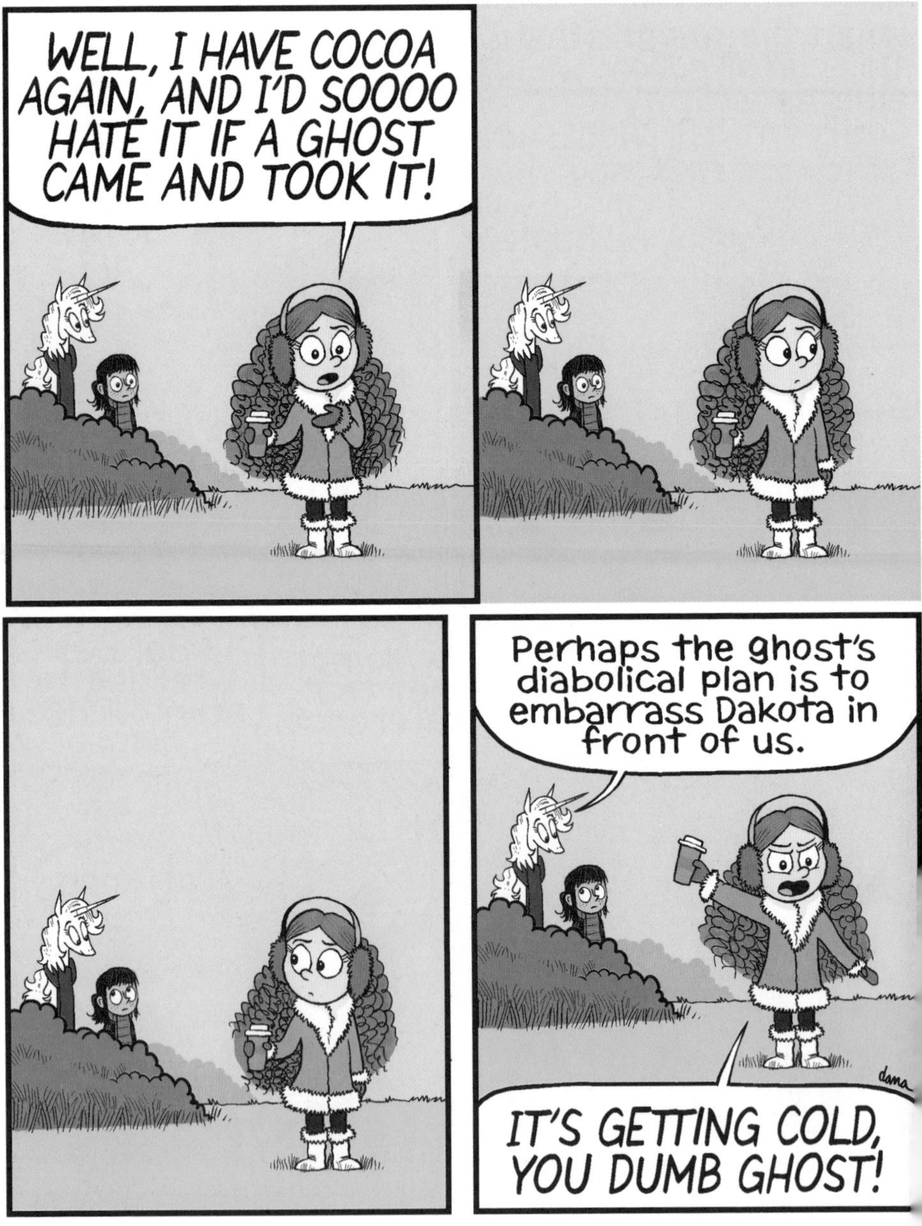
WELL, I HAVE COCOA AGAIN, AND I'D SOOOO HATE IT IF A GHOST CAME AND TOOK IT!
Perhaps the ghost's diabolical plan is to embarrass Dakota in front of us.
IT'S GETTING COLD, YOU DUMB GHOST!
dana

IT'S THE GHOST! QUICK! HIT IT WITH THE GHOST-REVEALING SPELL!!!
FLOUR
FLOUR
FOOMF
FLOUR
That's not a spell!
I did not SAY it was a spell. You just assumed that.
dana

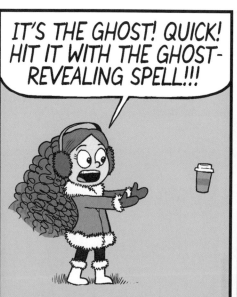

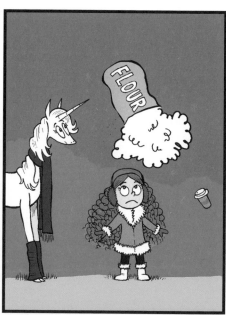

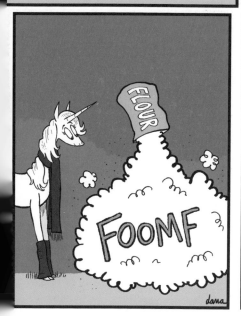

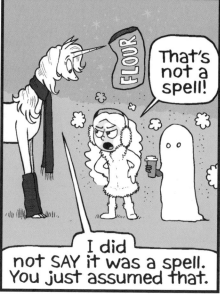

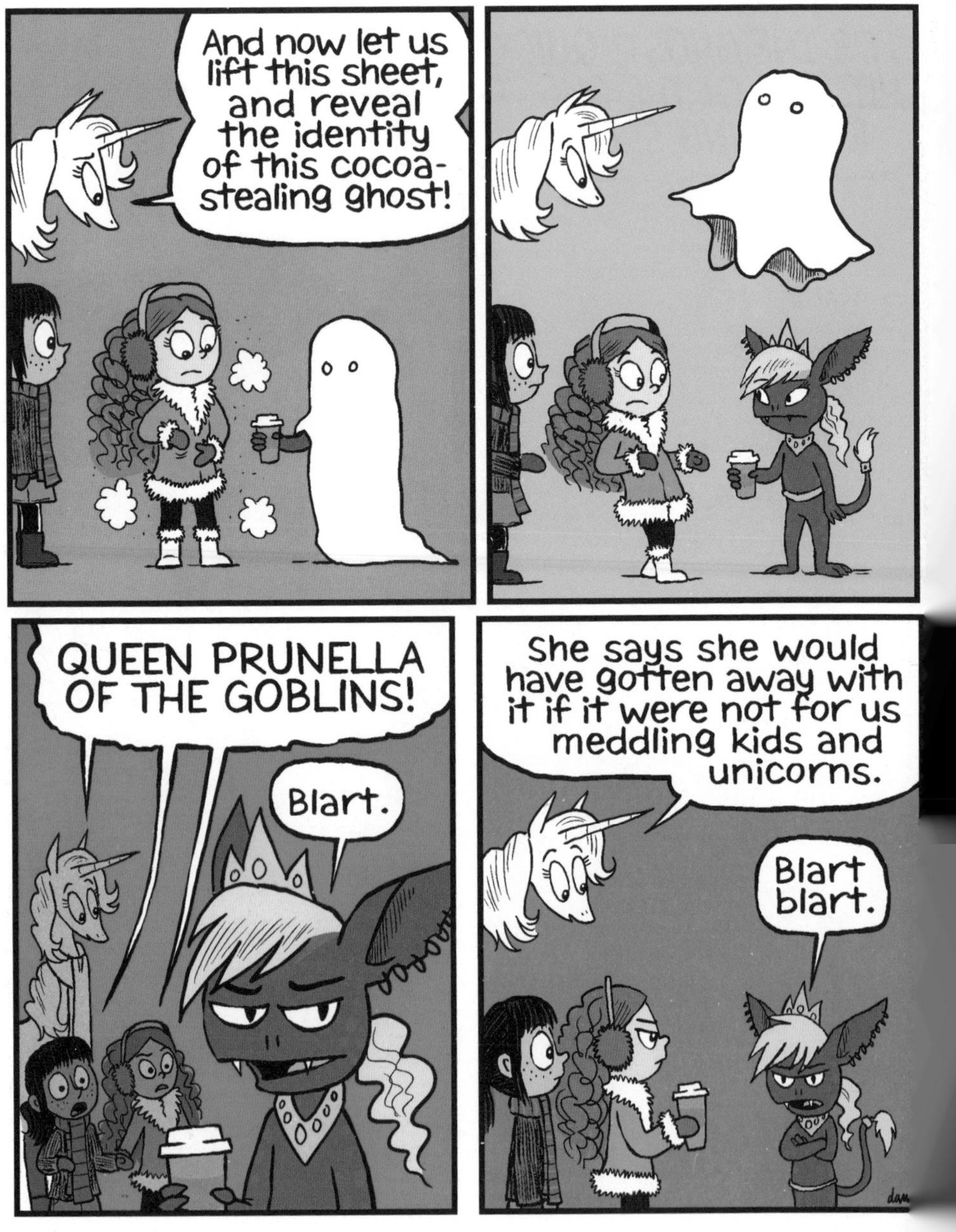
And now let us lift this sheet, and reveal the identity of this cocoa-stealing ghost!
QUEEN PRUNELLA OF THE GOBLINS!
Blart.
She says she would have gotten away with it if it were not for us meddling kids and unicorns.
Blart blart.

Blaart blart BLART, blärt blart blaart blärt blart.

Queen Prunella has been wearing an invisibility sheet and pretending to be a ghost and stealing your cocoa because...

BLÄAART.

Because.

Honestly, that does strike me as a good enough reason.

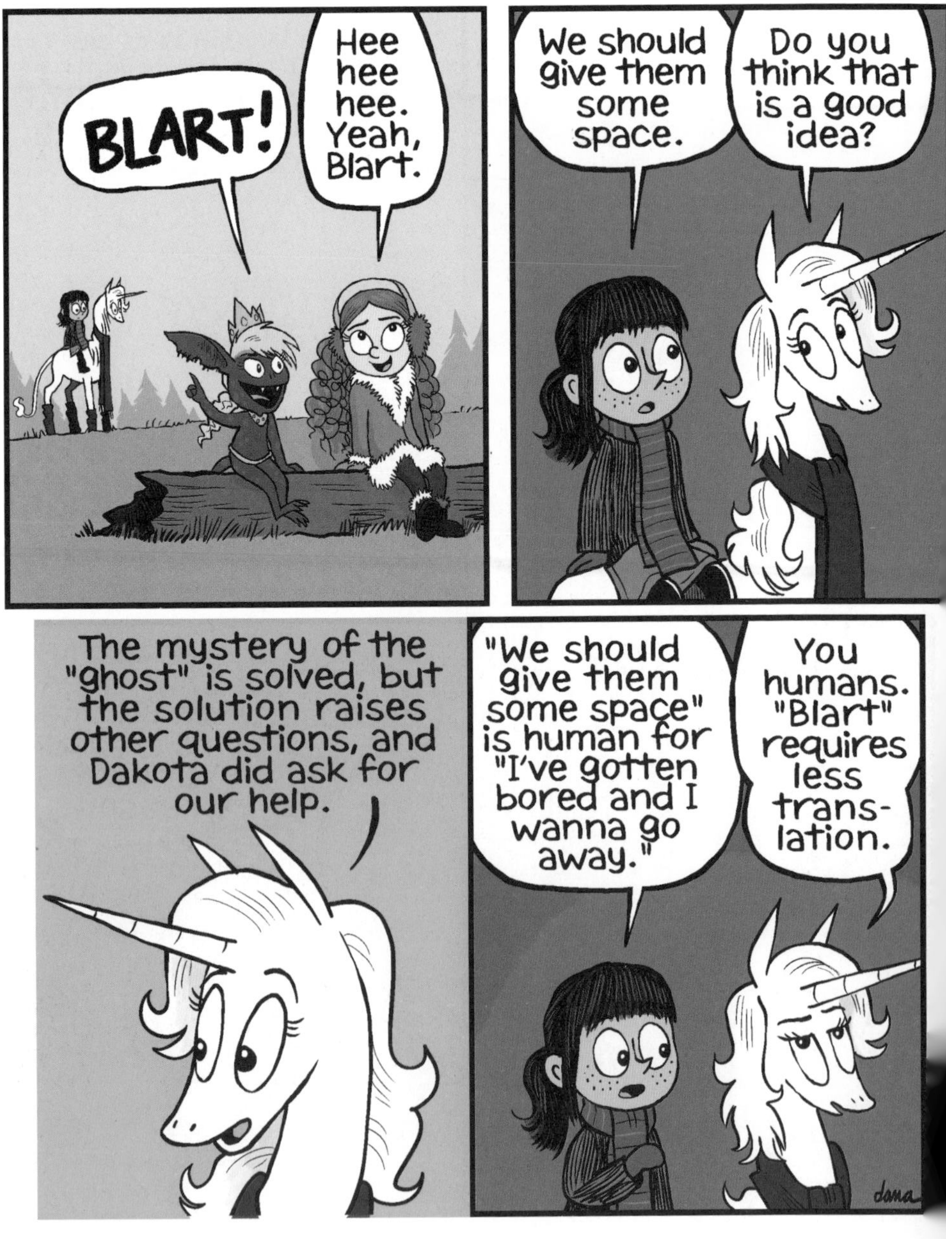
BLART!
Hee hee hee. Yeah, Blart.
We should give them some space.
Do you think that is a good idea?
The mystery of the "ghost" is solved, but the solution raises other questions, and Dakota did ask for our help.
"We should give them some space" is human for "I've gotten bored and I wanna go away."
You humans. "Blart" requires less trans-lation.
dana

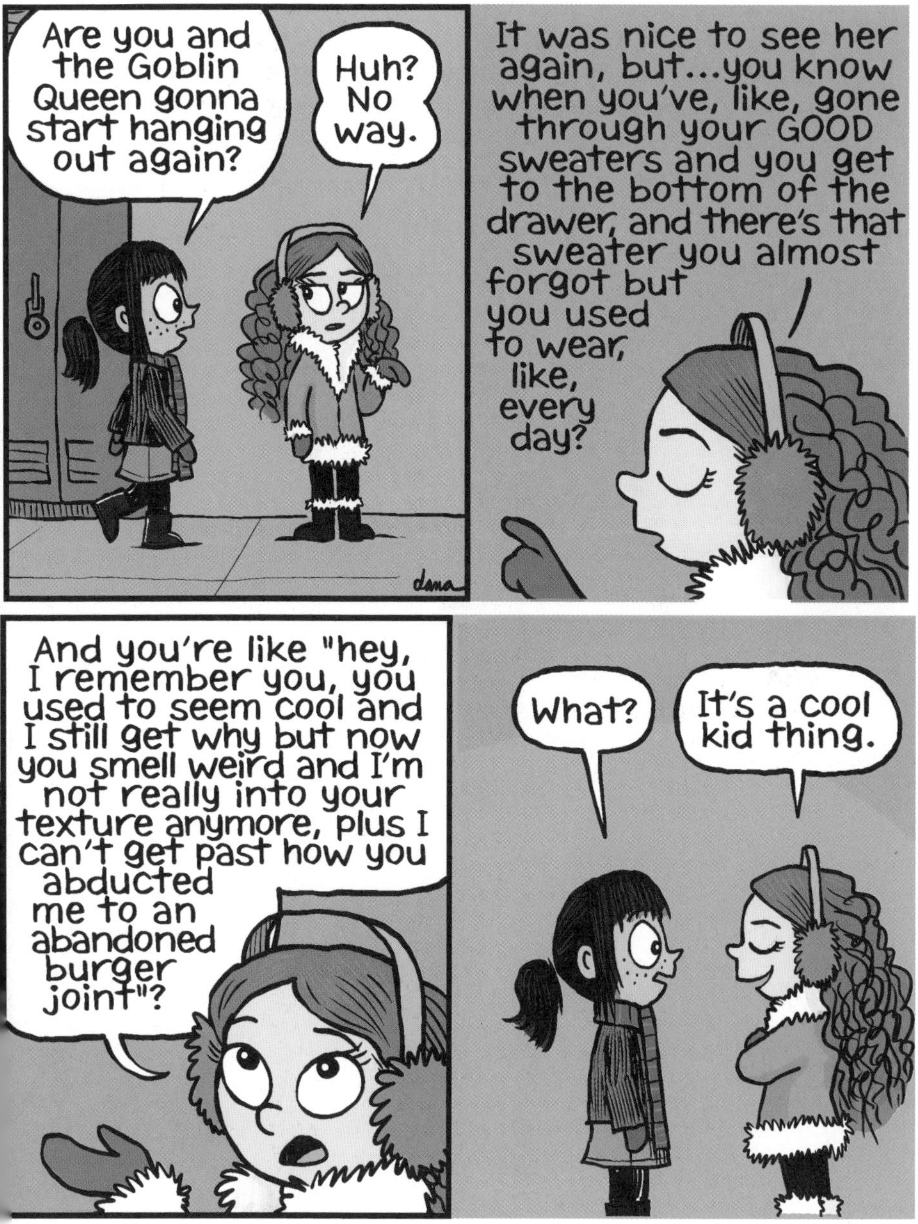
Are you and the Goblin Queen gonna start hanging out again?
Huh? No way.
dana
It was nice to see her again, but...you know when you've, like, gone through your GOOD sweaters and you get to the bottom of the drawer, and there's that sweater you almost forgot but you used to wear, like, every day?
And you're like "hey, I remember you, you used to seem cool and I still get why but now you smell weird and I'm not really into your texture anymore, plus I can't get past how you abducted me to an abandoned burger joint"?
What?
It's a cool kid thing.

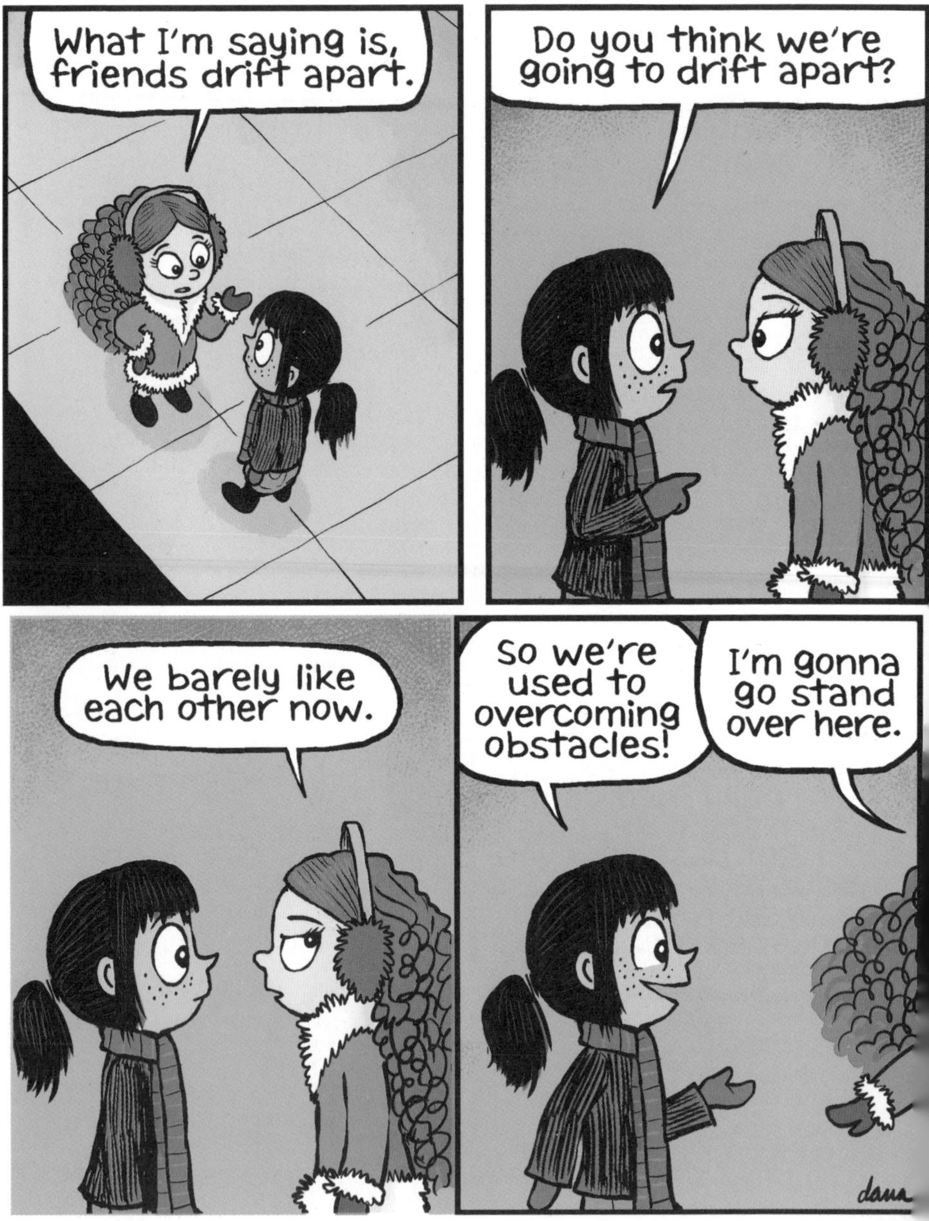
What I'm saying is, friends drift apart.
Do you think we're going to drift apart?
We barely like each other now.
So we're used to overcoming obstacles!
I'm gonna go stand over here.
dana

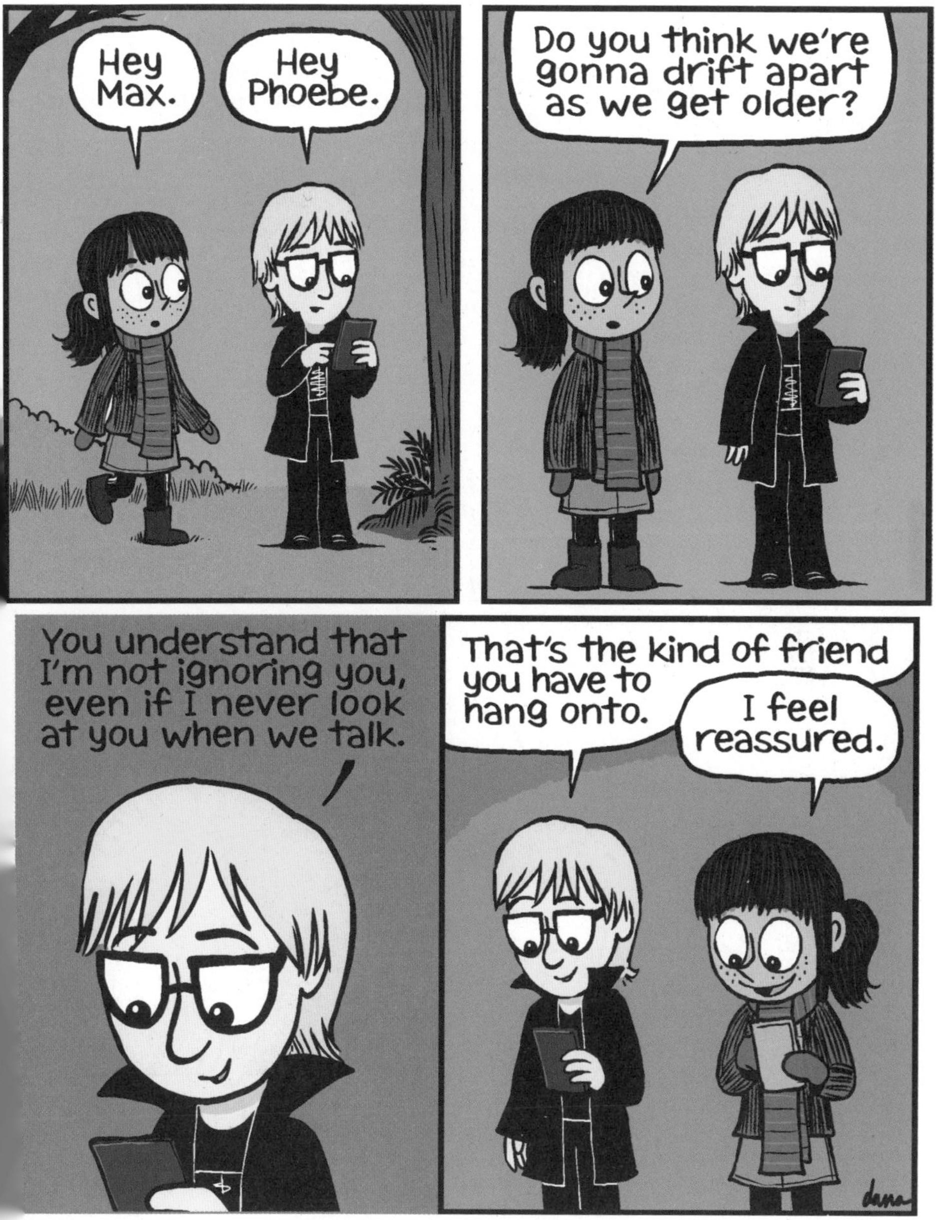
Hey Max.
Hey Phoebe.
Do you think we're gonna drift apart as we get older?
You understand that I'm not ignoring you, even if I never look at you when we talk.
That's the kind of friend you have to hang onto.
I feel reassured.
dana

Marigold? Do you think we're going to drift apart as we get older?
I...do not really think I GET older. I am an ageless magical being.
Do YOU plan to change as you get older?
I'll be a teenager in a few years.
AAAAA!!!
That isn't SUPER reassuring.
dana

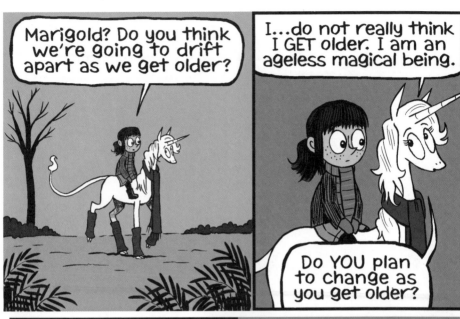

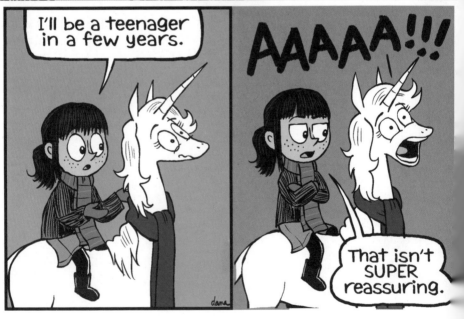

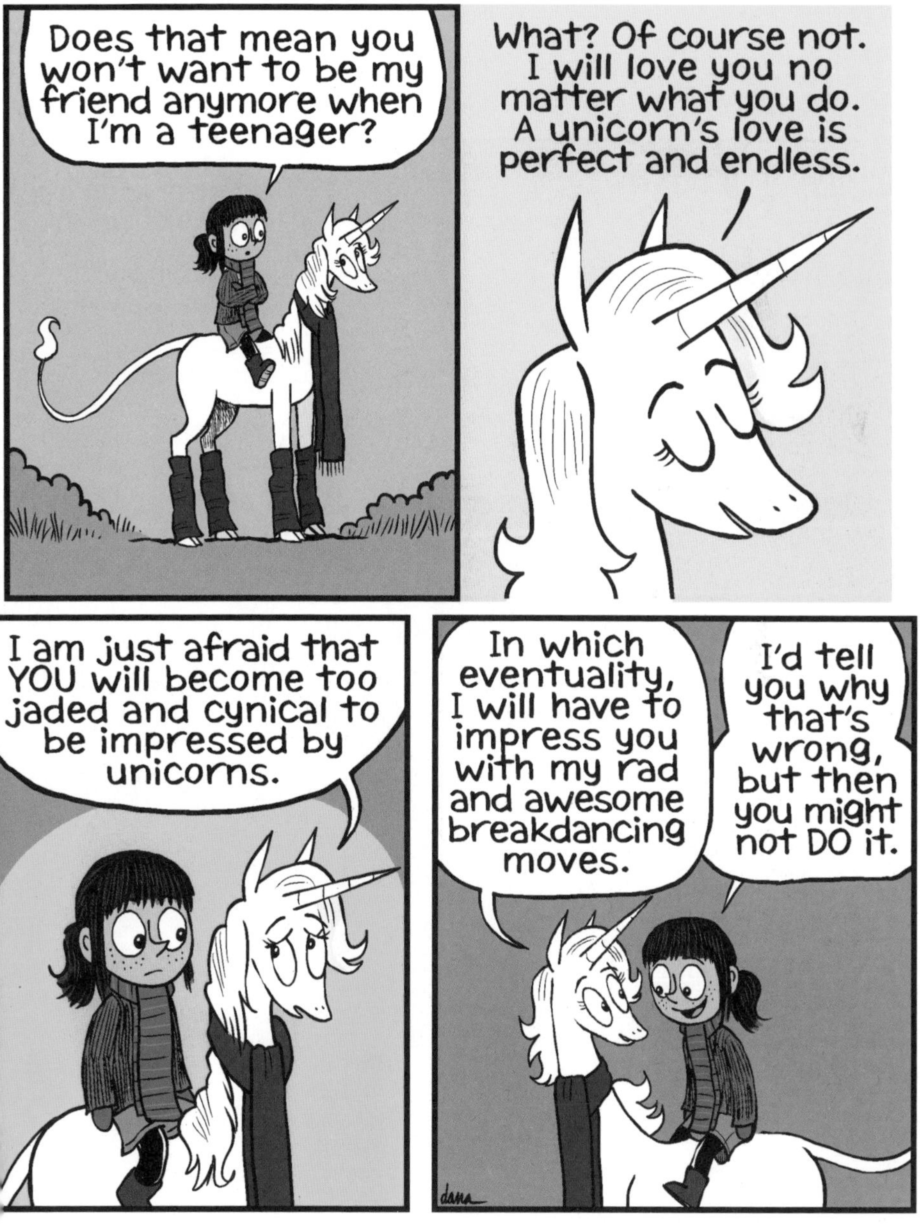
Does that mean you won't want to be my friend anymore when I'm a teenager?
What? Of course not. I will love you no matter what you do. A unicorn's love is perfect and endless.
I am just afraid that YOU will become too jaded and cynical to be impressed by unicorns.
In which eventuality, I will have to impress you with my rad and awesome breakdancing moves.
I'd tell you why that's wrong, but then you might not DO it.
dana

What if you're not really here?
But I am here.
Right, but what if you're a figment of my overactive young imagination?
If I am not real, who is carrying you down this forest path?
Maybe I *WALKED* here.
Your shoes.
What about them?

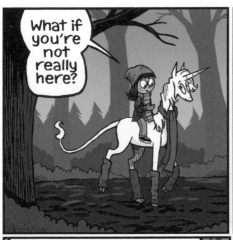

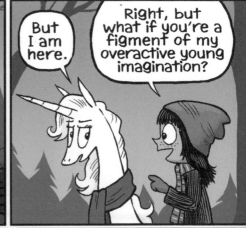

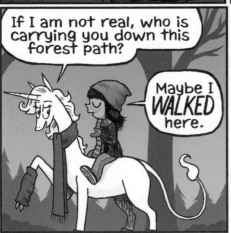

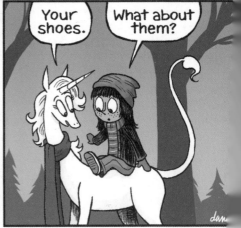

They are clean. If you had walked down this path today, they would be muddy.

That's true. Unless...

Maybe you're a figment of my imagination, and also I can FLY!

I am afraid you will have to accept that you rode here on a unicorn.

I guess we all gotta face reality sometime.

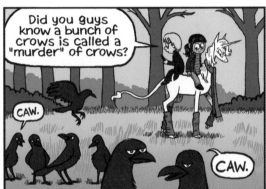

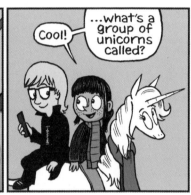

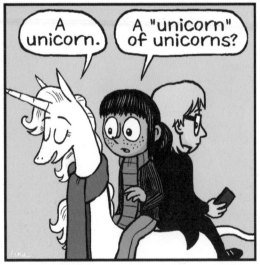

Did you guys know a bunch of crows is called a "murder" of crows?
CAW.
CAW.
Cool!
...what's a group of unicorns called?
A unicorn.
A "unicorn" of unicorns?
Every unicorn is perfect individually, so no word but "unicorn" could ever hope to describe us.

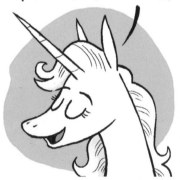

The internet thinks it's a "blessing" of unicorns.

The internet thinks a LOT of things.

Do...unicorns have a word for a bunch of humans?

We usually just say "an uncomfortably huge number of fingers."

Jealous much?

By the way, a word that means a group of something is called a "collective noun."

CAW.

CAW.

What're you watching?
A show we loved when we were younger.
You don't look happy.
It hasn't aged well.
Thanks for not saying "neither have you two."
I expect a raise in my allowance for that favor.
dana

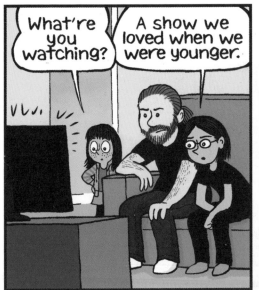

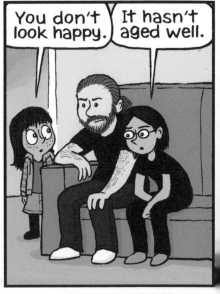

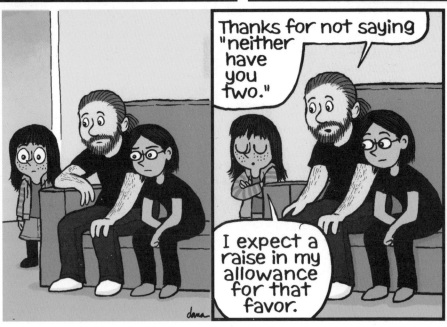

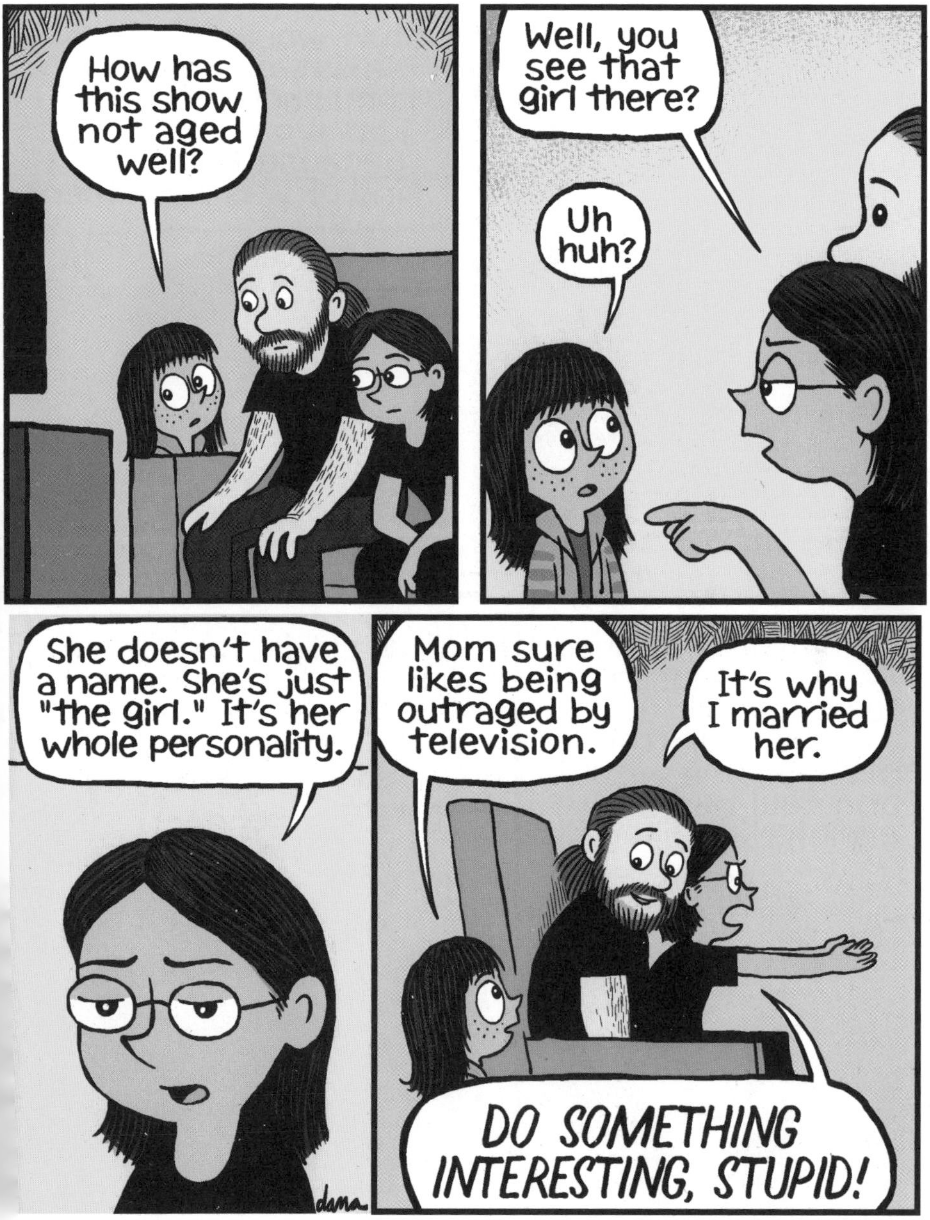
How has this show not aged well?
Well, you see that girl there?
Uh huh?
She doesn't have a name. She's just "the girl." It's her whole personality.
Mom sure likes being outraged by television.
It's why I married her.
DO SOMETHING INTERESTING, STUPID!
dana

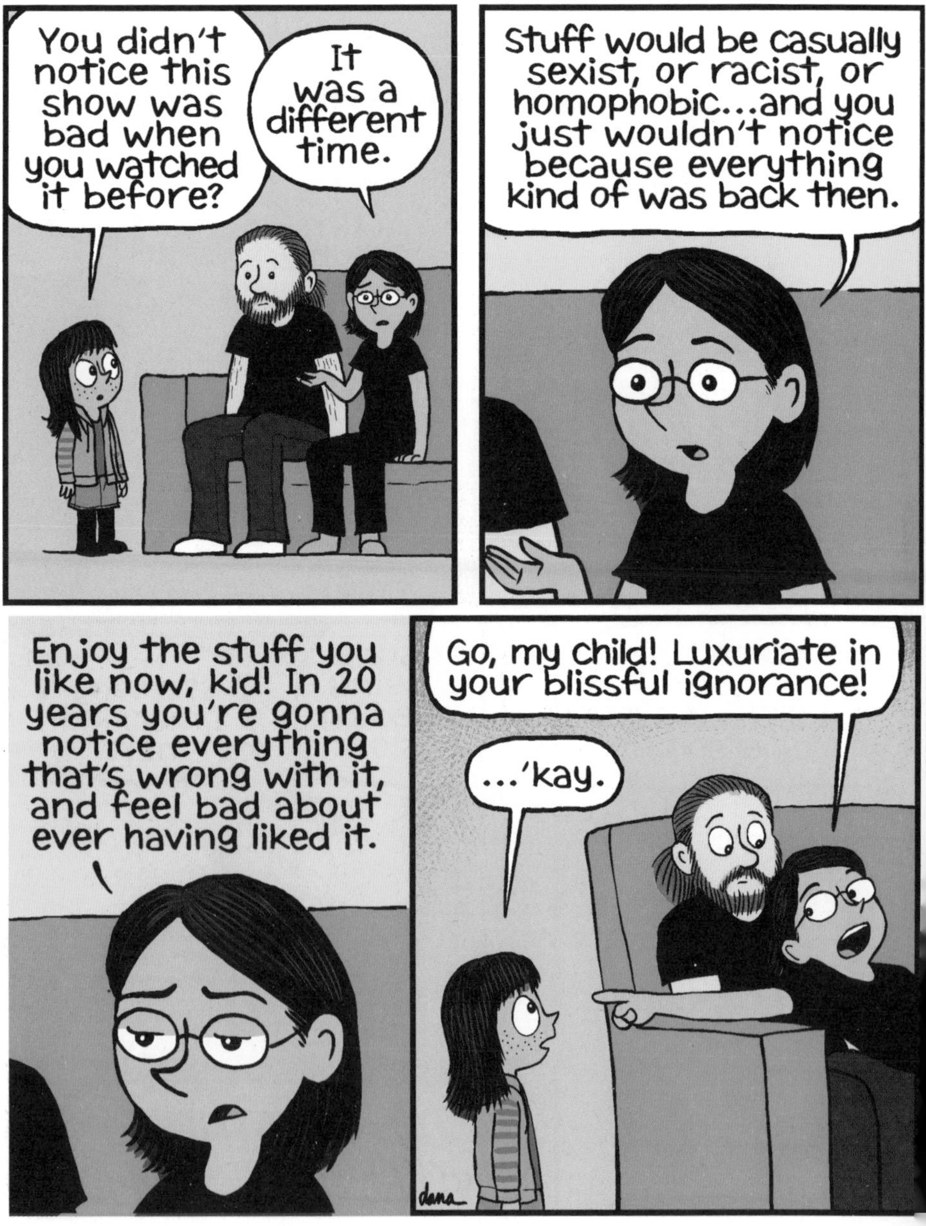
You didn't notice this show was bad when you watched it before?
It was a different time.
Stuff would be casually sexist, or racist, or homophobic...and you just wouldn't notice because everything kind of was back then.
Enjoy the stuff you like now, kid! In 20 years you're gonna notice everything that's wrong with it, and feel bad about ever having liked it.
Go, my child! Luxuriate in your blissful ignorance!
...'kay.
dana

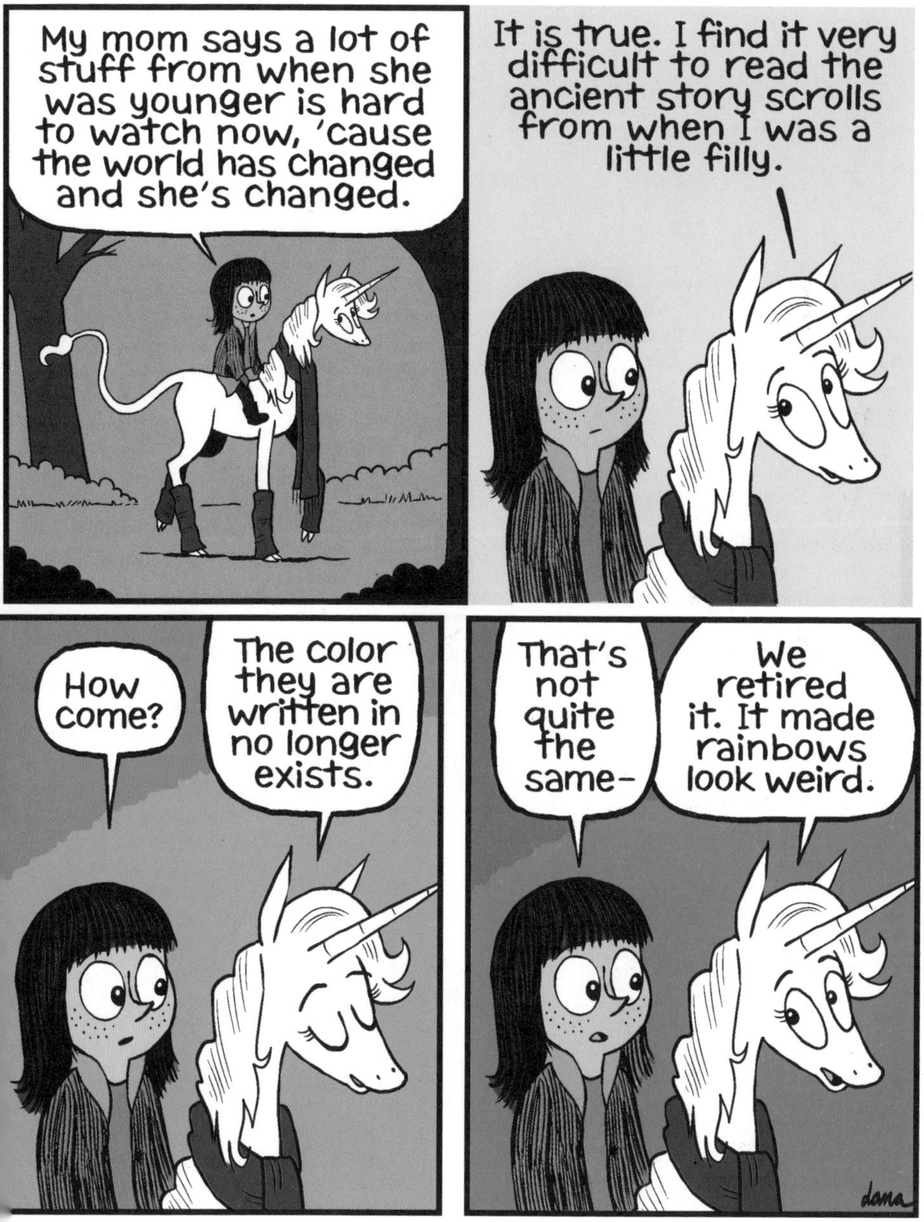
My mom says a lot of stuff from when she was younger is hard to watch now, 'cause the world has changed and she's changed.
It is true. I find it very difficult to read the ancient story scrolls from when I was a little filly.
How come?
The color they are written in no longer exists.
That's not quite the same-
We retired it. It made rainbows look weird.
dana

So you remember "Confetti Canyon"?

Your favorite television program?

It ended a while back.

And now I wonder if I'm still gonna like it when I watch it again! How long does it take for something to get problematic? Is a few months long enough?

We have to binge-watch it. For science.

For *Science*.

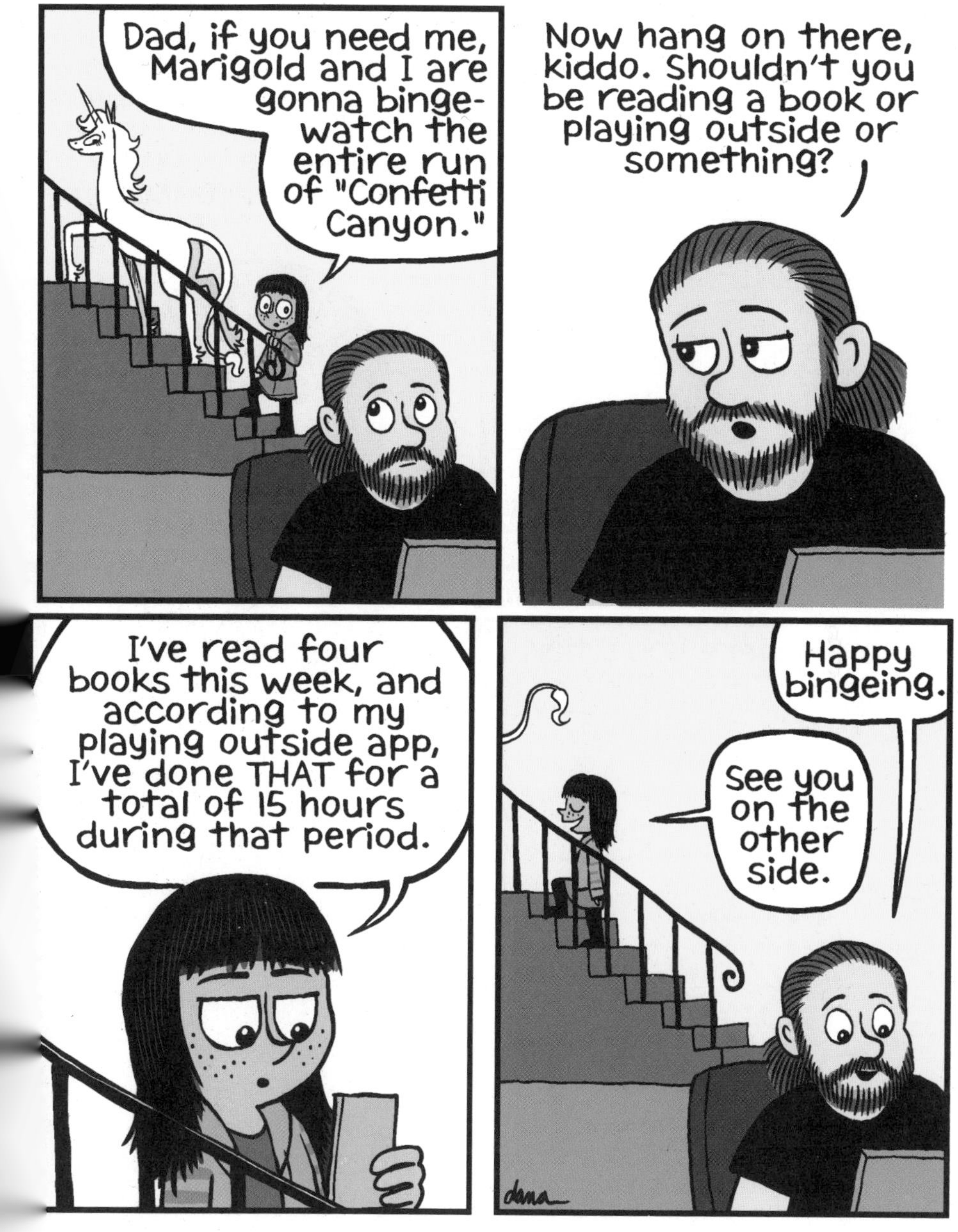
Dad, if you need me, Marigold and I are gonna binge-watch the entire run of "Confetti Canyon."
Now hang on there, kiddo. Shouldn't you be reading a book or playing outside or something?
I've read four books this week, and according to my playing outside app, I've done THAT for a total of 15 hours during that period.
Happy bingeing.
See you on the other side.
dana

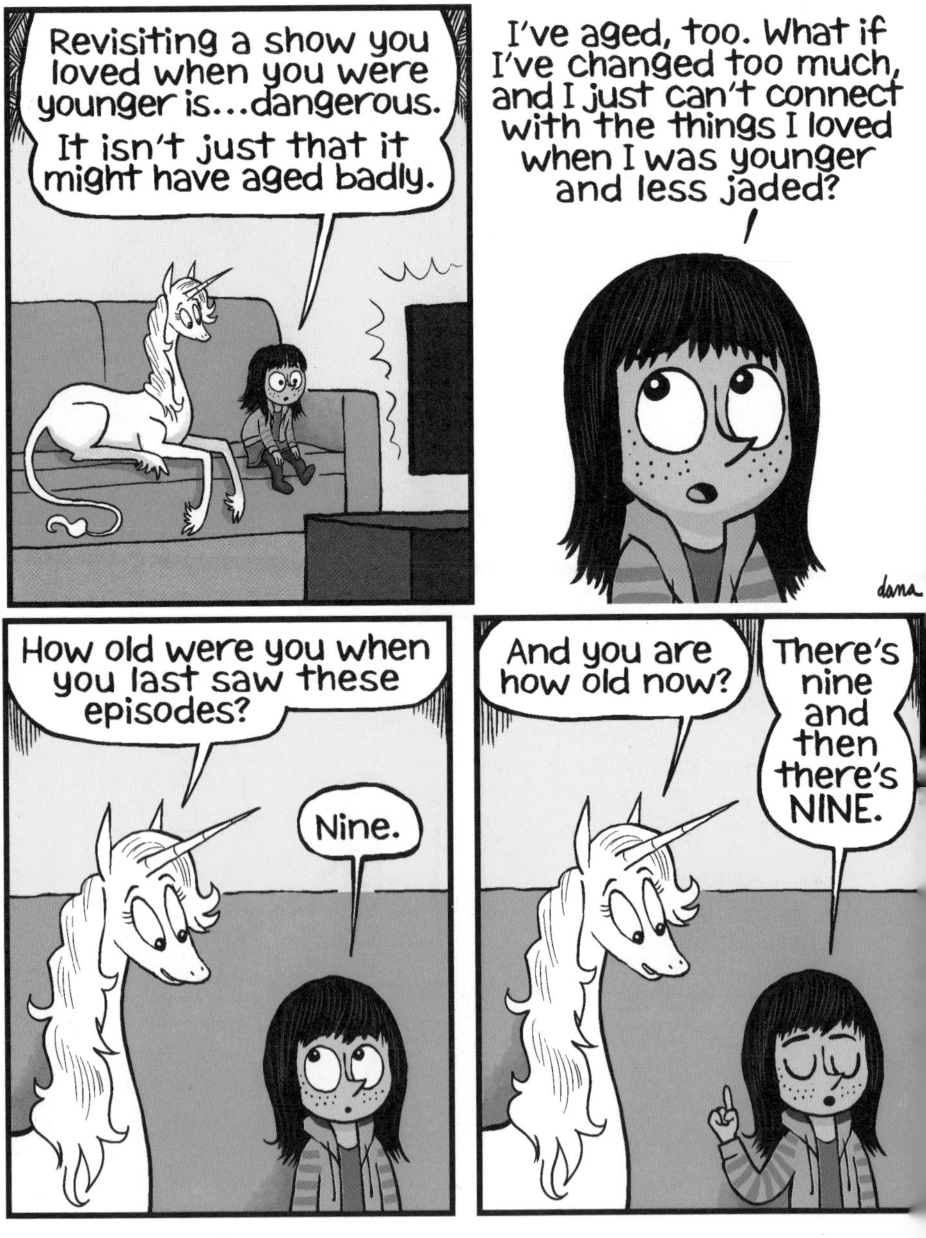
Revisiting a show you loved when you were younger is...dangerous.
It isn't just that it might have aged badly.
I've aged, too. What if I've changed too much, and I just can't connect with the things I loved when I was younger and less jaded?
dana
How old were you when you last saw these episodes?
Nine.
And you are how old now?
There's nine and then there's NINE.

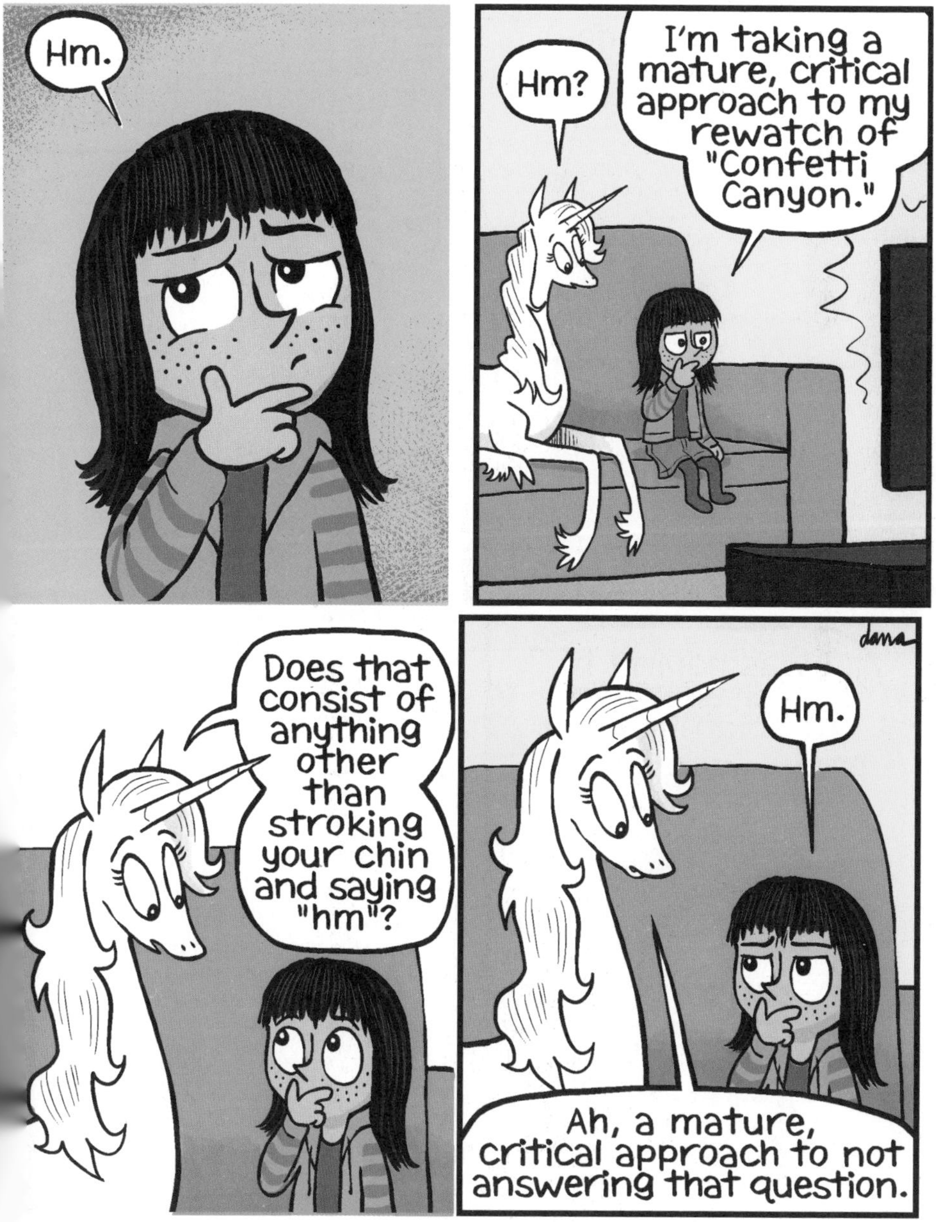
Hm.
Hm?
I'm taking a mature, critical approach to my rewatch of "Confetti Canyon."
Does that consist of anything other than stroking your chin and saying "hm"?
dana
Hm.
Ah, a mature, critical approach to not answering that question.

This show is still really good.

You do not look happy about that.

I am! It's just...

I was hoping to feel disappointed, but I didn't get to.

Then you should feel happy that you are disappointed by not being disappointed by a thing that makes you happy.

I might land there when I'm finished processing.

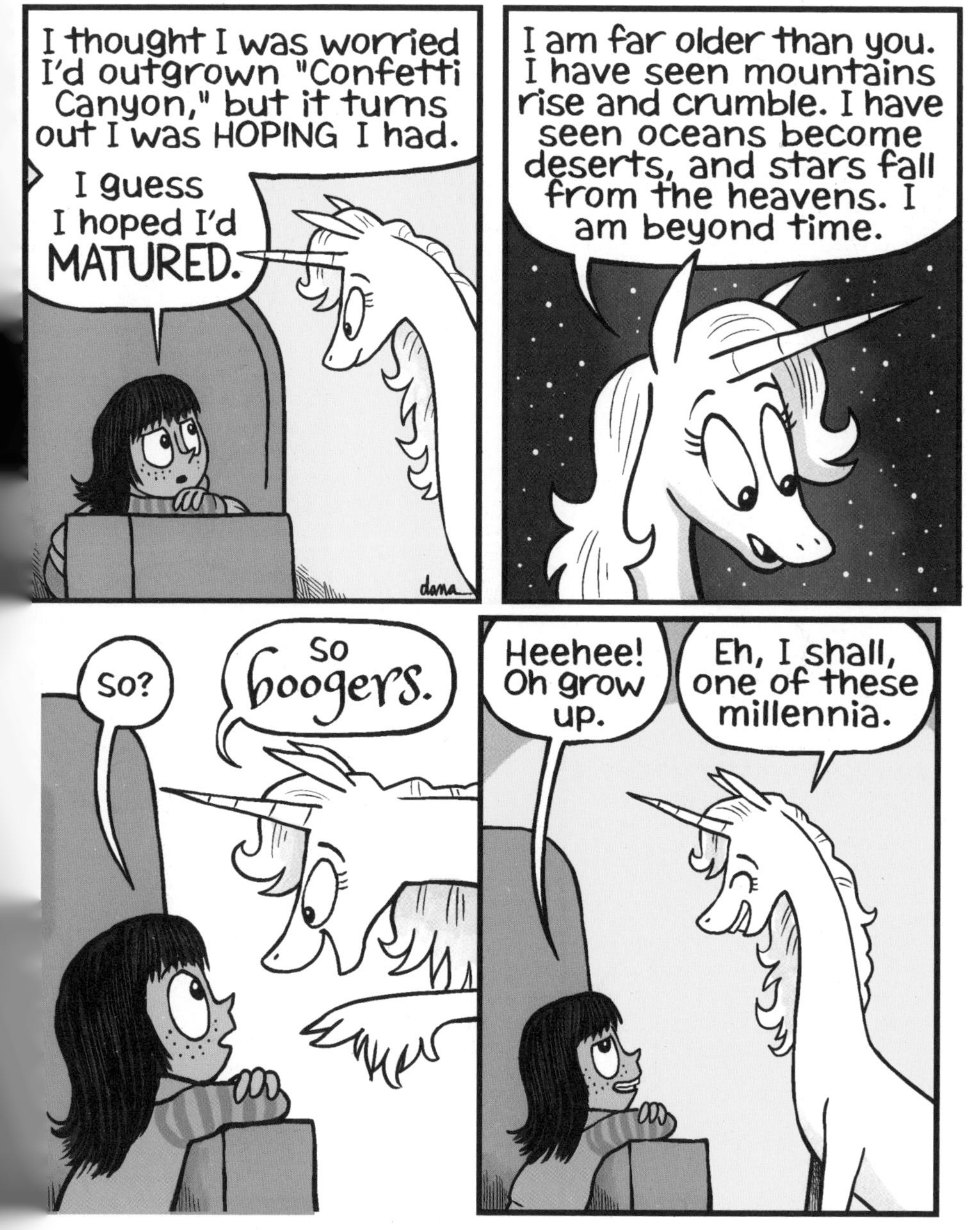
I thought I was worried I'd outgrown "Confetti Canyon," but it turns out I was HOPING I had.
I guess I hoped I'd MATURED.
dana
I am far older than you. I have seen mountains rise and crumble. I have seen oceans become deserts, and stars fall from the heavens. I am beyond time.
So?
So boogers.
Heehee! Oh grow up.
Eh, I shall, one of these millennia.

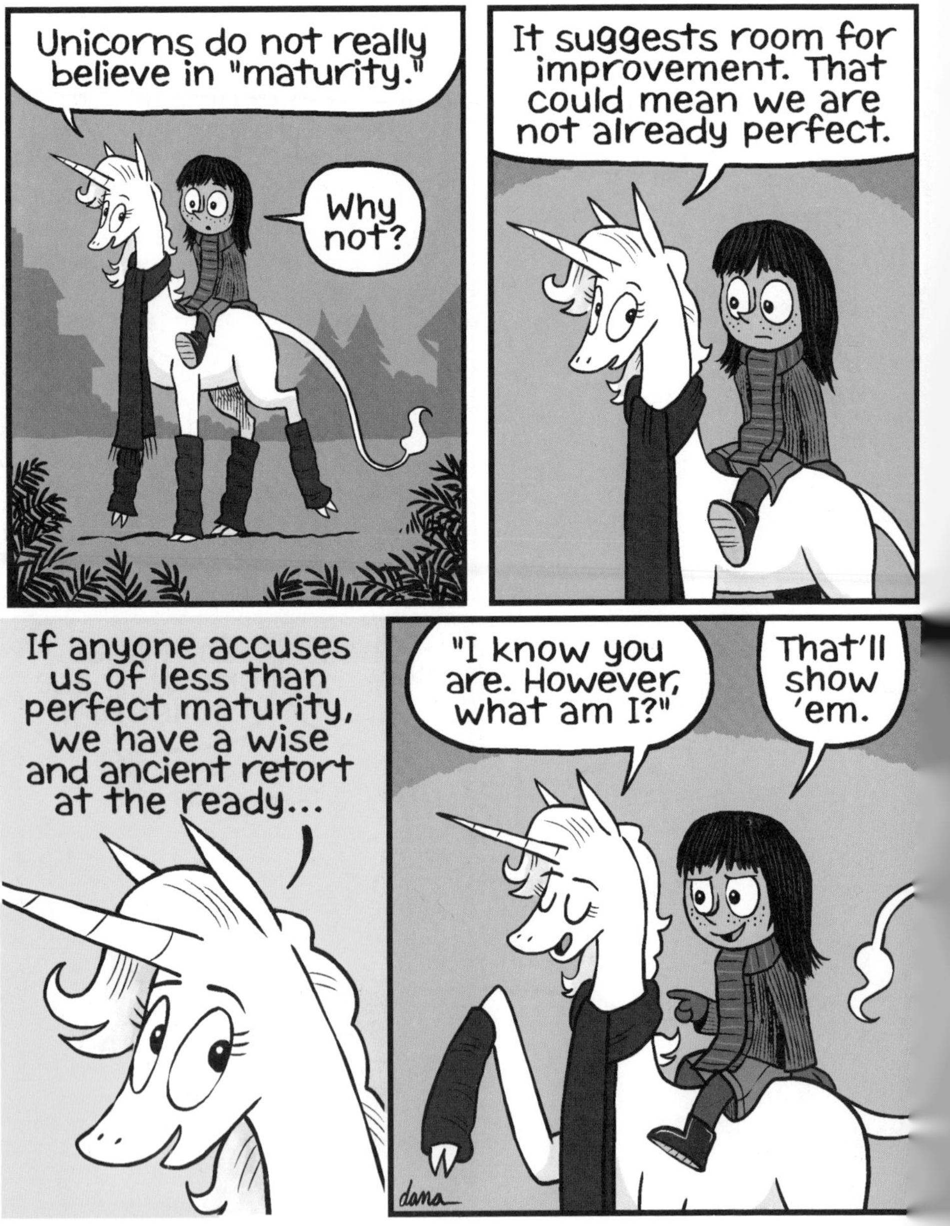
Unicorns do not really believe in "maturity."
Why not?
It suggests room for improvement. That could mean we are not already perfect.
If anyone accuses us of less than perfect maturity, we have a wise and ancient retort at the ready...
"I know you are. However, what am I?"
That'll show 'em.
dana

BLAAAH
NYEAH
THPPTPH
PHBBTB
BLAAH
HA! I stopped first! I win our maturity contest.
Or perhaps that is just what I, in my great maturity, am letting you believe.
dana

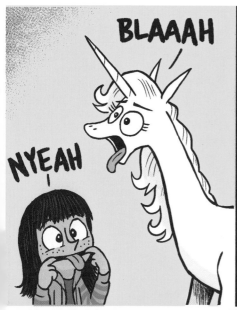

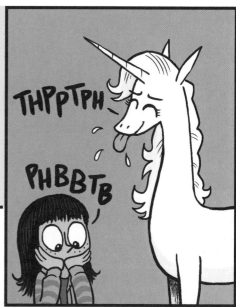

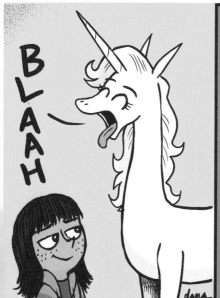

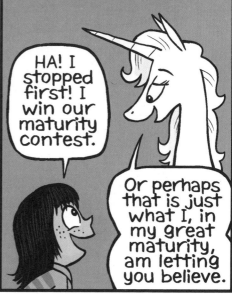

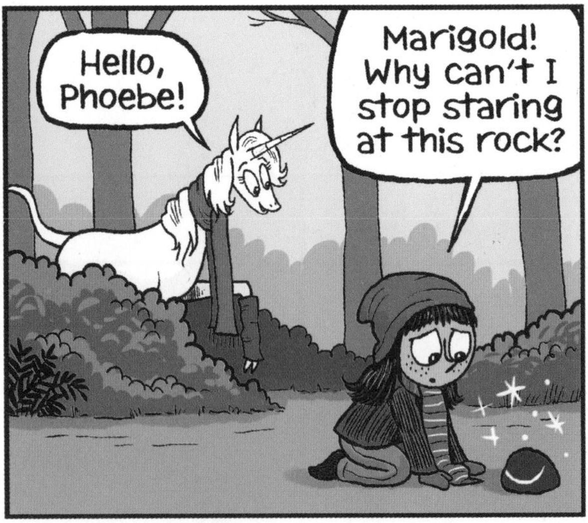
Hello, Phoebe!
Marigold! Why can't I stop staring at this rock?

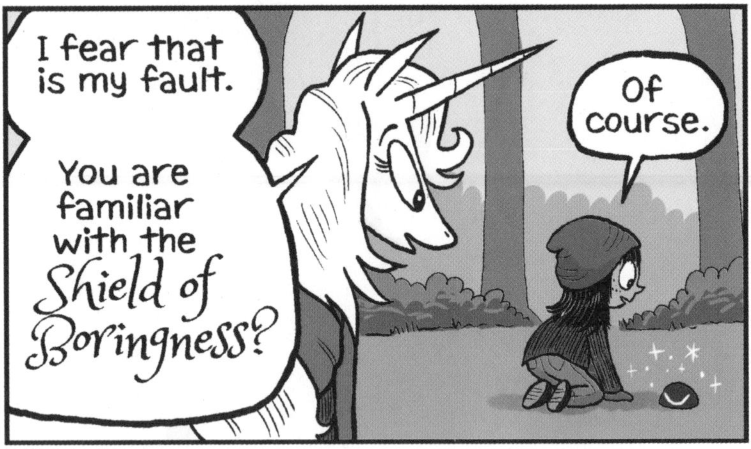
I fear that is my fault.
You are familiar with the Shield of Boringness?
Of course.

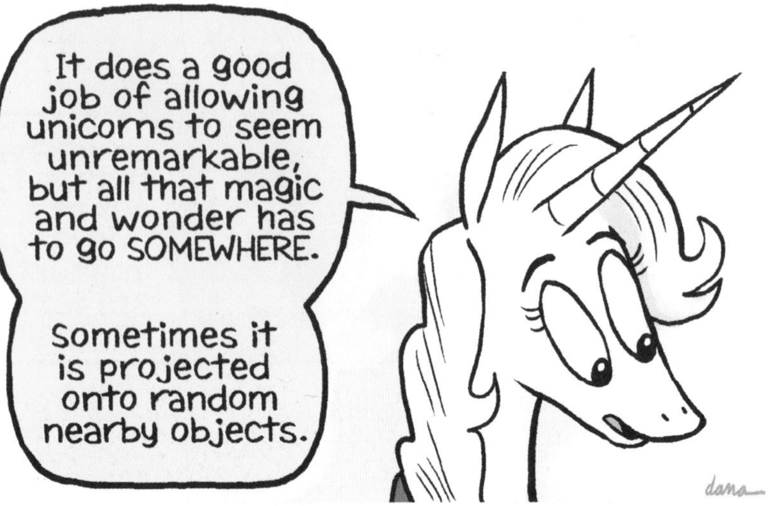
It does a good job of allowing unicorns to seem unremarkable, but all that magic and wonder has to go SOMEWHERE.
Sometimes it is projected onto random nearby objects.
dana

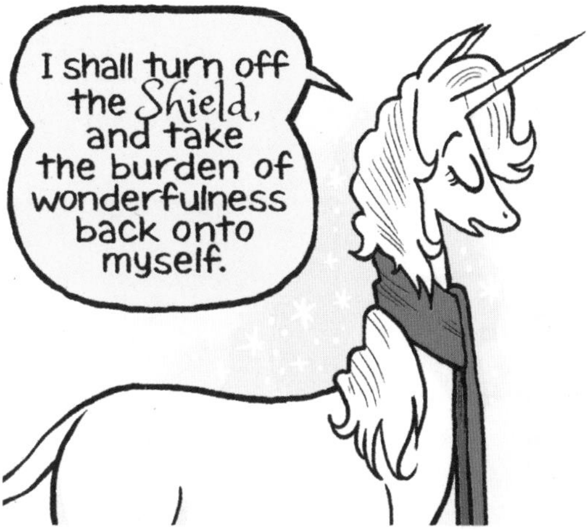
I shall turn off the Shield, and take the burden of wonderfulness back onto myself.

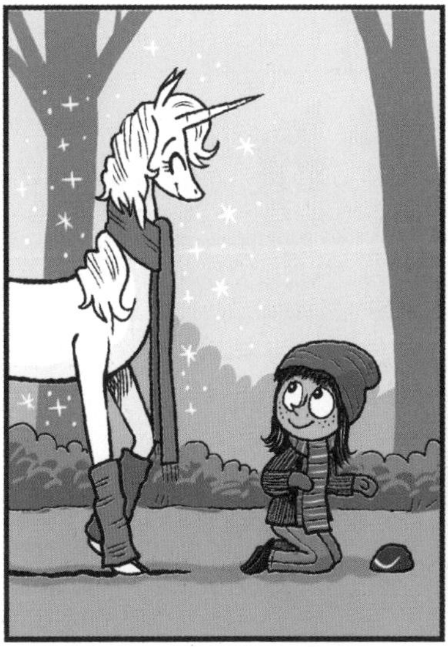

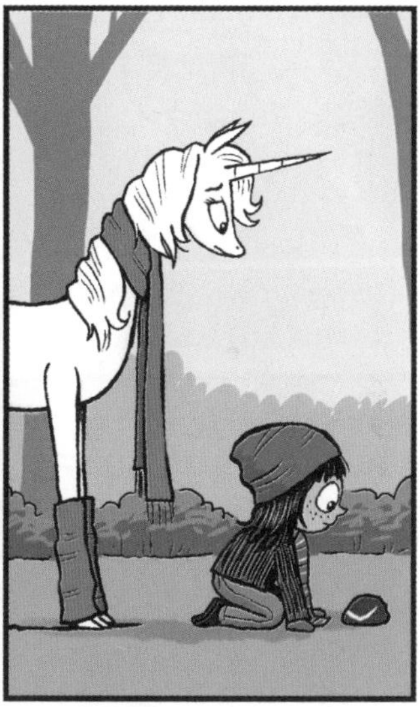

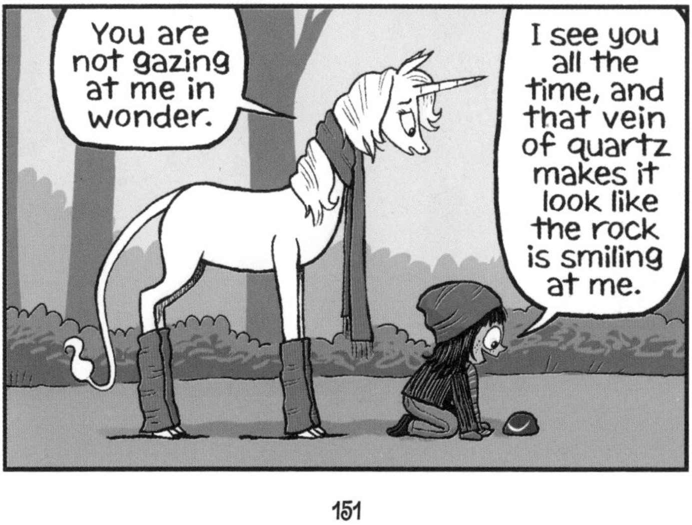
You are not gazing at me in wonder.
I see you all the time, and that vein of quartz makes it look like the rock is smiling at me.

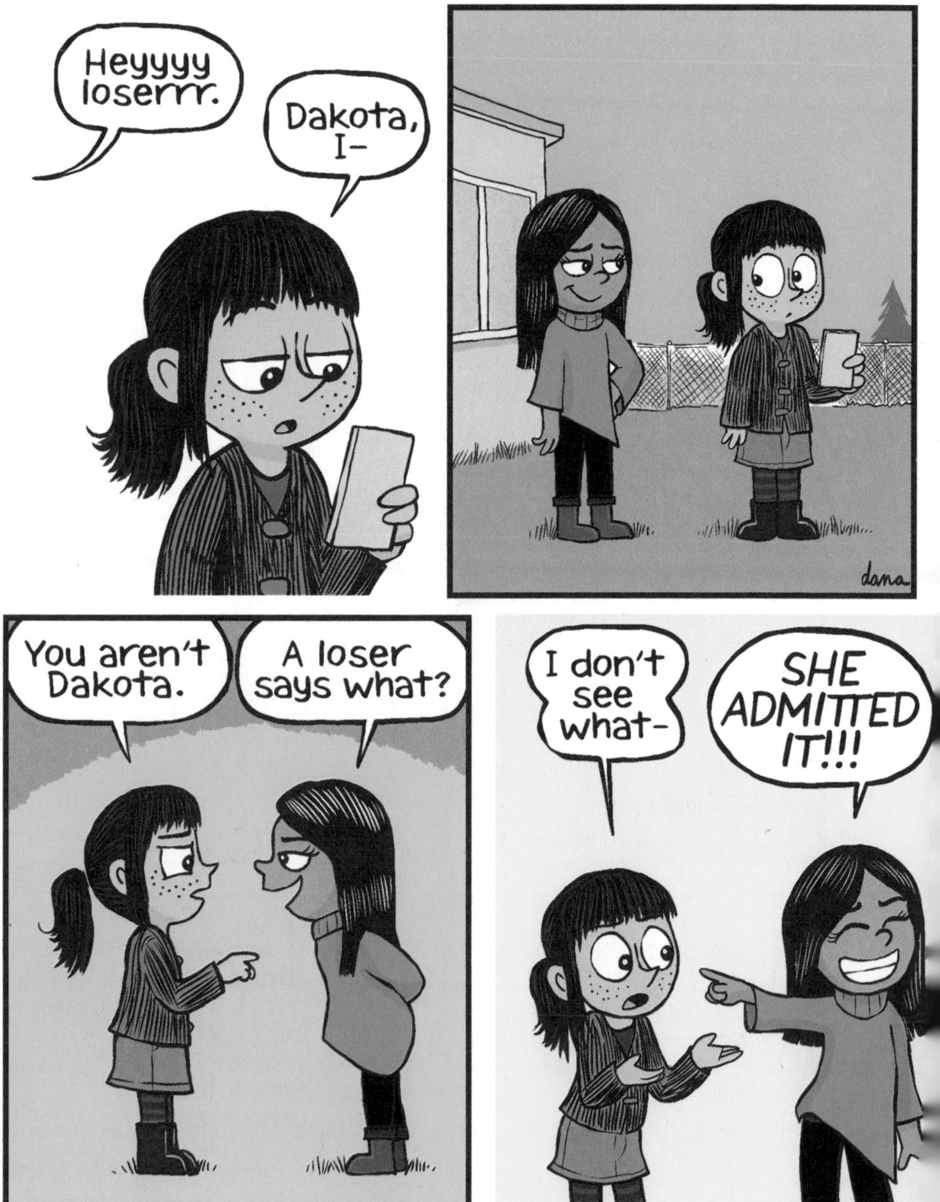
Heyyyy loserrr.
Dakota, I-
dana
You aren't Dakota.
A loser says what?
I don't see what-
SHE ADMITTED IT!!!

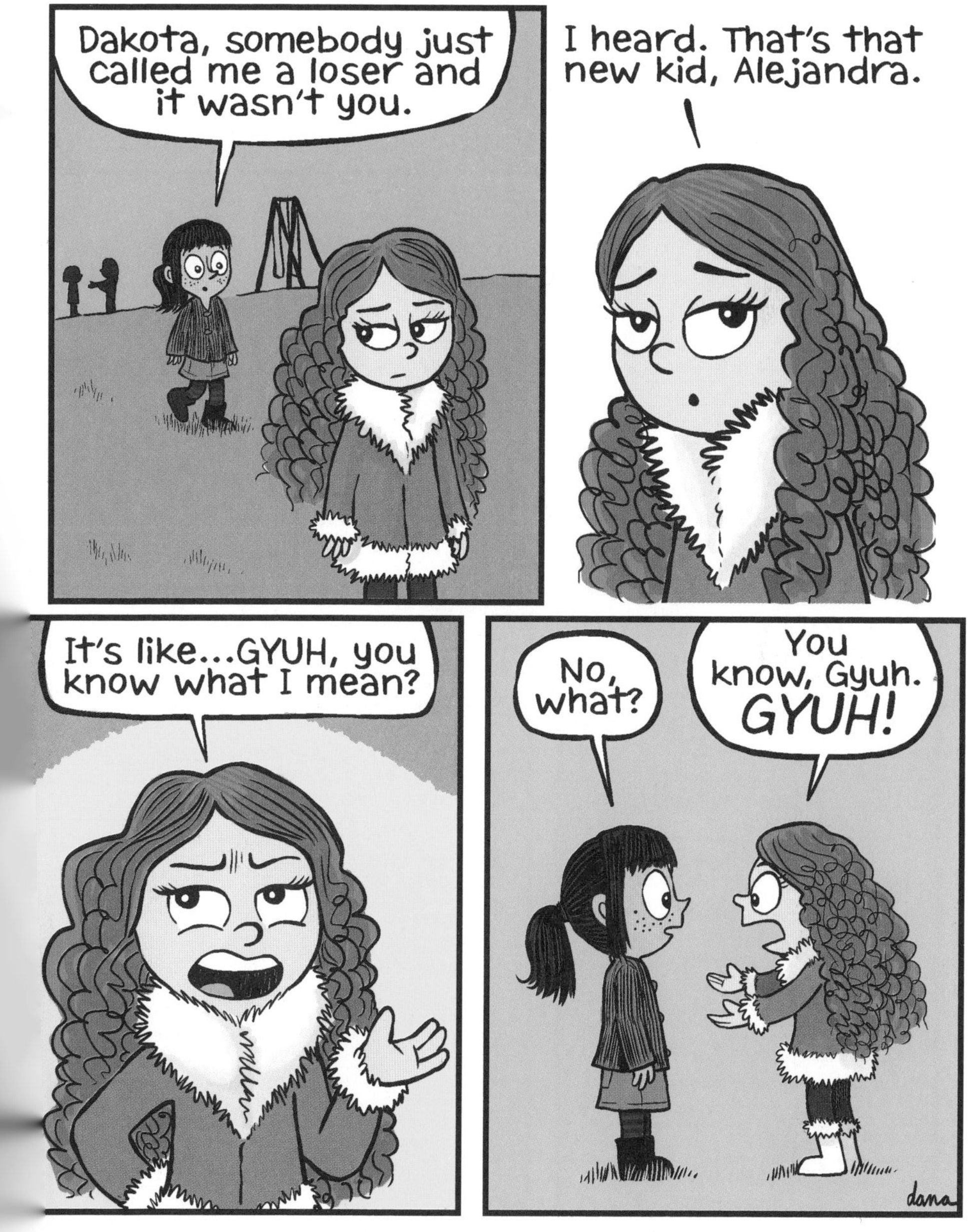
Dakota, somebody just called me a loser and it wasn't you.
I heard. That's that new kid, Alejandra.
It's like...GYUH, you know what I mean?
No, what?
You know, Gyuh. GYUH!
dana

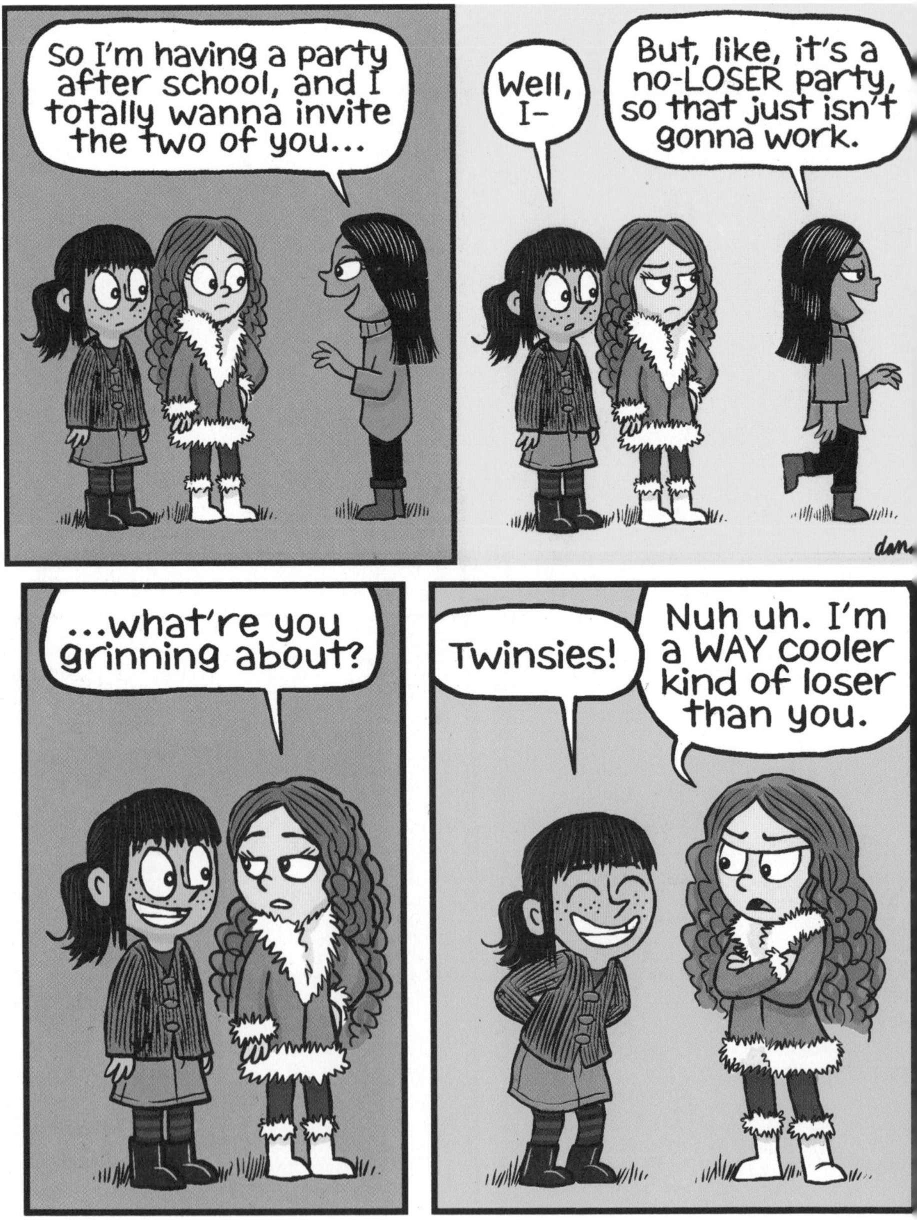

So I'm having a party after school, and I totally wanna invite the two of you...
Well, I-
But, like, it's a no-LOSER party, so that just isn't gonna work.
dan
...what're you grinning about?
Twinsies!
Nuh uh. I'm a WAY cooler kind of loser than you.

Alejandra is, like, a jerk.
She's just like YOU.
No way! We're TOTALLY different. I haven't called you a loser in like...
Did calling you "The Duchess of the Grand Duchy of Dweebington" count?
Yes, so 53 minutes.
dana

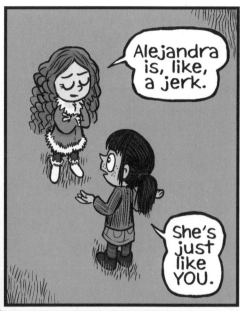

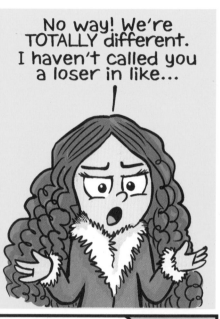

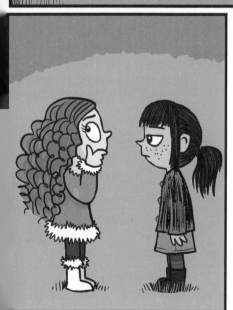

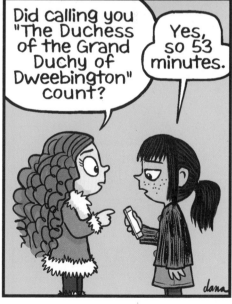

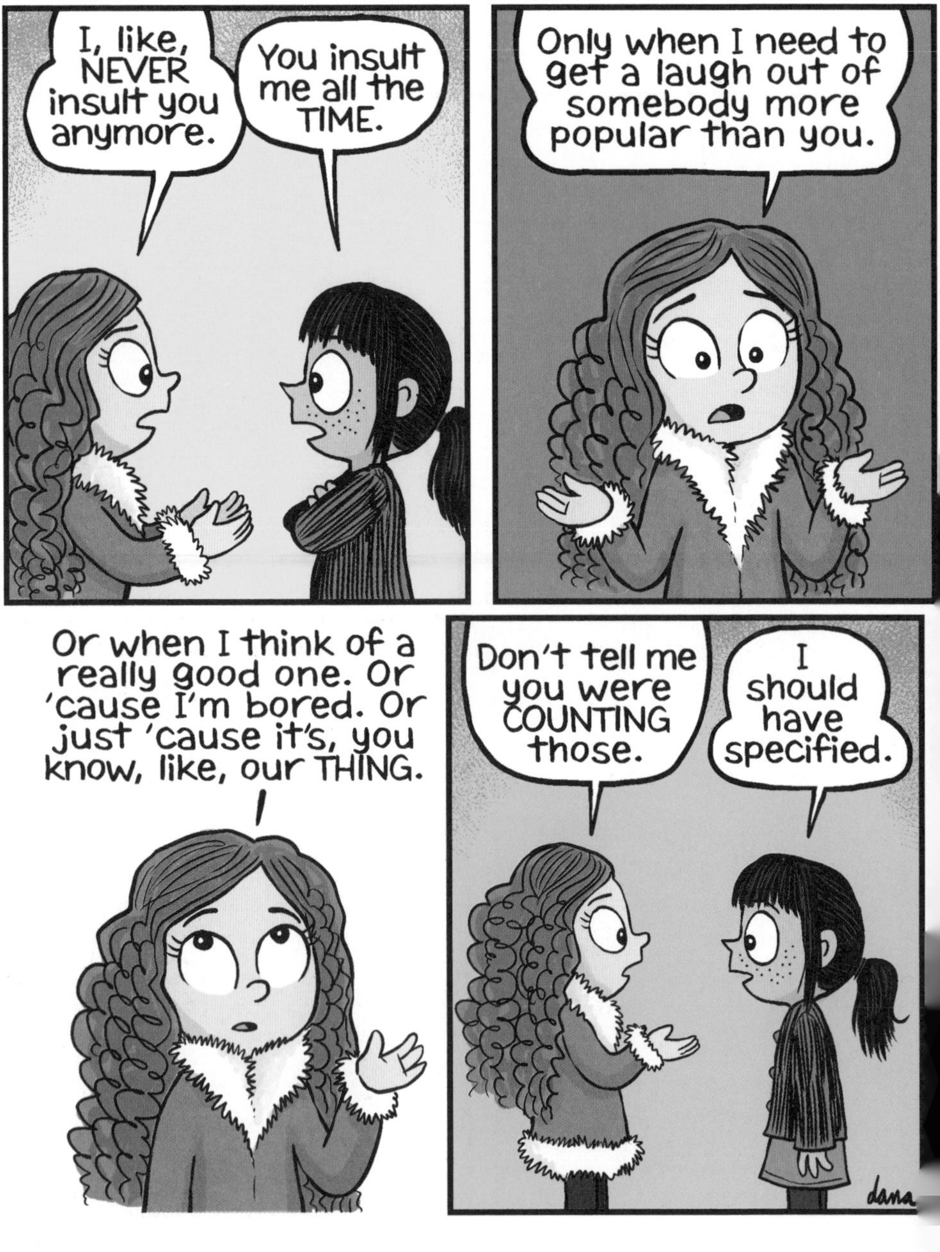

I, like, NEVER insult you anymore.
You insult me all the TIME.
Only when I need to get a laugh out of somebody more popular than you.
Or when I think of a really good one. Or 'cause I'm bored. Or just 'cause it's, you know, like, our THING.
Don't tell me you were COUNTING those.
I should have specified.
dana

Look, if it would make us more even...you can have a free one.
Insult me and I won't insult you back.
Okay.
Your right eyebrow is slightly wider than your left eyebrow and I notice it every time I look at you.
Thanks for making me self-conscious forever.
Merry Christmas.

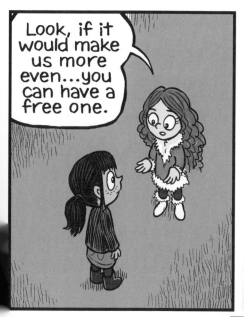

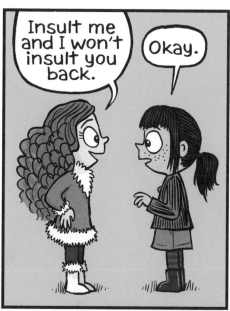

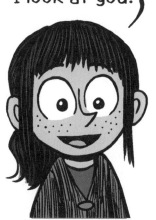

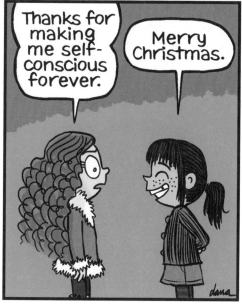

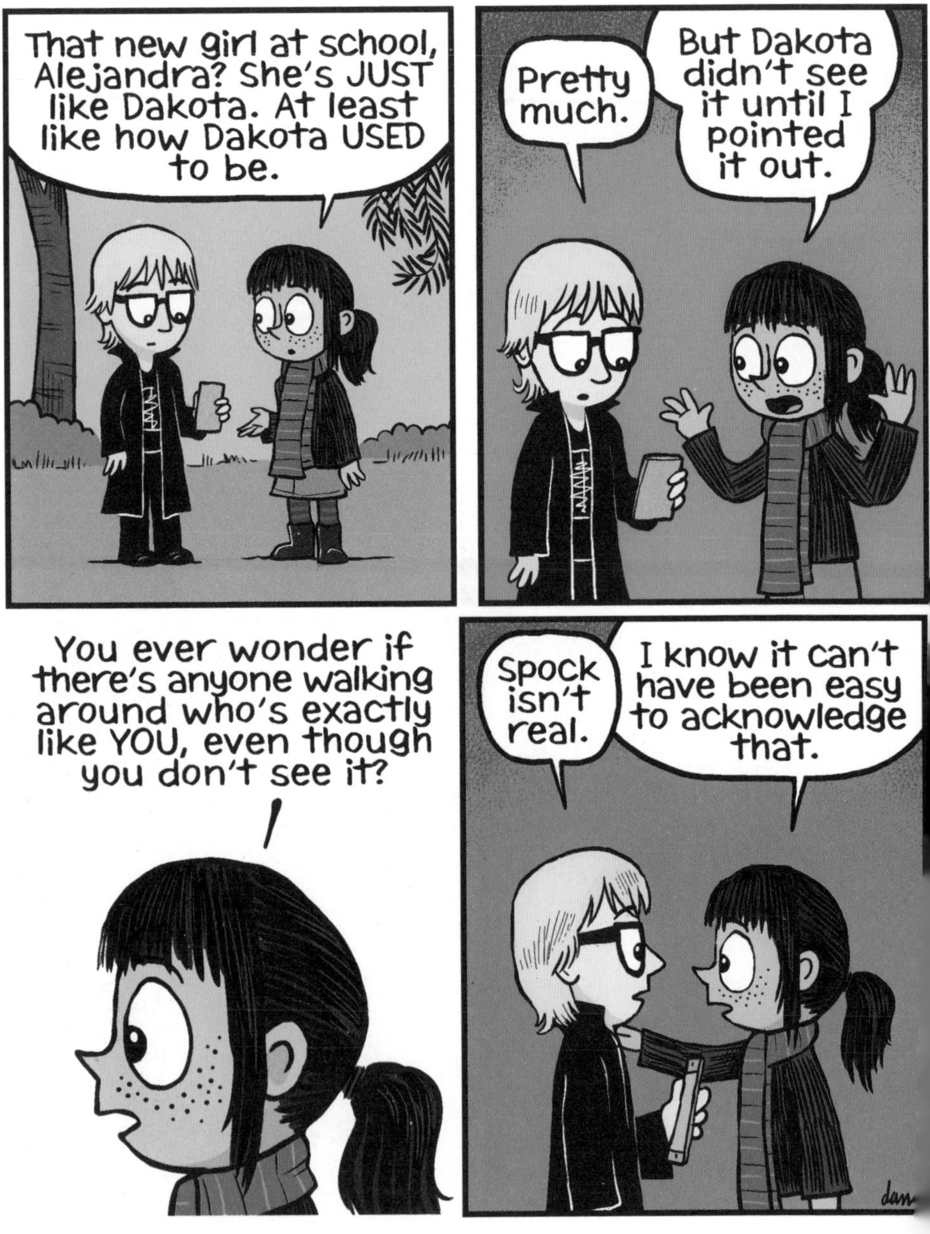
That new girl at school, Alejandra? She's JUST like Dakota. At least like how Dakota USED to be.
Pretty much.
But Dakota didn't see it until I pointed it out.
You ever wonder if there's anyone walking around who's exactly like YOU, even though you don't see it?
Spock isn't real.
I know it can't have been easy to acknowledge that.

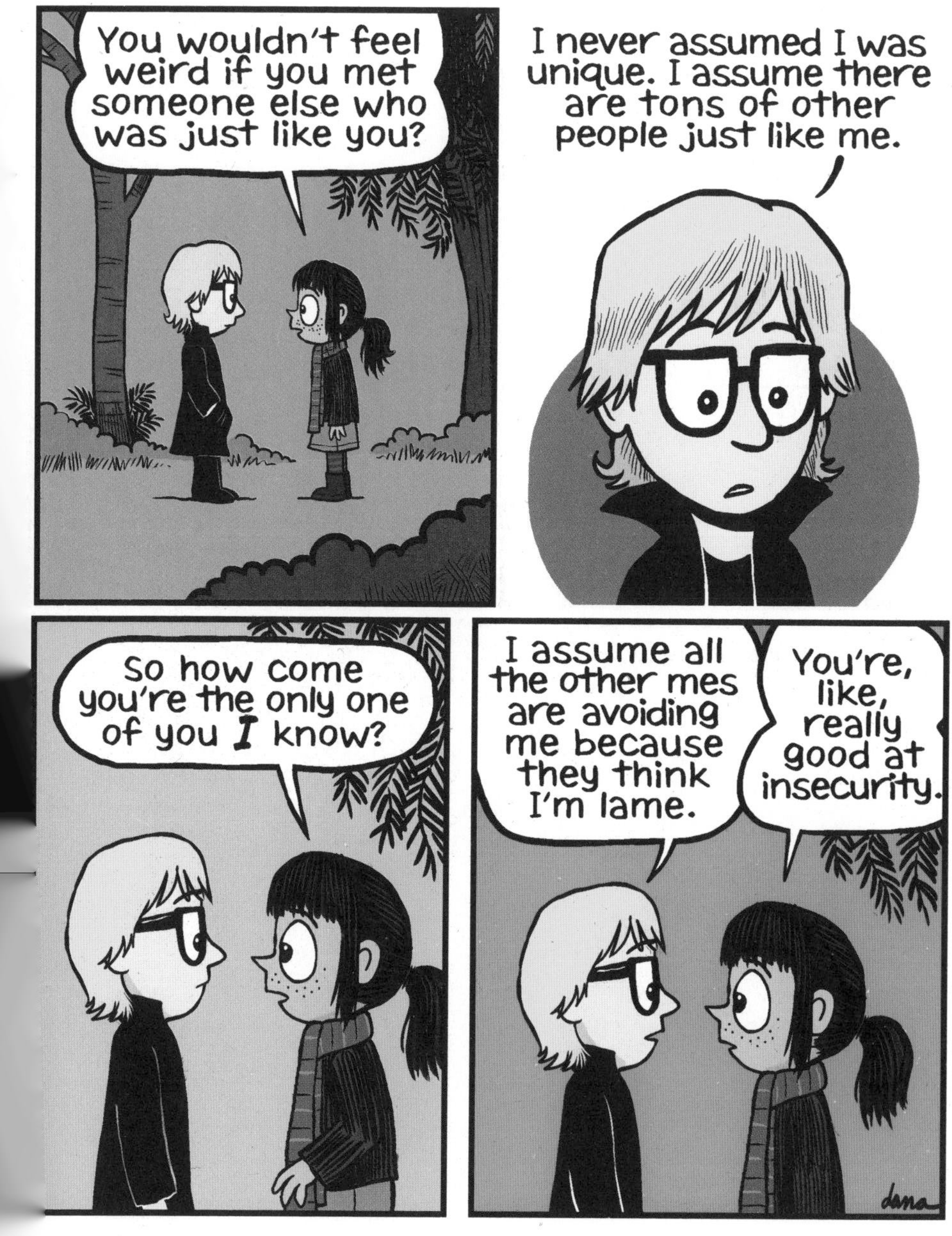
You wouldn't feel weird if you met someone else who was just like you?
I never assumed I was unique. I assume there are tons of other people just like me.
So how come you're the only one of you I know?
I assume all the other mes are avoiding me because they think I'm lame.
You're, like, really good at insecurity.
dana

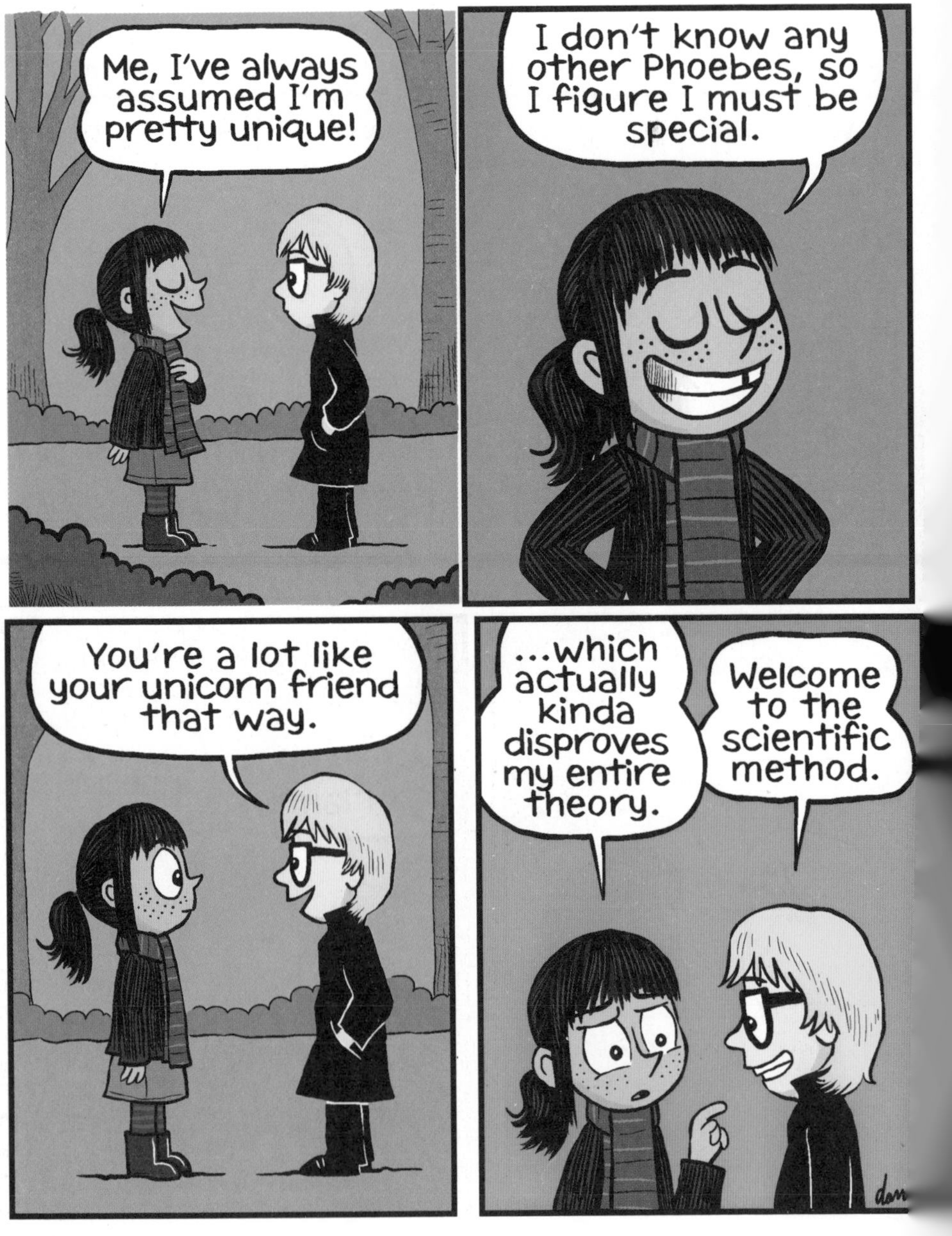
Me, I've always assumed I'm pretty unique!
I don't know any other Phoebes, so I figure I must be special.
You're a lot like your unicorn friend that way.
...which actually kinda disproves my entire theory.
Welcome to the scientific method.

I have gotten you something for the human gift holiday.

Now, I do not want to be one of those individuals who gives gifts that are all about themselves.

I thought, "What does Phoebe, as an individual who is NOT me, need most in the world?"

A mirror?

Merry Christmas!

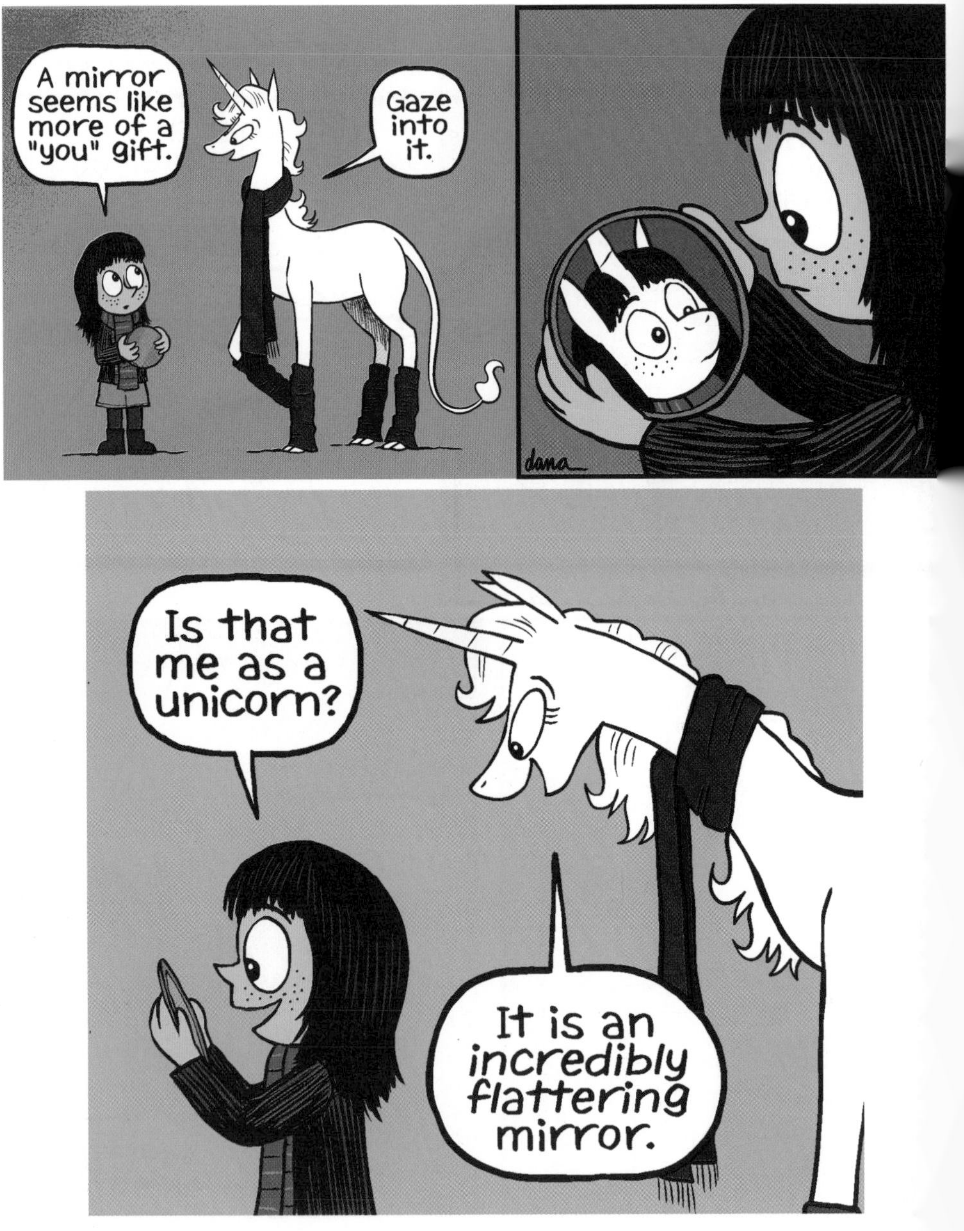
A mirror seems like more of a "you" gift.
Gaze into it.
dana
Is that me as a unicorn?
It is an incredibly flattering mirror.

So...this mirror shows people what they'd look like as unicorns?

Not precisely.

It shows YOU your inner unicorn. It is calibrated only to work on you.

You got me a fursona for Christmas!

I do not know that word, but I assume it conveys sparkliness.

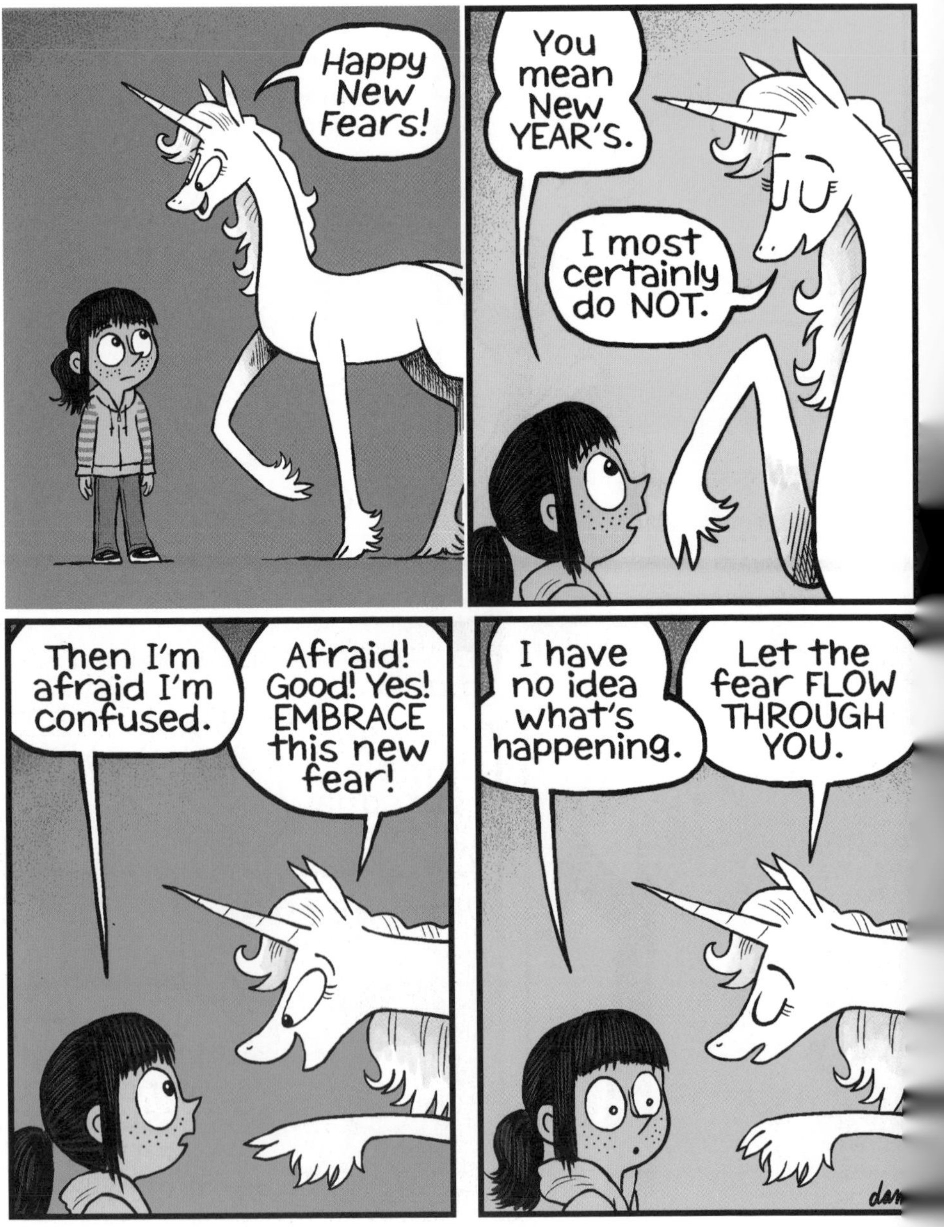
Happy New Fears!
You mean New YEAR'S.
I most certainly do NOT.
Then I'm afraid I'm confused.
Afraid! Good! Yes! EMBRACE this new fear!
I have no idea what's happening.
Let the fear FLOW THROUGH YOU.

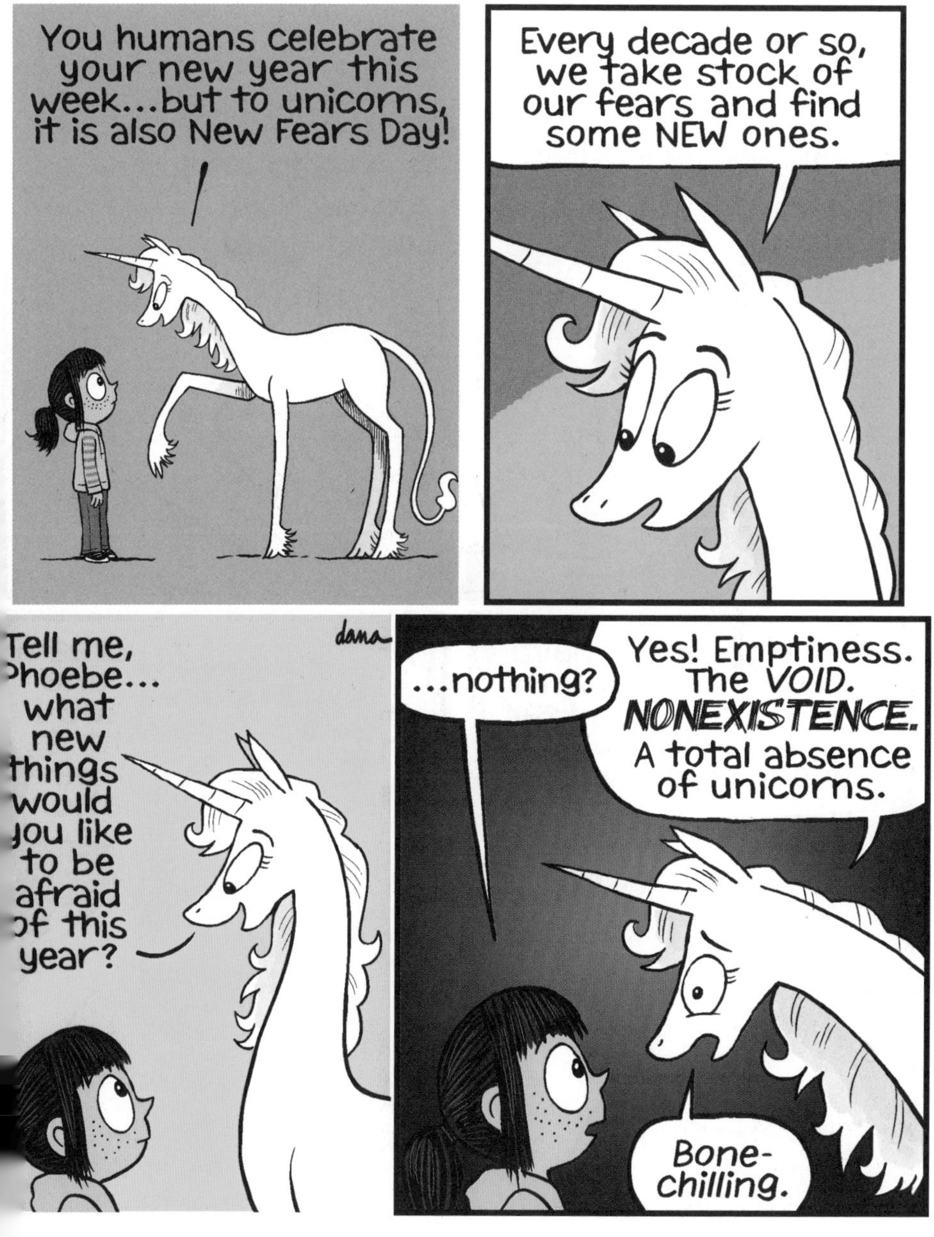
You humans celebrate your new year this week...but to unicorns, it is also New Fears Day!
Every decade or so, we take stock of our fears and find some NEW ones.
dana
Tell me, Phoebe... what new things would you like to be afraid of this year?
...nothing?
Yes! Emptiness. The *VOID*. ***NONEXISTENCE.*** A total absence of unicorns.
Bone-chilling.

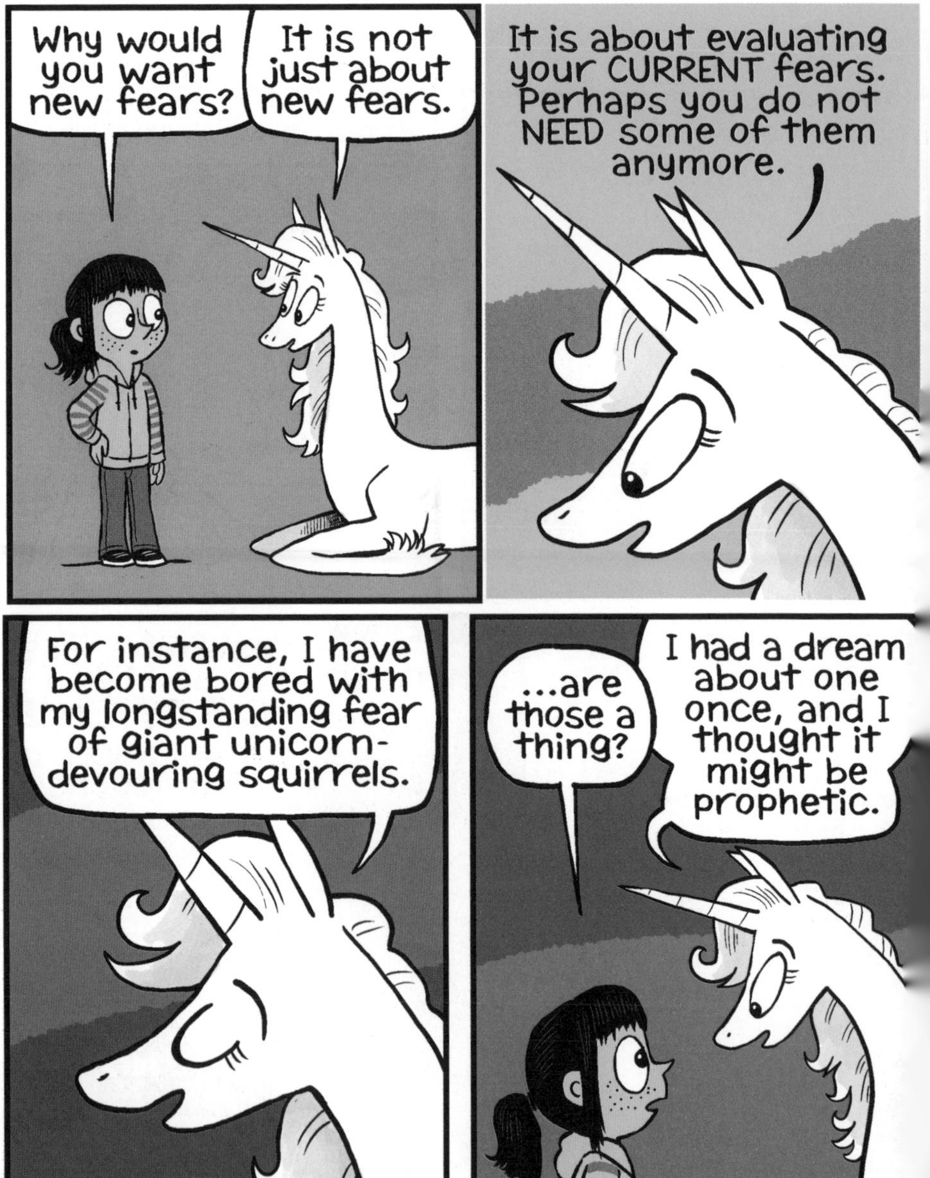
Why would you want new fears?
It is not just about new fears.
It is about evaluating your CURRENT fears. Perhaps you do not NEED some of them anymore.
For instance, I have become bored with my longstanding fear of giant unicorn-devouring squirrels.
...are those a thing?
I had a dream about one once, and I thought it might be prophetic.
dana

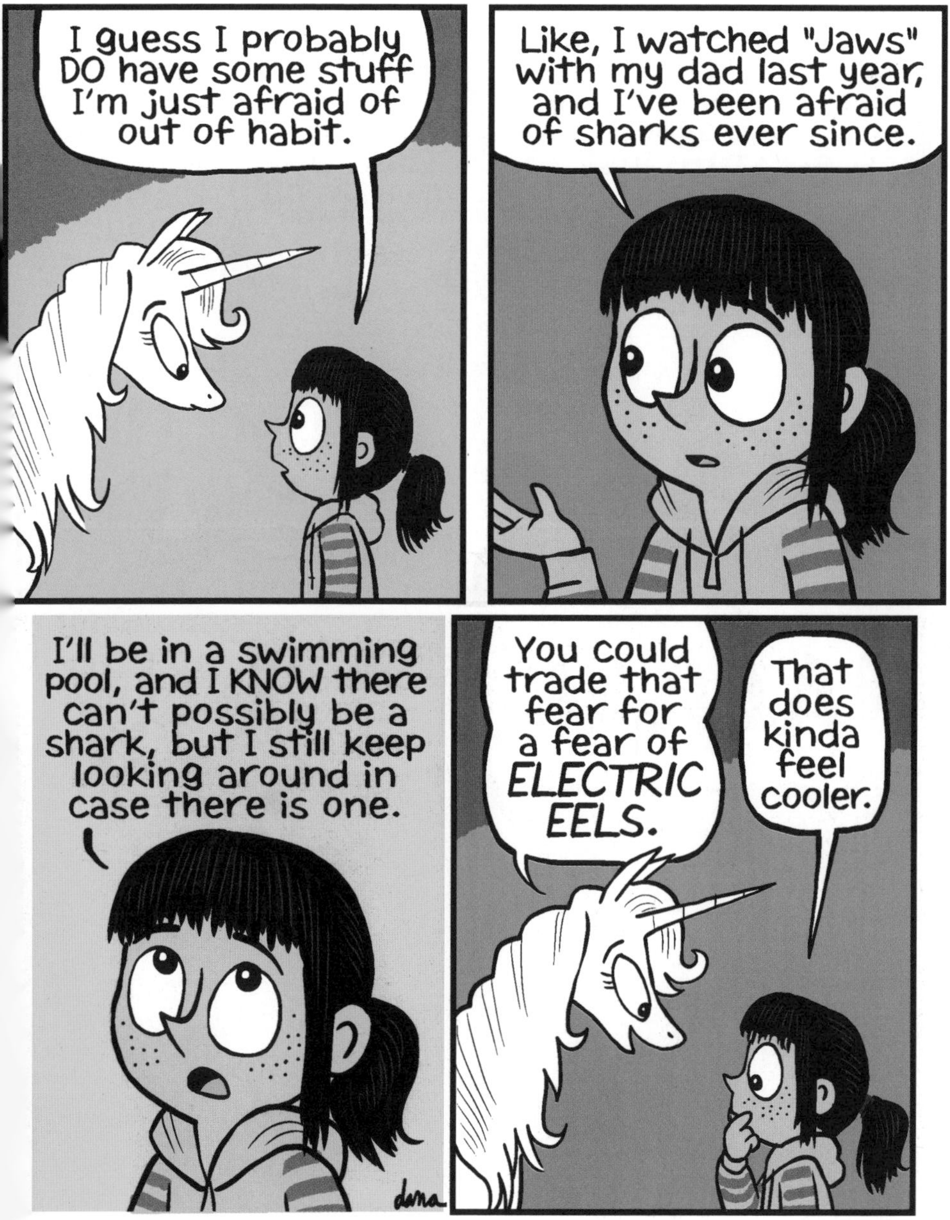
I guess I probably DO have some stuff I'm just afraid of out of habit.
Like, I watched "Jaws" with my dad last year, and I've been afraid of sharks ever since.
I'll be in a swimming pool, and I KNOW there can't possibly be a shark, but I still keep looking around in case there is one.
You could trade that fear for a fear of *ELECTRIC EELS.*
That does kinda feel cooler.
dana

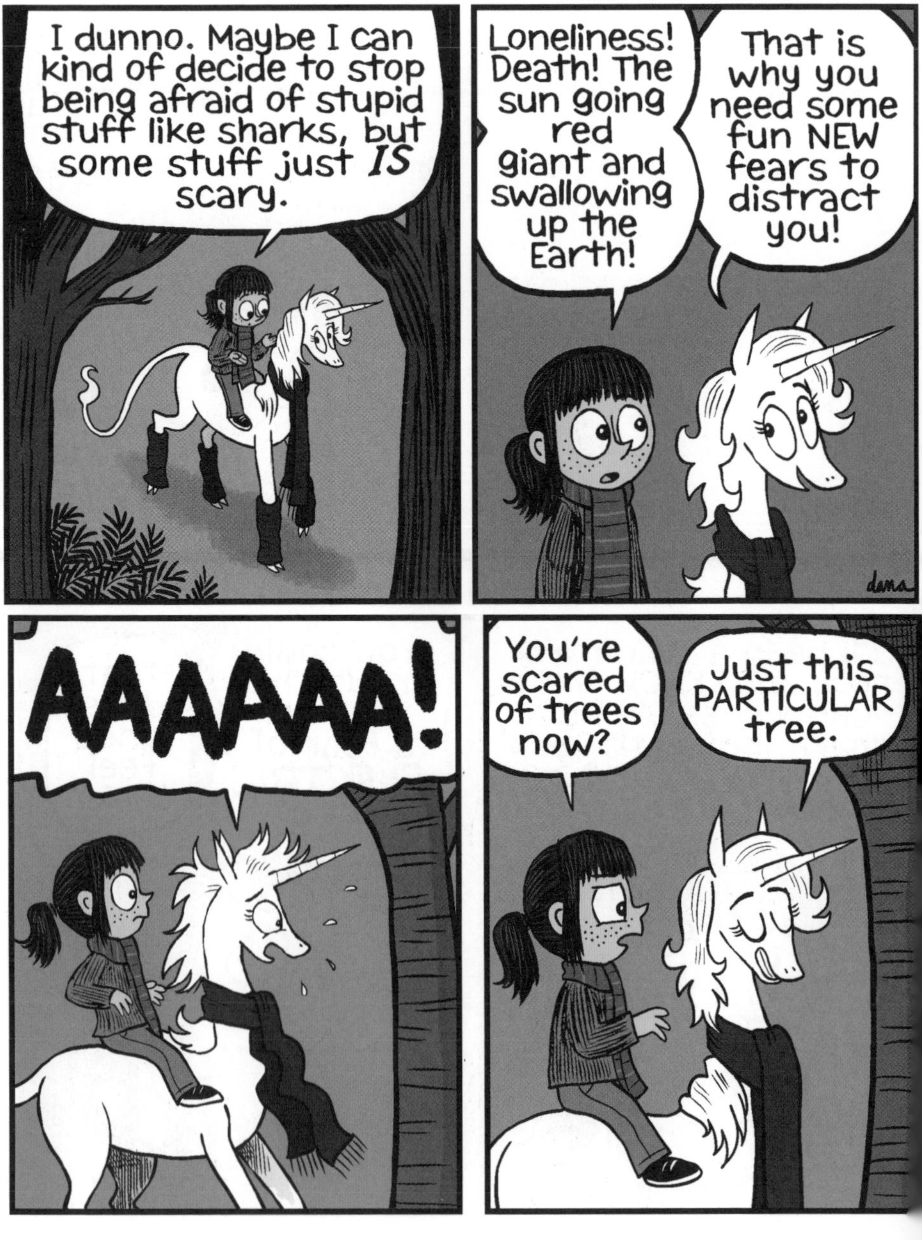
I dunno. Maybe I can kind of decide to stop being afraid of stupid stuff like sharks, but some stuff just *IS* scary.
Loneliness! Death! The sun going red giant and swallowing up the Earth!
That is why you need some fun NEW fears to distract you!
dana
AAAAAA!
You're scared of trees now?
Just this PARTICULAR tree.

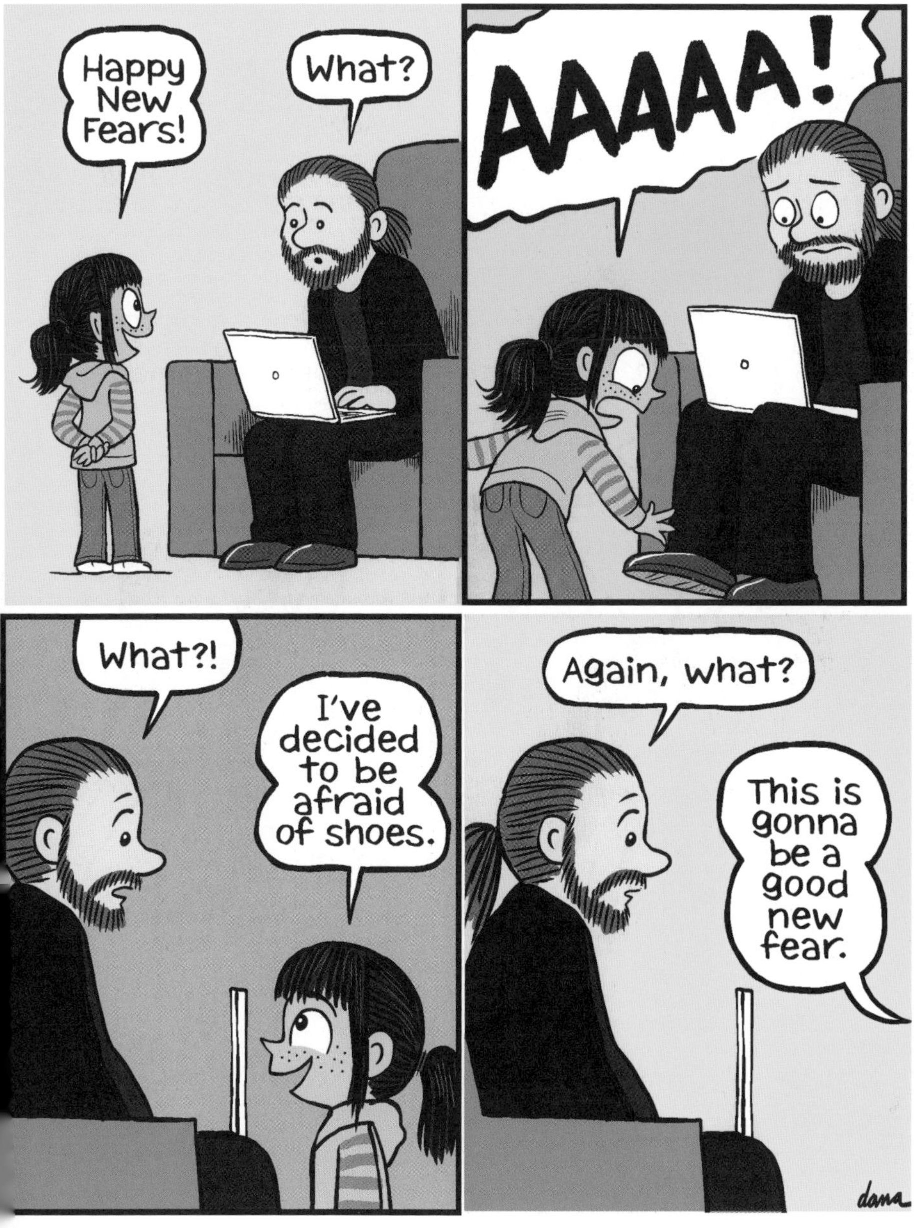
Happy New Fears!
What?
AAAAA!
What?!
I've decided to be afraid of shoes.
Again, what?
This is gonna be a good new fear.
dana

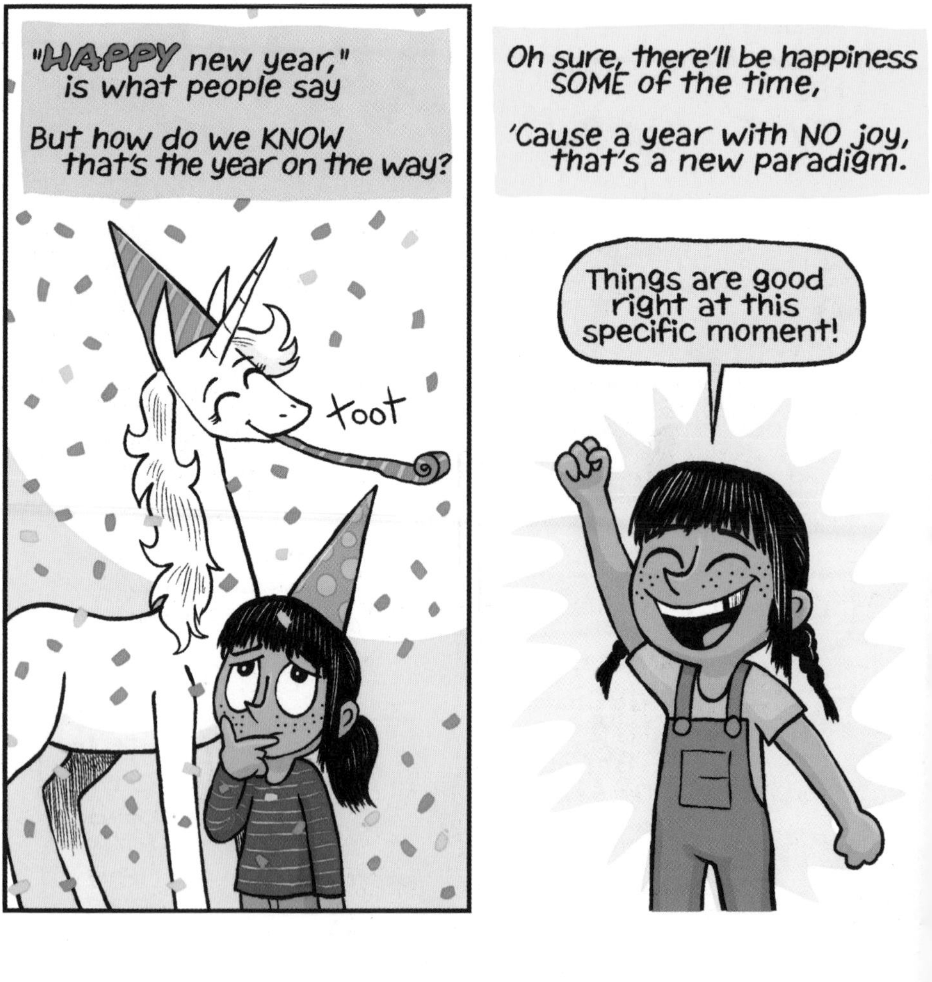
"HAPPY new year," is what people say
But how do we KNOW that's the year on the way?
toot
Oh sure, there'll be happiness SOME of the time,
'Cause a year with NO joy, that's a new paradigm.
Things are good right at this specific moment!

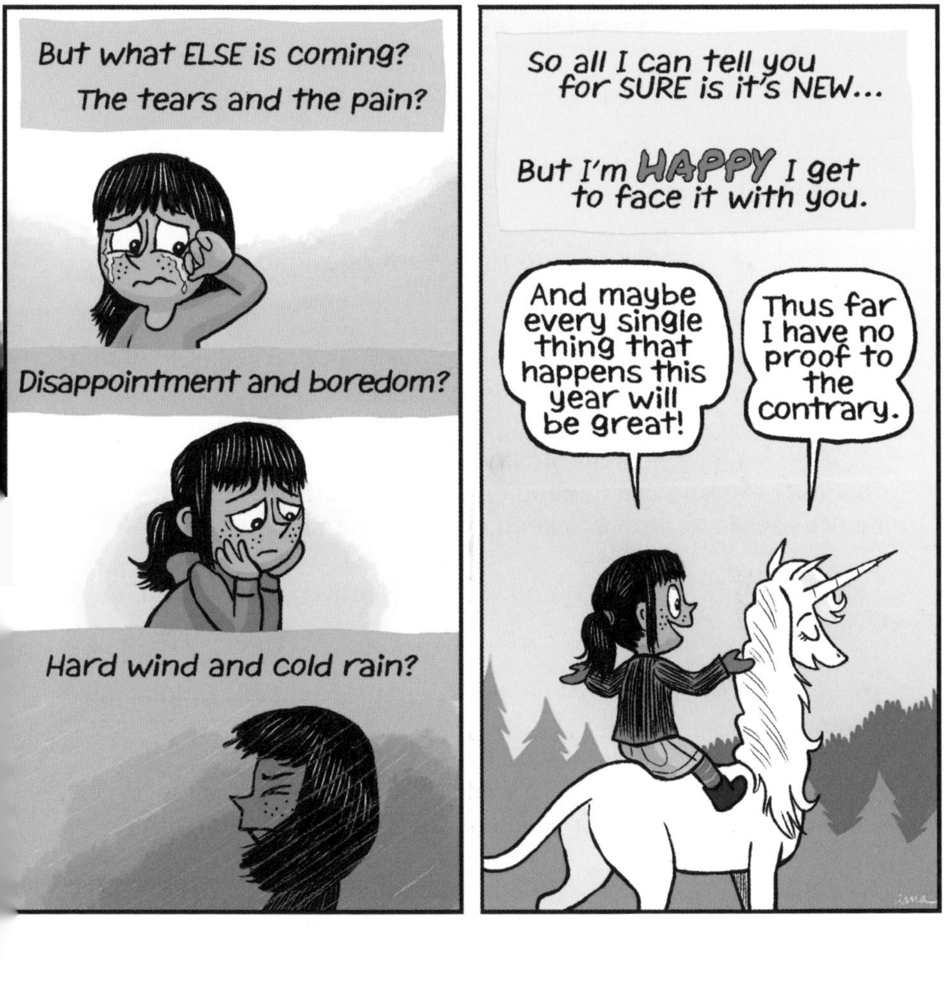
But what ELSE is coming?
The tears and the pain?
Disappointment and boredom?
Hard wind and cold rain?
So all I can tell you for SURE is it's NEW...
But I'm HAPPY I get to face it with you.
And maybe every single thing that happens this year will be great!
Thus far I have no proof to the contrary.

GLOSSARY

Ambivalence (am-bi-va-lents) pg. 97 – noun / mixed feelings or ideas about someone or something

Assuage (uh-sway-jd) pg. 33 – verb / to calm or smooth over

Bipedality (by-pe-dehl-it-ee) pg. 61 – noun / the ability to be bipedal, or walk on two feet

Calibrated (kal-ih-bray-tid) pg. 163 – verb / designed and adjusted to work a certain way

Coincidence (koh-win-seh-dense) pg. 118 – noun / an event or multiple events occurring at the same time by chance

Cozies (koh-zeez) pg. 83 – noun / a cozy is a drink holder that fits around a beverage can to keep one's hands warm. In Phoebe's case, she uses socks as cozies to keep her horn warm.

Diabolical (die-uh-ball-ick-ohl) pg. 124 – adjective / evil, wicked, or devilish

Doppelganger (dop-uhl-gang-er) pg. 7 – noun / a double or look-alike of someone

Etsy (et-see) pg. 68 – noun / a website and online marketplace where people sell crafts or products that are often handmade

Existential (eggz-ih-stent-shul) pg. 37 – adjective / relating to the belief that people are responsible for finding meaning in their lives and in existence

Homophobic (hoe-moe-phoe-bick) pg. 140 – adjective / something that shows prejudice or discrimination against people who are gay, lesbian, or bisexual

Jaded (jay-did) pg. 144 – adjective / tired of something or no longer having the same belief in it, often due to past negative experiences

Mortal (more-tuhl) pg. 106 – noun / another word (or adjective) for a person, a "mortal" is someone who will eventually die

Omen (oh-min) pg. 5 – noun / a sign or warning about something yet to come

Plaid (plad) pg. 78 – adjective / a pattern of lines and squares that is often found on clothing

Portend (pore-tend) pg. 6 – verb / to be a sign that something is going to happen

Quartz (kortz) pg. 149 – noun / a crystalline mineral that is sparkly and is prized as a decoration or a healing stone

Racist (race-ist) pg. 140 – adjective / something that shows prejudice or discrimination against people of a particular race, ethnicity, or country of origin

Sexist (sex-ist) pg. 140 – adjective / something that shows prejudice or discrimination against sex, usually against women

Spock (spawk) pg. 158 – proper noun / a character from the original *Star Trek* television series who was best known for the phrase "Live long and prosper"

Visage (viz-ij) pg. 22 – noun / face

Vulgarity (vull-gair-it-ee) pg. 59 – noun / bad words, curses, or profane statements

Andrews McMeel Publishing
a division of Andrews McMeel Universal
1130 Walnut Street, Kansas City, Missouri 64106

www.andrewsmcmeel.com

23 24 25 26 27 SDB 10 9 8 7 6 5 4 3 2 1

ISBN: 978-1-5248-8130-6

Library of Congress Control Number: 2023931628

Made by:
RR Donnelley (Guangdong) Printing Solutions Company Ltd
Address and location of manufacturer:
No. 2, Minzhu Road, Daning, Humen Town,
Dongguan City, Guangdong Province, China 523930
1st Printing – 5/8/23

ATTENTION: SCHOOLS AND BUSINESSES
Andrews McMeel books are available at quantity discounts with bulk purchase for educational, business, or sales promotional use. For information, please e-mail the Andrews McMeel Publishing Special Sales Department:
sales@amuniversal.com.

Look for these books!

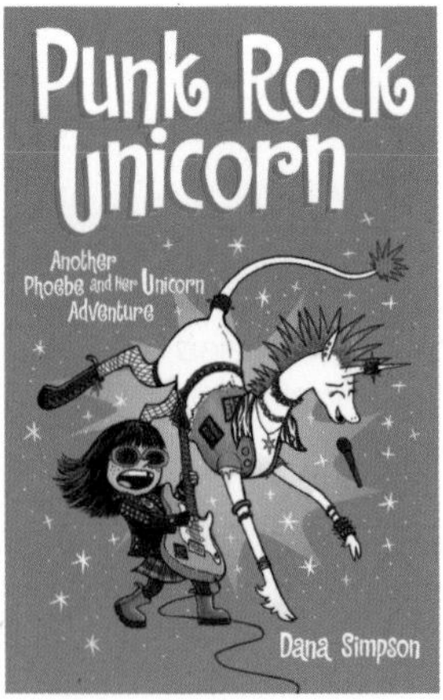
Punk Rock Unicorn
Another Phoebe and Her Unicorn Adventure
Dana Simpson

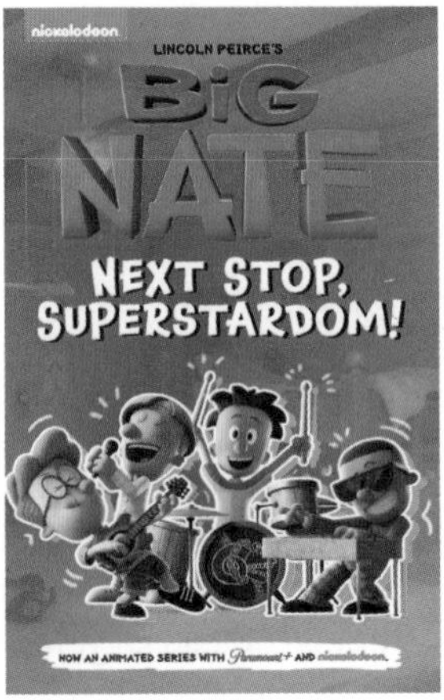
nickelodeon
LINCOLN PEIRCE'S
BIG NATE
NEXT STOP, SUPERSTARDOM!

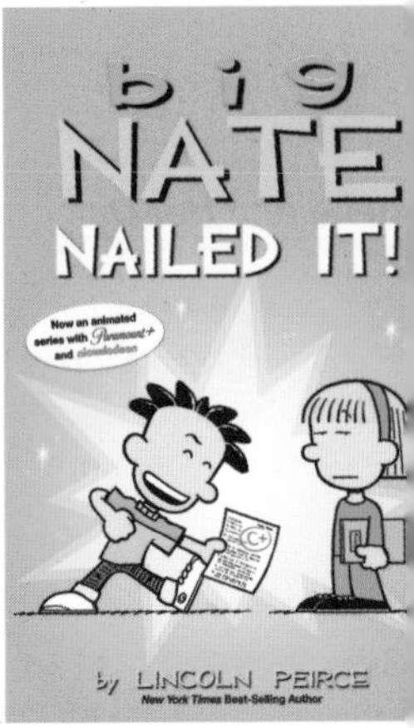
big NATE
NAILED IT!
by LINCOLN PEIRCE
New York Times Best-Selling Author

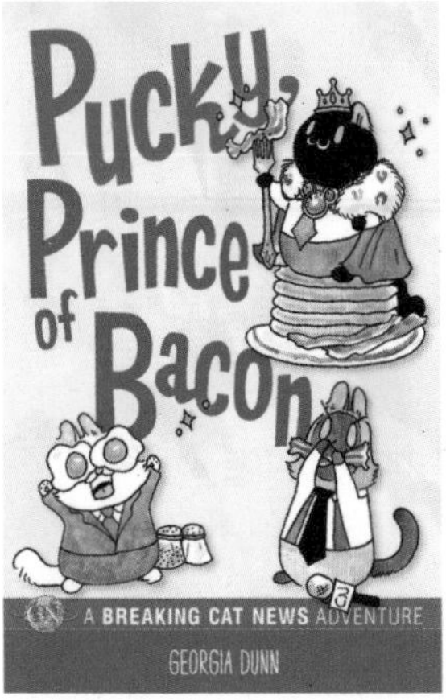
Pucky, Prince of Bacon
A BREAKING CAT NEWS ADVENTURE
GEORGIA DUNN

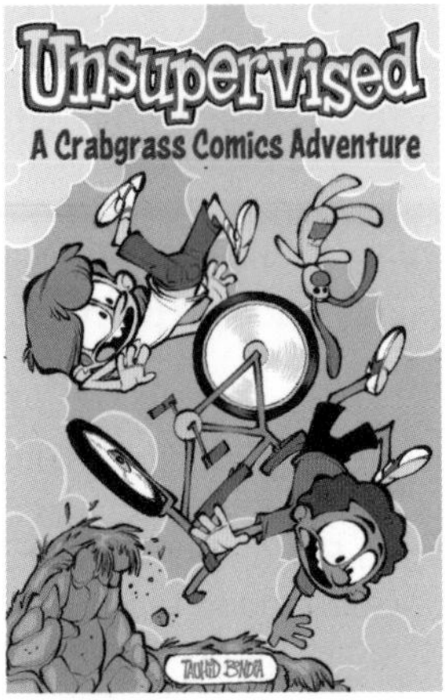
Unsupervised
A Crabgrass Comics Adventure
TAUHID BONDIA

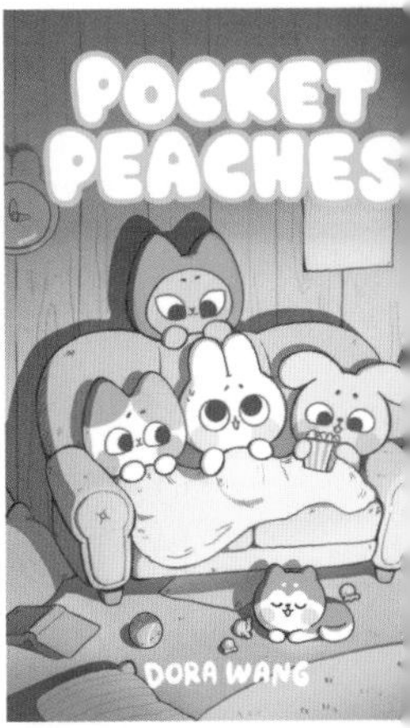
POCKET PEACHES
DORA WANG

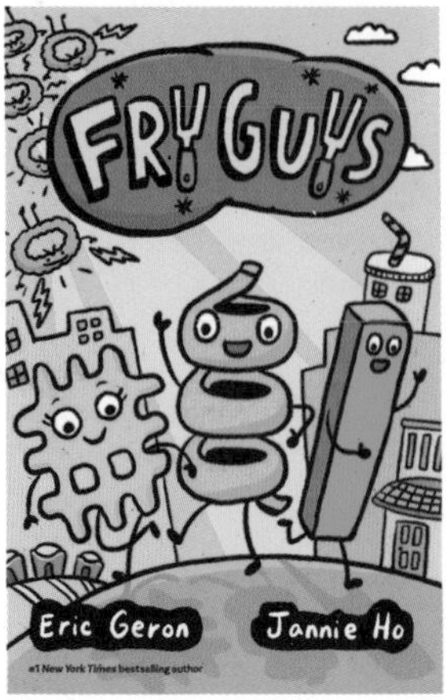
FRY GUYS
Eric Geron
Jannie Ho
#1 New York Times bestselling author

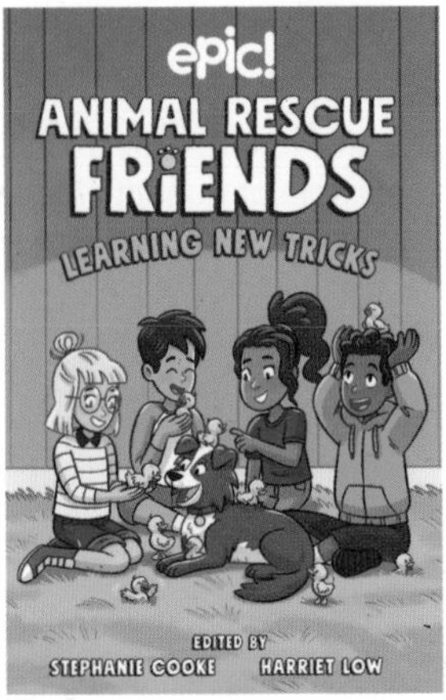
epic!
ANIMAL RESCUE FRIENDS
LEARNING NEW TRICKS
EDITED BY
STEPHANIE COOKE
HARRIET LOW

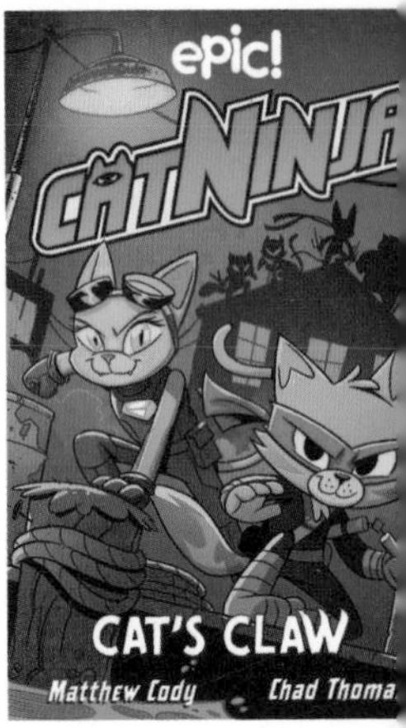
epic!
CAT NINJA
CAT'S CLAW
Matthew Cody
Chad Thoma